THE

KA...

AND

SEDUCING A SEAL
BY
JAMIE SOBRATO

Praise for Kate Hoffmann from
RT Book Reviews

"Fully developed characters and perfect pacing make
this story feel completely right."
—on *Your Bed or Mine?*

"Sexy and wildly romantic."
—on *Doing Ireland!*

"A very hot story mixes with great characters to make
every page a delight."
—on *The Mighty Quinns: Ian*

"Romantic, sexy and heart-warming."
—on *Who Needs Mistletoe?*

"Sexy, heartwarming and romantic…a story to settle
down with and enjoy—and then re-read."
—on *The Mighty Quinns: Teague*

THE SEXY DEVIL

BY
KATE HOFFMANN

First published in Great Britain 2011
by Mills & Boon, an imprint of Harlequin (UK) Limited,
Eton House, 18-24 Paradise Road, Richmond, Surrey TW9 1SR

© Peggy A. Hoffmann 2010

ISBN: 978 0 263 88064 9

14-0511

Harlequin (UK) policy is to use papers that are natural, renewable and
recyclable products and made from wood grown in sustainable forests. The
logging and manufacturing processes conform to the legal environmental
regulations of the country of origin.

Printed and bound in Spain
by Blackprint CPI, Barcelona

Kate Hoffmann began writing for Temptation in 1993. Since then she's published sixty books, primarily in the Temptation and Blaze® lines. When she isn't writing, she enjoys music, theater and musical theater. She is active working with school students in the performing arts. She lives in southeastern Wisconsin with her two cats, Chloe and Tally.

Dear Reader,

This book marks the end of another trilogy. I'm not sure why these sexy men always seem to find me in groups of three, but they do. I'm sure there's another trio waiting right around the corner to hop onto the pages of my next three books.

Readers often ask where I get my ideas. Thankfully, there's never a shortage of inspiration. The world is full of bad boys—Charmers and Drifters and Sexy Devils— all just waiting for their own story, and their own heroine to introduce them to the power of love.

I hope you've enjoyed reading the Smooth Operators trilogy as much as I've enjoyed writing it.

Happy reading,

Kate Hoffmann

1

"ALEXANDER NIKOLAS STAMOS of Chicago and Tenley Jacinda Marshall of Sawyer Bay, Wisconsin, were married on Saturday in a traditional ceremony at St. Andrew's Greek Orthodox Church. Stamos, president and CEO of Stamos Publishing, and his bride will reside in Lincoln Park after a honeymoon in Tahiti." Celia Peralto leaned back in her chair and sighed. "So they're going to live happily ever after."

Angela Weatherby glanced over her shoulder. "Alex Stamos was the exception to the rule," she said softly. "He's an aberration, part of the margin of error."

"And what about Charlie Templeton?" Ceci asked. "He's getting married, too."

"He's engaged. He's not married yet," Angela said stubbornly. She spun to face Ceci, her hands clutching the arms of her desk chair. "Listen, this isn't doing me any good. Every time this happens, I start to doubt the thesis of my book. Please, can you just keep these stories to yourself until I finish?"

This book was turning into a nightmare. Every time Angela thought she had her thesis nailed, something came along to screw it all up. She just needed to be right about this. These men—these smooth operators—weren't supposed to change. They weren't supposed to fall in love and get married and live happily ever after.

She hadn't set out to write a book about bad boys and the women who loved them. With her career as a freelance writer stalled, Angela had begun writing a blog, ruminating on the state of the male-female dynamic in contemporary dating. After hundreds of women had begun relating their own dating disaster stories, the blog had turned into a Web site, filled with profiles of thousands of men and a catalog of their dating atrocities. And now, Angela was about to put all of her theories and research into a book, *Smooth Operators: A Woman's Guide to Avoiding Dating Disasters*.

"Ever since you've started this book, you've been really tense," Ceci said.

"I should be tense. It was due at the publisher three months ago and I can't seem to finish."

"Maybe you should put it down for a while and reconsider your reasons for writing it."

"I know what you think," Angela said. "And I'm not doing this because I want to prove something to my parents."

"Oh, really?" Ceci asked. "Both your parents are psychologists who've written numerous books. They both teach at prestigious universities here in Chicago. Your older sister is a neurosurgeon and your younger sister is a physicist. This is your chance to step up to the Weatherby plate and hit a home run."

"A baseball metaphor?" Angela asked. Her thoughts shifted, an image of a handsome man flashing in her mind. Max Morgan. Professional baseball player. Classic smooth operator. And the subject of Chapter Five—the Sexy Devil.

"Sorry," Ceci said. "It's all Will can talk about. Baseball, baseball, baseball. He's in this ridiculous fantasy league and they get together every Monday night at some bar over in DePaul. I have no idea what they do, but he can't stop talking about it."

Angela turned back to her computer. Max Morgan. For such a long time, she'd barely thought of him. And then, one day, she'd been looking at profiles on the site and there he was. Twenty-six women had commented on him, and the comments were far from flattering. Since then, she couldn't keep from wondering what had turned her teenage Prince Charming into one of her bad-boy archetypes.

Throughout her childhood, Angela tried her best to please her parents, cultivating a rational and practical facade. But inside, Angela knew she wasn't like her sisters. They dreamed of academic glory while she secretly dreamed of romance and adventure, of being rescued from her dull existence by a white knight with a heart of gold.

As a young girl, she'd waited, secretly smuggling romantic novels into her backpack at the library— *Jane Eyre, Pride and Prejudice, Gone with the Wind.* As she devoured each one, she became the heroine, strong and feisty, the kind of girl every man wanted for his own.

And on the day she began high school, she'd met the man of her dreams, her prince, her white knight— Max Morgan. They'd bumped into each other in the registration line and from that moment on, Angela knew they were meant to be together. He'd been tall and beautiful, with chocolate-brown eyes and a mop of unruly, sun-streaked hair.

He'd said one word to her—"sorry"—and she'd fallen deeply and madly in love, or at least as deeply as a fifteen-year-old could. He'd never noticed her again. Forget about Mr. Rochester, Mr. Darcy and Rhett Butler. Max Morgan became the stuff of all her secret fantasies.

She'd followed him around high school, secretly watching everything he did. She attended his football games and baseball games, describing every moment in her diary in great detail so that she could relive it all over again when she was alone.

When it came time for college, she made a last minute decision to go to Northwestern in her hometown of Evanston, rather than an Ivy League school as her parents had wanted. Her self-respect denied that the only reason for the change was because Max had decided on Northwestern, securing both a football and baseball scholarship his freshman year.

"Hope springs eternal," Ceci said in a cheery voice. "It does give you hope, doesn't it? That maybe the men you've written off as...unsalvageable might just need the right woman?"

"No!" Angela said. "Our Web site proves my point every day. SmoothOperators has thousands of profiles of men who can't commit."

She couldn't be wrong. This was her one chance to prove to her parents that she wasn't wasting her time with this "silly Web site" as they called it. She saw it as a giant petri dish, a source of ever-evolving information about how men and women related in the world of dating. Her undergrad degree in psychology and her graduate degree in journalism made her the perfect person to write this book.

Ceci sighed. "I bet they both had a moment. Now, that would make good material for a book."

"Who? What are you talking about?"

Ceci rolled her chair over to Angela's desk. "Charlie Templeton and Alex Stamos. They had a moment and they were magically transformed into decent guys."

Angela rolled her eyes and shook her head. "There's nothing magical about this. They probably just decided they were tired of playing the field. The instinct to procreate kicked in. Once they've done that, they'll dump the wife and hit the bars again."

"I don't think so. Look at how fast it happened for them. They had a moment. You know, that instant when your eyes meet and you realize your life is about to change forever and there's nothing you can do about it. Maybe that deserves a chapter in your book. Chapter Fourteen. The Moment."

Though she didn't want to admit it, Angela knew exactly what Ceci was talking about. She'd experienced a moment…once, about four years ago. But it hadn't changed her life. "Have you ever had a moment?" Angela asked, keeping her gaze fixed on her work.

"No," Ceci admitted.

"Not even with Will?"

"Nope. It might happen, though. It doesn't have to be the moment you meet. That's love at first sight. For some people, it happens a little later. And sometimes it happens at different times for men and women. My brother-in-law said he fell in love with my sister when she burned a pot roast for his birthday dinner. She sat on the kitchen floor and cried for a half hour. And that was the moment he knew they'd be together forever."

Unfortunately, it had taken Angela six years to realize that she and Max would never have a moment. She'd even wrangled an interview with him for the college paper, but she'd been so nervous, she could barely remember the questions she'd planned to ask. After that, they'd passed each other on campus on numerous occasions, and even shared a sociology class. But he'd never once given her a second glance.

The summer after her sophomore year, Angela set out to transform herself into the kind of girl Max would notice. She studied the fashion magazines and bought a whole new wardrobe. She dyed her mousy brown hair a pretty shade of honey-blonde. She got herself a pair of contacts and lost ten pounds. She silently observed the girls that Max found attractive and she turned herself into one, then waited for her moment, determined to turn it into something special.

But it wasn't to be. At the end of his sophomore baseball season, Max left college for the minor leagues, signing with the Tampa Bay Devil Rays. He packed his bags and headed south for their farm system.

She knew her last chance at romance was gone, so she'd done exactly what the rational middle daughter of the Doctors Weatherby should do—she moved on. She started dating other guys and within a year, Max Morgan had become a distant memory from an all-too-foolish adolescence.

Until that night, four years ago. A night that could have changed the course of her life—except it hadn't. "There was a moment," Angela murmured. "With this one guy."

Ceci leaned forward. "Really? With who?"

"With whom," Angela corrected.

"With whom!" Ceci said.

"I was out with a coworker at a sports bar in Evanston. I came there to meet her cousin, a stockbroker. It was a blind date. Our eyes met across the bar and it was like I'd been struck by lightning. It took my breath away. We stared at each other for what seemed like forever. It was…frightening and exhilarating. And I felt like I was under some kind of…I don't know. Spell."

"See! You know exactly what I'm talking about! What happened?"

"Nothing. I got nervous and looked away. When I looked back, some other woman had captured his attention."

"But this guy was your blind date," Ceci said. "God, what a creep. He went off with another girl?"

"No!" Angela said. "My blind date was sitting next to me, rattling on about bond rates and investment strategies. This was a different guy."

It was the only real regret she had in her life. She'd let her one last chance at Max Morgan slip away. As his career in the majors blossomed that season, he became the stuff of tabloid legend, slowly transforming himself into her archetypical smooth operator— dating a long string of models and actresses and party girls, then tossing them aside when something more interesting came along.

Angela had gone home that night and wrote her first blog, talking about what she called "White Knight Syndrome," and her silly dream of finding the perfect man to rescue her from the horrors of single life.

Ceci reached out and took Angela's hand. "That's so tragic."

Angela shook her head, lost in thoughts of Max. "No, it isn't," she said stubbornly. "It wasn't meant to be. If he'd been interested, he would have walked across that bar and introduced himself."

"And you'd be married to him today," Ceci said.

"No!" Angela protested. "We might have gone out, had a nice time, maybe slept together, but then he would have turned out to be like all the others."

"You don't know that," Ceci said.

"I do." Angela paused, not sure of how much she wanted to reveal to Ceci. "He has a huge profile on our site. Nearly fifty women have commented. I would have been just another in a long line of broken hearts."

"You found him on the site?"

"Actually, he's the reason I started the blog," Angela admitted. "We went to high school and college together and I had this massive crush on him. He never noticed me. We had that moment in the bar and I realized what a ridiculous fool I was, still carrying a torch for him after all those years. That night, I went home and wrote my first blog."

"What's his name?" Ceci asked, turning back to her computer. "I want to look him up." She clicked on the search engine, then waited.

Why not tell Ceci? It's not like she had feelings for

him anymore. "He's the Sexy Devil," she murmured. "Chapter Five. Max Morgan."

Ceci's hands froze on her keyboard and she slowly turned to face Angela. "You know Max Morgan? The baseball player?" She sighed in frustration. "How many times have we talked about him? About his chapter in the book. And you never told me you knew him."

"I don't, exactly." Angela shrugged. "I've spoken to him…once. No, twice if you count the one word he said to me when we first met. I know almost everything there is to know about him. But we don't know each other. He's not even aware I exist."

"But you had a moment!" Ceci cried. "Maybe you were destined for each other."

"Love is not about magic moments and fairy-tale endings," Angela said. "It's about two people willing to work hard to make a relationship succeed. Two people sharing common interests and goals. And there are few truly decent men around willing to invest the time and effort to make a relationship work."

"You sound just like your mother," Ceci said. "So what are you going to do? Are you going to interview him?" She frowned. "Wait a second. Is that why you didn't go to that big charity event? The one he was hosting last month?"

"It wouldn't have been a good place to conduct an interview. I have to get him alone and talking, without any distractions." She swallowed hard. "And

I'm not sure I want to catch him. I have several other candidates for that chapter."

In truth, Angela had thought an interview would be the perfect opportunity to prove to herself that her feelings for Max Morgan were gone for good. She was adult now and she'd put all her teenage fantasies about love behind her. He wasn't her Prince Charming. Max Morgan was just another serial seducer, bent on bolstering his ego with an endless supply of willing women. It wouldn't take more than a few minutes in his presence to recognize that he was not the man of her dreams.

"I think the reason you made him the subject of Chapter Five is because you want to see him again," Ceci said. "You had a moment and you can't forget it. And don't bother lying to me. I'm your best friend. Whenever you lie, your face turns red."

Angela clapped her hands over her cheeks and shook her head. "I'll interview him. But my luck with interviews has been pretty bad lately. I can't help it if no one wants to talk to me."

"What if I could set you up with Max Morgan?" Ceci said.

"How would you do that?"

"Will hangs out at the Tenth Inning every Monday night with his fantasy league buddies. Max Morgan owns the Tenth Inning. And Will says that Max has been in occasionally these last few weeks. He's back in Chicago for the summer, recuperating after some sort of surgery he had during the off-season."

"How do you know all this?"

"Occasionally, I do listen to Will's rambling. He even met Max last week. Got a photo of him on his phone. I'm sure if you went in there, you could talk to him."

Angela felt her stomach flutter and she drew a sharp breath, pushing the surge of excitement aside. Ceci was right. She shouldn't be afraid to interview Max. She could certainly maintain a professional demeanor, even taking into account her former feelings about him.

"If I'm going to interview him, we have to develop a better strategy. He can't know he's being interviewed. I have to find a way to meet him and then get whatever I need from casual conversation." Angela stood. "He can't know that this is for a book."

"Conversation," Ceci said. "That's exactly what people do in a bar."

"I know. But I've never been very good at that. I don't flirt, I have a tendency to babble when I'm nervous, and I absolutely cannot hold my liquor."

"That's the least of your problems," Ceci said. "First, we have to go shopping and buy you the sexiest outfit on the planet. You're going to have to attract him first. From what I see on his profile, he doesn't have any shortage of women wanting to sleep with him. What do you think—legs, belly or cleavage? Pick one."

"For what?"

"It's my mother's rule. She always used to tell me

that if your outfit only showed one of the three, it was sexy. Two of the three makes the outfit sleazy. And showing all three makes it slutty. The rule of three has served me well. So, legs, belly or boobs?"

"What do you think?" Angela asked, staring down at her rather unremarkable body.

"Legs," Ceci said. "You have great legs. Let him fantasize about the boobs and the belly." Ceci grabbed her purse, then pulled Angela along toward the door. "What color?"

"Does your mom have a rule for that as well?"

"No. I do. Black is boring, red is desperate. An unusual color, like chartreuse or tangerine, says you're a strong, independent woman who doesn't care what other people say about her weird color choices. And men think that women who wear weird colors are kinky in bed."

"You have proof of this?" Angela asked.

"Yes." She pointed to her own mustard-colored top. "I was wearing pumpkin-orange when I met Will. He said he knew exactly what I was like in the bedroom."

"I'm not going to sleep with Max Morgan," Angela said.

"Of course not. But in order to get close to him, you're going to have to make him believe you just might."

They stepped out of the office onto the noisy bustle of Ashland Avenue. It was barely noon and the heat was already stifling. "There's this really nice boutique that just opened on North," Ceci said. "Let's start there. You'll need a nice pair of Do-me shoes, too. The dress will be demure but the shoes will say 'take my body now'."

"You are not my fairy godmother and I'm not Cinderella."

Ceci slipped her arm through Angela's. "Honey, we all want to be Cinderella. Every single girl I know is waiting for that guy to come calling with a glass slipper."

THE BAR WAS CROWDED for a Tuesday night. Max Morgan leaned over and motioned to Dave, his manager and big brother. "Is this a typical Tuesday night? This is the busiest I've seen it in ages. What's going on?"

"It's Ladies' Night. Women drink for half-price on Tuesdays. And when you're here, a lot of women show up, hoping they'll get lucky," Dave said, grinning. "Hey, you're better than a promotional giveaway. The women want to date you, the men want to talk baseball with you. Just sit yourself down at the end of the bar and be your usual charming self. Or better yet, hang out by the door and take a few pictures."

Max glanced over his shoulder. This wasn't exactly how he wanted to be viewed, as some kind of marketing tool. God, since his baseball career had taken off, he'd become a giant marketing machine—selling athletic shoes and luxury cars and expensive watches. He couldn't buy a pair of socks without having to think about the impact it would have on his endorsements. And every move he made in his personal life affected his ability to make money.

He hadn't really minded the notoriety that much... until the press showed it could also be nasty. Suddenly his day-to-day life had turned into fodder for media commentators. At first, he didn't care what was said about him because most of it had just been made up anyway. But when he'd learned his nieces and nephews were hearing about it at school, Max had decided to take a break from the spotlight.

A shoulder surgery he'd been putting off became the perfect chance to get out of the limelight, to give the media an opportunity to focus on someone else. And though he still had a few photographers waiting to catch him at a bad moment, his time in Chicago had given him a chance to really contemplate his future—after baseball.

Here, he could leave the temptations of New York and L.A. behind, the women, the partying, a nonstop glare of the camera flash. And the constant need to be selling something. "I'm just going to make a few calls," Max said. "I'll be in the office."

Max had purchased the bar in the DePaul neighborhood nearly a year ago, turning it over to his brother to renovate and run. Dave seemed to have a golden touch when it came to business. Whenever Max had money to invest, he turned it over to Dave, who managed to make them both rich.

At least Max didn't have to worry about how he was going to live after his baseball career ended. With seven years in the majors, he'd done pretty well for himself. Max smiled and shook hands as he walked back to the office, posing for a few photos along the way. When he finally closed the door behind him, he drew a deep breath and leaned back against it.

One day, he would be completely anonymous again. Max couldn't believe he'd ever been fearful of the moment when no one recognized him. Now, all he longed for was a normal life again. Since he'd been home, Max had quietly observed his three older siblings, all happily married with kids of their own, and wondered how they'd managed to find the key to the happiness.

They weren't famous, Max mused. Most of his old high school and college buddies envied him. He had everything they'd ever dreamed of having. Hell, he played a game for a living, traveling all over the country. He had more money than he'd ever need. And he was single. The women…well, the supply of beautiful women never seemed to wane.

Max reached up and rubbed his shoulder. There were a few drawbacks. He was in a constant fight with his aging body. And though he was a little more than a year shy of thirty, his body was already beginning to feel a lot older.

One thing always made the aches and pains disappear. Sex. And there were probably five or six girls sitting at the bar right now he could charm into his

bed. But the prospect of losing himself in the plea-
sures of a woman's body didn't seem all that exciting
right now. Lately, his sexual conquests had always
been followed by a juicy story in the tabloids. He
couldn't completely trust anyone anymore, outside
of his own family.

And since he'd returned, there hadn't been a single
woman who'd caught his eye. Instead, he'd spent his
time reviewing his business investments, rehabbing
his shoulder and visiting with family. It's the injury,
he thought to himself. The team doctor warned him
he might experience some mild depression, that he'd
need to focus more intently on his rehab and his return in the second half of the season.

Max sat down at the desk and pulled out his cell
phone, scrolling through the list of missed calls. Even
though he was off the media radar, women were still
interested. "Sophia," he murmured. An Italian model
he met last month at a charity event. "Christina."
A flight attendant who'd charmed him on his flight
home from Tampa. "Helena." An actress he'd dated
in New York during the off-season. Though a night
in bed with a beautiful woman would certainly make
him feel better, it just wasn't worth the hassle.

Max cursed softly and shut his phone, tossing it
on the desk. What the hell was wrong with him?
Making decisions about anything had become nearly
impossible. He pushed to his feet and restlessly paced
back and forth in the tiny office. "Do something," he
muttered to himself. "Pick a lane and hit the Gas."

A soft knock sounded at the door and he looked up to see Dave peering inside. "Sorry to disturb, but Greg Wilbern, our liquor salesman is here and he'd really like to meet you. He brought his teenage son. This guy gives us great—"

Max held up his hand. "Say no more. I'll tell him his son looks like a future major leaguer."

"I wouldn't go that far. His son showed me how to reprogram our cash registers. I suspect he has a better chance working for Microsoft than in the major leagues."

Max followed Dave, closing the office door behind him. He glanced across the bar, scanning the crowd. Suddenly, his breath caught in his throat. She was sitting with a friend, sipping a drink, her warm blond hair softly falling around her face. She looked up and their gazes met and Max had an overwhelming feeling of déjà vu.

He stood, fixed in one spot, staring at her. They'd met before. Or maybe not. Yes, there had been a lot of women, but he remembered all of them—at least he thought he did. But, he'd never forgotten a woman he'd slept with.

"Are you coming?" Dave asked.

"Yeah, just give me a sec," Max murmured. "I'll be right over."

Had he ever touched her…or kissed her? His fingers twitched as he tried to recall the feel of her skin, her hair. What was the scent of her perfume? He had

an uncanny memory for smells, but he couldn't recall hers.

Max smiled and she returned it, tilting her head
slightly. Whoever this woman was, he had to meet
her. Maybe he did know her. "Think," he murmured.
If he walked over and introduced himself and they'd
already met, she'd be insulted. But if he acted as if
he knew her, then she might be put off. "Best to be
upfront." He took a step in her direction, finally picking a lane and hitting the Gas.

"Max!"

Max blinked and looked at his brother motioning
him toward the bar. He glanced back and the connection was broken. A strange sensation came over
him. It was déjà vu. This had happened once before.
When? Where had it been? He recalled the odd sense
of loss he'd felt at the time.

Frustrated, Max approached the bar. Dave made
the introductions, then handed Max a baseball from
the stock they kept handy. "See that woman over there
in the green dress? Send her a drink from me."

"Champagne?"

"No," Max said, as he scribbled his name the ball.
"Never mind. That's too cheesy." He handed the boy
the baseball, then shook the liquor salesman's hand.
"I'll just go talk to her. Do I look all right? How's
my breath? Shit, I shouldn't have had onions on that
burger."

"What is wrong with you? Since when do you

worry about your appearance?" Dave looked over his shoulder. "That girl? She's not your type."

"What's my type?" Max asked.

"There's a ten sitting at the end of the bar. Fake hair, fake boobs, fake nails. She's your type."

"Shut up, Dave."

Max walked away from his brother and circled the bar slowly. Keeping his gaze fixed on her. Since the connection between them had been broken, she'd gone back to chatting with her girlfriend, a petite dark-haired woman with trendy glasses perched on her nose.

When he finally reached them, Max slipped into a spot next to her at the bar. But the patrons standing around her thought he'd come to socialize with them, wanting to shake his hand and pose for pictures. When the celebrity posturing was finally finished, he turned back to her.

"Hi," he said. Max waited for her to respond and began to think that she hadn't heard him, but then she slowly turned and faced him. She was even more beautiful up close. She had the greenest eyes he'd ever seen. And her shoulder-length hair, the color of honey, smelled like peaches.

"Hello," she said.

"Do I know you?"

She paused, then smiled quizzically. "I don't know. Do you?"

Max frowned. "I'm not sure. I can't believe I would have forgotten you if we'd met before." He held out his hand. "I'm Max. And forget what I just said. It sounded really lame."

"Angela," she said, resting her hand in his. She had beautiful fingers, long and slender, tipped with pretty red polish. No, Max thought. He'd never had those hands on his body. Though they might have met, they'd never been intimate. "And this is my friend, Celia. Ceci."

Max reached around to Ceci and shook her hand. "Hello, Ceci. It's nice to meet you." He turned back to Angela. "Can I buy you two a drink?"

Angela held up her margarita. "I have a drink. But thanks anyway."

"And I have to go," Ceci said. "I—I have to drive my mother—I mean, my brother to—shopping. I have to take my mother grocery shopping. She's completely out of…bananas." She forced a smile as she slid off her barstool. "Sorry, I forgot."

"Stay," Angela whispered, grabbing her hand. "How will you get home?"

"I'll grab a cab," Ceci said. "You just enjoy your drink." She picked up her purse, then gave Max a clever grin. "It was nice meeting you, Max. She likes her margaritas unblended, no salt. And she can't hold her liquor, so make the next one a virgin, all right?"

Max watched as Ceci hurried to the door. In any other instance, he would have been glad to have

Angela all to himself. But he felt strangely nervous. What the hell was that all about? Max Morgan never got nervous around women.

2

ANGELA TOOK A QUICK SIP of her drink. This was not part of the plan. Ceci wasn't supposed to leave the moment Max noticed her. They were supposed to stay together until Angela felt comfortable. They'd even worked out a series of signs and a plan to escape to the ladies' room to regroup if things got too complicated.

And they were already way too complicated. Her heart was slamming against the inside of her chest and she couldn't seem to catch her breath. And as she tried to calm herself, she felt light-headed and unable to think. Oh, God, she was having a...moment.

No, this wasn't supposed to happen! Angela knew exactly what Max Morgan was—a smooth operator. And yet she was allowing herself to be overwhelmed by his obvious magnetism. Get a grip, she scolded silently. You're a grown woman with a job to do. This is no time for silly fantasies.

But if she couldn't even think of something clever

to say, how would she keep him interested long enough to get all her questions answered? What if he decided to move on to someone else after just a few short minutes? She'd be left sitting alone at the bar feeling like a fool, humiliated in public.

But then, maybe that would be for the best. If he dumped her for someone prettier, it would only prove her point—Max Morgan was a class-A jerk.

"So," Max said. "Do you come here often?"

Angela swallowed hard. How many times had she heard that line? He was supposed to be an expert at seduction and that was the best he could come up with? "You really need to work on your pick-up lines."

The words were out of her mouth before she had a chance to think. Oh, hell, she'd just insulted him. And given him an excuse to move on to the redhead at the end of the bar.

At first, he seemed a bit taken aback by her comment. But then Max laughed and slid onto the stool vacated by Ceci. He thought she was teasing him. She could use that to her advantage. Keep him off balance. He was obviously used to having women agree with everything he said. She'd do the opposite. Reverse psychology.

"I do," Max said. "And that was really bad. Maybe I should move right on to astrological signs. Wait, here's a good one. I think I need to call heaven because they're missing one of their angels. How does that work for you?"

Angela had to admit, he'd gone from cheesy to charming in a heartbeat. Max had a way of looking at her with those dark and dangerous eyes that made her feel as though she was the most captivating female on the planet. But that was all part of the package that was Max Morgan, Sexy Devil. He could tempt even the most steadfast of women. "Sweet and not at all suggestive. A good effort. I'd give it a seven out of ten."

"Oh, you want suggestive? You must be the reason for global warming because you're hot."

"No," Angela said, shaking her head. "Not good to reference the looks. It makes you appear shallow and desperate. That one deserves a two."

"I lost my number, can I have yours?"

"Clever. Not as trite as the previous attempt."

"If I followed you home, would you keep me?"

Angela groaned. All right, he was impossibly charming. But she certainly wasn't going to let that affect her in the least. "Do you have a database of these? Or is your memory really that good?"

He leaned closer. "I have more. Maybe if you'd tell me what would work, I could choose more wisely."

He was obviously interested. But how far was he planning to take this, she wondered. Was he simply having a little fun or was he looking for something more. Angela gathered her nerve. "Sorry. Pick-up lines don't work with me," she said.

"What's the worst you've ever heard?" he asked.

"If I had a garden, I'd put your tulips and my tulips together? Just how is that supposed to work?"

Max leaned forward and brushed his lips across hers, lingering there for a brief moment before stepping back. "I think it worked pretty well."

Stunned, Angela stared at him. Yes, it was an innocent kiss, so quick it barely warranted mention. But she hadn't had a chance to prepare herself. Max Morgan, the man of her teenage dreams, had just kissed her! That simple touch had a startling effect on her body. Her pulse began racing and a warm flush crept up her cheeks. She opened her mouth, then quickly snapped it shut. Any attempt to put together a clever comeback would result in a string of incoherent babble.

His expression shifted suddenly and she thought she saw a flash of regret cross his deeply tanned face. "Hey, I'm sorry," he said. "I didn't mean anything by that. Really." He grabbed her hand. "Maybe we could start over? I'm Max Morgan. And the reason I came over here was to tell you that you look incredible in that dress. The color is…amazing."

Angela cleared her throat, trying to regain her composure. Rewind. Begin again. Gather your composure and act as if the kiss meant nothing. It didn't mean anything at all! "That was a pretty good line. Honesty. I like that."

"I was an Eagle Scout. We're big on honesty."

"I know," she said. She knew every arcane detail about Max. "I mean, Eagle Scouts are supposed to be trustworthy, right? You should have probably led with that instead of the angel line."

He held out his hand. "Hello, I'm Max Morgan, former Eagle Scout."

"Angela Weatherby," she replied. "Former …" What could she say. Wallflower? Introvert? Stalker? "President of the Latin Club."

"Really?" he asked. "So, you're smart and beautiful."

"And you're cheeky and charming," Angela replied.

Max pushed away from the bar. "Would you like to get out of here? It's a nice night. Why don't we take a walk?"

She felt a tremor run through her. This was the moment of truth. She could turn and run or she could hang in there and get her interview. Angela pointed to her shoes. "I'm not going far in these heels."

"I know the perfect place, then," he said.

She wasn't sure she'd be able to handle Max on her own, without the distractions of the bar to fill the silences. But this was her chance, to figure out this guy who'd had such a hold on her. And to rationalize her crazy reaction to him. "Sure," she said. "That sounds nice." In truth, it sounded impossibly romantic.

"All right, here's the plan. Where is your car parked?"

"In the ramp just down the block."

"Why don't you leave through the front door and

start walking toward the ramp. I'll go out the back and meet you outside. That way, nobody will see us leaving together."

Angela frowned. "That was not a good line," she said. "In fact, it was kind of insulting."

"No!" he cried, taking her hand again. "No, no. That's not what I meant. It's just that if we leave together, there will be all kinds of speculation, maybe even some mention of it in the papers. I don't want you to get pulled into that." He paused. "You know who I am, don't you?"

Angela decided not to lie. What would be the point? She just stared at him silently and shrugged. "You're Max Morgan," she replied. "You play baseball."

He grabbed her hand. "Come on, we'll both go out the back." He laced his fingers between hers and pulled her along behind him, through the crowd to the kitchen and then out the rear door to the alley. "We'll take my car." He pointed to a black BMW sedan with tinted windows, parked against the building.

Max opened the passenger side door for her and helped her inside, then hopped in behind the wheel. Angela wasn't sure what to say to him. She'd expected they might chat at the bar. She'd been prepared to ask him a few questions, to get a sense of the man he was. She'd even predicted it would take approximately thirty minutes for her to realize, once and for all, that he was not the man of her post-adolescent dreams.

The night was definitely not going as planned. "Nice car," she murmured.

He laughed as he reached for the ignition. "Now, I'm going to have to start calling you out on the cheesy lines."

"Sorry," Angela said, relaxing a bit. "I'm not the best flirt. And I'm sure that's what you're used to."

Max turned to her. "Maybe I don't like what I'm used to," he said. "Maybe I don't want you to flirt with me." He shook his head. "Sometimes I just wish people could forget all that celebrity stuff and be normal."

"Well, if you're looking for normal, then I'm definitely it," Angela said. "Nothing very special here."

"You were president of the Latin Club," he said, grinning. "I think that's kind of special."

"You're very strange," Angela said. As he pulled out of the parking spot, she took the opportunity to observe him, his profile outlined by the light from the street lamps.

He was even more beautiful than she remembered, his features so perfectly. His hair was darker and his body more mature, but there was still a bit of the handsome boy left inside him—especially in the smile and in the teasing tone of his voice.

"Tell me something completely random about yourself. Let's start there."

Angela knew she'd have to come up with something intriguing and humorous. Something to show him that an evening with her could be fun. "I can list all the states in the Union."

"Impressive," Max said.

"In alphabetical order, in reverse alpha order, in order of entrance into the union, and in order of geographical size. Plus I know all of the capitals by heart." She drew a deep breath. "What can I say, I was a geek and my parents thought it was an interesting party trick."

"You are a very interesting woman, Angela." He turned on some music, flipping through the CDs in his player until he found something soothing.

She was going to make a complete mess of things. In another hour, he'd be dropping her off at the parking ramp and heading back to the bar, looking for someone more intriguing. It was time to start asking questions. "So you're famous," she ventured. "What's that like?"

"It's about what you'd expect," he said with a shrug. "Sometimes bad, sometimes good."

"Tell me the bad," Angela said.

"I hate the press. I hate that they can make up stories about my life without any thought of how it affects the people I love. I hate that people wonder who I date or where I eat dinner or where I sleep at night. I hate that I don't have much of a life outside of baseball."

"Tell me the good," she said.

"If I wasn't famous, you might not have given

me a second look at the bar," he said. "I'm glad you did."

"Oh, you think I'm impressed by your fame?" Angela asked. "I've spent time with much more famous people than you—Churchill, Gandhi, Hemingway. You don't impress me."

"Obviously not," Max said with a devilish grin. "Since you seem intent on poking holes in my ego." He opened all the windows in the BMW, letting the warm summer wind blow through the car. "I love Chicago in the summer. The smell, the sounds. I never get to enjoy my summers anymore. It's always about work, the next game, the next at bat. This is the first summer in my memory that I haven't played baseball."

"Isn't it fun?" she asked, anxious to keep him talking about himself.

"It's a job. It can be fun. It certainly looks like fun. But it's not…normal. I'd like to lead a normal life."

"Normal is boring," Angela said. "Take it from me."

"Normal might be nice for a change." He glanced over at her. "What would you be doing on a normal Tuesday night?"

"Laundry," she said.

"You made the right decision," he teased. "I'm much more interesting than laundry."

The conversation was going well. Maybe it was time to get a bit more personal. "Can I ask you a question?" Angela began.

"Anything," he said.

"Why did you choose me? That bar was full of women more beautiful. More interested in a guy like you. Why me?"

"I don't know," Max said. "I just got this feeling. When I saw you and our eyes met, there was this… moment."

Angela's breath froze in her throat. Oh, God. He'd had a moment, too? What did that mean? No, there was no need to get excited. Maybe a guy like him had multiple moments. Maybe it didn't mean anything at all. Of course, they'd been attracted to each other. But a "moment" was more than just sexual attraction, wasn't it?

They chatted about a variety of subjects for the rest of the ride—the latest festivals on the lakefront, the best ethnic restaurants in town, the traffic, the weather. But Angela couldn't get her mind off the "moment."

The conversation turned to his injury and his rehab efforts, but she found herself transfixed by a careful study of his mouth. He asked her about her work and she told him she was in communications, before changing the subject to the music he liked.

By the time they reached the lake, the conversation had become surprisingly relaxed, at least to the casual observer. But Angela was in the midst of an internal crisis. She found herself completely charmed by Max Morgan. He was sweet and funny and smart. And when he smiled at her, she felt as if she might just melt into a big puddle of goo on his leather seat.

No, Angela thought to herself. Max Morgan was supposed to be the enemy. And all this charm was expected from a smooth operator. Of course, he would try to weaken her defenses, to turn himself into the perfect guy. He knew exactly how to read the signs. And if she weren't careful, she'd fall for it, hook, line and sinker.

Max found a place to park, then helped her out of the car. It was dark on the beach, but the city was alive with light behind them. He held onto her arm as she kicked off her shoes and stepped into the sand. Then he laced his fingers through hers and they walked toward the water.

"I never come to the beach," she said. "I just drive by." She closed her eyes and drew a deep breath. "It doesn't smell like the city."

"I have a place on the water in Florida," he said. "And a place on a small lake in Wisconsin. And my apartment here in Chicago overlooks the lake. I'm a water guy, I guess. Where do you live?"

"I have a flat in Wicker Park." This guy was seriously out of her league, Angela thought to herself. He had at least three homes, maybe even more. She lived in a tiny, one-bedroom flat with leaky pipes and a noisy radiator.

When they reached the water's edge, Max slipped out of his shoes and socks and rolled up his pant legs, then waded in. "Cold," he said, wincing. "I can't believe I used to swim in this."

"It's always cold," Angela said, backing away from his invitation to join him. He ran out and grabbed her, pulling her along until her toes touched the water too.

"No!" she cried, trying to twist out of his grasp. But he pulled her closer until she was caught in his embrace. He stared down into her eyes, then bent closer and kissed her.

Angela tried to remain calm, hoping to remember every little detail of the kiss. It was sweet and simple and filled with a delicious anticipation. She parted her lips and he took the invitation to tease at her tongue. He'd obviously had a lot of experience kissing women and it had paid off. When he finally drew away, she felt as if her legs were about to buckle beneath her.

"I've been thinking about doing that ever since we left the bar," he murmured, smoothing his hand through her hair. His gaze scanned her features and he smiled. "I don't know what it is. I feel like we know each other. Is that strange?"

"Yes," Angela said. The one word was all she could manage for the moment. Oh, it was wonderful kissing him. And though she'd tried to maintain her defenses, it was all it took to make her realize that she was totally and utterly at his mercy.

He pulled her back into his arms and kissed her

again, this time more playfully. "So, what are we going to do for our next date?"

"What?"

"Where are we going to go? You probably have to work tomorrow, but I'm free tomorrow night. We can go to dinner or take in a concert. I haven't been to the aquarium for years."

Angela wasn't sure what to say. This was so unexpected. Although, maybe he'd do the same thing all the other smooth operators did—promise to call her tomorrow to firm up their plans and then never call. "I—I don't know. I'd have to check my—"

He placed a finger over her lips. "No. We're going to plan it now. I'll pick you up at six."

Angela took a deep breath. She wasn't sure she wanted to believe what he was saying. She'd have more than just this night to get to know Max. All the questions spinning around in her head didn't have to be asked tonight. Tonight, she could just enjoy herself. "Six," she said in a shaky voice. "Sounds good."

THEY SAT ON THE SAND for two hours, talking, joking, laughing. Max couldn't remember the last time he'd been so completely fascinated by a woman. What was it about Angela that he found so sexy? Had he passed her on the street or seen her at a party, he might have considered her ordinary.

But for the first time, he found himself looking a bit deeper. She was a study in contrasts. One moment she was confident and outspoken and the next, shy and nervous. She didn't play games, but she did enjoy poking at his ego every so often. And though she wasn't the kind of woman he usually found himself attracted to, he was beginning to think she was the most beautiful woman he'd ever met.

"This is going to be a great summer," Max said.

"Will you have the entire summer off?" Angie asked.

"If rehab goes well, I should be on my way back to the club by September. Maybe August. But I'm thinking I need time, not just to heal physically, but to figure out a few things."

"Like what?" Angie asked, turning to face him.

He grabbed her legs and pulled them over his, drawing her close to kiss her. The impulse to seduce her was overwhelming. He wanted to explore her body, to learn what made her shudder with desire. There was something between them that he'd never experienced before. Yet, he didn't want her to be just another notch on his bedpost.

"Like life," he said. "I've been living in an alternate reality. I see my brothers and sisters and their families and they're happy. Really happy, not just artificially happy."

"How can you be artificially happy?" she asked.

"You know. When you buy a new car and you think you're happy, and maybe you are for a day or so. But then you realize it's just a car."

Angela leaned against him, the warmth from her

body seeping into his. "So what makes you really happy?"

"Kissing you does it for me," he said.

"Then do it," she said.

This time, he put aside the gentle, sweet kisses they'd shared. Max wanted her to know exactly how he felt about her. His lips found hers and he slowly lowered her into the sand, stretching out beside her.

His hand smoothed over her arms and then lower, to her hip. As she drew her leg up, her skirt fell away and he touched the silky length of her calf. It was so easy to get lost in the feel and taste of her. At first, he didn't notice the wind picking up, swirling the sand around him.

And then, a moment later, the clouds opened and it began to rain. Max rolled to his side and looked up at the sky. Nature had decided to mess with his perfect date. But to his surprise, Angela didn't seem to care. Instead, she sat up, turned her face to the sky and laughed.

The downpour had already drenched her hair and her dress, and droplet clung to her lashes. She opened her mouth to catch the rain with her tongue and Max could only watch her. Any other woman would be racing for cover, hoping to preserve her carefully tended appearance. But that obviously hadn't occurred to Angela.

Thunder rumbled in the distance and when lightning flashed, Max leapt to his feet and grabbed her hand. "Come on. Let's get out of here before we get zapped."

As they ran to the car, pedestrians were rushing for cover. He unlocked the door and pulled it open, then helped her inside. When he finally slipped in behind the wheel, she was raking her fingers through her dripping hair. "I'm getting your car all wet," she said. "And my dress is covered with sand."

"Don't worry." He pulled out into traffic and headed north on Lakeshore Drive. "My condo is just on the other side of the zoo," he said. "We'll stop there, get dried off and then decide what we want to do with the rest of the night." He glanced over at the clock in the dashboard and was surprised to see that it was past midnight. "Or, I could drop you back at your car," he added. "You probably have to be up early for work tomorrow."

"I really wouldn't mind getting dry," she said.

Good, Max thought to himself. He didn't want the night to end, either. Not yet. Not until he was absolutely sure she wanted him as much as he wanted her.

Minutes later, he pulled into the underground garage of his Lincoln Park high rise. As they rode the elevator up, he pressed her back against the wall and kissed her again, his fingers tangling in her damp hair. "This has been the most amazing night," he whispered.

She stared up at him, a strange look in her eyes. Didn't she believe him? Hell, that was all he needed.

The first time he found a woman he was truly interested in and she thought he was playing her. So how could he prove he wasn't, Max wondered. He could forget about luring her into his bed. That would be a good start.

"Your lips taste like rain," he murmured. When the elevator doors opened, he took her hand and walked with her to the door of his apartment. He pushed the key into the lock, then stepped aside to let her enter. The apartment was dark, rain glittering on the wide wall of windows overlooking the lake.

He wanted to draw her into his arms again, now that they were completely alone, and find out just how deep their attraction for each other went. Instead, he flipped on the lights. "The bathroom is just down that hall," Max said. "There are towels in the cabinet and I'll find you some dry clothes."

He watched as she walked away from him, her wet dress clinging to her slender body. Somehow, he knew the night wasn't over. It was just beginning.

Max hurried to his bedroom and rummaged through his clothes for something to give her. He found a team sweatshirt and some warm-up pants, then grabbed a pair of socks from the clean laundry.

When he knocked softly on the bathroom door, Angie opened it a crack and he held the clothes out. "It's the best I can do," he said. "They're warm and they're dry."

"Is it all right if I take a quick shower?" she asked. "I'm covered with sand."

"No problem," he said. "I'm just going to make us something to eat. Are you hungry?"

"Yeah," she said with a winsome smile. "That would be great." She took the clothes and shut the door. He glanced at his watch. He had about ten minutes tops to shower, get dressed and cook something. Max headed to the galley kitchen and to his relief, found a container of gourmet mac and cheese he'd bought at Whole Foods. He popped it into the oven and headed for the guest bathroom.

As he stepped beneath the hot water, his mind wandered down the hall, to the woman who was showering in his bathroom. With any other woman, he wouldn't have thought twice about joining her there. And with any other woman, he knew he'd have been welcome. But he didn't want to move too fast with Angela. He was having trouble reading her signals and a single mistake might win it all.

Max glanced down and groaned. Just the thought of the two of them naked together brought a physical reaction. He turned up the cold water and stood beneath it until the spray stung his skin. Then he stepped out, grabbed a towel and wrapped it around his waist.

He hurried back through the living room, dripping water on the hardwood floors. But he stopped suddenly when he saw Angela standing at the windows, peering down at the street. She turned and her eyes went wide when she noticed he was dressed only in a damp towel.

To his relief, the cold water had done the trick and there wasn't an embarrassing bulge in the front of that damp towel. "Sorry," Max muttered, clutching at the cotton where it was tucked around his waist. "I thought you'd take a little longer in the shower."

"I didn't want to take advantage," she said. "It's a nice shower. Big…enough for two."

"I—I'm just going to go get dressed. I'll be right back."

When he returned from the bedroom, wearing basketball shorts and a T-shirt, Angela was still standing at the window. He stepped up behind her, then slipped his arms around her waist. "What do you see out there?"

"It's a beautiful view. It's so quiet up here."

Max rested his chin on her shoulder. "The minute I saw this place, I knew I had to have it. And there was no way I'd stay at my parents' place. My mother would drive me crazy and my father would expect me to help him with all of his household repair projects. I needed a place of my own here in Chicago."

"So you dropped a few million on a condo? Why not rent?"

"It seemed like a good investment," Max said. "And now that I've been here for a while, I like it. It feels like home." He turned her around to face him. "What can I get you to drink? I have wine. And beer. Energy drinks and mineral water."

"A glass of wine would be nice," Angela said. "Red, if you have it."

As Max walked to the kitchen, he smiled to himself. This was going well. She could have asked for a ride home. But instead, she'd stay at least long enough to finish a glass of wine and eat some mac and cheese. He found a bottle, struggled with the cork, then filled a wineglass nearly to the brim.

It would take her longer to drink a big glass of wine, giving him more time. But at the last minute he dumped half of it in the sink. She might think he was trying to get her drunk. He didn't want to confirm all the worst things the press had to say about him.

"Take it slow," he reminded himself. "And don't make an ass of yourself."

Angela pressed her hand to her chest. Ever since he'd walked into the room, dressed in a only a towel, she hadn't been able to breathe. It had been a long time since she'd been in the presence of a naked man—or a nearly naked one. Almost a year. And she'd never been near a man with a body like Max's. The fact that it was Max, the man of her teenage fantasies, made the entire incident surreal.

After he'd walked away, she'd thought about following him, about tugging the towel off the lower part of his body and exploring everything underneath. If she were only bolder, she could do something like that.

But Angela knew the dangers of allowing herself

to surrender to a guy like Max. Though she wanted to believe that he genuinely liked her, she couldn't help but wonder if this stop at his apartment was all part of a grand plan to seduce her. There was no ignoring the profiles on her Web site. Max did have an amazing capacity to separate a woman from her panties.

If he wasn't interested in sex, then why had he brought her here? Angela suspected it had nothing to do with getting warm and dry. He'd probably waltzed through in a towel on purpose, just to tempt her. And she was tempted. It would be so easy to fall into his trap, to make the first move so he couldn't be blamed for the seduction.

Angela had indulged in a few one-night stands over the years, only to regret her behavior the next day. But would she regret sleeping with Max? She'd finally have a chance to make her teenage fantasies come true. How many women would pass up a chance like that? If he were great, then she'd have a memory to keep for the rest of her life. And if he wasn't, maybe she could finally consign her fantasies to the past.

If he offered, she'd accept, Angela decided. But what if he didn't offer? What would that mean? Was she not woman enough to satisfy him? Though she hadn't had the number of experiences that he'd had, Angela knew how to pleasure a man. She was good in bed. Not porn-star good, but she could get a little kinky when called for.

"Here. Red wine. Dinner should be ready in about ten minutes."

Angela jumped at the sound of his voice. She turned and took the glass from his hand. "What are you cooking? It smells good."

"Mac and cheese. I buy it in bulk from Whole Foods."

"I love their mac and cheese," she said. "And I am a little hungry. I haven't stayed up this late for a long time."

"You don't go out much?"

Angela shook her head. "No. I don't really like the bar scene."

"What were you doing out tonight?"

"It was just a whim," she lied. "Ceci convinced me to go. What about you? Do you do this often?"

"Drink wine?"

"Bring a girl home?" She might as well get a few more of her questions answered. "You're very difficult to resist. Very...charming."

"I'm having a nice time just talking to you, Angela. I'm not looking for anything else."

"You aren't?"

"No. I mean, I think it's a little early to—not that I wouldn't want to. You're beautiful. Any man would want to...you know. But I think we should just let things happen...."

Angela set her wineglass down on the windowsill. So how did he feel? Was he having second thoughts about seducing her? Didn't he think she could handle it? Well, she was just as capable of enjoying it as any other woman. "Why don't you kiss me again and we'll see what happens?"

She'd be crazy not to take the chance when she had it, right? Forget the book, forget all the questions she wanted to ask. Her curiosity had completely overwhelmed her common sense and she wanted to enjoy what so many other women had.

It didn't take him more than a heartbeat to change his mind. His fingers slipped through her hair and he pulled her mouth to his, steering her toward the sofa. This time, his kiss left no doubt in her mind as to where they were headed. He couldn't seem to get enough of her lips and her tongue. Max was like a man, parched with thirst and desperately searching for a cool taste of water.

They tumbled onto the leather cushions and he pulled her down on top of him, his hands roaming freely over her body. There wasn't much between them. Angela had left her underwear to dry in the bathroom and Max hadn't bothered with his, either.

When he slipped his hand beneath the hem of the sweatshirt and skimmed it up her back, she moaned. It was the most delicious sensation in the world. Every nerve seemed to tingle as his touch drifted from one spot to the next.

In the past, Angela had always kept a small part of herself detached from the man sharing her bed, afraid to commit herself completely, afraid that she might be making a mistake. But with Max, she wanted to surrender, wanted to offer him every pleasure that he might find her in body. It was just one night, that's all. Why not enjoy it completely?

She was breathless and giddy. Though Angela knew the risks, her body was on fire, the desire so hot that the only way to survive was to tear off all her clothes. Straddling his hips, she sat up and tugged the sweatshirt over her head. Her hair tumbled around her face as she tossed the sweatshirt aside. Angela watched as he slowly reached out to cup her breast in his palm. She closed her eyes and tipped her head back, losing touch with reality.

Was this a dream? Would she wake up suddenly, alone in her bed, and realize that once again, her fantasies of him were just an illusion? No, Angela thought. She felt her skin tingle where he touched and she heard the pulse pounding through her veins. She smelled the scent of his cologne and heard the sound of his breathing.

If this wasn't real, it was the most vivid dream she'd ever experienced. Angela stared into his eyes, daring the image to fade before her. But instead, he drew her down again, into another kiss, this one, more powerful than the last.

"What are we doing?" he whispered

"Touching," she said. "Kissing."

He groaned softly as she shifted above him, his hard shaft pressed against the spot between her legs. It wouldn't take much to rid themselves of the rest of their clothes. Angela knew so much about him, yet all of it was purely superficial. She wanted to see him naked, to touch him intimately and to have those images burned into her memory. "Take your shirt off," she whispered.

Max pushed up on his elbows and she pulled his shirt over his head, then dropped it on the floor. Angela ran her palms over his torso, from his belly to his chest, the muscle rippling beneath her fingers.

He was absolute perfection, his skin smooth and warm and burnished brown by the sun. Angela smiled, wondering at how this fantasy had suddenly become reality. Every time she thought it might end, it just got better and better. Perhaps this was the way it was meant to happen between them. This was the time when they'd both be at their best, the time when they could both walk away with out any regrets.

She ran her hands along his arms, then laced her fingers between his, drawing his arms up above her head. Nuzzling her face into the curve of his neck, she leaned closer, her breasts rubbing against his chest.

Max groaned, then grabbed her around the waist. Before she knew what was happening, he was standing beside the sofa, her legs wrapped around his hips. He carried her down the hall, toward his bedroom. Angela knew if she had any doubts, now was the time to call an end to this. But she wanted to go the rest of the way, to share the ultimate intimacy with him.

He stopped halfway down the hall and gently pushed her into the wall, his mouth coming down on hers for a deep, demanding kiss. She arched against him until they were nearly joined, their clothes providing the last barrier between anticipation and release.

Max groaned again, then suddenly went still. Angela waited, wondering what had happened. Then with a sinking feeling, she knew what it was. The excitement had been too much for him. "It's all right," she whispered, toying with a lock of his damp hair. "We can just wait a bit."

He drew back and a gasp slipped from his throat. "What?"

"I understand. It happens. Things were pretty intense there."

"You think I …" His voice trailed off and then he laughed. "No, I'm fine. Everything is still fully… functional."

"Then why did you stop?"

"Because I'm really not sure we should be doing this, Angela. In fact, I'm positive we shouldn't be doing this. Not yet. Not that I don't really, really want to do this. Believe me, I do. But, I think if we both take a step back and—"

Angela quickly unwound her legs from his waist and dropped to her feet. As her body slid against his, she noticed that the bulge in his shorts wasn't subsiding. Oh, God. She'd just assumed he'd— "Right," she said, nodding frantically. "You're absolutely right. I mean, we've just met. And I understand you probably have women coming on to you all the time. It must be so—"

"No!" Max said, reaching out to touch her face. "It's not that. Believe me." He drew a deep breath, then let it out slowly. "I'm just going to get the rest of our clothes. Then we can—talk. We'll talk. And eat."

As he strode toward the living room, Angela braced herself against the wall, holding her arms over her breasts. What was going on? Didn't he want her? Wasn't she attractive enough for him to take to bed? This was not the behavior of a smooth operator.

First Alex Stamos, then Charlie Templeton and now, Max Morgan. Why couldn't these men behave the way they were supposed to? What was happening to the world as she knew it? Every assumption she'd made about these seducers was being shattered. And now, Max Morgan was acting all upright and honorable.

When he returned, Max was wearing his T-shirt again. He helped her into the sweatshirt, then took her hand and led her back to the sofa. He sat down next to her, then grabbed her hands and kissed the tips of her fingers.

"I had a really nice time tonight," he said. "I want to see you again. And I don't want to mess anything up by sleeping together just a few hours after we met."

"Is that really why you stopped," Angela asked.

"Or is that just the story you think I'll buy until you can get me out of your apartment?"

"I don't know how much you know about me, or my rather formidable reputation with the ladies. But most of it is greatly exaggerated by the press." He paused. "Well, some of it is true, but a lot isn't."

"So, when you bring a woman home, you usually sleep with her?"

He drew in a sharp breath, then nodded. "Usually."

"Why not me?" Angela asked, desperate to know the answer.

"Because you're someone I'd like to know better. That is, if you want to get to know me."

She searched his eyes for the truth in his words, but Angela didn't know him well enough to guess at what was really beneath his reluctance. No man, not even the most well-intentioned red-blooded male, would turn down the chance at sex. There had to be something more to this.

She forced a smile, then quickly stood. "I—I have to get up early for work tomorrow. I should really get home."

"You're not hungry?"

"No."

Max cupped her face with his hand, his forehead meeting hers. Then he kissed her, the contact soft and fleeting. "All right. I'll take you back to your car."

"No," Angela said. "I can get a cab."

"I'll take you," Max insisted, his tone firm, yet betraying a hint of irritation.

"I'll just get my things." She stepped around him and walked back to the bathroom. When she got inside, she closed the door behind her. Angela caught sight of herself in the wide mirror that hung on the wall above the sinks. She leaned closer to examine her face.

She was still flushed, her cheeks pink and her lips red and puffy. Her hair, though mussed, didn't look that bad. Objectively, she should have been pretty enough to tempt Max into sex.

Angela fought back a wave of anger. She knew exactly what kind of man Max Morgan was and she'd allowed herself to get carried away by his charm. It was all there in black-and-white on her Web site. What made her think that he'd be any different with her?

This was all Ceci's fault, all of her talk about "moments" and "hope springing eternal." Max was exactly what she knew him to be—a smooth operator. Of course, he wouldn't want a woman like her. He never noticed the girl she'd been, so why would he even consider the woman she'd become?

She wouldn't get her fantasy night with Max Morgan after all. Tomorrow, she'd wait for his call and it wouldn't come. And in a few weeks, she'd find out he was dating another woman—a model or an actress, someone more befitting his status in the celebrity world.

He was everything she knew him to be—a rogue, a cad, a seducer and the shallowest man she'd ever met. But she would get one thing she wanted from this night—an end to all of her silly fantasies. She'd never have to think of him again and wonder what may have been. Though they might have shared a moment, it was *the* moment.

Angela pulled off his clothes and slipped into her own underwear and dress. She winced at the cold, damp fabric against her skin, the sand still caught in the seams and folds. The sooner this night was over, the better.

3

MAX GLANCED OVER AT Angela, her profile outlined by the lights from the street. They'd made a quick exit from his place and an uneasy silence had enveloped them. He wasn't quite sure how to read her expression. At first glance, she seemed unbothered by what had happened between them. But experience had taught him that how a woman acted and how she really felt could be two completely different things.

The night had been so promising, but it was ending on a sour note. Maybe he should have taken her to bed. She seemed almost insulted that he hadn't. But for the first time in his life, Max had looked past his urges and put aside his need for release. He wanted a good life after baseball and a woman to share it with. Seducing every woman who caught his eye wasn't getting him there. So maybe it was time to try a different approach.

It was his mistake. He shouldn't have started what he didn't want to finish. They should have kept their clothes on, sipped their wine and eaten a little mac and cheese. He would have driven her back, they would have kissed good-night and he could have looked forward to a second date. Now, he wasn't even sure he ought to try to kiss her again.

Max glanced over to see Angela rub her bare arms and he reached for the air conditioner. "Are you cold?" he asked.

"No," she said.

"You're rubbing your arms."

She forced a smile. "I'm fine."

With a muttered curse, he shut off the air conditioner and rolled down the windows, letting the warm night breeze flow through the car. Was this what he deserved for trying to be a gentleman? That's what women were supposed to want, right? A guy who wasn't focused on getting into their pants? It wasn't just supposed to be about sex. There was trust and friendship, too.

He'd wanted to explain his reasoning to her, but Max suspected he'd only make things worse. So, for now, he'd just stay quiet, get her number before he dropped her off, and they would start fresh on their next date.

As they neared the parking ramp, he began to worry that she might not give him her number at all. He pulled into the ramp and grabbed the ticket, then turned to her. "Where are you parked?" he asked.

"Level 3B," she said. "It's a blue Volkswagen Jetta."

Max carefully steered up the spiral ramp and exited on the third level, then squinted in the low light, looking for her car.

"It's right there," she said, pointing to the left.

Max took an empty spot nearby, then turned off the BMW. She made to get out of the car, but he reached out and took her arm. "Hang on." He grabbed his cell phone from the center console. "I don't have your number."

"Why do you need my number?" she asked.

She was angry. Much angrier than he'd ever suspected. "Because we have a date tomorrow and I want to call you and work out the details."

"We made those plans before..." Her voice trailed off and she waited for him to reply.

He sent her an inquiring look. "Before what? Before I decided we shouldn't sleep together?" He shook his head. "It isn't always about sex, no matter what you might have read in the press."

With an impatient sigh, she rattled off a series of numbers. He punched them into his cell phone, then smiled in relief. "All right. I'll call you. Tomorrow."

She made a move for the door again, but Max wasn't about to let her get away without one last kiss. He smoothed his hand along the length of her arm, then tangled his fingers in her hair. Angela turned toward him. He leaned forward and dropped a simple kiss on her lips. "I'll see you tomorrow."

"Tomorrow," she murmured. With that, she made

her escape. Max turned on the BMW and waited until she was safely inside her car, before pulling out behind her. He followed her down to street level. She turned left and he thought about following her home. But at the last minute, he decided to go back to the bar and help his brother close. Right now, he needed some advice from a guy who had actually managed to find a woman to love.

When he pulled into his parking spot behind the bar, he reached for his phone. On a whim, he decided to call her, just to see if he could smooth things over a bit more. He dialed the number and waited. It rang twice.

"Thai Express," the voice on the other end of the line said. "Pick-up or delivery?"

"Shit," he muttered.

"May I help you?"

"Sorry," Max said. "Wrong number." He checked the call against her number. He'd dialed the digits she'd given him. Either he'd messed up entering it on his phone or she'd deliberately given him a bad number.

He got out of the car and walked through the back door of the bar. The kitchen had closed an hour before and a few members of the staff were still cleaning up. When he entered the bar, there was still a crowd, but it wasn't nearly as busy as it had been earlier. He noticed Caroline, one of their best bartenders, behind the bar. "Is Dave still here?"

"In the office," she said. "Can you tell him we're

running low on rimming salt. I used the last container to make the rim mix for the Bloody Marys."

"No problem," Max said. A few people caught him on the way to the office but he still managed to get through the crowd pretty quickly. When he shut the door behind him, he found Dave on the computer, clicking through the liquor inventory.

"Caroline says you need more rimming salt. She used the last of it for the Bloody Mary stuff. Why don't you just order Bloody Mary salt?"

"Because we mix our own," Dave murmured. "We're known for our Bloody Marys. We sell a ton of them on Bloody Sundays. Ten bucks a pop."

"For tomato juice and vodka?" Max asked.

"Not just that. It's the garbage we add. A special salt on the rim, a shot of stuff that packs a punch, and a skewer that includes all kinds of pickled veggies. You should try one."

"I could use one right now," Max said, flopping down in a nearby chair.

Dave grabbed the phone and buzzed the bar. "Carrie, can you bring Max one of our Bloodies. Make it a good one." He hung up the phone, then turned to face his brother. "What are you doing back here?"

"I thought I'd come back and help you close."

His brother's eyebrow shot up and he gave Max a dubious look. "You left with a woman. I figured you'd be busy for the rest of the evening."

"I don't sleep with every woman I meet," Max said.

"Yes, you do. All the magazines say you do."

"Screw the magazines," Max muttered. "They said I was Madonna's new boytoy. I've never even met the woman. Don't believe everything you read."

"It didn't work out with the girl?" Dave asked.

"No, the girl was great. We made a date for tomorrow night—I guess that would be tonight."

"So, you two didn't …"

"No. This girl is…different. I don't know what it is. She's really sweet and kind of shy. But she sees right through me. I mean, she doesn't fall for my bullshit. And I feel like I know her." He paused. "Do you believe in reincarnation?"

"You think you shared a past life?"

"No. But it's like that." He sighed. "The only problem is, I don't have her phone number. I must have entered it wrong in my phone. I tried calling and I got a Thai restaurant."

"She gave you a bad number," Dave said, chuckling. "Oh, isn't that sweet. You finally meet a girl worth dating and she doesn't want you. Max Morgan has lost his mojo."

"It was probably just an innocent mistake."

"You think?" Dave asked.

"I'll just look her up in the book."

"What's her name?" Dave asked, turning back to the computer. "I'll look her up online."

"Angela Weatherly. Or maybe it's Weatherby." He groaned. "Shit. It's Weather-something." As Dave was searching the online phone book, Caroline came in with a huge glass, filled with Dave's version of a Bloody Mary. "Jeez, this thing is a meal," Max muttered.

"There isn't an A. Weatherby listed. There is an A. Weatherly listed."

"That must be it," Max said. "What's the address?"

"Looks like Lakeview," he said.

"She said she lives in Wicker Park," Max said. "You think I should try that one?"

"At two in the morning? No." Dave paused. "Give me her number. The one she gave you."

Max read off the number and Dave dialed it into his phone. When he got an answer on the other end, he grinned. "Hi there. This is kind of an odd request, but do you have a regular customer named Angela Weatherly?" He waited. "Weatherby. Yeah, that's it. Well, I want to send her dinner. She's not feeling well and could really use some hot soup." Dave ordered the soup, then gave them his credit card number. "And can I double-check the address on that?" He grabbed a pen and scribbled the address on a notepad. "Thanks. Don't tell her who it's from. It's a surprise."

When he hung up the phone, he spun around in his chair and tossed the notepad at Max, grinning triumphantly. "She lives on Ashland Avenue in Wicker Park. They deliver to her all the time. You want her phone number, you're going to have to get it on your own."

"You should have been a detective," Max said.

"I know. I've missed my calling. And you owe me fifteen bucks for the soup."

Max stared at the address. He'd stop by tomorrow morning with breakfast, maybe a latte and a Danish. And this time, he'd make sure he got the right number. He raked his hand through his hair. "I should go."

"I thought you were going to help me clean up," Dave said.

"Another time," Max said. "I have things to do."

"You're going to drive by her place, aren't you?"

"Maybe. If the light is on, maybe I'll ring the bell and get this all straightened out tonight."

"Man, you must have it really bad for this girl."

"Yeah," Max said. "Maybe I do." He started to the door, but Dave's voice stopped him.

"Lauren called earlier. She said Mom and Dad are throwing a barbecue a week from Saturday and Mom wants you there. They've invited all their friends. I'm not supposed to tell you, but I think she has a girl she wants you to meet. She's the daughter of one of her tennis partners."

"No," Max said. "I don't need my mother finding dates for me. I'm perfectly capable."

"She's not looking for dates, she's looking for a wife for you. If you marry a Chicago girl, then you'll be sure to come back to Chicago when you retire."

"You have to tell her to stop this," Max said. "The last time I was there, she was showing me pictures of her hairdresser's daughter. She had pink hair."

"You're her baby boy. She wants to see you happy."

"I'm happy. At least for now."

"You've got one shot with this girl," Dave warned. "You better not mess it up. Court her. Woo her. Take your time and do it right."

"That's easier said than done. When I'm with her, all I can think about is dragging her to bed." He stepped out of the office and headed right for the door, his gaze fixed on the address Dave had given him.

When he got to his car, he punched the address into his GPS, then pulled out onto the street. He'd just cruise by and see where she lived. He'd be able to scope out a Starbucks in the neighborhood and make a plan for the next morning.

When he reached Ashland Avenue, he watched the GPS as it counted down the distance. Right on cue, he found the address and pulled up to the curb in front of the building. But it wasn't a house or an apartment building.

"Wicker Park Tech Centre," he read from the sign over the front entrance. This must be where she worked. It made sense. She'd work late and send out for Thai. Unfortunately, the delivery guy was going to end up taking the soup back to the restaurant.

Still fifteen dollars was a small price to pay for locating the girl of his dreams. And tomorrow morning, he'd be waiting for her.

"I JUST THOUGHT, what the hell. Why not turn those old fantasies into reality. And everything was moving along. And then he just—stopped."

"Stopped what?" Ceci asked.

"Stopped seducing me. He just stopped. He tried to make it seem like the chivalrous thing to do. He said he didn't want to ruin things between us. It was so humiliating," Angela said. "I couldn't have made what I wanted any clearer if I'd sent him an engraved invitation. Angela Weatherby cordially invites you to rip her clothes off, ravage her body and leave her gasping for more."

Angela and Ceci paused and waited to cross the street, the morning rush hour alive around them. Horns honked, brakes squealed and a bus rolled to a stop near the intersection. They walked to work most mornings. Ceci and Will's flat was only five blocks from Angela's, so they used the walk to get a bit of exercise before starting the workday.

"It's better that everything turned out this way. I couldn't maintain my journalistic integrity after sleeping with him. And, considering his frustration with the press, he wouldn't be happy to learn that I'm one of the people intruding into his private life."

"That's different," Ceci said. "You're not seeking these women out. You're not making up these stories. You're just giving them a place to vent."

"I don't think Max Morgan would see it that way," Angela countered. She took a deep breath and smiled. "So, I'm going to move on. I'll revise the chapter, choose a new subject to interview and forget I ever met Max Morgan."

It was time to put her childish fantasies behind her. After all, in sixteen months, she'd celebrate her thirtieth birthday. How pathetic would it be if she were still carrying a torch for her high school crush?

Although… Angela was certain she hadn't misread the signals. He'd wanted her as much as she'd wanted him. Something wasn't right, but she didn't know him well enough to figure it out.

"It wasn't like I have some deformity he discovered. Everything was in the right place and it looked good." She glanced down at her chest. "Maybe it was my boobs. He's probably used to really big ones."

"You have nice boobs," Ceci said. "You didn't have anything hanging from your nose or stuck in your teeth, did you? 'Cause that can really wreck the mood."

"No! I looked at myself in the mirror and I thought I looked really good. And I know I was turning him on. I mean, that much was evident. He's very well-endowed, from what I could see."

"Really," Ceci said. "You saw him naked?"

"No. He was wearing those silky basketball shorts with nothing underneath. You could see everything. And I looked—a few times—but I didn't get a chance to touch." A shiver skittered down her spine. Just the thought of Max naked was enough to set her heart racing.

This was crazy. She'd gone into this ready to

finally put Max Morgan in the past, to prove that all her fantasies were just that, silly dreams about a man who didn't exist. How was she supposed to stop thinking about him now? She hadn't slept last night at all and since she'd crawled out of bed, he'd been the only thing on her mind.

"I feel like I'm moving backward. Like I'm going back to that time when he just consumed my life. I'd lay on my bed and make up long, elaborate stories about our dream life together."

"Stop thinking about him!" Ceci said.

"Easier said than done."

"So where did you leave it?"

"He asked me out for tonight, but after what happened, I knew he wasn't going to call. If he was really interested, he wouldn't have stopped when he did." Angela smiled weakly. "And now, I can finally put him behind me, for good."

If she said it enough times, maybe that would make it true. Except, there were all sorts of beautiful memories she had of their night together. And even though it ended badly, the beginning and middle was pure heaven.

"Maybe it's better that he did stop. I mean, how would you have felt this morning if you'd slept with him last night?"

"If we'd had sex, it probably would have been incredible. Then when he dumped me, I would have been left a lot angrier than I am now."

"So what are you going to do if he calls you? What are you going to say?"

"He won't call," Angela said. "He can't. I gave him a bad number."

Ceci stopped short with a little gasp. "You what?"

"I gave him the number for the Thai place down the block from our office. See, this way, it's kind of like I dumped him. It's finally over. I've put my obsession with Max Morgan in the past and I can go on with my life."

"Well, you had one night," Ceci said in a bright tone. "That's better than nothing."

Angela's cell phone rang and her heart skipped a beat. But when she flipped it open, she noticed her mother's number. She glanced up at Ceci. "My mother. She wants me to come to Evanston for a barbecue next weekend. One of her tennis ladies is throwing it and I guess she has a son she wants me to meet. We'd be perfect for each other, she says."

Angela turned the phone on. "Hi, Mom. You're up early." She listened patiently as her mother laid out a very logical case for meeting this man, reminding Angela that the prospects for marriage were diminishing with each year that passed. It had always been a point of conflict between the two of them. Her two sisters were already married, but Angela didn't see anything in their marriages that she envied.

Both of her brothers-in-law were dull, unromantic men who didn't know half of what Max Morgan did about seducing a woman. If Angela was going to have a man in her life, he was going to be sexy and exciting and fabulous in bed. Otherwise, what was the point?

Angela held her hand over the phone. "Now, we're moving into the guilt phase. My mother knows exactly how to pull my strings."

When Kathleen Weatherby set her mind on something, there was no changing it. "Just meet him, Angie. He's a very successful fellow. He's actually a bit of a celebrity, at least your father thinks so. He plays baseball. Now I know, you might think he's some kind of arrested adolescent, but from what his mother tells me, he's made some very wise investments."

Angela stopped, grabbing Ceci's arm. "He plays baseball?"

"Yes. On some team in Florida. What was the name of that team, Jack? The Deviled...Eggs?"

"Devil Rays?" Angela asked. "He plays for the Devil Rays?"

"You know the team? Yes, that's it. Your dad says it's the Devil Rays. His name is Max. His mother and I have become such good friends and we just got to talking. He's single and you're single and it would be perfect for both of you. It's a week from this Saturday. Surely, you can fit it into your schedule."

"Mom, I really can't. I have to—"

"You cannot continue to avoid social situations

like this." She paused. "Your sisters are both happily married. Don't you want that for yourself?"

"Mom, I'm not going to marry a guy just so I can say I'm married. I'm happy. I have my work and—"

"That silly Web site of yours is not a career. You spend your whole day with all those nasty men and when a good one comes along, you won't even try."

Angela's expression must have looked worrisome, because Ceci grabbed her arm. "Just hang up," she whispered.

"I'll have to call you back, Mom," Angela said. "The reception here is really bad. Ceci and I are on our way to the office. I'll talk to you later."

Angela hung up the phone, then bent over at her waist, desperately trying to draw her next breath. "You won't believe this. This is so, so weird. I mean, it's like, spooky weird." She looked up at Ceci. "My mother is trying to set me up with Max Morgan."

Ceci dragged her over to a nearby bench and pulled her down. "Oh, my God. Angie, this is like all the karmic forces in the universe have finally converged. I was reading about this at that New Age bookstore on Damen. You can't mess with this. No matter what happens, you and Max are destined to be together."

Angela stood up. "Don't be ridiculous," she said, starting back down the street. "It's a coincidence. Don't forget, we grew up in the same town, went to the same high school. Our parents live ten blocks away from each other. They belong to the same tennis club. They'd have met sooner or later. It just happened later."

She picked up her pace. The quicker she got to the office the better. She needed to get back into her routine, work hard and put all thoughts of Max out of her head. As they approached the office, Ceci grabbed her arm again, but this time, she pulled her behind a bus shelter.

"What are you doing?" Angela asked, twisting out of her grasp.

"Look! Isn't that him?"

Angela peered through the Plexiglas wall of the shelter, then quickly turned around. "What is he doing?"

Ceci looked over her shoulder. "He's sitting on the steps, reading the paper and drinking a latte, I think. He's really cute, Angie. I mean, I thought he was cute at the bar last night. But he's cute in actual daylight. See, I told you. Karmic forces. They cannot be denied."

"Stop it. He didn't come here for me. He's probably just taking a run and stopped to rest for a bit. He doesn't know where I work."

"It wouldn't be hard to figure it out," Ceci said. "All he'd have to do is put an Internet search out for your name and SmoothOperators would come up. There was that article in the Trib six months ago. And you were on that news show in January."

"Oh, God. Maybe he's seen the Web site. Maybe

he read his profile. What am I going to do? Does he look angry?"

"Go talk to him," Ceci said. "He's sitting there waiting for you. How sweet is that? Maybe he brought you a donut. Oh, that would be so romantic."

"Why are you so determined to put us together? You're going to be the one picking up the pieces when he dumps me. And you know he will. And that's when I'm going to say, I told you so."

"Oh, boo freaking hoo. I feel so sorry for you. You have a gorgeous man who wants to take you out on a date and you're grumbling about how miserable he's going to make you. Well, don't fall in love with him then. Go out, have a nice time and see what happens. And quit being such a beeyotch or no one is going to want to date you." She paused. "Ever again."

"You're the beeyotch," Angela whispered. "And I'll hate you forever if this blows up in my face."

"I may be a bitch, but I'm your best friend," Ceci replied in a low voice. "And I love you. Now go talk to him or I will."

When Angela refused to move, Ceci stepped back out on the sidewalk and started toward the office. As she approached, Max stood up. Angela watched as they chatted for a bit, then Ceci turned back and waved at Angela. Left with no choice, Angela walked up to the pair, a smile pasted on her face.

"There she is," Ceci said, with a cheery expression. "What was wrong? Did you have a pebble in your shoe?"

"It came untied," Angela said. "My shoe." She looked up at Max. "Hi. What are you doing here?"

"He came to see you," Ceci said. "You gave him the wrong phone number last night. I always have trouble remembering my own cell phone number. I mean, you never call yourself, right? Why would you remember it." She gave Max a cute little wave, then reached for the door. "I'll see you in a bit, Angie. Don't hurry."

"What are you doing here?" Angela asked.

"I thought I'd bring you some breakfast. But I've been sitting here so long, I ate the cheese Danish and drank the latte I bought you. Do you want to walk down to Starbucks with me?"

Angela knew she could use work as an excuse to beg off. This had disaster written all over it. Even if he didn't know about the Web site, chances were he'd find out sooner or later. And she already knew the effect he had on her. When she was with Max, she forgot all the reasons she was supposed to mistrust him. Still, she couldn't help but be a little curious as to what he was planning to say. "Sure," she said.

"They won't miss you at work?"

"I'm the boss. No one will miss me," she assured him.

"Good."

They strolled down the sidewalk in the direction of the coffee shop. "You didn't answer my question," she said.

"Which one?"

"Why are you here?"

"You gave me a bogus number last night. I was wondering if you'd done it on purpose or by accident. By the way, I already know you gave me the number of your favorite Thai restaurant, so don't bother lying. That's how I found you. I sent some chicken soup to this address last night at 1:00 a.m. I thought this was where you lived."

"Chicken soup?"

"It's a long story. So why did you give me a bad number?"

Angela knew she ought to make up some excuse, but for some reason, she wanted him to know what kind of effect his behavior had on women. "I didn't want to be disappointed when you didn't call," she finally said.

"But I asked you to dinner. We had a date."

"In the heat of passion, you asked me to dinner. Things look different the morning after."

"God, you must really think I'm a jerk," he said. "And you don't even know me."

His words brought her up short. True. She didn't know him. She was lumping him in with all the other misogynists she catalogued on her Web site and wrote about in her book. And she was accepting the opinions of women she didn't know. Maybe she ought to put more trust in her own observations.

"Man, you must have dated some real scumbags to be so cynical," he said.

"No," she said. "I'm sorry. It's just that…I don't

understand why you're interested in me. I know about you, Max Morgan. I'm not your type."

"Maybe I'm looking for a new type," he said. "And maybe you're exactly what I'm looking for."

Angela smiled and shook her head. "You are smooth, I'll give you that. I'm not sure whether to believe you or to run away as fast and as far as I can."

"Give me a chance," Max pleaded. "Just one date. And after that, maybe another five or twenty. And if you don't like the way things are going, you can dump me. I promise I won't kick up a fuss."

"I'll get to dump you?"

"Yes."

She thought about the offer for a long moment. Every fiber in her being told her to refuse. She knew the danger of spending time with Max. But curiosity overwhelmed common sense. "Okay, it's a deal," Angela said, holding out her hand. "I'll give you three dates to convince me of your honorable intentions. If you don't make the grade, I'm going to cut you loose."

"Five dates," he said.

"Four," she countered.

"Does last night count?"

Angela thought about it then shook her head. "No."

"What about this morning?"

"Yes," she said.

"All right. I guess that's fair." He grabbed her hand

as they continued to walk down the sidewalk. "So, how am I doing so far?" Max asked. "Are we having fun?"

"You'd be doing better if you hadn't eaten my Danish," she said. "And drank my coffee. But I'll forgive you for that."

He grinned, then wrapped his arm around her neck and pulled her close, kissing the top of her head. "I'm glad we got this all straightened out. I was beginning to think you didn't like me."

How could she not fall hopelessly in love with this man? He was sweet and charming and funny. And he knew exactly what to say to make her feel like she was the only woman who could make him happy.

She couldn't fall in love with him. At least not completely. But a little bit wouldn't hurt, would it?

THEIR FIRST DATE WAS going well, Max mused as they sat at an outdoor table sipping coffee and sharing a cinnamon roll. He hadn't had such a simple date since…well, ever. When he dated, it usually came along with cameras and curious onlookers. Today, he felt like a regular guy, enjoying the company of a beautiful woman on a breezy summer morning.

"Tell me about your work," Max said, taking another bite of the cinnamon roll. "You said it had to do with Web design."

"I'd rather not talk about work, if that's okay," Angela said.

"You said you're the boss."

"It's only the two of us," she said. "Me and Ceci. And occasionally we have a part-time programmer working for us."

"Some of the guys on the team have their own Web sites," he said. "I never thought much of doing it myself, though. It just seems like a lot of work."

"I suppose it depends on what you want to accomplish. If you want your name to become a brand of sorts, then a Web site is a good idea."

"I don't think we have a Web site for the bar. Maybe you could help us out with something like that?"

Angela shook her head. "We really have all the work we can handle right now. But I can put you in touch with someone if you're really interested."

She glanced at her watch and frowned. They'd been sitting at the coffee shop for nearly two hours. Max had hoped she wasn't noticing the time. "It's almost lunch time," she said. "I should really get to work."

"You're the boss, right?" he asked. "Skip work for the day. Let's go to the ballpark. The Sox are playing. I can probably get us seats in one of the luxury boxes." He wasn't sure if she even liked baseball, but the word *luxury* usually appealed to women.

Angela wagged her finger at him. "I know what you're doing. You think that if you run this date into the next and then into dinner it will only count as one date," she teased.

He sat back in his hair, thoroughly amused. Man,

she just didn't let him get away with anything, did she? Most guys might call her a ball-buster, but he liked that about Angela. She kept it real. "I never thought of that. Thanks for the idea." He pulled out his cell phone and handed it to her. "Call Ceci and tell her you won't be coming in. In fact, call her and ask her to join us."

"Really?"

"Yeah, and tell her to invite someone else along. Does she have a boyfriend?"

"Will," Angie said. "He's the one who told us about your bar. He hangs out there on Monday nights with a bunch of his friends. You've met him. He took a picture with you."

"Invite him. I'll get four tickets and we'll make a day of it."

He waited while she called Ceci and when she handed him the phone back, she had a bemused smile on her face. "So this is how famous people do things," she said. "You just make a few phone calls and it's done."

"Usually," he said. "Being a celebrity is good for some things. But most of the time, it's a huge pain in the ass."

"What else could you do?" she asked. "Could you get us a table tonight at Charlie Trotter's?"

"You want to eat at Charlie Trotter's?"

"No. I'm just wondering if you could get a table there."

"Probably," he said.

"Could you get us a table at any restaurant in Chicago?"

"Probably," he said. Max knew it sounded conceited, but she wanted the truth. And maybe it was better she understood from the start what it was like to be with him. "The thing is, it can get complicated if people know where I'm going to be ahead of time. Then there are cameras and questions. Like, if we were to go sit in regular seats at the game, we'd both be in the news tomorrow. I hate that they're always in my business."

"Are you really that good a baseball player?"

"This has nothing to do with my skills on the playing field," he said. "It has everything to do with my skills playing the field."

She smiled at the joke. "It's about the women."

"Yeah, it's all about the women. Unfortunately, I realized that too late and now that's all anybody's interested in. A few months back, they wrote that I was addicted to painkillers and I was rushed to the hospital after overdosing. My nephew heard about it at school and flipped. He couldn't stop crying. They're such leeches. I hate it."

"Why would they be interested in me?" she asked. "I'm not famous."

"They're interested in anyone I'm interested in. I can't believe there was a time when I thought I wanted that kind of notoriety. I thought it would be cool to date famous women—models and actresses. Have my face in the magazines. And for a while it was pretty much fun. Unfortunately, a nice guy isn't all that interesting to the press. And if they can't find any dirt, they invent it."

"Then stop dating actresses and models," she said.

"They're going to be just as interested in you. I'm giving you fair warning. It hasn't been that bad here in Chicago. The press has kept a respectable distance. And since I told them I was thinking about retiring, I'm not such a hot story."

"Are you retiring?"

"I haven't decided," he said. "Depends upon the rehab." He paused. "Hopefully, they won't bother us. But if they do, expect that there will be some pretty silly stories."

"Like what?"

"That we're engaged, fighting, expecting a baby, hooked on drugs, dependant on booze, having plastic surgery, planning our wedding, moving to Europe, buying a mansion in Beverly Hills, looking at a condo in Manhattan, getting a dog. I don't know. It could be anything."

Angela giggled. "Wow. All that after just one date."

"It's not so funny when you're in the middle of it," Max warned.

"But we'll know what's true," she said. "It shouldn't make any difference what they say."

She was wonderfully naive about it all. And maybe she wouldn't have to endure the scrutiny of the media.

He could only hope they'd be able to get to know each other without having to deal with it.

"So, if I wanted to watch the Fourth of July fireworks from the deck of a yacht on Lake Michigan, you could arrange that?"

"Is that what you'd like to do?" he asked.

"I've heard it's really cool to watch them from out on the lake."

"I'll see what I can do," Max replied.

"I was just kidding," she said.

The fourth of July was a month away. If they were still together after a month, then it would be one of the longest relationships he'd ever had with a woman. And if Angela wanted to see fireworks from a yacht, he'd make it happen. "But today, we're going to the game." Max stood and held out his hand to her. "Now, I have to run home and change. But I'll come back in about an hour to get you and your friends."

"Where is your car?"

"At home. I ran here. I needed the exercise. Can you make it back to the office on your own?"

"No, I might get lost," Angela said, shaking her head. "I walk here all the time by myself."

"Oh, sarcasm," he said. "I like you even more now. I have a great appreciation for sarcasm." He leaned close and kissed her cheek. "I'll see you in a little while." With that, he pulled his sunglasses off the brim of his cap and slid them on. "Look both ways before crossing the street. And don't talk to strangers." He jogged backward down the sidewalk, waving to her as he went. "And prepare yourself for a great afternoon." Then he turned and headed toward home.

As he ran, he felt a wonderful energy pulsing through him. For the first time in a very long time, he was…happy. Over the past three or four years, he hadn't found much pure joy in his life. Everything he achieved seemed to come with strings attached. But this feeling he had when he was around Angela was simple to understand.

There were so many different things they could do together. The fact that she ran her own business was a big plus. They both had the freedom to come and go as they pleased. They could take off for a weekend in New York or fly down to Florida for a few days. He could steal her away to San Francisco for a romantic getaway.

As he jogged at a stoplight, waiting for the traffic to pass, Max realized he was getting ahead of himself. He needed to take this slowly. "Woo her," he said. "Court her."

But how easy would that be? The more time he spent with Angela, the more he wanted to learn everything about her—including what made her pulse beat fast and her body ache with desire. He had no doubt he could pleasure her in bed. In truth, he was much better at that than he was at dating.

"Hey, Max Morgan! Rock on!"

Max glanced up to see a truck driving by with a

kid hanging out of the passenger window. He waved and smiled. "Rock on!" he called.

The driver beeped his horn and before long, there were other drivers staring at him and waving. As soon as the light turned, Max jogged across the intersection. Though Max wanted to be a different person here in Chicago, there were always reminders that he had a different life in Florida, and a career that paid very well.

This would be a stolen summer, a time when he could experience life the way it was meant to be lived. His time wouldn't be wasted. He'd figure out the man he planned to be once baseball was over. And Angela was going to be a part of his summer. He could learn a lot from her. And maybe, if things went well, they'd have more than just this summer.

4

"WILL IS IN HEAVEN," Ceci said.

They sat together in the back row of seats in the luxury box. Will and Max were sitting outside, their arms braced on the railing as Max pointed to the scoreboard.

"Look at him," Ceci continued. "He's like a little kid." She tipped her head and fanned her face with her program. "I think I'm having a moment."

"Really?"

"How can I not love that man? He's got a pennant in one hand, a foam finger on the other and a big old mustard stain on his shirt. Who else is going to love him?"

Angela giggled. "Will is a pretty nice guy. In all the time you two have been going together, he's never done anything to make me doubt his feelings for you. There's something to be said for that."

"Max is a nice guy, too," Ceci said. "I didn't expect that. I mean, after reading his profile, I thought he'd be full of himself. But he's really sweet. And it was so nice of him to invite us here. Will is going to be talking about this for months."

"You told Will to keep quiet about our business, right?"

Ceci nodded. "Yes. And he understands completely. Besides, he's not about to do anything to mess up his chances for future fun with Max Morgan."

"Good," Angela said. "I was thinking that…well, maybe we should take Max's profile off the site. Just until…you know, we're over."

"Really? We've never done that, Angie. Don't you think we have a responsibility to be completely objective?"

"Of course," she said. "But I know how he'd feel about this. He wouldn't be happy. He'd feel like it was a betrayal."

"Well then, he shouldn't have treated those women so badly," Ceci said.

"Maybe he didn't," Angela said. "It's their word against his. And you said it yourself, he's a nice guy."

"To you. That doesn't mean he was nice to those other women." Ceci sighed. "Secrets aren't a good thing, Angie. They have a tendency to blow up in your face. Maybe you should just tell him. If he really likes you, it shouldn't make a difference."

"I'm not going to tell him," she said. "If he finds out, I'll disarm that bomb when the time comes."

They watched as Max and Will stood and walked

back into the box. They were in a heated discussion about something called a sacrifice bunt. But when they got inside, Max's attention turned toward her. He sent her a warm smile. "You having fun?"

"I am," she said.

"Me, too," Ceci replied.

Will pulled off his Sox cap, the foam finger still stuck on his hand. "Max is going to take me down to the clubhouse to meet some of the players. Is that all right? I mean, you don't want to leave right away, do you?"

"The game is over?" Angela asked.

"Yeah," Max said. "The Sox won, 4-3."

Ceci shook her head. "Nope, we're free all day."

He grinned. "Okay, then. Let's go, Max."

"Honey, you might want to clean up that mustard stain before you go," Ceci suggested.

He glanced down at the front of his shirt, then groaned. "Oh, man. I knew I shouldn't have had that fourth hot dog."

"Don't worry," Max said. "We'll pick up something for you to wear on the way."

"Right," he said. "We can do that?"

"Are you ladies interested in meeting some of the players, too?" Max asked.

"I think we'll wait here," Angela said.

Max bent close and kissed her, lingering for a long moment, before drawing away. "We won't be long. If you want anything, just pick up that phone over there and order it."

"There's plenty to eat here already," Angela said, nodding at the luxurious buffet set up along the wall. "Did you pay for all that food?"

Max shook his head. "Nope. One of my buddies on the team took care of it. My contract is up at the end of this season. I'll be a free agent and I think he wants me to come play in Chicago."

"You'd leave the Devil Rays?"

"Who knows? They might just release me if I can't come back from the injury. It might be fun to play in my hometown. At least for a year or two." He kissed her again. "Oh, and the team is called the Rays. They changed the name a few years ago."

"Oh." Angela frowned. "So there's no devil in it anymore?"

"Nope, just the Rays."

After he and Will left, she went back to sit beside Ceci. "I'm going to have to change the title of Chapter Five. He's not a Devil Ray anymore. He's just a—Ray."

"I don't think it makes much difference, do you? I mean, no one is supposed to know his identity anyway. And he is a sexy devil, that's for sure."

"I guess it doesn't matter."

"Are you really going to write about him, Angie? I think you're losing your objectivity. You wanted to take him off the site a minute ago."

She sighed softly. "I know. But despite his behavior here in Chicago, he has been the typical smooth operator. Then again, maybe he's the exception to the rule. Maybe he can change." She sighed. "The only way I can see to move forward with the book is to focus on the person he was before we met at the bar. Who's to say that he wouldn't have gone home with a different girl that night and broken her heart?" Angela reached for her beer and took a sip.

"I'm not sure what I'm going to do. He just told me he's considering moving back to Chicago to play. His contract is up at the end of this season."

"Really? So, there's a chance you could be together for a lot longer than you anticipated."

"No," she said. "I'm not going to start planning a future with him. This could all be over tomorrow. I'm not making any decisions about the site or the book or Max Morgan today. Or tomorrow."

"I hope it's not over tomorrow," Ceci said, crawling over Angela. She stood in front of the buffet. "I like being around famous people. They eat for free. They drink for free. They sit in luxury boxes and drive in fancy European sedans with tinted windows."

"I can see how fame would be addictive. Life is so easy when you have money and connections."

"Admit it, Angie. You must have imagined what it would be like to have a future with this guy. What girl wouldn't? He's gorgeous, rich, and really nice. If you're not thinking of snatching him up, then you are in serious denial."

"No, I haven't. I can't. And I won't. I'm not some silly teenager anymore. I understand the realities of relationships and what's going on here is simple infatuation. We're in that phase when we're both perfect for each other. But that will wear off. I know it will." She held up her hand when Ceci opened her mouth. "And don't go all karmic on me."

"The reality is, this guy really likes you. The way he looks at you is proof. He treats you like a princess. When he opened your car door for you, I thought Will was going to hurt himself hurrying to open my door for me. What guy in this day and age has decent manners?"

"He can have manners and still be a creep."

"Will you just give him a chance? Don't always be looking for faults. He might not be perfect for those other women, but he might be perfect for you." Ceci sighed. "Now, come over here and help me eat some of this food. We can't just leave it here. Do you think they have take-out containers?"

Angela got out of her seat and joined Ceci in front of the table. "I'm starving. I didn't want to act like I was too impressed by all this, so I didn't eat much." She paused, then groaned. "Ceci, what am I doing here? I want to hate him. I should hate him. But I can't. I feel like I'm drowning here."

Ceci nodded. "Yeah. I can see how you'd have a hard time resisting him." She popped an éclair in her mouth and considered her next words as she chewed. "Maybe you're right. Maybe he is the exception to the rule. And maybe he's been waiting for you his whole life."

Angela rubbed her forehead. "I can't think about

this now. I need chocolate. Are those éclairs?" She reached out and grabbed one, then took a bite of the custard-filled pastry. "Oh, my God. This is so good. We have to take these home. Find something to wrap them in, Ceci. I can put them in my bag."

For the next fifteen minutes, Angela and Ceci worked their way through the buffet, tasting every item at least twice. They kept an eye on the door, ready to scamper back to their seats if the boys came back. The cream puffs and éclairs and a few brownies were safely hidden in Angela's bag, carefully wrapped in a linen napkin, and the sushi rolls were nearly gone when Max and Will walked back in.

Will looked like a kid who'd just spent the day in a candy store. He showed them the baseball he'd gotten autographed and was telling Ceci about everyone he'd met, while Max stepped behind Angela and wrapped his arms around her waist. "Are you ready to go?" he asked.

"Sure." She turned around and faced him, then dropped a kiss on his lips. "Thank you for today. They both had a great time."

"How about you?"

"Me, too," she said.

"Good. Then I guess our first date has been a success. I'm batting .200 so far." He rested his hands on her hips. "I thought we could get some dinner. What about you two? Are you hungry?" he called, looking over her shoulder.

"Sure," Will said. "I could eat."

"No," Ceci said. "We have a previous commitment. We're going to have to take a rain check on dinner."

"Rain check?" Will frowned. "We don't have anything going on."

"Yes, we do," Ceci insisted. "We have that thing at that place. You know. I told you about it last week."

"You told me we didn't have anything going on today and—" He stopped short, realizing what Ceci was trying to do. "Oh, right. That thing. Now I remember." Will gave Max an apologetic shrug. "Yeah, we can't miss that thing."

"I thought you were going to tell me you had to take your mother—or was it your brother—shopping," Max said. "There's no reason for excuses. We'd love to have you come to dinner with us, right Angela?" He turned to look at her and for a second she couldn't speak. This was another moment! She was looking at Max, watching him treat her friends with such warmth and kindness and she was having a moment.

She swallowed hard. "We'd love to have you come with us," she said softly, trying to keep the emotion from tightening her throat. "I know you're not doing anything, Ceci, so don't bother making a fuss."

"No," Will said. "We'll do dinner another time. Our treat. Besides, I should check in at work. Unlike the rest of you, I have a boss who doesn't take kindly to afternoons off."

They walked out to the parking lot, chatting about

the game and laughing together like they'd known each other for years. Angela was amazed at how easily Max fit in. She'd always felt like a third wheel when she spent time with Will and Ceci, but now the wagon was perfectly balanced.

They dropped Will and Ceci at their flat and after saying their goodbyes, they got back in the car. "Dinner," Max said. "What are you thinking?"

She drew a deep breath. After everything she'd eaten that afternoon, she wasn't really hungry. And it was so hot and sticky outside, she really didn't want to get dressed up. "We could send out for a pizza," she suggested.

"I could eat pizza," Max said with a grin. "Besides, it's too hot to get dressed up and go out. Why don't we swing by your place, grab your suit and we'll take a swim?"

"The lake is really cold," Angela said.

"I've got a pool on the roof of my building. They don't allow kids, so no one ever uses it. Especially at night."

Max continued to amaze her. He knew exactly what she wanted and he'd offered it to her. She couldn't think of anything more refreshing than a swim on a summer evening like this. And pizza would be the perfect meal. "How do you do that?"

"Do what?" he asked.

"Know exactly the right thing to say. Did you take a class when you were younger? Or is there some secret handbook that they pass out to you guys?"

"I like pizza," he said. "And swimming seemed like a good idea. Would you rather do something else? Just tell me what."

"See, there you go again," Angela said. "You make it so easy for me to like you."

"Isn't that the point?" Max asked. "If I did stuff you didn't like, then you wouldn't want to go out with me."

"No, no," Angela said, shaking her head. "It's the way you do it. You make it sound like eating pizza with me is the only thing in the world you want to do."

"It is," Max said. "But if you don't want pizza, we can order Thai or Chinese. There's a really good—"

"No!" Angela cried. "It's not about what we eat."

"What is it about then?"

"If one of your buddies called you right now and told you there were some hot Swedish swimsuit models waiting for you at some bar and they were a sure thing, you'd go, right? You blow me off to hang out with them, right?"

"No," Max said, frowning.

"You're lying," Angela accused. "You would so go."

He twisted around in his seat to face her. "I would not. I'm spending time with you, because I choose to, Angie. I don't want to be with anyone else. Besides, I don't think there are many Swedish swimsuit models out there. They're too pale to tan." He turned the car on. "Now, let's go get your swimsuit and then we'll decide about dinner. What do you like on your pizza?"

This was exactly what she expected of him. With absolute ease, he could make her believe she was the most important woman in his life. That his entire world revolved around her. And that eating pizza next to a pool with her was better than dining at a gourmet restaurant with a movie star.

She knew the sexy devil was charming. But she'd never realized just how insidious that charm could be. With every moment they spent together, she was more convinced Max wasn't the man with the profile on her site.

She wanted to throw her arms around his neck and kiss him until her lips were sore. She wanted to run her fingers through his hair and smooth her palms over his chest and discover the body beneath the clothes.

Was it so wrong to want him? Why not admit she'd been taken in, just like all those other girls? Why not enjoy it while it lasted? Angela knew the risks of surrender, but right now, looking into his gorgeous eyes, the rewards far outweighed any risk to her heart.

THE UNDERWATER LIGHTS cast wavering shadows on the pool deck. Max sank below the surface then swam underwater to the opposite end, popping up in front of Angela. Bracing his hands on either side of her legs, he boosted himself up and kissed her before dropping back down into the water. "Are you going to come in?" he asked. "It's really nice."

"I'm having more fun watching you," Angela replied with a wicked grin. She swirled her feet around in the water in front of him and he grabbed her foot, kissing the arch. "It would be much more fun if you didn't have those shorts on."

Max glanced up at her, his lips pressed against her ankle. "What would be the point if you won't get in the water. I won't let you drown. I promise."

"I'm not worried about that," she said.

"What are you worried about then? I've already seen you wet and you look beautiful with your hair all stringy. Unless you don't want to get that suit wet."

She wore a pretty flowered two-piece that left just enough to the imagination. It was the first chance he'd had to really appreciate the beauty of Angie's body. She was fit, not thin, with curves in all the right places. Unlike a lot of the girls he'd dated, she boasted no surgical enhancements. Her breasts, her nose and her lips were all completely natural.

Angie leaned back and stared up at the sky, kicking her feet in the water. "This is so nice. It's like we're not even in the city anymore. I can't believe people don't use this pool. I'd be up here every night."

"It would be more fun if it belonged exclusively to us," he said. "I have a pool at my place in Florida. Bigger than this one." He kicked off the side and swam toward her. "With a hot tub. And a big, tall fence around it."

"I have bathtub," Angela teased. "I do laps every morning."

"All right," Max said. "That might have sounded a bit egotistical. Maybe I was hoping to impress you." In truth, he was thinking about how much fun it would be to take off his shorts and her suit and enjoy the feel of her body against his in the water. If they were in Florida, he wouldn't have to worry about anyone barging in on them. After swimming for a while, they could lie down on one of the comfortable chaises on the deck and continue what they'd started in the pool.

Max pulled himself out of the water and sat down next to her, pushing aside the fantasy. "You're very hard to impress."

"That's not true," she said.

"What do you like about me, Angela?"

She regarded him with a cool stare, her eyebrow arched. Max had never met a woman like her before. She certainly kept him on his toes. He wasn't sure from one moment to the next what she was thinking. But then, when she turned that smile on him, he could almost believe she was as captivated by him as he was by her. "I like your...hair," she said, lowering her gaze in mock innocence. "And you have a very nice body. And your voice. That's nice, too."

"Nice?" He jumped back down into the pool, then pulled her along with him. She cried out in surprise, but he held tight, cradling her body against his. "I told you the water was nice."

"It's warm. Like bathwater," she said. Angela wrapped her arms around his neck and kissed him, deliberately taking her time before drawing away. Her body rubbed against his provocatively and Max wondered if she knew what she was doing to him. "I like your mouth," she said. "And the way you kiss me."

Max growled softly as he pulled her into another kiss. Beneath the water, her skin felt like silk. He ran his palms from her shoulders to the small of her back, then drew her hips against his. "What about the way I touch you?" he asked.

"I like that, too," she whispered. "See, there's a lot about you that I appreciate."

Something had changed. The moment she'd kissed him, he felt her grow pliant in his arms. A silent surrender. He slipped his hand between them to cup her breast, softly teasing at her nipple through the fabric of her suit. Angela watched him, and then to his surprise, she reached back and untied the top, letting it fall in front of her.

Max bit back a groan. It took every ounce of his will to resist. But she'd given him an invitation to touch. How could he refuse? Sinking down further, he traced a line of kisses from her shoulder to her breast. And then, his mouth found her nipple, peaked from his caress.

Angela moaned, tipping her head back and

furrowing her fingers through his hair. Max pulled her legs up around his waist as they bobbed in the water, his lips gently exploring the exposed flesh. But as he continued, Max knew they were reaching the point of no return.

He drew back and waited until she opened her eyes and looked at him. "Are you hungry? We could go down and order the pizza."

Angela sent him a puzzled looked, the same one she'd given him that first night when he'd stopped mid-seduction. "No. Let's stay up here a bit longer. It's so relaxing." She undid the back of her suit and tossed it on the deck, then closed her eyes and leaned back, holding her arms out until she floated in front of him, her hair fanning out around her. He moved his palm up her belly, then back again.

It was so easy to get caught up in his desire, Max mused. Though he tried to ignore his need to possess her, there were moments when he let himself imagine what they might share, what it would feel like to move inside her. He'd always followed his instincts, taking pleasure where it was offered without any regrets.

But what had seemed so casual with women he barely knew, took on much more meaning with Angela. He wanted her, not to satisfy his own needs, but so that he might know everything about her. The impulse to strip off the rest of their clothes was too intense to ignore.

She opened her eyes and he pulled her back into

his arms. "I'm hungry," he murmured. "We should go down."

Confused, Angela watched him for a moment, then reluctantly nodded. He slipped his hands around her waist and set her on the edge of the pool, then crawled out next to her. Straightening, Max helped her to her feet and collected the towels he'd brought with him, wrapping one beneath Angie's arms to hide her naked breasts.

They rode the elevator down three floors to his twenty-second floor apartment. When they opened the door, the chill from the air conditioning rushed out.

"You should get out of that wet suit," he said softly, his gaze fixed on her mouth. Max rubbed her arms and her skin prickled beneath his touch. "I'll get you something warmer to wear."

She stared at him, silently, as if she were waiting for something more than words. "Here we are again," she said. "With just a towel between us."

"I don't—"

"The last time we were in your apartment, you were wearing it." She reached down and slipped out of the bottom to her suit, letting it drop to the floor before kicking it aside.

This was crazy, Max thought. They were both consenting adults. Why wait any longer? And she was right. All it would take was just a flick of his finger and the towel would be gone. He reached down, smoothing his hand over her shoulder. "You really want to do this? I can wait."

"Why are you waiting?" she asked.

"I don't want to mess this up," he said. "But if you really want—"

Angie nodded. "Yes, I really want this. Do you?"

"Oh, God, yes," he said.

A moment later, the towel fell to the floor and she stood in front of him, naked. Max wasn't quite sure what to do first. He picked up the towel and rubbed it over her body. He'd never denied himself before, never even considered the consequences of indulging in recreational sex. But it was different now. He needed this to be right between them.

She grabbed the towel from his hands and began to rub it over his chest. Then she hooked her finger in the waistband of his board shorts. "You should get out of your wet suit," she murmured.

He slowly shoved the shorts down over his hips, then let them fall to his feet. Drawing a deep breath Max waited, allowing her to make the next move. She made work of drying him off and every time she came close to his growing erection, he held his breath. There was no ignoring the fact that he was aroused, but she was doing a pretty good job of it.

When she finally tossed the towel aside, Max slipped his arm around her waist and pulled her body against his. The contact was everything he'd expected it to be, electric and overwhelming, so powerful that he thought he might come before she even touched him.

With nothing between them, they were both free to explore each other's body and they did, slowly, silently, each caress a tantalizing prelude to the next. There was nothing of the practiced seducer in him anymore. He wanted to proceed at her speed, making sure that his pleasure was secondary to hers.

The distance that she usually kept between them was suddenly gone, dissolving the moment her naked body touched his. She arched into his touch, her breathing quick and shallow, her lips searching for his. And when her fingers finally grazed his rigid cock, Max was ready to explode.

He clenched his jaw and drew a deep breath, thinking about the embarrassment he'd suffer if he let himself go to soon. The thought was enough to temper his need.

Slowly, she stroked him, her touch soft, but firm, and he grew even harder beneath her caress. Max pressed his lips into the curve of her neck, listening to her soft gasps and tiny sighs. And when he finally touched her between her legs, the gasps turned into a moan of such intensity that he thought she'd reached her peak already.

He stopped, then began again, this time his caress more gentle. If they only had one night together, it would be the best night she'd ever experienced. He'd bring her to an orgasm so powerful that she'd never forget it. So powerful that she'd want to experience it over and over again.

ANGELA KNEW SHE WAS CLOSE. His gentle assault sent wild sensations coursing through her body. She could barely form a rational thought, yet she was almost afraid to let go.

If she did, everything she'd ever thought about him, every negative stereotype she'd attached to him, would be gone. She'd never be able to think of him without remembering this. He wanted her, needed her as much as she needed him. This wasn't just a casual seduction; they shared something between them, something special.

A current flashed through her body and suddenly, she was there, on the edge again. Let go, her mind screamed. Surrender and everything will be all right. But could she trust that he'd be there to catch her?

A slow ache built inside of her, a tension she could no longer deny. Casting caution and common sense to the wind, Angela surrendered, her mind completely focused on the feel of his fingers between her legs.

The first spasm hit her hard and by complete surprise. She cried out, grabbing his shoulders to maintain her balance. When the shudders came, she jerked away, unable to take it anymore. But he was there again, drawing her orgasm out, making her give him every last bit of her soul.

When it was finally over, she leaned against him, her legs weak, her body completely spent. She'd never experienced anything so powerful before. Angela closed her eyes and felt the tears well up in her throat. If she was wrong about him, if this was the end instead of the beginning, then she'd regret this night for her entire life.

"Are you all right?" he whispered.

She nodded, her cheek pressed against his chest. "I think so."

"Would you like to continue or do you want to rest for a while?"

She pressed a kiss to his chest, amused by the question. "I think I can continue."

"Good," he growled, scooping her up into his arms. He carried her down the hall to his bedroom, then dropped her onto the bed, stretching out on top of her and trapping her body beneath his, his hands braced on either side of her head. "You know that once we do this, we're going to want to do it again. And again."

"I'm counting on that," Angela said.

He bent his elbows, his mouth hovering over hers. "Are you ready?"

"Yes," Angela murmured.

He kissed her, his lips soft against hers, his tongue tracing the shape of her lower lip. As she lost herself in the tantalizing taste of his mouth, he reached down and pulled her leg up beside his hip. Angela knew that with just one shift of her body, he could be inside of her. But she was willing to wait, allowing Max to choose the moment.

As his mouth drifted over her body, Angela closed her eyes and enjoyed the fresh rush of need that pulsed through her veins. Though the after-effects of her orgasm still controlled her responses, she felt a new desire begin to grow inside her.

Again and again, he brought her close, with his fingers, with his tongue, until she was whispering his name, pleading for relief. When she tried to finish it herself, he gently drew her hand away and then began again.

When she finally couldn't take any more, he sensed her need. Before she could open her eyes, he had retrieved a condom from the bedside table and sheathed himself. She waited, arching against him as he settled between her legs. And then he was there, softly, slowly entering her, inch by delicious inch.

Angela held her breath, the pleasure so intense every nerve in her body was on fire. Max began to move, drawing away and then driving into her in a languid rhythm that betrayed his own desire.

She looked up at him and he smiled sleepily, his eyes drifting shut with each thrust. Her pleasure only intensified and she was surprised at how quickly he brought her back to the edge again.

Her fingers dug into his shoulders as she urged him on, deeper and faster, bringing her closer and closer. And then, to Angela's astonishment, another orgasm wracked her body. But this time, he was with her, tensing, then shuddering as he thrust deep and hard.

When it was over, Max kissed her softly, nuzzling

his nose against hers. It had been everything she'd dreamed it might be and so much more. Maybe Ceci was right, Angela mused. Maybe this was some kind of karma. They seemed to fit together so perfectly, as if they'd been made for each other.

He lay down beside her, his hand clutching hers, his gaze fixed on the ceiling. "I'm really, really hungry." His stomach growled and he pulled her hand up and kissed it. "Sorry. There are just certain parts of my body I can't control."

Angela turned over and patted his belly. "We can order pizza now."

"Pizza will take too long. I want something sweet," he said. "Not that your body wasn't delicious, but I need carbs right now if we're going to do this again."

"Are we going to do this again?" Angela asked.

"Damn right we are," he said, sitting up. "Do you think we could send out for ice cream? Does Dairy Queen deliver?"

"No," Angela said. "But I have another idea. Go get my bag. I think I left it next to the door."

He crawled out of bed and Angela watched as he walked out of the room, admiring his wide shoulders and tight backside. He really did have an incredible body, so perfect. Except for the surgical scar on his shoulder, he could pass for one of those Greek statues. She wondered how many other women had admired his butt from the seats of various baseball stadiums.

When he returned, Max set the bag on the bed. "Please, tell me you have a candy bar in there."

"Nope. Do you have milk? We need milk."

He left again and Angela pulled out the desserts she'd pilfered from the stadium. Spreading the napkins on the bed, she rearranged the miniature cream puffs and éclairs and frosted brownies on the napkin, then waited for him to return.

When he did, he stopped at the door of the bedroom, staring at the feast laid out on his bed. "I've never understood the mysteries that lie at the bottom of a woman's bag, but I won't question this one."

Angela patted the spot beside her. "Sit."

He handed her the half-gallon of milk and she set it down beside her bag. "Is there a fully-equipped pastry kitchen in your purse?"

"No, I took these from the table at the ball game. They were just going to go to waste and they were so good."

He tipped his head back and laughed. "I swear the surprises never end with you, Angela. And just when I think I have you figured out."

"What's surprising? That I'd steal goodies for future consumption? I'm a very practical girl, Max. You should know that by now."

"That you'd admit it with such unabashed glee. Besides it's not stealing when it belonged to you in the first place. It's relocating. Or even liberating. You liberated those éclairs."

She picked one up and held it out to him. "Taste."

Max bit into it and then moaned softly. "These are good."

"Better than sex?"

Max pretended to consider his answer, furrowing his brow. "Better than bad sex. Doesn't touch what we have, though. That would take a double chocolate cheesecake with raspberry sauce and whipped cream."

Angela pretended she was insulted, then playfully pushed an éclair into his nose, leaving custard dripping onto his chin. But before he could return the favor, she leaned forward and caught the dripping custard with her tongue. Slowly, she licked the rest of the mess off his face.

"Do that again," he murmured.

Angela straddled his crossed legs, facing him, the éclair in her hand. She touched the chocolate to his nose, then licked it off. Dotting custard and chocolate on different parts of his body, his shoulder, his chest, his biceps, she used it to explore the perfection of his form.

When she was through, she took a huge bite of the éclair and handed it to him. "Yum," she said with a wicked grin.

"Now I'm all sticky," he said.

"We could go back up to the roof for a swim."

"That sounds like a plan," he said. "Or we could just take a shower."

She lay down next to him and groaned. "I love éclairs but I don't think they love me." Angela rubbed her belly. "Let's stay here a bit longer. I'm not sure my legs are fully functional yet."

He grabbed the milk and took a long drink, then set it aside. "I could get used to this," he said.

"Eating éclairs in bed?"

"No, having you in my bed. Naked and happy. I like it."

Angela smiled to herself. She'd expected to feel a tiny bit of guilt over what they'd done, a sliver of doubt over her choice. But there was nothing about what happened between them she could regret.

"I guess our second date went pretty well," he said, staring up at the ceiling again. "Swimming, sex and dessert. My batting average is quickly rising."

She reached out and smoothed her hand over his belly, coming to rest at his groin. "You've got a few more innings left to play, Max," she said.

5

MAX ROLLED OVER IN BED, opening one eye to the morning light. A sharp pain in his shoulder caused him to curse and he rolled back again, working out the twinge. Though the surgery had been nearly four months ago, he still had pain. Either the swimming or the sex had been too much for him and considering how much time he spent at both last night, Max was sure it wasn't the swimming.

When the ache had subsided, he sat up and found the other side of the bed empty. "Angela?" he called. His voice echoed through the silent apartment. Then he noticed the note on her pillow. Max snatched it up. "I have to work sometime. Date number two tonight. Better make it good."

He chuckled, then flopped back down onto his pillow. Smiling seemed to be the only thing he could manage. His body was exhausted, his desire completely sated and he felt completely transformed. He reached for the phone beside the bed, ready to call her, merely to hear her voice. Then he realized he didn't know her number by memory yet.

At that very moment, the phone rang and he reached out and grabbed it. "You better have a very good reason for leaving my bed this morning," he said.

"Some of us have to work," Angie replied. "And with all the noise I made, you didn't even move. You were snoring."

"I'm sure that was attractive," he said. "What time did you leave?"

"About an hour ago. I caught a cab. I just got home. I'm going to shower and then head into work."

"Why don't you shower and head back here?" he said. "You're the boss, you can take the day off."

"I took yesterday off," she said. "And if the boss doesn't work, the boss doesn't make money."

"I have plenty of money for both of us," Max said.

"I'm not dating you for your money," she said.

"Why are you dating me?" he asked.

"For your body. Call me later. Tonight, I get to choose what we do. Go back to sleep."

"Bye, baby," he said.

"Bye," she cooed.

The line went dead. He switched off the phone and tossed it aside. But almost immediately, it rang again. "She can't get enough of me," Max murmured. He pushed the button and held it to his ear. "I knew you'd change your mind. My bed is so lonely without you."

"That is not what a mother wants to hear first thing in the morning, Max."

He winced, biting back a curse. "Hi, Mom."

"Hello, darling. I won't bother asking you what you've been doing."

"It's not what you think," he said.

"I prefer not to think about it," she said. "Get out of bed and get dressed. I'm on my way to your place. We're going to have coffee. I'll pick you up out front in five minutes."

Max ran his hand over his chest. He was still sticky from last night's adventure with the éclairs. "Give me ten. I have to hop in the shower."

"All right. I'll see you in a few minutes." Max drew a deep breath and rolled out of bed. Reaching behind his head, he stretched the kinks out of his shoulder, then rubbed at the scar as he walked to the bathroom.

Five minutes was all he needed for a shower and five minutes after that, he was downstairs, watching for his mother's car. When the Saab pulled up, he hopped in the passenger side, then leaned over and gave his mom a kiss on the cheek.

"Where's the nearest coffee shop?" she asked.

"Out the driveway, then take your first left. As long as we're in the car, we'll go to my favorite place."

Max gave her directions as they drove west. The coffee shop, Beanie's, was in a busy part of the

Lincoln Park neighborhood. He kept his eye out for a parking place, but knew that at this time of the day, it would be a while before they found something close. To his surprise, his mother pulled into a spot a few moments later.

"Why is it I can search forever for a spot and you always find one the minute you start looking?"

"You're buying me coffee," Maggie Morgan said as she stepped out of the car.

"It's free," Max said. "I own this place."

"Really?" She stared up the facade. "It's very nice. So you feed them drinks at night and soothe their hangovers in the morning. Your father would call that smart business." She walked past him. "Too bad you don't conduct your personal life with such care."

"Here we go," Max muttered. All of this because he'd made a mistake answering the phone. He followed his mother inside, then ordered coffees and pastries for them both. They found a table near the window and he pulled out her chair for her. "Before you start in on me, I'll just say that the woman I was with last night is someone pretty special."

"Movie star or model?"

"Neither. Just a regular, normal girl. Well, not normal. Very pretty. And nice. You'd like her."

"Maxwell Morgan, it is time you seriously reevaluated your social life. You can't keep sleeping with these women and expect any good to come of it. You're not going to find a nice girl that way."

"Oh, I know what this is about," Max said. He took

a bite of his pastry and slowly chewed. "David told me you want to set me up on a date. That's why you're here. To convince me to come to your barbecue. I'm not interested. I'm busy that weekend."

"Just consider this girl. She's lovely and she's from a good family. And she's not the sort to go sleeping around."

"You've met her?"

"No, but her mother has shown me photos. She owns her own business and has a master's degree. You went to high school with her. You might even remember her."

"I went to high school with 3,000 kids," Max said. "I didn't know all of them."

"She went to Northwestern, too. Although she finished all four years." His mother grabbed her bag. "I brought your yearbook along. We'll look her up and see if you remember her." She flipped through the pages. "Here she is." She paused. "Oh, my. This isn't a very flattering picture. She looks nothing like this anymore." She slammed the book shut. "Just trust me. Besides, if you don't hit it off, you haven't lost anything."

Max grabbed the yearbook. "Show me. I'd like to know what you consider a lovely girl."

Reluctantly, she found the page again and then held it out to Max. "Top row, second to the last."

"Where?" Max asked, scanning the photos.

"There," his mother said. "She had braces and

she's wearing glasses. She looks so much better now. She's blond. You seem to prefer blondes."

The photo looked strangely familiar, but he shook his head. "Oh, Mom, no. This girl I'm dating is really great. I was thinking about bringing her to the barbecue. Her name is Angela."

"Yes, dear. Angela Weatherby. I know."

Max blinked in surprise. "How did you know that? Did Dave mention her?"

"It's right there, next to the photo."

"What?" Max shook his head. "What photo?"

His mother pointed to the list of names in the yearbook. "Angela Weatherby. That's her name. Kathy Weatherby is my tennis partner."

Max stared at the picture for a long moment, dumbfounded. If he squinted his eyes, he could almost believe this was the woman who'd shared his bed last night. He bit back a curse. What the hell did this mean?

When they'd met, Angela had acted as if they'd been strangers. How could she have gone through four years of high school without— No, everyone in school knew who he was. And that wasn't just ego talking, it was the truth. He'd been class president his junior year and student body president his senior year.

His brain scrambled to make sense of it. What had seemed so simple last night was suddenly incredibly complicated. Max had to question Angela's motives and rewind every comment she made. Was this part of some clever manipulation?

Some of his buddies in the league had some experience with stalkers. Was Angela one of those? He slowly worked through the events of their short time together. No, she'd given him a bogus phone number. Why would she do that? Unless she knew his interest would be piqued and he'd come looking.

And she had been evasive about her background. She'd never mentioned where she went to high school or college. "Can I keep this?" he asked.

"Of course. Now, you'll be coming to the barbecue, right?"

"Yes," he murmured, his gaze still fixed on the photo.

"Alone?"

"Yes," Max replied. "I'm very anxious to meet this girl. There's something very familiar about her. In fact, I feel as if I know her quite…intimately." He stood up. "I have to go, Mom."

"But we've barely started our coffee."

Max bent over and gave his mother a kiss on the cheek. "I have a lot of things to do today. Don't worry, I'll walk home."

"All right," she said. "I'll see you a week from Saturday. Come about one. And wear something nice. I hate seeing you in those silly basketball shorts all the time. Wear a shirt. In fact, buy a new shirt. Then send it to the cleaners to be pressed. And no jeans. Khakis."

"Are you going to pick out my underwear for me, too?" Max asked.

"You don't have to be snippy," she warned.

"Sorry. I'm tired."

"I just want you to be happy," she said, her expression softening.

"And that's all I want for you, Mom. I'll be at your barbecue. I promise." He walked out of the coffee shop and onto the busy sidewalk. For a long moment, Max wasn't sure what he wanted to do. He wasn't even sure how he felt. Angry? Confused? Shocked?

He pulled his sunglasses down and headed east, toward the lake. "Let's review," he murmured. "I didn't know her, but she knew me…maybe. We went to high school and college together, but we never—" He cursed softly. "We might have met." There was a reason he'd thought he knew her that first night. They had met. But when?

"Think." He'd only been in college for two years. She probably hadn't looked much different from her high school graduation picture, with the exception of the braces. And maybe the glasses. She'd told him she'd been the president of the Latin Club. Max stopped and paged through the yearbook until he found the photo. "There she is," he murmured. "Angela Weatherby. President."

This was all too strange. Like it had all been planned out ahead of time. He'd known women— baseball groupies—who'd gone to great lengths to meet him, but was Angela one of them? Had she walked into the bar that night hoping that she'd catch his eye? The groupies he'd encountered were much more obvious about their intentions. Unless she was so good at manipulating men that she knew how he'd react if he were forced to chase her.

Max needed some straight answers. Now. But he wasn't even sure what questions he ought to be asking. It would be better to wait and let things between him and Angela play out. A few well-timed questions about high school and college might shake the truth out of her. And then he'd know if this was a complicated manipulation or just a simple misunderstanding.

Max hoped it was the latter. Right now, he didn't want to consider anything that might mess up the good thing they had going.

"I LOVE THIS PLACE," Angela said, staring into the penguin tank at the Shedd Aquarium. "Whenever I need to clear my mind, I come here and watch the penguins. Life seems so perfect for them. Swim and eat, swim and eat."

She glanced over at Max, her gaze taking in his perfect profile. They'd been together for two days and she'd done her best to resist his charms. But his constant assault on her defenses had left her feeling exposed and vulnerable.

It was just sex, incredible as it was. But it was the simple moments like this one, when she'd look at him and saw the man behind all the hype and celebrity that threw her. He was just a regular guy who loved pizza and swimming and watching penguins. He was completely content to spend a quiet afternoon with her.

"They're like us," Max said. "But we threw a little sex in there for variety."

"Penguins mate for life, you know."

"I didn't know that," Max said.

"It's true. They search for that one special penguin they're meant to be with and when they find each other, they settle down, build a nest and have a little penguin family."

It was only after she relayed the penguin information that she realized how he might interpret her words. Did he think that's what she was after? Was she even sure what she wanted? Angela had been so careful not to think about the future. Whenever her thoughts spun out to the weeks and months ahead, she stopped herself.

Two days. Forty-eight hours. And already she was in serious trouble. It wasn't going to last, Angela told herself. In a week or two, he'd give her some sort of lame explanation and he'd move on. Why not just enjoy what they shared for what it was?

"It must take them a while to find their mate," Max said. "They all look alike."

"They know. They can feel it." He looked at her and Angela smiled. "They stick together through sickness and bad weather, protecting each other. From the time they meet until the time they hatch their first baby, they don't even eat. And then, the couple shares all the responsibilities for the newborn."

Max slipped his arm around her shoulders and they silently watched the birds leap into the water and jump back out again. If only life could be so simple for humans. She'd already made so many mistakes and now, Angela wasn't sure she'd be able to go back and fix them.

How would she explain everything to Max—how she'd been in love with when they were teenagers? How she'd once dreamed about a day when they'd be doing just this. How she'd decided to write about him in her book and how his personal life was splashed all over her Web site.

No matter how she fashioned her explanation, she could never make it sound better than common stalking. But it wasn't like that. What had begun as a complicated mess was now perfectly simple—she wanted him, he wanted her, and they'd found each other.

If she really believed they had a future together, then she'd have to come clean. The barbecue would be difficult to navigate with all her secrets still intact, so she'd have to tell him before then. Either that, or break up with him.

"What do you think about that?" Max asked.

Startled out of her thoughts, she blinked, then turned to him. "Think about what?"

"About mating for life? Is it possible?"

"Of course. Zoologists have studied penguin colonies and—"

"I meant for humans. Is it the natural order of things to spend your life with just one person?"

"I don't know," she said. "Look at the divorce rate nowadays. All those couples went into marriage thinking it was forever. And then it wasn't. Relationships are hard. I think two people have to be temperamentally suited for each other. And then they have to work at it, every day, forever."

"Have you ever thought about getting married?"

"No one has ever asked me," Angela admitted. "But I do believe in the penguins. I think there's one person out there for each of us and we spend our life trying to find that person. Sometimes, we think we've found them, and then we realize we were wrong. But when we actually do, it's…perfect." She forced a smile. "And what do you think? Are you a believer in the penguin theory of love or do you side with my parents?"

"Your parents don't believe in romance?" he asked.

"They think I need to choose someone to marry for practical purposes, not because of some overwhelming passion. I was the oddball in our family. My parents and sisters were the scientists, always looking at life with a purely objective, rational eye. I spent my whole childhood lost in silly romantic fantasies. I loved fairy tales. My mother thought they were horrible stories that sent young girls all the wrong messages. She banned certain books from my reading list and I'd just sneak them out of the library with my best friend's library card. She wouldn't allow me to read Wuthering Heights because Cathy commits suicide over her love for Heathcliff."

"Do your parents have a happy marriage?"

"No," Angela said. "Maybe. I don't see any passion there. I know they respect each other, but I was never really sure if they loved each other. What about yours? Are they happy?"

Max nodded. "Yeah, I know they are. They have their disagreements, but they love spending time together. They golf and play tennis. And I'm pretty sure they still have sex, so that's a good thing, right?"

"I think so," she said. "I hope that when I'm older, my husband still wants me."

"You want to get married, then?" Max asked.

She shrugged. "I don't know. I suppose if the right man comes along."

"And the perfect guy. He would be..."

Angela laughed. "You want a list? I don't know. He'd be honest and kind. Funny. I think humor is important."

"Rich?"

Angela shook her head. "No. I'd want him to be passionate about his work, but money isn't a deal breaker. I guess that's it. Honest, kind and funny. And maybe spontaneous and romantic, too." She frowned. "It doesn't seem like much. I really should have found a guy by now, don't you think?"

"Maybe you're like that penguin right there," Max said, pointing to the tank. "Maybe you're still searching."

She slipped her arm around his. And maybe she'd found him already and was just too stubborn to acknowledge it, Angela mused. "Let's go get some lunch. And then I have to get back to the office. I've been taking too much time off work and leaving everything to Ceci. It's really not fair."

"Do you ever take a vacation?" Max asked.

Angela shook her head. "Not really."

"Then why don't we go somewhere this weekend, just the two of us."

"I don't know," she said. "Maybe next weekend?" If they were both out of town next weekend, then neither one of them could attend the barbecue. "I'd have more time then."

He shook his head. "That doesn't work. I've got plans. My parents are throwing a barbecue." He paused. "You wouldn't want to come with me, would you?"

"No!" Angela quickly replied. "I mean if I'm in town, I should probably get some work done."

"It's probably for the better," Max said. "There's this woman they want me to meet. The daughter of one of my mother's friends. I'll just go and say hello."

Angela's breath caught in her throat. This was where her real life intersected with the life they'd created for themselves. She risked a sideways glance, trying to read his expression. Was it possible that his mother hadn't mentioned the name of this woman? "So you have a blind date?" she asked. "What's her name?"

This was it. The truth was about to come out, right here in front of the penguin tank. Angela was glad. She hated all of the secrets between them. She'd make her explanations and if he couldn't except them, then it would be over.

He paused, then shrugged. "I don't know. She went to high school with me, but I don't remember her."

Relief washed over her. He didn't know it was her. Though the urge to tell him was still there, Angela decided to take more time to consider her approach. She loved the penguin tank and didn't want one of her favorites spot ruined by a bad memory.

"She can't possibly be as beautiful as you," he said.

Angela felt guilt snake through her. Did he know? Had Max already figured everything out? This was her fault for hiding things from him in the first place. She should have walked into the bar and admitted her reasons for being there. If she had, she certainly wouldn't be stuck in this mess now. No, considering his hatred of the press, he probably would have tossed her out on her ear.

"I wouldn't be so sure about that," Angela said. She'd tell him at lunch. She'd confess everything and then let the chips fall. If he was still in her life at the end of the day, then they might actually have a future together.

"DATE NUMBER THREE," he said. "Let me see. Penguins at the aquarium, a long swim, take-out pasta for dinner, and early to bed. I think I deserve top scores, don't you?"

Angela nuzzled her face into his shoulder, her naked body pressed against his. "You're getting awfully confident. You expect top scores for take-out pasta?"

"It was from a great restaurant. Face it. You like me. You think I'm hot. I'm irresistible. I managed to talk you out of going back to work, didn't I?"

"You're not that irresistible," she said.

She'd been awfully quiet since they'd left the aquarium. Max knew what was on her mind. She was trying to work up the courage to admit that she'd known him all along. His first impulse was to attach some ulterior motive to their meeting at the bar that night. But after he thought about it for a while, Max realized that there might be another reason she didn't want to admit their common past. She'd been one of those girls that nobody noticed in high school, the girls who watched from the sidelines. The girls that a guy like Max wouldn't have bothered to talk to.

Max ran his hand along her body, cupping her backside and pulling her up to lie on top of him. All that had changed. And not because she was beautiful, but because he had finally found a reason to see beyond mere physical beauty.

This stolen summer had changed him. He'd grown up, become an adult. And he was finally beginning to realize what life was all about. It wasn't about money or fame. It was about this—the small, perfect moments that he shared with Angela. The quiet conversations and long silences. The simple kisses and the passion that followed.

"I am irresistible," Max said, searching for her mouth. His lips brushed against hers and he moved above her, his shaft growing harder between them. "Admit it."

"No," she said. "I can resist. Just watch me."

Her wicked smile was an outright challenge to him. And though they were only teasing, Max suddenly needed her to acknowledge what was happening between them, the power that their attraction generated. Did she want him as much as he wanted her? How deep did her feelings run?

Their conversation at the penguin exhibit had given him a few clues. She wanted a relationship, something that would last, even though she hadn't come right out and said it. And wasn't that what was going on here? A relationship?

With all the other women in his life, he saw their time together in finite terms, with a beginning and an end. But he wasn't able to contemplate ending things with Angela. Though she hadn't been completely honest with him, her actions certainly weren't enough to drive him away. In truth, he felt even more attracted to her knowing how vulnerable she felt about her past.

Still, there were two sides to every relationship. What would drive her away? Would it be his celebrity? The long periods apart? Her past? There were plenty of things on his side of the board that she might find unbearable.

Max pulled her into a long, deep kiss, doing his best to seduce her with his lips and tongue. "Say it," he whispered. "Tell me you need me."

"I don't," she said, still teasing.

Max took her face between his hands and stared into her eyes. "Tell me," he said.

She paused, clearly confused by the intensity of his request. Then she drew a ragged breath. "I need you," she murmured.

"Only me," he said.

"Only you," she replied. Her smile widened. "Unless you have someone else under the covers. Another man? Oh my, a threesome. I suppose I could spread the need around."

It was clear she wasn't about to engage in a serious conversation. And maybe it wasn't fair of him to press her. After all, they'd only known each other forty-eight hours. What did he expect?

"I have something for you," Max said. "In the envelope on by the lamp."

"What is it?"

"Open it," he said.

Angela shook her head. "We shouldn't be giving each other gifts. It's too soon."

"It's not really a gift," Max said. "Just open it."

She grabbed the envelope and slowly withdrew the airline ticket. "It's a ticket," she said. "Are you going somewhere?"

"I have to fly to Florida tomorrow and I was hoping you'd come with me. We could spend the weekend there. I could show you the city, then we could relax and have some fun."

At first Max thought she'd accept, but slowly her expression changed. "We talked about this earlier. I—I can't."

"Why not? It's just a couple days. I want to show you where I live."

"I just can't," she said. She rolled off him, grabbing his T-shirt from the end of the bed and tugging it over her head. "I—I'm going to go get some orange juice. Do you want some?"

Max pushed up on his elbow. "Angela, wait."

"I'll be right back," she said, forcing a smile.

He watched her walk out of the bedroom, then flopped back on the pillow. What was this all about? He thought she'd enjoy a little vacation. Since he had to be in Florida for a few days, why not take her along? There was something else at work here.

When she returned, Angela sat down at the edge of the bed. "I'm sorry," she said. "It's a lovely…gift."

"No, it's not a gift. Jewelry is a gift. This is just me being selfish," Max said. "I have to be away for a few days and I knew how much I'd miss you. I thought if you came along, I wouldn't miss you so much." He reached out and touched her arm. "Is that so bad?"

She shook her head. "Not really." Angela took a sip of the orange juice. "But that's your other life. Down there, you're famous, you have girls and paparazzi trailing after you. I can't compete with that life. It's so…big. But here in Chicago, everything works."

"Angela, I might have to go back to that life. It's my job. What's going to happen then?"

She shrugged. "I don't know. We'll deal with that when the time comes, I guess."

"I want to know now," he said.

"We've known each other for—how long?"

"Forty-eight hours," he muttered.

She blinked in surprise. "Really. That's all? I've had stomach viruses that have lasted longer than that. I've had headaches that have lasted—"

Max pressed a finger to her lips. "I get it. But you forget, we've spent nearly all that time together. If you were dating some other guy, you might have had dates that lasted for five hours max."

"Yeah," she said.

"Right. Well, we've had the equivalent of…" He tried to do the math in his head. Nine times five was forty-five so—

"Nine point six," she said. "I'm good in math, too."

"All right. We've been on the equivalent of 9.6 dates. Now, if you figure two dates a week, we've been dating for almost five weeks. Five weeks is not too early to take a trip together."

"It's too early for me," she said.

Slowly, it became clear to Max what she was saying. "You don't trust me," he said. "Go ahead. Say it. You don't trust me."

"I don't trust you," she said. "And not because you're not a great guy. I don't trust you because I barely know you, Max. And I don't trust myself. I don't want to get hurt. I don't want to see the wonderful life you lead in Florida. I don't want to be reminded of the differences between us."

Differences? Damn it, they'd grown up in the same hometown, attended the same schools. Their parents were friends. If she were going to use that as an excuse, then he'd have to call her on it. Or maybe that was the reason she'd kept a few secrets from him. After dating starlets and pop stars, what could he possibly find interesting about a hometown girl?

"Forty-eight hours," she repeated. "That's barely enough time to figure out how you like your coffee."

"You know how I like my coffee," he said.

"And it doesn't help that we spend most of our time in bed. I know a lot about your body and about how you like to be touched. But I don't know how you got that scar on your knee."

"Bike accident when I was twelve," he said.

"Or what you like to read," she added.

"Mostly non-fiction." He sighed. "All right. I get

your point. So, let's get to know each other right now."

"I'm still not going to Florida with you," she said.

"I know you're stubborn," Max said.

"Cautious," she countered.

He bent close and kissed her. "And your lips are incredibly soft."

"You're getting off track again," Angela warned.

Max cupped her breast in his hand. "And that your body seems to fit perfectly against mine. As if it were made for my touch."

She sighed softly. "Why don't we play a game? I'll ask you a question—any question—and you have to answer. We each get ten questions and two passes."

"Passes?"

"We can refuse to answer twice. I'll start."

"All right." Max sat up and crossed his legs in front of him, then pulled a pillow over his lap. "Shoot."

"How many women have you slept with?"

He laughed. "Really? You want to know? I'm not sure I ever counted, but it's not as many as you'd think."

"More than five hundred?"

"No," Max said. God, his reputation must be a lot worse than he'd ever imagined. "Where did you hear I'd slept with five hundred women?"

"More than two hundred?"

"Absolutely not," he said.

"More than one hundred?"

Max shook his head. "I don't think so. I've had some long dry spells and I've had some short-term relationships. Maybe ninety." He paused. "Jeez, even that sounds like a lot. But it's really not. If you figure ten on average a year. And that's since the beginning. A lot of what you hear in the press isn't true. If it were, I'd be up in the thousands. How many questions was that for you—four?"

"No, just one."

"Actually, it was four. One main question and three sub-questions."

With an astonished laugh, she reached out and slapped him on the chest. "You don't play fair."

"My turn," he said. "Same question."

"None," she replied.

"None?"

"That's question two according to your rules. And my answer is none."

"You've slept with me, so it has to be at least one."

"Oh, but you're a man. You said same question. So I answered the same question—how many women have I had sex with."

He grabbed her and threw her down on the bed, stretching out on top of her. "Oh, so this is the way it's going to be. You're going to trick me. I might as well give up right now. You're much too clever, Angela Weatherby."

"All right, all right, no more tricks."

For the next two hours, they talked, asking

questions, laughing at answers, and learning more about each other than they needed to know. Max carefully avoided questions about her hometown and her high school and college education, waiting for her to volunteer that information herself. And though she had plenty of opportunity, she never once mentioned she'd known him in the past.

When it came time to ask his last question, Max paused. "I think I'm going to save it," he said.

"For what?"

"For later. For when I really want to know something."

"I can always pass on it."

"No, you can't. You've had your two passes, remember?" Max pulled her into his arms and kissed her. "Now, can we please just stop talking and start getting down to business?"

She growled playfully, then grabbed his face and kissed him long and hard. "Max, if kissing is your business, then I think I'd like to invest."

6

ANGELA SAT AT HER DESK and stared at her computer screen. As hard as she tried, she couldn't seem to concentrate on work. Max had been gone for two whole days. He'd called a few times, but their phone conversations had been stilted and short, like two strangers trying to find something interesting to say to each other.

He hadn't been sure when he was going to get back and though she'd been anxious to see him again, she didn't want to press him on the matter. She'd tried her very best not to want him too much, but the effort was taking a toll on her heart and her body.

"Look at this," Ceci said. "Someone posted another comment on Max. SunkissedGrl goes into great detail about how he charmed her, then never called her again."

"It didn't take him long," Angela said.

"You don't think he went out with this girl this weekend?" Ceci said.

"He could have," Angela said. "How do I know what he's been doing? He could be having an orgy down in Florida for all I know."

"Angie, you need to accept the fact that this guy might really like you. You can't automatically think the worst of him."

"Why not? What makes me different from all those other girls? He's here in Chicago for the summer. Obviously, he wants to find someone to…seduce. Why not me? I was handy, willing." Angela moaned, burying her face in her hands. "And stupid. I was stupid."

Ceci reached out and rubbed her arm. "No, you weren't. You just led with your heart instead of your brain."

"And now, I'm falling in love with him. After just a few days together. I try to stop these feelings but I can't. It's like I'm sitting on the Metro tracks and there's a big train coming and I can't move. All I can do is wait for the impact."

"There's nothing wrong with falling in love," Ceci said. "Sometimes you have to take a risk."

"But don't you see how ridiculous this is. I'm doomed to fail, yet I can't help myself. When he finds out about the Web site, he'll hate me. When he finds out we went to high school and college together, he'll mistrust me. And when he finds out I'm falling in love with him, he'll run away as fast as he can."

"You don't know that. He may be the exception."

"Stop saying that!"

"You just assume everything will fall apart," Ceci said.

"It's much easier than thinking about a real future with Max." She paused. "I can't believe I just said those two words in the same sentence. Max. Future. Sometimes this does seem like a dream."

"It's real. I was at the ballgame. He was there. In the flesh."

A shiver skittered down Angela's spine. Putting the words *Max* and *flesh* together created a brand new flood of sensation. "I can't think about him right now," she said. "It's making my brain hurt."

Angela picked up her cell phone. She'd checked it at least a hundred times already that day. "Stop it," she scolded. "I feel like some silly teenager. I was this silly teenager, mooning over him, wondering where he was and what he was doing every minute of the day." She stood up. "I have to go home."

"We could get some lunch. Eating always takes your mind off your worries."

Angela shook her head. "No, I'm not hungry. Maybe I need a nap. I haven't really been sleeping the last few nights."

"Nothing to tire you out?" Ceci asked.

"Right." Angela forced a smile. She grabbed her bag and threw it over her shoulder. "I'll see you tomorrow."

"Tomorrow is Sunday. Will and I were going to drive out to—"

"Sunday," Angela said. "I knew that. Monday, then."

She stepped out into the heat of a Chicago summer day, the street busy and the sidewalk crowded with pedestrians. Angela walked to work most days and had done it so many times that she could find her way home with her eyes closed.

She stopped at the grocery store and picked up a deli container of chicken pasta salad. At the last minute, she bought a bottle of wine. Maybe a few drinks would put her mind at rest and allow her to sleep.

Angela walked home slowly, her thoughts focused on Max. She'd been thinking about him all day, waiting for him to call, wondering why he hadn't. Of course, she could have called him. There wasn't anything improper in that. They were sleeping together. The rulebook had been burned the moment they tore off their clothes and jumped into bed together.

She reached into her bag and searched around for her cell phone, then checked again to see if she had any messages. "What does this mean?" Angela murmured. Was this how it would end? He'd just stop calling and move on to another girl?

As she turned the corner and approached her flat, she noticed a BMW sedan double parked on the street. Angela's heart skipped a beat. It couldn't be him. Just wishful thinking. He would have called to tell her he was coming back.

She slowly approached and when she was beside

the car, the passenger-side window lowered and Max leaned over the seat, a wide grin on his face. "Get in," he said.

"You're back. Why didn't you call?"

"I did. Three or four times. And I just called the office. Ceci said you were on your way home."

"You called? I didn't get any messages."

"Something's wrong with your cell phone," he said. "Come on, let's go."

She reached for the door. "Where are we going?"

"Away," he said.

"How far away?"

"I thought we'd drive up to my cabin and spend a few days," he said. "It's not a vacation. Just a long drive with a bed at the other end. And a lake. And a boat."

This time, Angela wasn't about to refuse. He'd been gone for two days and she'd barely survived his absence. Another two days apart and she'd be ready for the psych ward. "Shouldn't I pack some clothes?"

He shook his head. "You won't need any. And if you do, we'll buy them on the way."

Angela stared at him for a long moment. This was exactly what she'd always wanted from a man—excitement, spontaneity, romance. How was it possible to go from the depths of doubt and despair to this, all in the course of a few minutes? This is exactly why people ended up going crazy over love. "You just want to leave, right now?"

"Yeah," he said, waving her inside. "Let's get out of the city and have some fun."

She opened the door, then hopped inside the car. "All right, let's go."

Before long they were racing north through the sparse Sunday traffic. Inside the cool interior of the sedan, soft music played beneath their conversation. He was back and it was as if he'd never left. Everything was exactly the same between them.

Yet everything that she'd gone through in the past few days wasn't that easily forgotten. Angela couldn't imagine surviving another separation without a better understanding of how he felt about her. She drew a deep breath and turned to him. "What's going on with us?" she said.

He glanced over at her. "What? We're going to my cabin."

"No, I meant, with us. You and me."

"Oh, no," he said, shaking his head.

"I just asked a question," she said. "I mean, we're dating, I know that. But are we exclusively dating? Would you be angry if I told you I went out with another guy while you were gone?"

"You went out with another guy while I was gone?" he asked, his brow arching in surprise. His jaw twitched and his gaze remained fixed on the road.

"No. Did you go out with another girl?"

He shook his head. "No."

"So...we're dating."

"Exclusively," he said.

"You could say we're having a...relationship?"

"Yes, you could say that," Max replied.

"Would you say that?"

He nodded. "Yes, I would say we're having a relationship. It's a little weird at times, but it's interesting."

Angela sank back into the leather seat and smiled. "All right."

He reached across and slipped his hand around her nape, furrowing his fingers in her hair. "Feeling better?"

"Absolutely," she said. "I'm glad we got that cleared up."

"THIS IS AMAZING," she murmured. "It's so beautiful. And quiet. It's hard to believe Chicago is only four hours away."

Max handed Angela a glass of wine, then drew her over to one of the Adirondack chairs on the porch. "Sit," he said.

She shook her head. "No. Let's walk down to the lake. We can sit on the pier."

"All right," he said. He laced his fingers through hers and they strolled down the steps to the dirt path that led to the water. "I haven't spent much time up here since I bought the place six years ago. My brothers come up and fish a few times each summer. And my sister brings her kids up, but the place is closed most of the time."

She drew a deep breath. "I love the smell. The trees and the lake."

"You act like you've never been on vacation," he said.

"I haven't," Angela said. "I've traveled for business. And I spent the usual semester abroad. But, until recently, I didn't have the money for a real vacation."

"You've never gone on vacation with your family?"

She shook her head. "Not a relaxing vacation. When my family vacationed, it was always a teaching opportunity. We visited museums and historical sites. I can't tell you how many times we've been to Washington, D.C. We never just sat on a beach and relaxed. My parents believed that sitting around was a waste of time."

"We had the best vacations when I was a kid," Max said. "We'd all pile into the family van and we'd just go. Four kids, my parents, and the dog. We'd camp and hike and cook over a open fire and spend as much time as we could outside."

"Sounds nice. There were times when I seriously wondered if I'd been adopted. I never fit in with my family. My two sisters and I are so different."

"How?" he asked.

They sat down at the end of the pier and stared out at the setting sun. "They were so focused in everything. From the moment they exited the womb, they had a plan. My parents were so proud."

"They weren't proud of you?"

Angela laughed. "Sure. But my parents never really knew who I was. I pretended to be one thing for them, but inside I was different. I was a dreamer. I lived in my own little world. When I was a kid, I didn't have just one imaginary friend, I had a whole roomful of them. An alternate family, with brothers who took me horseback riding and sisters who loved to play dress-up."

"What's wrong with that?"

"My parents and sisters don't have any imagination. I used to think my name was magical and that's why I was so different. I was like an angel. My sisters are Susan and Mary. Very practical names. But my name was...romantic."

"I like your name. You look like an angel."

Angela laughed, remembering his attempts the night they met. "And you are so full of it, I can barely tolerate you," she teased.

"You don't take compliments well at all."

"I'm not used to them. My parents never complimented us. We were expected to be confident and self-possessed. We weren't supposed to need coddling." She paused. "I love my parents, don't get me wrong, but sometimes I think I could do a better job raising a child."

"I think you're perfect just the way you are," he said. "And if you ever need me to tell you that, you just speak up." Max kissed the end of her nose. "Do you want to go for a swim?"

Angela shook her head. "I'm hungry. Maybe we can make some dinner first?"

Max stood up and grabbed her hand, pulling her to her feet. As they walked up the rise to the cabin, he lagged behind her, taking in the view. "You have a very lovely ass, too," he said.

She turned and looked at him, a bemused smile curling her lips. "Don't think that's going to get you anywhere, buddy," she said.

He caught up with her, grabbed her around the waist and tossed her over his shoulder. "We'll see about that," he said.

When they reached the house, it only took them a few seconds to strip off the clothes they wore. Max lifted her up on the kitchen island, his lips wandering over her body. She was perfect, every inch of her a delicious revelation.

This was exactly how he imagined weekends at the lake. A little wine, a little conversation and a lot of sex. He'd just never found the right companion, until now.

"I'll bring the cooler in. It's too heavy for you!"

The sound of his brother's voice shocked Max out of his haze of passion. Angela jumped, then quickly slid down beside Max. A moment later, the screen door opened and Dave and his family bustled inside.

A tiny scream burst from Angela's throat and Max

cursed beneath his breath. They both dropped down to the floor, their heads poking above the countertop. "Ah, Dave?"

His brother glanced over into the kitchen, then stopped. The kids and Lauren ran into him from behind. "Max? There you are. We saw the car. What are you doing up here?"

"I could ask you the same."

"We thought we'd come up for a few days. Lauren doesn't have to work on Monday and Tuesday, so we wanted to take a long weekend. I thought I told you."

"Why is Uncle Max hiding?" six-year-old Brittany asked. "Can I play, too?"

"If you don't want your kids to get an eyeful, I think you'd better take them outside," Max warned.

"Everybody out." Dave and Lauren quickly hustled back out the door and a moment later, the cabin was silent.

"Oh, no," Angela moaned. "This is not the way I imagined meeting your family."

He turned to her. "You've imagined meeting my family?"

"No! I was speaking generically. Do you think they saw anything?"

"No. But I'm pretty sure Dave and Lauren have a good idea what was going on. And it wasn't hide and seek."

"Go get my clothes," she whispered. "I'm staying right here."

Max hurried out to the living room and gathered everything up in his arms, then returned to the kitchen. The clothes went on more quickly than they'd come off and when they were both fully dressed, he grabbed her hand and pulled her toward the door. "Come on, I'll introduce you."

Angela dug in her heels. "No. I don't want to meet them. Not right now."

"They'll be fine."

When Max got to the door, he pushed it open. Angela shook her head, but followed him, stepping outside. The kids were already down at the lake with Lauren and Dave was sitting on the porch steps. He stood when he saw Angela.

"Hey, I'm sorry," he said, holding out his hand. "I'm Dave, Max's very rude older brother."

"This is Angela," Max said.

"Weatherly?" Dave asked.

"Weatherby," she said. She glanced at Max, a questioning look in her eyes.

"Dave helped me track you down after you gave me that bogus phone number. You really made an impression on him."

"I'm going down to the lake and introduce myself to your wife and children," Angela said. She walked down the steps and followed the path across the lawn.

"I didn't see anything," Dave called to her. "I swear."

Max jabbed him in the ribs with his elbow. "Don't make it worse than it already is."

"I lied," Dave muttered. "I got an eyeful. But don't tell her that. And for God's sake, don't tell Lauren. By the way, that girl has got a nice body. She's the first naked woman I've seen since I've been married. I mean, except for pictures in magazines. And porn."

"If you don't shut up right now, I'm going to kick the shit out of you," Max warned.

"Okay," Dave said. "I just never thought you'd be up here. When we saw the car, I figured we'd have a nice family weekend."

"I do own the place," Max said. "Is it so difficult to believe that I might want a little privacy?"

"Of course not. But I just assumed you'd be in the city." He picked up a football from the pile of toys he'd brought along and tossed it up in the air. "Hey, go out for a pass."

"I'm not in the mood," Max said. He had been in the mood for sex until a few minutes ago. The interruption had made things a bit uncomfortable for the moment.

"Come on," Dave said. "Don't be a pussy. I'll take it easy on you. You won't hurt yourself."

Max trotted across the lawn for twenty yards, then caught a perfect spiral from his older brother. Though Max had played football throughout high school and his first year of college, he'd never liked it as much as baseball. He did remember how to catch a ball, though. "Nice," he called.

"Throw it back," Dave said.

Without thinking, Max heaved a pass, then realized he probably shouldn't be stressing his shoulder outside of his rehab exercises. He rubbed the spot just beyond his collarbone, surprised there'd been no pain.

"You all right?" Dave called.

"I'm fine." Frowning, he walked over to his brother. "It didn't hurt. In fact, it felt good. Strong. It hurts when I wake up in the morning, but after I warm up, it feels pretty good."

"What did the team doctors say?"

"They did an MRI and a few other tests. They said it's healed and I can start to throw again. I just have to start real easy."

"Hey, that's great," Dave said, clapping him on his back.

"Yeah," Max murmured.

"You don't sound thrilled. How come?"

He shrugged. "I guess I just assumed it wouldn't come back, that I wouldn't have to make a decision about going back. That the decision would be made for me. But now they're saying I could start training with the team again mid-July if everything goes well."

His stolen summer would be over before it really began. He'd have another month with Angela and then they'd go their separate ways, at least until the end of the baseball season.

Max grabbed the football and started toward

the water. When he'd come to Chicago for rehab, he'd mentally moved on with his life. Once he'd met Angela, a future without baseball seem even more attractive.

He sat down at the edge of the water. A moment later, Dave joined him. "You want to tell me what this is all about? I thought you were determined to get back in the game."

"I was. Not so much anymore."

"Is it the girl?"

"Her name is Angela. And she's not just one of my girls. She's different."

"I can see that. But you say that about every girl you date."

Max cursed beneath his breath. "This time, I mean it. I can see myself with her…for a long time. Maybe even married to her."

"What do you know about her? You've been together, what? A week? Maybe you ought to check her out before you fall in love," Dave suggested.

"What do you mean? Like, hire a private investigator?"

"It couldn't hurt, Max. You've got a lot of money. You need to make sure she's interested in you for the right reasons."

"You never suggested this with any of the other girls I dated."

"Because those relationships were doomed from the start. But you really seem to like this girl."

"Woman," Max insisted. "She's not a girl, she's a woman."

"I can arrange for it," Dave said. "I work with a firm that does background checks on our bartenders. It's a simple process."

Max shoved the football into Dave's lap and stood up. "Nope, there's no need. I've got everything under control."

He walked along the pier toward Angela. Everything wasn't under control. There were still a lot of questions that needed to be answered. And he was running out of patience.

ANGELA PICKED A CARD, then showed it to the two girls. "Blue," she said. She moved her Candyland marker to the next blue square. "I'm winning. You better watch out."

Brittany grabbed the next card. "No, it's my turn," Bethany cried.

"She's right," Angela said. She glanced over at Max and he smiled at her, then cocked his head toward the door. Angela nodded and a moment later, Max squatted down next to the coffee table. "I'm going to steal Angela away for a little while," he said. He held out his hand and pulled her to her feet. "Come on. We're going for ice cream."

"Me, too!" Bethany cried, scrambling to her feet.

"Take us. We wanna go," Brittany added.

"No, it's late," Max said. "And it's almost bedtime

for you two. We'll go tomorrow, I promise. But to-night, Angela and I want to go by ourselves."

"I bet they're going to get naked again," Brittany whispered as she and Bethany walked off.

"Mama says they weren't naked. They had their swimsuits on."

As they stepped outside, Max slipped his arm around her shoulders. "We may have scarred them for life." When they got up to the driveway, Dave's SUV was parked behind the BMW. Max pulled her along to the road. "We'll walk into town. It's only a mile. And it's a nice night."

The winding road through the woods was quiet, with only the occasional rabbit or squirrel to interrupt the silence. "My family used to come up here when we were kids. We'd rent a place on the other side of the lake. It was just a small cabin. My folks would stay inside and we'd get to sleep in tents. I tried to buy the place when I was looking, but the family that owned it didn't want to sell."

"This place is nice," she said.

"I remember how much fun it was up here, the freedom we had. My folks would go to bed early and we'd be out until all hours of the night, prowling around in the woods, playing in the water, walking into town."

As they approached town, the sky grew a bit brighter from the lights. The ice cream stand was a beacon in the dark, neon outlining the facade. The parking lot was crowded with cars and kids. "We came here for ice cream almost every day. Back then a cone was just fifty cents. The place hasn't changed at all. What do you want—cone or bowl?"

"Bowl," Angela said.

"Chocolate, vanilla or strawberry?"

"Strawberry," Angela said. "With just a tiny bit of chocolate on the side."

Max nodded. "I learn something new every day. I would have pegged you for a pure chocolate girl." He walked up to the window and placed their order. A few moments later, he returned and they found a seat at a table beneath a tall maple tree.

"This is nice," she said, licking a bit of ice cream off her spoon.

"It's nice to be alone again. I feel like we haven't been able to talk all evening. I'm sorry about Dave and the kids showing up," Max said. "I had no idea they'd be here."

"It's not a problem. I kind of like it. It's a real family vacation. Lauren was saying that she was happy to see you using the place. She said the family likes having you around."

"Tell me more about your family," he said. "Where did you grow up?"

The question seemed to come out of nowhere and Angela coughed, a blob of ice cream catching in her throat. Suddenly, a blinding headache pierced her temple. "Ow," she said. "Brain freeze."

Her discomfort distracted him for a moment and

Max reached out and rubbed her forehead. "Just breathe real deep," he said.

When the ache subsided, she took another bite of her ice cream, letting it melt in her mouth. "Around Chicago. The suburbs."

He stared across the table at her, his spoon poised in midair. "Which suburb? There are so many."

She glanced up at him, trying to read the odd expression on his face. Did she really want to spoil this wonderful weekend with a fight? "Does it make a difference?"

"Yes," he said. "I think it does. This is my last question, Angie. The one I was saving?"

Angela took a ragged breath. He knew the answer already, she could see it in his eyes. Somewhere along the line, he recognized her, remembered her or simply figured out she was hiding something. "You know, don't you? You know exactly where I grew up."

Max nodded. "Yeah. I do. You're from Evanston. We went to high school together. And college, at least for the two years I was there. And you know that next Saturday we're supposed to meet at a barbecue?"

Angela nodded. "At your parents' house. Your mother and my mother are tennis partners. My mother called me the day after we'd met to invite me."

"A little strange, isn't it?"

A tiny smile curved the corners of her mouth.

"But you don't remember me, do you. Don't worry, I wasn't very memorable. I blended into the walls."

He stood up and they started their walk back to the cabin, still eating ice cream as they strolled. "Why didn't you mention this when we met?" Max asked. "Why weren't you just honest with me?"

She sent him a sideways glance, wondering how honest she ought to be. There was a bit more to her story than just a high school crush. "Maybe I wanted you to think I was beautiful and alluring and a little bit mysterious. Maybe I didn't want you to remember the plain, nervous girl I used to be."

"I wouldn't have remembered that girl. We'd never met."

"But we have," Angela said. "A number of times."

"When?"

"You bumped into me during freshman orientation for high school. You said sorry, and then walked away. And once, I handed you a book you'd dropped in the library. And you sat in front of me for a whole semester in physics class."

"That's it?"

She shook her head. "I once interviewed you for the college newspaper. It was right after they started scouting you for the pros. You'd just done that calendar for the athletic scholarship fund."

"Oh, my God, that's it," Max said. "That's where I knew you from." He reached out and pulled her into his arms. "When I saw you at the bar that night, I felt as if we'd met before, but I couldn't remember when. That was it."

"There was one other time. A few years ago. I was at a sports bar in Evanston, waiting for a table and you were there. And…you looked at me. Across the bar."

An odd expression, and then one of slow realization crossed his face. "I remember that. I remember how I felt when you looked away. There had been this connection and it shocked me. I'd never had that happen before. Not since then, either." He paused. "That was you?"

"That was me," she said.

"I should have introduced myself. I was tempted, but I was with—"

"Another woman," she said. "Several, I think."

"My sister," he said. "I think Lauren and Dave were there, too. It was around Christmas and I was home for the holidays."

"It's probably better you didn't come over. I would have babbled something stupid and you would have walked away wondering who'd let me out of the asylum for the night. I would have been that stupid, silly girl who watched your every move and went home at night dreaming about kissing you."

"What?"

Now that she had the opening, Angela didn't want to stop. It was time to tell him everything. Or almost everything. "You might as well know the rest of the story. I had a crush on you in high school. And in

college. In fact, that's why I went to Northwestern.
I was supposed to go to Sarah Lawrence, but when
I heard you were going to Northwestern instead of
straight into the minors, I followed you there. I know,
it sounds pathetic, and it really was."

Max stared at her, his gaze fixing on her mouth.
She wanted him to kiss her right then, to reassure her
that nothing had changed between them, to put a stop
to her clumsy explanations. In all the moments they'd
shared over the past week, she'd never felt quite so
vulnerable.

"A crush?"

"I suppose this changes everything," Angela said,
her voice trembling with emotion. "I'm not the person
you thought I was. I'm not exciting or interesting or
even the tiniest bit mysterious. I'm just a girl from
your hometown who was once hopelessly infatuated
with you."

"How long did the crush last?"

"I don't know. Six years. Then you went into the
minors and I decided to move on."

"So, you were in love with me and I was just going
about my life without ever knowing you had these
feelings? You were watching me and dreaming about
me and hoping I'd talk to you and—"

"You can stop now," Angela said. "I'm going to
crawl off into the woods and die." Now that she'd
completely humiliated herself, she needed the conversation to move to a new subject. "This is really
good ice cream. The sign said it was custard. What's

the difference between ice cream and custard? I never could figure that out."

"And that night, in the bar, when we met," Max continued. "That was it. That was probably the last chance for us. If I hadn't come over to talk to you, you would have left and we never would have met."

"Well, there's always your parents' barbecue," she said.

"I would have found an excuse not to go," Max replied.

He seemed a bit stunned by her revelation, by the series of coincidences that had brought them together. Angela knew she ought to continue, to tell him about the Web site and the interview for the book, but he'd already been given too much to absorb. Maybe tomorrow.

Max drew a deep breath, then nodded. "I guess we were lucky."

"How is that?"

"I was lucky. To have finally recognized what I'd been missing all those years."

A blush warmed her cheeks. He didn't seem angry, or offended, or deceived, just…bewildered. A bit amazed. "You're not angry that I wasn't honest from the start?"

Max shook his head. "Nope. Hey, I know I have a reputation. Maybe if you'd admitted everything up front, I might not have been…intrigued. But you have me now. And you're stuck with me."

Tears swam in Angela's eyes. "Really? You're not

going to dump me because I'm Angela Weatherby, former Evanston High School wallflower."

Max hooked his finger beneath her chin and drew her closer, then dropped a kiss on her lips. "As long as you don't drop me because I'm Max Morgan, former jackass and serial seducer from Evanston High School."

"Deal," she said.

"So I guess we've told all our secrets and we're officially in a relationship," Max said.

She swallowed hard. "I guess so."

Max dipped his spoon into her ice cream. "You know that means that we can share our ice cream. Can I have some of your strawberry?"

Right now, Max could have anything he wanted, Angela mused. Her heart, her soul, her body. Everything she wanted to believe about him was proving true. He was kind and honest and romantic. And she was falling in love with him all over again.

7

MAX PACED BACK AND FORTH in front of the fireplace. The night was warm and all the windows in the cabin had been thrown open to catch the breeze. Outside, the trees rustled and he could hear the gentle lap of water on the shore.

He loved nights like this, when everything was so still. He glanced over at the rack that held a selection of fishing poles. He could sit on the end of the pier and fish, but Max suspected that it wouldn't put thoughts of Angela out of his head. They'd be leaving for Chicago in the morning and he wanted to share this place with her, to show her what her life might be like with him in it.

Instead, they'd been sent off to separate bedrooms, for the sake of the children. Angela was in one room with Brit and Beth while he'd been given another room with Davey, his three-year-old nephew. Of course, Dave and Lauren took the big bedroom, with the comfortable bed, the bed Max should have been sharing with Angela.

Max opened the closet and pulled out a pair of sleeping bags and set them next to the door. If they couldn't sleep together inside the cabin, then they'd sleep together outside.

He walked down to the pier and tossed the sleeping bags into the boat, then jumped down into the cockpit. The aft seat folded out into a comfortable lounge, almost as wide a bed. He unzipped the sleeping bags and laid them out, then surveyed his work in the pale moonlight. It wasn't the Ritz, but it was certainly better than what they'd been given.

If Max had had his way, they would have driven back to Chicago as soon as Dave and Lauren arrived with the kids. But Angela had insisted on staying and she seemed to enjoy the time with his family, even if it meant playing endless games of Chutes and Ladders and Candyland with the girls.

Now that they were officially in a relationship, family would probably become part of the picture and strangely enough, Max didn't mind. He hadn't introduced a girl to his family since his senior prom date in high school, but he felt reasonably certain that Angela would be in his life for more than just a few months.

As he walked back up to the cabin, he contemplated the possibility that he'd met the girl he was going to marry. Max had always thought once he found her, everything would fall into place. He never considered that he might have to convince her to take a chance on him.

When he walked back inside, he headed for her bedroom. Max knocked on the knotty pine planks, but the knock was met with silence. Was she already asleep? He knocked a bit louder and a moment later the door opened. She looked at him through sleepy eyes. "What are you doing? You're going to wake the girls," she whispered.

"What are you doing?" Max asked, his gaze taking in her pretty face and tumbled hair.

"Trying to sleep," she said. "But it's impossible. They keep wriggling around every time I close my eyes. They're all arms and legs. Between the lumpy mattress and their elbows and knees, I feel like I'm being assaulted."

"If you come and sleep with me, I'll be much nicer," he said.

She peeked out the door. "Where are we going to sleep? On the floor?"

"Come on. Come with me." He reached out and grabbed her hand, pulling her along through the dark cabin. When they reached the door, he pulled her into his embrace and they stumbled out onto the porch, caught in a desperate kiss.

He furrowed his hands through her hair and molded her mouth to his. It had been at least two hours since he'd last kissed her. "I don't like sleeping alone."

"You weren't alone."

"I didn't have you there. That's alone."

"Where are we going?"

The moon was nearly full, lighting the way for part of their escape, before disappearing behind a cloud. Though the air was still warm, there was a damp breeze coming off the lake. Angela shivered and Max slipped his arm around her shoulders, pulling her close.

They hurried down to the pier, then laughing softly, stripped off their clothes and jumped in the water. Though the air was chilly, the water was warm. Max stood on the sandy bottom, his arms wrapped around her naked body, his face nuzzled into the curve of her neck. "Someday, I'm going to steal you away to a deserted island. Just you and me. No one else."

"Why?"

"I just want to see what it would be like to be completely alone with you," he said. "With no distractions or interruptions."

"We're alone now," she said.

Max looked out across the lake. In the distance, a light from a motorboat was visible, slowly skimming across the water. He furrowed his hands through her hair and pulled her into a fierce kiss. "Do you know how difficult it is being around you without touching you?" he asked, sliding his hand over her breast. "I like being able to do this whenever I want."

Angela sighed softly. "I like it, too. I like falling asleep with you and waking up with you. And swimming naked with you."

His lips found her breast and he teased her nipple to a peak. She shivered and he pulled her closer. "The very first time I kissed a girl, I was sitting on a pier on the other side of the this lake." Max pointed to a light across the water. "The white light to the left of the blue one. We met on that pier and I kissed her."

"So this is where it all began?" Angela asked.

"I guess you could say that. God, I was so nervous I thought I was going to throw up. I didn't know what to do with my hands. I wasn't sure where to put them."

"I see you've figured that out," she teased.

"I remember how exciting it was. My heart was pounding so hard, I thought it would burst out of my chest." He kissed her again. "Kind of like now."

"I was a junior in college before I got my first kiss," Angela admitted.

"Really? How can that be? You're so damn kissable."

"I was a very late bloomer. As you know, I lived in a fantasy world throughout my teen years, dreaming of this gorgeous baseball player I knew."

"I feel bad," he said. "I wish I'd have known you back then."

Angela shook her head. "No. You would have thought I was just pathetic. I wouldn't have been able to put together a coherent sentence. Believe me, it's much better that we met now."

"I guess so," he said. "So, when did you bloom?"

"Are you asking me when I first had sex?"

"Yes."

"You answer first."

"Well, surprisingly late. I fooled around a lot, but I didn't want to do anything that might mess up my future in the major leagues. It was the summer after I graduated from high school. She was the older sister of one of my teammates. After that, there was no going back. What about you?"

"I was twenty-one. By my junior year in college, I'd decided it was time to put a little effort into my appearance. I tossed aside the ugly duckling and tried to become a swan. And it worked. Sort of."

"It sure did," he murmured.

He kissed her again and when he drew back, he fought the urge to tell her exactly how he felt. Whether he wanted to admit it or not, he was falling in love with Angela. By tomorrow night, they'd have known each other a week. He was already imagining what it would be like to know her for the rest of his life.

"Are you cold?"

"It's a little chilly out here."

"I've reserved a private room for us." He pointed to the boat. "It's got a beautiful lake view, a nice big bed and all the privacy we could want." He helped her back onto the pier and then held her hand as she stepped down into the boat.

He grabbed a towel and dried them both off,

admiring the sight of her naked body in the moonlight. Then they crawled beneath the sleeping bags and pressed their naked bodies together for warmth. "What do you think?"

"I've never slept outside before."

"Never?"

She shook her head. "What if I have to go to the bathroom?"

"You walk back up to the house," he said.

"But aren't there animals outside?"

"Wake me up. I'll come with you."

She drew a deep breath, then relaxed. "No pillows?"

"Do you want a pillow?" Max asked.

"Yes, please. And a bottle of water. And my lip balm. I left it on the beside table in the bedroom."

"We're supposed to be roughing it," Max said. "I don't think lip balm and bottled water qualify."

"But I'm very particular about my sleeping environment," she said. "Things have to be just right, or I don't sleep at all."

"You don't have any trouble sleeping in my bed," he said.

"That's because your bedroom has solid walls, an adjoining bathroom, 600-count sheets and really nice down pillows. But I did have trouble sleeping that first night. Mostly because we were up so high and I felt the building swaying. Kind of like this boat. And, your clock makes this funny humming sound, so I had to put it inside the drawer." She paused. "Lip balm?"

"All right," Max said. "Lip balm, water, pillow. I'll be right back. If you see any bears, just give me a call."

"There are bears?"

"No," he said. "But if you see any, I want to know." Max grabbed his clothes, then stepped out of the boat to dress on the pier. "You're very high maintenance. Did anyone ever tell you that?"

"Never," she said. "Lip balm, please."

Max walked back to the cabin, laughing softly. This was interesting, he thought to himself. The more comfortable they became with each other, the more he began to discover about her. She was a bit odd, but he liked that about Angela. All her idiosyncrasies were so damn lovable.

He tiptoed into her bedroom and retrieved the tube of lip balm and a pillow, then fetched her a bottle of water. But by the time he got back to the boat, she was asleep. Max stripped off his shorts, then pulled the sleeping bag up around them both.

She sighed softly as she curled her body into his, pressing her face against his shoulder. "Good night, sweetheart," he whispered.

As her breathing slowed, Max silently stroked her back, his eyes closed, his body completely relaxed. Though it always seemed like the most natural thing in the world to make love to Angela, lying beside her like this felt just as good. He could spend his entire life like this, if he chose. He could have her forever.

He'd have to get her to agree, but Max didn't see that as an insurmountable problem. After all, he was a charming guy. And women loved him. But, there was only one woman he wanted and he had to figure out a way to make her need him as much as he needed her.

MAX SAT AT THE BAR, the Tribune sports page spread out in front of him. He scanned the box scores for the Rays, then went though the rest of the scores for the teams in his division.

He and Angela had driven back from Chicago the previous morning and spent the entire day and night in his apartment, curled up in bed watching old movies, eating Szechwan, and reading the Sunday paper.

But when he suggested they spend Tuesday in bed as well, she'd put her foot down. She had to at least make an attempt to go to work on occasion. The more she left for Ceci to do, the further behind they got, she'd argued. So Max had reluctantly kissed her goodbye, pulled on shorts and a T-shirt and gone for a run.

"Hey there!"

Max glanced up to see Dave strolling in through the kitchen door. "Hey. I didn't expect you back until later. It's not even eleven."

"Lauren got us up at the crack of dawn," he said.

She said she wanted to do some gardening. And the kids have swimming lessons this afternoon." Dave tossed his keys on the bar then poured himself a glass of lemonade from the pitcher in the refrigerator. "So, did you have a nice weekend?"

"It was great until my bozo of a brother showed up and ruined it all."

"Sorry. I guess now that you're home, we'll have to schedule our weekends at the cabin. Lauren extends her deepest apologies, as well. Although she was really glad she got a chance to meet Angela. Lauren said you two met in high school. I didn't know Angela went to Evanston. But now that I think of it, I remember a Susan Weatherby. She was really smart."

"We didn't know each other back then."

"Lauren also mentioned that she thought she recognized her from somewhere."

"Susan?"

"No, Angela."

Max looked up from his paper to find Dave watching him with a cautious expression. "From where?"

His older brother winced. "Well, that's the thing. She couldn't remember. So she did an Internet search and…well, she remembered seeing Angela on a morning news show last winter."

Max felt his gut twist as he recognized the look in his brother's eyes. This was not going to be good. Was she a criminal? A bunny boiler? Or even worse—a reporter? "What?"

"Lauren found a video clip. It turns out Angela

Weatherby is writing a book. About dating disasters. I think she might be writing about you."

Max braced his elbow on the edge of the bar, frowning. "Angela? No, she would have told me about that."

"She has a Web site, Max. It's a big collection of dating horror stories. They have files on thousands and thousands of guys, all written by the women they've screwed over. And guess who's on the Web site?"

"Me?"

Dave nodded. "Yeah. You've got a really fat file. Lots of women have a helluva lot to say about you. And none of it is very nice."

"Nah, Lauren must have it wrong. There's probably another Angela Weatherby."

"Look for yourself," Dave said. "You can use the computer in my office. I'm just saying, if you're going to invest time in this girl, maybe you ought to get to know her a little better."

"It's not going to make a difference," Max said. "So she's writing a book."

"And maybe you're just research?"

"Jeez, David, give me a break. We're sleeping together. Don't you think that's a little extreme to be research? She's a nice girl. She wouldn't do that."

"I'm just looking out for you, man. You have to admit that you haven't made a lot of sensible choices when it comes to women. Half of them were flat out crazy, and the other half were only interested in sex."

"And you think Angela fits in one of those two categories?"

"Just go take a look and form your own opinion. I just think you might have a few questions you want answered."

Max stared at his brother for a long moment, then cursed beneath his breath. "All right. I'll go look. But it's not going to make any difference." He shoved away from the bar and stalked back to the office, slamming the door behind him.

Over the next half hour, he looked at every Google link that had to do with Angela Weatherby of Chicago, Illinois. By the time he was finished, Max was forced to admit that he didn't know her at all.

Who the hell was this woman? She seemed to be determined to exact some kind of revenge on any guy who didn't automatically fall in love with the woman he was dating. His own profile was filled with detailed stories of Max Morgan's pathological inability to commit.

Hell, if she'd read his profile, why in the world would she want to date him? If he were a woman, he'd stay as far away from himself as possible. But was he really that bad? He'd never made any promises and then broken them. All the girls he dated knew he wasn't interested in marriage. But they'd all been certain they'd be the one to change him. It's not like he forced them to hop into bed with him. They were perfectly willing partners.

Max leaned back in the desk chair, rubbing his hands over his face. Now that he knew, what was he going to do about it? He could pretend it didn't make a difference, but he knew it did.

How had he missed this? His experience being in the public eye had given him a keen radarlike sense that detected anyone with suspicious motives. When he'd come home to Chicago, he'd let his guard down and shut the radar off. And now, he was left to wonder just who Angela Weatherby really was.

Max pushed away from the desk and walked back out into the bar. "I'll see you later," he muttered as he passed Dave.

"Hey, didn't I tell you? It's weird, huh?"

Max's jaw tensed as he fought the impulse to turn around and curse a blue streak at his brother. Though he ought to appreciate the fraternal loyalty, he didn't like his family interfering in his social life. But wasn't that what he'd come to Chicago for—to be closer to his family? When it came down to it, he'd always trust them first.

When he got out to the street, Max realized he didn't have his car. He'd either have to run back home or run all the way to Wicker Park to talk to Angela. He turned west, toward Angela, and toward the answers he needed.

By the time he reached Angela's office, he was drenched in sweat and even angrier than he was when he'd left the bar. He wiped his face on his T-shirt, then walked inside. A receptionist sat at a desk in the lobby, her gaze fixed on her computer. She turned and smiled and then caught her breath in surprise. "Hello," she said. "You're—"

"Angela Weatherby," Max interrupted. "Can you tell me where her office is?"

"Down that hall and to your right. Last door."

When he found the office, Max drew a deep breath and then opened the door. Though he wasn't sure what he planned to say, he knew he'd come up with something the moment he saw her. Unfortunately, he saw Ceci first. She stood beside a table, a sheaf of papers in her hand, a stunned expression on her face.

"Max. Hi."

"Ceci." He glanced around. "So this is where you two work." The tension had seeped into his voice and Ceci forced a smile as she glanced around nervously.

Ceci's shoulders slumped and she sent him an apologetic smile. "Max, believe me, she never thought anything would happen with you two. She just wanted to interview you. And I think, part of her wanted to see if the feelings she had for you so long ago were finally gone. I talked her into going out that night. If I hadn't, you two would have never met. She wouldn't have gone on her own."

"Why do I feel like I'm only getting half the story? First, she doesn't know me. Then she does. Then she was madly in love with me. And now—I don't know what's going on now."

"Maybe you better talk to her. She just went out to get coffee. She'll be back in a few minutes." Ceci grabbed her purse from a nearby chair. "I'm just going to leave you two alone."

"That would probably be best," he muttered.

She stopped halfway out the door, then turned back. "For what it's worth, I really do think she loves you. She just wasn't prepared to still feel that way. And certainly not after a week. You caught her by surprise."

"Everything seems to be catching me by surprise," Max said.

The door swung closed and Max was left in the silent office. He sat down in one of the desk chairs, bracing his elbows on his knees as he shoved his fingers through his damp hair. He wasn't sure whether to believe Ceci or not. Did Angela love him or was Ceci simply trying to cover for her friend?

A minute later, the door opened again. Angela froze when she saw him, two large paper cups in her left hand. For a moment, her arm wavered and Max jumped up and grabbed the coffees from her, setting them on a nearby desk.

"Tell me something," Max said, his gaze fixed on the coffees.

"Anything," she said in a shaky voice.

He looked at her, his eyes locking on hers. "Are you writing about me in your book?"

"Am I or was I?" she asked. "There's a difference."

Max cursed softly. "We are not going to play word games, Angela. Am I in your book? Yes or no?"

"Yes," she said. "But it's not you. I mean I don't use your name. There's no way anyone would—well, maybe a few people would make the connection, but—no, you're not. Not anymore. I decided to take you out."

"And all that happened between us? Was that just research? Or was all this just some elaborate scheme to meet me?"

"It wasn't research. And it wasn't a scheme." She took a step toward him, then stopped when he held out his hand. "I know this all looks bad," Angela continued, "but it's not. I have never done anything more than love you. It sounds stupid, but I think I knew the moment we met that we belonged together. All those years ago. And then again, in the bar that night. Ceci thinks it's karma and I have no idea if she's right. But I think I've been waiting for you my whole life. Kind of like those penguins."

"And this is the way you get my attention? By trashing my name on the Internet?"

"It wasn't me," Angela explained. "Those women have a right to their opinions. I—I don't happen to share their views, but that doesn't make their feelings any less valid. Max, I didn't expect to feel this way. I just wanted to prove that you were everything they said you were. And that these feelings I had for you were silly and childish. Only you weren't…and my feelings weren't. I didn't know what to do."

"The truth might have been nice."

Angela nodded, a tear sliding down her cheek. "Probably. But after a while, I just didn't want to ruin it. I figured you'd put an end to it sooner or later. I guess this is it."

Max closed his eyes and leaned back in the chair. "You knew how I felt about the press. What you're doing here isn't much different."

"No," Angela said. "It's not. And I can understand how you might think it's an invasion of your privacy. But maybe you need to see a bit of truth in it as well. These women all felt they had a good reason for writing about you. And I think, if you're honest with yourself, you know you didn't treat them well."

"So you think I deserve to have my reputation trashed?"

"No. But I think my opinion of you might be a bit prejudiced. We are sleeping together." Angela took a ragged breath. "I didn't know what to do. Being with you was like a fantasy come true. I couldn't help myself from getting caught up in it."

"That doesn't make me feel any better."

"I'm not going to make excuses," Angela said. "This is what I do for a living. You don't have to like it."

"But you're doing it to me," he said. "What does that say about us?"

"There was no *us* a week ago," Angela said. "And

I'm not sure there'll be an *us* next week. I don't know how this is going to turn out, Max, but if your profile is any evidence, it's not going to turn out well. I'm going to be just another notch on your bedpost."

"How can you be such an optimist and a cynic at the same time?" he asked, shaking his head.

"That's always been my problem. I want the fantasy, but I'm too practical to believe it when I get it." She closed the door and crossed the office. Kneeling down in front of him, she placed her hands on his knees. "I know I've probably messed this up. And I don't know if you can forgive me. But if you can't, I'm all right with that. I had my chance and I blew it. But at least I had my chance. No matter what you say to me, I don't regret it."

Max looked down at her, his anger waning. He wanted to gather her in his arms and kiss her until all the confusion went away, until he was sure of his feelings again. But at the moment, he wasn't certain of anything. He quickly stood, stepping around her, and walked to the door before he could touch her.

"I have to go. I'll talk to you later."

Angela sat down on the floor, then nodded as he closed the door. Max stopped, bracing his hand on the wall as he looked back at office. Every instinct told him to go back inside, to begin again, to forget everything that had happened. This was a woman who had just admitted she loved him and he was ready to throw that all away because of—of what?

He needed time to sort this all out. Time to figure

out exactly where Angela belonged in his life. She'd been a part of his past. Would she be a part of his future, too?

"YOU KNEW THIS MIGHT HAPPEN," Ceci said. "There is no such thing as anonymity in the age of Google. So how did you leave it?"

"He walked out."

"That's it?"

"He said, see you later. But he says that to everyone."

Ceci smiled wanly. "Well, maybe he means it this time. Maybe he just needs time to think this out."

"No. It's definitely over," said Angela, shaking her head. "And that's good. I accomplished what I set out to do. I got to know him. I turned the fantasy into reality. He seduced me and he dumped me. My thesis is proved."

"And that makes you happy?"

"No," Angela said. "But I'm back to where I was before we met. Only now, I won't have to compare every guy I meet to Max Morgan. He will not be the standard by which every other man in my life is judged."

Ceci leaned up against the edge of Angela's desk. "You seem to be handling this very well."

She swallowed back her tears and tried to put on a brave face. "What's there to handle? We were together a week. For Max Morgan, that's pretty good." A tear trickled down her cheek and then, a sob slipped out.

Angela couldn't seem to stop herself. Her composure was shattered.

Ceci gathered her in her arms. "Oh, sweetie, I'm sorry."

"You should be," Angela replied, forcing a laugh. "I told you you'd have to pick up the pieces." She wiped her damp cheeks with her fingers. "I tried not to fall in love with him but it was so difficult. He is a devil. He tempted me and I just…cracked." Angela drew a ragged breath. "But I had fun. The sex was great. And I got to do some interesting things."

A soft knock sounded on the office door and a few moments later, Will stepped inside. Ceci turned, her arms still around Angela. "Hi. You're early."

"Yeah. I thought you'd be too excited to wait."

Angela glanced back and forth between them. "Excited about what?"

Ceci shook her head, stepping away to grab her purse. "Now's not a good time," she said. "We'll tell you later."

"Tell me what? I'm fine, really."

"She just broke up with Max," Ceci explained. "I really don't think—"

Angela cursed softly. "What?"

Ceci bit her bottom lip. "Will and I are engaged. He proposed last night and I said yes."

Angela felt the tears start again, only these were tears of happiness. "Oh, Ceci, that's wonderful. So you had your moment?"

"The mustard stain at the baseball game. That was it."

Angela hugged Will. "You'll be so happy. I know you will. You picked the best girl."

Ceci wrapped her arms around Will's waist and they all hugged each other. "He's my guy! Besides, if I didn't marry him, who would?"

"I think it's perfect," Angela said through her tears.

"Stop crying or I'm going to start. Why don't we all go out for a glass of wine?"

Angela drew a calming breath. "You two go. I'll be fine. I have some work to do on the book." She gave them a little wave as they walked out. Then, pressing her lips together, she fought back another surge of tears. She was happy for them, really she was. But she couldn't help but wonder if she'd ever find a guy who loved her as much as Will loved Ceci.

She sat down at her desk, cupping her chin in her palm as she scrolled through the site. She clicked to the main menu and then typed in a search for Max's name. His profile came up, along with a series of photos that the women had posted.

As she looked at each one, Angela was struck by how none of the photos resembled the man she knew. For all she could tell, she was looking at a complete stranger. Max's smile was warmer, and his eyes darker, and the dimple in his cheek deeper.

She knew every post in his profile by heart but as she read through them again, it was clear that they'd never known the real Max Morgan. Angela closed her eyes and cursed softly. Or maybe she was the one who'd never known him.

When she'd finally regained her composure, Angela opened the site maintenance program and found the tab to delete a profile. Then she clicked over to Max's. She and Ceci had always been adamant about their own neutrality in editing the site. Profiles were meant to inform, not to slander. It was a fine line to walk, but Angela had been proud of the job they'd done so far.

Deleting a profile had never been an option. If one of the men got married, the profile was tagged, but not deleted. She drew a deep breath, the pointer hovering over the delete button. It was the least she could do for him. And if someone complained, they could always write it off as a technical glitch.

Drawing a deep breath, Angela clicked and Max Morgan disappeared from SmoothOperators.com. She felt as if an unbearable weight had been lifted. The deception, though not forgotten, was at least undone. She pulled up the manuscript for her book and found Chapter Five. Unfortunately, this wasn't quite as easy to delete.

It was just one chapter. Would he even recognize himself in her words? There were eleven other archetypes in the book. No, she wouldn't delete it. She'd simply change the title of the chapter. "The Sexy Sinner," she murmured. "The Sexy Scoundrel." Angela nodded. That would work.

When she'd saved her change, Angela turned off her computer and grabbed her bag. The past week had been a whirlwind of emotion. It was time to get her life back on track. Tuesday night was laundry night. She'd have time to give herself a pedicure, catch up on all her reading, and take a long hot bath.

There was a time she'd actually enjoyed her single life. She could find that happiness again. Angela walked to the door, but as she opened it, the office phone rang. She hesitated, desperate to leave business behind. But then she walked back inside.

"Hello, this is Angela."

"Angela! Kelly Caulfield at Daybreak Chicago. How are you?"

"Hello. I'm fine. How are you?"

"Well, we have an opening in our schedule for Thursday morning. One of our guests cancelled. And since you were so great when you were on with us in January, I was hoping you might come back and do another segment."

"Thursday morning?"

"Yes. I know it's short notice, but I'm really desperate. This would be a huge favor and I promise that we'll have you on again to plug your book when it comes out. In fact, you can pick the date."

"I don't know, I—"

"Please," Kelly said. "Did I mention we're desperate?"

"Yes. All right. What time do I need to be there?"

"We're going to give you a later spot, so if you arrive by 7:15, we'll be fine. Thank you so much! Our graphic guy is going to pull some shots from the Web site. If you have a cover for the book and a solid release date, we can mention that, too."

"I do have a cover," Angela said. "But I'm really not sure of the release date."

"Bring it along and we'll get it up anyway. Thank you again. I'll see you Thursday morning."

Angela hung up the phone. This was beyond strange. It was as if her life was rewinding, back to a time when everything seemed to be moving along quite nicely. But could she really go back after what she'd experienced in the last week?

She walked out into the warm evening, heading toward her flat. She'd spend the night alone. It felt strange to have no plans, nothing to look forward to. Just her empty bed and a quiet house.

On her way home, she stopped at the grocery store and picked up dinner, a salad, soup and some freshly baked bread. As she passed the dessert case, she picked up a small strawberry cheesecake.

At times like this, when her life looked a little bleak, eating an entire cheesecake was the only prescription for happiness. And it was just a small cheesecake.

Her flat was silent and cool as she stepped inside. The place was a bit messy. Over the past week, she'd run in and out, to dress, to shower, to get ready for fun with Max. She kicked her sandals off and walked into the kitchen, setting the bags on the granite countertop.

She picked up her phone, then set it down before listening to her voice mail signal. He wasn't going to call. And waiting for him was only going to drive her crazy. But her curiosity got the better of her and she picked up and dialed. "One message," she murmured, listening to the number. It was Max's home number and he'd left the message early that morning. She held her breath, then replayed the message.

"Hi. It's me. You just left for work and I'm lying here in my bed wondering what we're going to do tonight. I think you should put on your prettiest dress and I'll take you out for dinner. I have something I need to talk to you about. Don't worry. Nothing bad. I'll see you later. Love you."

"Love me," she muttered. "Not anymore."

She hung up the phone, then retrieved the bottle of wine from the fridge and yanked out the cork. Not bothering with a glass, Angela took a drink of the Chardonnay, straight from the bottle. There was a half bottle left. She'd have to be careful. The last thing she wanted to do was drink too much and start drunk dialing.

Setting the wine down, Angela grabbed the bag with the cheesecake in it. She retrieved a fork and dug in, then carried the box with her to her bedroom. When she'd settled herself in the center of the bed, she flipped on the television and began to devour the cheesecake. "So this is my life," she murmured. "Empty calories and reality television."

There was one bright spot. It could only get better from here.

8

THE ACHE IN HIS HEAD throbbed along with his pulse, an incessant rhythm that kept him from falling back asleep. Max rolled over in bed and pulled the pillow over his head, blocking out the early morning rays of the sun. He peeked at the bedside clock then groaned. Four hours of sleep was usually not enough for him, especially if it came after a night of too many beers.

He threw his arm out on the opposite side of the bed, just to make sure there was no one else in the room with him. He'd been almost drunk enough to bring a woman home. But not quite. In truth, he probably would have passed out before he drank enough to put Angela out of his mind for good.

He'd spent the last couple days trying desperately to forget her. When beer didn't do the trick, he ran, miles and miles, pushing his body until he couldn't run any longer. Running, drinking, sleeping and then doing it all over again. Anything to wear his body out so his mind wouldn't have the energy to remember how good he'd had it.

Reaching out again, he searched the bed for the remote control, then flipped on the television, anxious for the drone of the morning news to put him back to sleep. Max closed his eyes and drew a deep breath.

But just as he was drifting back into unconsciousness, he heard her voice, soft, sweet, a sound he'd come to crave over the last few days. Cursing softly, he threw aside the pillow and sat up. A groan rumbled in his chest as his head threatened to explode with the pain. But her voice was still there.

Max stared at the television, giving his eyes a moment to focus. When they did, he realized Angela really was there, on television, talking about her Web site. He sat numbly, listening to her voice but not bothering to comprehend the words she was saying.

She looked tired, he thought to himself. But she was still beautiful, her honey-blond hair falling around her shoulders, her lush lips forming each word. Max crawled to the end of the bed to get a better look. He stared at her eyes, fascinated by the color. High definition plasma televisions were a wonderful invention, he mused.

Before long, the hostess wrapped up the interview and Angela was gone. An odd sense of loss settled in his gut. Was that the last time he'd ever see her? Max had fought with himself over the past few days, wanting to call her, thinking that they might be able to work it out, and then knowing that he'd be heading back to Florida in a few weeks to rejoin the team.

What was the use? Long distance relationships never worked. They'd be apart at least until the end of the regular season. And if the team made it into the playoffs, until late October.

After that, he was in charge. Free agency was a complicated affair, but Max had an ace to play. He was willing to walk away from the game if he didn't get what he wanted. If he was going to play another year, Max wanted to finish his career in Chicago. If he could get the Rays to trade him or release him, he'd be able to negotiate a deal to make the move. Money didn't make a difference anymore, so chances were, he could make it work.

But what was the use coming back to Chicago if he wasn't going to be with Angela. Sure, he wanted to be near his family, but Angela was the reason he was considering a move north. But right now, they weren't even talking to each other.

His phone rang beside the bed and Max frowned. Only one person called him this early in the morning—his mother. No doubt she wanted to firm up plans for Saturday's barbecue. He'd decided to attend, hoping some time with the family would take his mind off Angela. And maybe, just maybe, she might decide to come.

"Hi, Mom," he said. "What's up?"

"She was just on the news. Did you catch it? Channel Seven."

"Actually, I did catch it."

"She's lovely, isn't she? I told you. Now why wouldn't you want to go out with a woman like that?"

"I'm coming on Saturday," he said.

"These models and actresses. They just have their minds on other things. They don't—"

"Mom, I said I'd be there."

"Really?" Max heard her cover the phone with her hand and shout to his father. "Max is coming to the barbecue!"

"What time do you want me to come around?" he asked.

"Noon. She's coming at one. And wear something nice. Not those raggedy shorts you always have on."

"We've already discussed the wardrobe, Mom." He paused, fighting back an impulse. In the end, though, Max decided that if his mother was going to run his social life anyway, he might as well get something out of the deal. "Make sure you call this girl and let her know that I'm anxious to meet her. Tell her I'm really looking forward to it."

"Really?"

"Of course. If she's as great as you say she is, then I'm sure I'll like her. But I'm not going to come if she doesn't come. Tell her that."

"All right," Maggie Morgan said. "I'll see you Saturday."

She hung up and Max tossed the cordless phone onto the bed. Then he flopped down and covered his face with the pillow again. What was the use in trying to stay away? He needed to see Angela again.

The anger he'd felt a few days ago had dissolved with time and now, he was left with the realization that what had happened hadn't changed his feelings for her. He really liked Angela. He probably even loved her. Not probably, he did love her. And Max had never felt that way about a woman before.

He crawled out of bed and grabbed a pair of running shorts from the pile of clean clothes on a nearby chair, then tugged on a T-shirt. His shoes were next to the door and once he got them on, Max headed out, jogging slowly to warm-up, then began to run in earnest.

It was like some invisible force was drawing him toward her. He just wanted to make sure she was all right. Max wasn't sure what he planned to do once he got to her neighborhood, but he felt an overwhelming need to see her again.

He stopped in for a latte and a Danish at the Starbucks closest to her place, then walked to her flat carrying her breakfast in a bag. As he waited on her stoop, Max wasn't sure he was ready to talk to her. What was he supposed to say? He needed a plan, something to offer her, a way that they could move forward.

Maybe it would have been better to have just waited until Saturday. Max left the coffee and Danish on the step and started down the block. But before he turned the corner, he glanced back. He saw her, walking toward her flat, dressed in the clothes she'd worn on television.

Max hid behind a nearby tree, watching her. "Now who's the stalker?" he muttered.

Angela stopped short when she saw the coffee and the paper bag with the Danish. She looked up and down the street, then slowly picked it up. Max smiled to himself. She had to know where it had come from. He wondered what was going through her mind.

A few moments later, she took one last look around, then disappeared inside. Max decided to wait and see her when she came out again. If he ran around the block, he'd be able to run into her, as if it were an accidental meeting. They could chat, he could read her mood and maybe figure out where he stood.

But his wait was interrupted when he heard the piercing sound of a police siren. The noise startled him and he spun around to see a patrol car parked right behind him. The policeman rolled down his window and leaned out.

"You wanna tell me what—" He paused. "Hey, you're Max Morgan, aren't you?"

Max nodded. "Yeah, I am."

"What are you doing here?"

"Just standing," he said. Max pointed to his leg. "Cramp."

"Oh, yeah? You eat bananas? I find that if I eat a banana a day, I don't have trouble with leg cramps. I think it's the potassium."

"Thanks for the advice," Max said.

"No problem." He nodded. "I'm gonna have to tell you to move along, though. We had a call from one of the neighbors. She's worried you might be casing her place for a burglary. These older folks get a little nervous when they see strangers on the street."

"No problem," Max said.

The policeman nodded. "A lot of burglars pose as runners. If they get caught, they can escape pretty quick." The guy chuckled. "But, hey, I don't think you'd need to burgle in order to make money. You've got a nice contract down there in Florida, don't you?"

"Actually, I'm a free agent after this season."

"Aw, man, you've gotta come back and play for the Sox. They could use a hitter like you." The radio on his shoulder crackled. He pushed a button and listened to the call. "Gotta go. Fender bender on North. Take care now."

Max chuckled to himself as he took one last look down the street. After another ten minutes, Angela still hadn't emerged. Maybe she'd gone back to bed, Max thought. He stretched out his calf muscle, then jogged across the street and headed back toward the lake.

"I'll see you soon, Angela," he murmured.

THE MORGANS LIVED IN a beautiful old house near Ingleside Park in Evanston. As Angela searched for a place to park on the street, she drove past a familiar black BMW. "Oh dear. What am I doing here?" She drew a deep breath. She'd been invited. If she didn't go, she'd never hear the end of it from her mother.

If she did go, then she'd definitely be seeing Max again. Just once more, just enough time to set things straight. Angela was certain she could finally put their relationship in perspective. There were no hard feelings, at least on her part, and she hoped he felt the same way.

After she parked, Angela twisted the rearview mirror toward her and examined her hair and make-up. This would be his last memory of her and she wanted it to be a good one. Not that he'd give her a second thought once he found a new woman to occupy his time. But someday, he might look back on what they shared and realize it had been good—for a little while, at least.

Angela hopped out of her car and hurried down the sidewalk toward the house. The barbecue had started at one, but she'd spent some time driving around her hometown in an attempt to work up her courage. She'd turned the car south more than once, but in the end, she'd decided she wanted to end this with no regrets. She wouldn't spend another fourteen years thinking about what might have been if she'd only attended the Morgan barbecue.

The front door was open and she recognized the two girls standing behind the screen. Angela smiled and waved at Brit and Beth. "Hello there."

"Angela!" they shouted as they shoved open the door and stumbled outside. They met her in the middle of the walk, each grabbing a hand and pulling her toward the house. "You're here," Brit said. "Why didn't you come with Uncle Max?"

"Can we play a game?" Beth asked. "Grammy has Chutes and Ladders. Have you ever played Apples to Apples? Grammy has that game, too. Do you want to play that?"

They ushered her into the spacious foyer and then through a beautiful living room. When they reached a great room at the back of the house, she could see the party through the wall of windows that overlooked the backyard. "We brought our dog," Brittany said. "We don't take him to the cabin because he throws up in the car on long trips. His name is Elwood."

"Girls, take the guests to the backyard, please. That's your job."

Angela held her breath at the sound of his voice and when Max came around the corner from the kitchen, their eyes met. A long silence grew between them and the little girls looked back and forth, their expressions curious.

"It's Angela," Beth said. "Say hello to her, Uncle Max."

"Right," Max said, forcing a smile. "Hello. I wasn't sure you'd be coming."

"Duh," Brittany said, rolling her eyes. "She's your girlfriend. Why wouldn't she come?"

"Maybe she had a tummy ache," Bethany said. "I had a tummy ache and I couldn't go to day camp yesterday."

"Girls, head back to the door. I'll show Angela out to the backyard." Max shooed them off, then turned to Angela. His gaze searched her face and Angela felt a flush warm her cheeks. "I'm glad you came," he murmured.

"I thought we needed to see each other once more," she said. "Just to…settle things."

Max glanced over his shoulder at the crowd in the backyard. Then he grabbed her hand and pulled her along after him. But instead of going outside, he took her up a rear stairway that led from the kitchen to the second floor. At the end of the hall, they stepped inside a bedroom and he closed the door behind them both.

Angela looked around at the shelves of baseball trophies that lined the walls. This was his room. She walked over to the dresser and studied the items displayed on the top. "This looks a lot different than your condo," she said. Angela pointed to the trophies. "You should move these down there. They'd impress the girls you bring home."

"Maybe," he said. "Would they have impressed you?"

She turned and smiled at him. "Nothing impresses me."

"That's right," he said. "I forgot."

Angela sat down on the edge of the bed and looked up at him. He looked so handsome in a blue oxford shirt and khakis. She'd become so accustomed to seeing him in various states of undress that she'd never appreciated how well he wore clothes. "I wanted to tell you I'm sorry I wasn't completely honest with you from the start. I guess I never thought we'd even speak to each other, much less spend any time together. And then, things started happening so fast, there never seemed to be the right moment."

He sat down beside her. "I may have overreacted," Max said. "The truth is, until you came along, I didn't much think about the impression I was leaving with the women I knew. I didn't really care."

"And now you do?"

Max took her hand and wove his fingers through hers. "I care about what you think," he said. "I don't want you to have any regrets."

"I don't," Angela said.

He brought her hand to his lips and kissed the back of her wrist, his warm mouth lingering on her skin. Angela's heart fluttered and a tiny sigh slipped from her throat. The sensation was so familiar. Her mind flashed back to a time when his lips had traveled all over her naked body.

How difficult would it be to just pull him down on the bed and kiss him? How would he react? Angela didn't have to guess. The answer was in his touch, in the gentle caress of his fingers on her wrist. He still wanted her as much as she wanted him. "How is your shoulder?" she asked.

"Better."

"So, you'll be going back to Florida soon?"

He nodded. "Actually, I'm flying back tomorrow." He paused. "But I don't have to. I mean, I could fly back—"

"I'm glad," she said, pasting a bright smile on her face.

"That I'm leaving?"

Angela shook her head. "No, that your shoulder has healed."

Without warning, Max took her face in his hands and kissed her. Angela drew back, startled, staring up into his gaze without blinking. But then, he tried again and she felt her defenses crumble. Why go on fooling herself? She wanted to kiss him. She wanted to rip off all her clothes and make love to him on his baseball bedspread.

He must have had the same thought because as the kiss spun out, he gently drew her down onto the bed. It amazed her how perfectly they read each other's desires. Her fingers fumbled with the buttons on his shirt and when she'd managed to undo three or four, Angela smoothed her hand over his muscled chest.

"I've missed you," he murmured, furrowing

his fingers through her hair and pulling her into a deeper kiss.

"You better find a way to stop that," she said. He frowned, meeting her gaze. "You're going back to Florida tomorrow."

"If you ask me to stay, I will." He kissed her again, his passion rising. "Ask me."

It was just one word. "Stay." And her entire life would change. But it wasn't that simple. He had a job in Florida, a life, and a career. And everything she'd built for herself was here in Chicago. But for a chance at love—at real, forever love—wouldn't she give it all up?

"I can't," she said. "You have to go back."

"You could come with me?"

Angela shook her head. "We've known each other for…well, it hasn't been two weeks yet."

"It doesn't make a difference," Max said.

"Yes, it does," Angela said. "We're in that stage when all our flaws are hidden and we think we're perfect for each other."

"You have no flaws," he said, finding a spot just below her ear to kiss.

Angela gently pushed him away. For once in her life, she wasn't going to give in to her fantasies. She was going to do the right thing, the practical thing. "You need to go back, Max. And then, when the season is over, we can see how we feel."

"I already know how I'll feel," Max said. "I need you."

She opened her mouth, then paused before speaking. "Do you need me? Or do you just need a woman? Maybe you need to find out for sure."

An astonished look crossed his face and he regarded her warily. "That's a lovely offer, but I don't think I'll be taking advantage of that. Now that I've decided which woman I want, another one won't do." He reached out and cupped her face in his hand. "I've fallen in love with you, Angela. There won't be any other women in my life from now on."

Angela felt emotion clog her throat. How long had she waited to hear those words? Every dream she'd had about him had always ended in a sweet confession of his feelings for her. But now, she couldn't quite bring herself to believe him.

Ceci was right. The Web site had changed her. She couldn't look at love without a healthy dose of cynicism. She wanted to believe it could exist, but Angela needed proof. If he went back to his life and then returned, she'd know for sure. "I think you should go," she said.

"We'll both go."

She shook her head, but Max kissed her again. "I was about to leave anyway. I came to meet this girl and she didn't show up. Besides, I only have a day left in Chicago. I don't want to spend it with my parents and their friends. I want to spend it with you."

They walked to the door. "I should at least go in and say hello to my parents," Angela said.

He took her hand and led her to the stairs in the

front of the house. "If we sneak out, no one will even know where we've gone."

"Where are we going?" Angela asked.

"Somewhere we can be alone."

The girls were waiting at the front door. Max ruffled their hair. "Go tell Grammy that I really like the girl she found for me and I'm taking her home with me."

The two girls giggled and ran off as Max pulled Angela out the front door. Every shred of common sense had fled. Angela knew she shouldn't jump into bed with him, but that's all she really wanted—to feel his naked body next to hers. To lose herself in the delicious sensations of their lovemaking. She'd survived it all before. One last time couldn't hurt her.

"I'll meet you at your place," she said.

MAX STARED OUT AT THE water of the Gulf, watching a trio of pelicans float lazily on the surface. He ran his hands through his hair, waiting for that sense of calm to settle in. That's what he loved about his house in Florida. He could just open the door and listen to the waves on the shore, Everything was perfect.

But since he'd returned, that calm had been disrupted by nearly constant thoughts of Angela. They'd spent one last day and night together and then she was gone, sneaking out of his bed in the predawn hours.

In truth, Max had been glad there wouldn't be any

dramatic good-byes. It would be as if she'd just gone to work while he slept late. A day would pass, he'd call her and they'd pretend they weren't miles apart. The months would pass and the season would end and they'd be together again.

They'd talked on the phone a few times, but once again, they never seemed to have the same connection. She sounded distant and he fumbled for things to talk about. He needed to be able to reach out and touch her, to let his hands and his lips say the things he couldn't put into words.

The team had a three-game series in Chicago next month. Even though he was still on the disabled list, the series would give him a good excuse to fly back to Chicago for the weekend and see her.

Max sighed. He shouldn't need an excuse, but there was so much unsettled between them. It was clear that Angela was not hopeful about their future. Already, she'd begun preparing for the worst, assuming that everything would fall apart once they were apart. Somewhere along the line, the fantasy had disappeared and she'd begun to see the reality in front of her.

Max's doorbell buzzed and he glanced at the clock on the mantel. He walked to the front door, his footsteps silent on the cool tile. His agent, Bruce Carmichael, was standing on the other side, dressed in a ridiculous Hawaiian shirt and cargo shorts. "You look hot," Max said, stepping aside to let him in. "And I don't mean that in a sexual way."

"I love you, too, Max, but I hate where you live. You know, it's exactly the same temperature here as it is in L.A. And yet this feels so much more like hell."

"It's the humidity," Max said walking back into the airy living room. "Sit. Do you want something to drink?"

"Ice water. Lots of ice," he said.

In the kitchen, Max filled a huge glass at the sink and then grabbed a beer for himself before returning to the living room. He sat down and took a long swallow of his beer.

"What's up?" Bruce said. "Why did you make me fly all the way out here?"

"I've got some plans and I need you to make them happen," he said.

"Plans? What kind of plans?"

"I want to play in Chicago next season."

"What? No, I don't think that's going to happen. You're a marquee player and the Rays—"

"I'm a marquee player with a bad shoulder," Max reminded him. "I might not come back."

"Still, if they trade you, they're going to expect a draft pick and some major money. There isn't a team out there who'll bite unless you finish the season strong."

"But if I tell them I'm going to retire if they don't trade me, they might think differently."

Bruce leaned forward, concern etched deeply into his expression. "You're thinking about retiring?"

"It's an option. I might not have a choice if the shoulder doesn't come back. This can work," Max said. "We have the advantage. We just have to play it right."

"If you recover completely, you could play another five or six years. I thought you liked playing for the Rays."

"I do. They're a great team. But I have other reasons for wanting to play for Chicago. You do what it takes to get me there, all right?"

"You have to at least consider other offers," Bruce said. "If the Rays give you the best offer, then you have to take it."

"No, I don't. I'd retire. I'm looking at the end of my career, Bruce. And for once, I want to make a decision that doesn't involve money. I want to make a decision because my heart tells me it's right."

Bruce frowned. "Is this about a girl?"

"No!" Max replied. "Well, yeah, I guess it is. But what's wrong with that? I've made enough money to keep both of us comfortable for the rest of our lives. I've invested well. Now, I want to do something that would make me happy."

Bruce sighed. "I suppose I can put out some feelers and see what they'd be willing to do," he said. "But you're tying my hands. I'm supposed to get you the best deal and this won't be it."

"Do your magic. If I'm playing next year, I want to play in Chicago." Max got to his feet. "Now that we have the rest of my life settled, do you want to do some fishing? I haven't had the boat out in months. And it's much cooler on the water."

Bruce nodded. "Sure. What are we going to fish for?"

"We'll figure that out when we get there," Max said with a shrug.

His agent chuckled. "What is wrong with you? Where is the Max Morgan I know and love? I'm not used to seeing you so...relaxed."

"I'm getting ready to live the rest of my life," Max said. "I've got new priorities." He pulled the door open and Bruce walked through. "I'm thinking I might even get married. Maybe start a family."

"I don't know," Bruce said. "With this kind of attitude, how are you ever going to find someone to marry? You're not going to have a job and you'll be hanging around the house all day. Once you stop working out, you're going to put on some weight. And if you stop with the women, you're going to lose all your charm. Who would marry that?"

"I have someone in mind," Max said. "I just need some time to convince her. But I can't do that if I'm living in Florida."

"What are you going to do with this house?"

"I don't know. Maybe keep it as a vacation home. I need to have somewhere to escape to during those Chicago winters. And this place has a pool with a very high privacy fence."

Bruce frowned. "What the hell does that have to do with anything?"

"Nothing," Max said with a chuckle. At least nothing he wanted to discuss with his agent. His mind wandered back to the night he and Angela had spent skinny-dipping in the lake. Really, it didn't matter where they lived.

He could be happy in her little one-bedroom flat in Wicker Park. As long as she crawled into bed with him at night and woke up in his arms in the morning, Max would be content. "One more thing. I need you to keep this quiet," Max said. "No press speculation, no interviews about why I'm thinking of moving. When it's done, we can talk, but not until then."

"I don't know. Everyone is already wondering what's going to happen with you. It'll be difficult to keep the press out of it."

Max chuckled, clapping Bruce on the shoulder. His life was falling into place. He was only missing one thing—the girl. "I know you can handle it. That's why I pay you the big bucks, right?"

9

"WHAT IS THIS?" Ceci stared at the manila envelope Angela was holding out to her across the table.

They'd had a leisurely lunch, sitting at an outdoor café, but Angela had been anxious to get back to business. "It's an early wedding present," she said with a smile.

Ceci laughed, then rolled her eyes. "Will and I are not getting married tomorrow. We haven't even set a date yet. Or agreed on a concept. Will wants to elope to Vegas. And I'm beginning to think I look really fat in white, so I'm pushing for the beach in September. Kind of a hippie-retro wedding."

"Open it," Angela said.

Ceci pulled the legal papers out and frowned. "Are we being sued?"

"I'm turning the Web site over to you," Angela said. "It's all yours."

"What?"

"You can have it all, Ceci. I can't do this anymore.

I want to believe I can fall in love. I did fall in love for a little while. But this Web site is just a reminder of how wrong I was."

"That doesn't mean you have to give up everything we've worked for." Ceci stared at the papers in disbelief.

"I need to move on," Angela said. "I have a couple of job prospects. The neighborhood business association is looking for a director and I applied for the job. I've also got a freelance offer to write a relationship column for a women's magazine."

"But you could do those things and still work here. I can't do this on my own, Angie. I don't want to. I love coming to work with you. It's fun. Who am I going to walk with in the morning? Who am I going to have coffee with? And all our lunches and late dinners."

"Whom," Angela said.

"Stop! I'm serious."

"None of that will change," Angela said. "I'm not going anywhere. If I work for the neighborhood association, their office is in our building, just up the stairs."

"You're thinking about him, aren't you," Ceci said. "You're thinking you might leave Chicago and move to Florida. That's it, isn't it? We can't have coffee if you're in Florida!"

Angela took a quick sip of her lemonade. "I'm not going to Florida. Max and I aren't going to work this out. He'll soon forget all about me. I'm here to stay and I'll always be your best friend."

"What about the book?"

"It was a bad idea. I was completely wrong about my thesis, but my editor says it will still sell. So, I'm putting your name on the cover."

"Mine?"

"You were my coauthor and you've helped me with a lot of the research. You can do all the press for it and promote the site. It'll be fun. Besides, you like doing that stuff much more than I do."

"This is about Max, isn't it," Ceci said. "Are you doing this because you still love him?"

"No, I'm doing this because he might still love me," Angela said. "If he does and he comes back, then I don't want anything to get between us."

"Are you sure about this?" Ceci asked.

"I am. It's time to be more optimistic, Ceci. You've always been optimistic about love and look where you are. You're about to marry Will and start a wonderful new life."

Ceci stared down at the papers, a dejected look on her face. "I wasn't going to mention this, but we had a call last month from someone who wanted to buy the site. He wasn't offering much and I figured you wouldn't want to sell, but it would be enough to start up a new business for both of us. We work so well together. Between the two of us, we could come up with a really great idea."

"We'll talk about it," Angela said. "For now, I'm going to keep my options open."

Ceci jumped up and leaned over the table, throwing her arms around Angela and giving her a fierce hug. "I hope things turn out with Max. I really like him."

"And if they don't turn out, then there will be another guy," Angela said. "Optimism. I'm thinking positively. There will be another guy. I'm sure of it. Because for every woman, there is the perfect man waiting for her...somewhere. I just have to find him."

They were still hugging each other when Will walked up to the table. He grinned. "This is the second time I've caught you two in a passionate embrace. Should I be worried?"

Angela laughed. "You caught us. If you're going to marry Ceci, you get me in the deal. We're best friends and I'm not going anywhere. Isn't that every man's fantasy?"

"I can live with that," Will teased. "Although we're going to need a bigger bed."

"Stop," Ceci said. "I'm not sharing my husband with anyone, not even my best friend. How did you know we were here?"

"It's a nice day, you love the chicken salad at the place, and I saw you when I drove by," Will said.

"Sit," Angela said.

"I don't have time. I have to get back to work, but I came here to tell Angela something. Something big.

Really big." He lowered his voice. "This is a secret. Well, not really a secret, since I heard it on the radio, but more like a rumor. Max Morgan may be coming back to Chicago to play for the Sox."

Angela's jaw dropped and she stared at Will, not certain she heard him right. "He can just leave his team and come here?"

"No, there are all sorts of restrictions. He's a free agent at the end of this season. And because of his value to the team, they might not want to let him go. But, if the Rays release him or trade him because of his injury, he could end up back here in Chicago."

Ceci clapped her hands. "He needs to come here. It would be perfect. Like destiny."

"Karma," Angela said. She wasn't sure what to do with the news. In her heart, she wanted to believe she was the reason for his move back to Chicago. But they hadn't really talked about a future together and Max wouldn't make a move like that unless he was sure, would he?

Maybe Max had mastered what Angela still struggled with—optimism. Maybe he was certain they'd be able to work things out once he was back in Chicago. "I should call him," Angela murmured. "I'm going to go home and think about this. It's a lot to take in." She smiled. "Are you sure you heard right, Will?"

Will nodded. "Oh, and you might want to try him on his cell phone because the guy on the radio mentioned that Max is in town and was seen having dinner with a couple Sox players last night."

Angela's heart fell. He was in town and he hadn't bothered to call. If he was doing this for her, wouldn't he have contacted her the moment his plane landed? Wouldn't he have rushed over and dragged her off to the bedroom before doing anything else?

"I'll see you two later." She rubbed her forehead. "Too many things to think about."

Angela walked outside and started in the direction of her flat. But at the last minute, she stepped out to the curb and hailed a passing cab. She gave the cabbie Max's address, then sat back and stared out the window as they made their way east toward the lake.

If he really was thinking about moving back, then Angela needed to know why. He couldn't expect her to start things up again simply because he was living in the same city. There was more than just location keeping them apart.

Or was there? She closed her eyes and drew a deep breath, wrinkling her nose at the smell of air freshener in the cab. She still loved him. Even though she'd tried to convince herself otherwise, the feelings were still there, as strong as ever. Only now, that love was based on an actual relationship and not just a silly fantasy. The Max Morgan she'd dreamed about for years had turned into a man who just might want to spend the rest of his life with her.

Her hands clutched the edge of her seat and she

wiggled her foot nervously. She ought to think about what she was going to say to him. But the only plan she could come up with was to throw herself into his arms and kiss him. After that, it didn't really matter what they said. Kissing always seemed to do the trick with Max.

When she reached his building, Angela paid the cabbie and hurried inside. The doorman was standing behind his desk. He recognized her immediately. "Hello, Miss Weatherby. Is Mr. Morgan with you?"

"No," Angela said. "Actually, I'm supposed to meet him. Do you think I might go upstairs and wait? I'm dying of thirst and I need something cool to drink."

He nodded. "Mr. Morgan left a key with me. He said if you ever needed to get in, I should just give it to you."

"He did? When did he do that?"

"Right after the first time you were here," the doorman said. He handed her a fob with the key dangling from it. "Here you go. You can leave it with me when you go back out."

Angela rode the elevator up and when she got to Max's door, she knocked. Though the doorman implied that Max was out, he could have missed him. After a minute, she put the key in the lock and stepped inside.

It had been over a month since she'd been in his apartment. Angela drew another deep breath and smiled. The place smelled like Max—a wonderful mix of his favorite cologne, leather furniture and the vanilla candles he had scattered on the dining room table.

She dropped her bag on the chair nearest the door and wandered inside. When she got to the bedroom, Angela flopped face down into the rumpled sheets, pulling a pillow under her nose. Strangely enough, the pillow smelled like her shampoo and not Max's cologne.

She stretched out, kicking her sandals off. It felt so good to be back in his bed again. Her eyes fluttered shut. Though she didn't think she'd fallen asleep, Angela had a sense that time had passed when she opened her eyes again. She rolled over and found Max sitting in the chair at the end of the bed, his legs stretched out in front of him, his gaze fixed on her.

"Was I asleep?" she asked, sitting up and smoothing her hand through her mussed hair.

He nodded.

"How long?"

Max smiled. "I've been here for about fifteen minutes. You were asleep when I got here." He stood up and walked across the room, then sat down beside her and smoothed his hand over her bare arm. "What are you doing here, Angela?"

"I came to talk to you."

"How did you know I'd be here?"

"Will said you were in town. I figured you'd have to come home sooner or later. He said you were here to talk about playing in Chicago. Is that true?"

"Unnamed sources," Max said. "Boy, it didn't take the press long. Although, eating lunch with a couple of the players probably wasn't such a great idea."

Angela reached out and rubbed his chest through the crisp fabric of his shirt. It seemed so natural to touch him. She didn't even have to consider how he'd react. "How's the shoulder?"

He shrugged. "It's all right. I've been practicing with the team. I might be able to start playing next month. Then we'll see how it goes."

"Good," she said. "I'm glad everything is turning out all right."

"Almost everything," he said. Max leaned forward and dropped a gentle kiss on her lips. "I think about you all the time, Angela. I think about how good we are together. And how I just want to go back to where things got messed up and figure out how to fix it all. I want you in my life and I'm willing to do whatever it takes to make that happen. If Chicago doesn't make an offer, then I'm going to retire. I'll come back here when my contract runs out and we'll start all over again. Only this time, we won't make any mistakes."

Angela stared into his eyes. The truth was there, so brilliant and clear. "I'm the one who made the mistakes. I didn't believe in what I felt. I couldn't trust my feelings." She reached out and smoothed her hand against his cheek. How many times had she touched him like this and taken it for granted. She'd never do that again. "I'm giving up the Web site. And the book. I don't believe in my thesis anymore."

"What was your thesis?"

"That most men are creeps and they'll take advantage of women if given the opportunity. I believe that men never change and women who think they can change them are just deluded fools. That, for some people, there is no happily ever after."

"So, what do you think about us?" he asked. "Is there reason to be hopeful?"

"Maybe," Angela said. "It would help if you'd kiss me again."

He leaned forward and touched his lips to hers. But what started as a simple contact dissolved into a whirlwind of passion. All the feelings Angela had kept pent up over the past few weeks came pouring out and she wrapped her arms around his neck, surrendering to the feel of his mouth on hers.

They tumbled back onto the bed, pushing aside clothes so that they could touch bare flesh. When they both finally came up for air, Angela sighed. "Oh, that was nice. I've missed you."

Max kissed her bare shoulder. "I'm a nice guy. And I'm sorry I acted like such a jerk. I guess I do deserve to be on your Web site."

"I took you off," she said.

"You did?"

She nodded. "I don't want anyone saying anything bad about my boyfriend."

"I'm your boyfriend?"

Angela nodded. "Yes, you are officially my boyfriend."

"And since I'm your boyfriend, can I take all your clothes off now?"

She nodded again. "Yes, you may. But only if you take your clothes off, too."

"We operate so much better when we're naked, don't we."

Angela laughed, then pulled him on top of her. She wrapped her arms around his neck and kissed him hard. Fourteen years ago, she touched him for the first time and her life had changed. Maybe they were meant to be together. And maybe the fates had just been waiting for the right time.

Now that she had him, Angela didn't intend to let him go.

* * * * *

SEDUCING A SEAL

BY
JAMIE SOBRATO

Dear Reader,

Throughout my life I've been drawn again and again to the romance of the ocean. There's something about its rhythms and depths I find irresistible. So I really enjoyed creating Drew and Kylie, who share my love of the sea. And while the icy Pacific of the California coast is the ocean I experience in my daily life, I think you can guess by the content of this book that I simply adore the warmer water of the tropics. What better setting for a steamy romance?

I love to hear from readers, so write and let me know what you think of *Seducing a SEAL*. You can reach me through my website, www.jamiesobrato.com, or via e-mail at jamiesobrato@yahoo.com. I'm also on Myspace at www.myspace.com/jamiesobrato.

Sincerely,

Jamie Sobrato

Jamie Sobrato's first aspiration as a young child was to join the navy, mostly because she wanted to explore the world by sea and she thought the uniforms were cute. Luckily, she went on to use her primary talents—daydreaming and procrastinating—to become a writer instead. Jamie lives in Northern California with her two young children and two house rabbits who think they rule the world. *Seducing a SEAL* is her fifteenth novel.

To my dad, Russ Bush, a true survivor.
Thank you for all your love and support.

Prologue

KYLIE HEARD the gunshots first, then the screams.

Shots? This was not a war zone. She was a Naval officer, yes. But she was in San Diego, not Baghdad.

Her fingers halted on the computer keyboard, and as adrenaline kicked in, she pushed back from her desk and sent her wheeled chair careening across the room as she shot out of it toward the door. Her instincts had her taking inventory of the soldiers and civilians at work, then Ensign MacLeod raced past her door, calling out for everyone to take cover.

But this was her office, her people. And as lieutenant commander, it was her job to defuse the situation. She ran toward the sounds of chaos coming from the reception area at the front of the building. A man yelling, another gunshot, more screams.

She couldn't let anyone get hurt on her watch.

Her hand slipped into her pocket and pulled out a cell phone, dialed the military police. As she entered another hallway, she was met by a wall of chest. Hands grabbing her and pulling her into an office. She struggled, then realized it was Ensign MacLeod who held her.

"Stay here," he ordered, his voice low. "There's a gunman in the building."

Kylie looked at him, confused. How could this be happening? Despite the evidence, her mind struggled to grasp the situation. A voice on her cell phone focused her thoughts. "A gunman," she repeated into the phone. "I'm in Building 2024. There's a gunman. He's already fired several rounds. People may be hurt. We need help *right now!*"

She didn't hear what the dispatcher said next. All she heard was the round of gunfire, another scream and a man's voice demanding, "Where's Thomas?"

That was her.

She had to get out there. She had to face that man and figure out how to disarm him before anyone else got in his way.

But Ensign MacLeod was tugging her across the room, away from the door he'd just closed behind them and cursed for its lack of a lock. "Out the window," he said.

"No. He wants me. I have to confront him so no one else gets hurt."

Before either of them could argue further, the door swung open, and they faced a man pointing an assault rifle at them.

Not just a nameless stranger, though. He was a seaman who'd been under Kylie's command until a week ago, when she'd filed dishonorable discharge papers on him for his having raped a fellow sailor.

"Seaman Caldwell," she forced herself to say calmly. "Please put down the gun and tell me why you're here."

"Shut up, bitch. Both of you on the floor, now!"

1

HE WAS MUCH TOO YOUNG for her. Eight years too young, according to his military record.

Off-limits for her.

And there was the fact that he worked for her. This was the U.S. Navy, not a daytime soap opera, so rank was huge.

Definitely off-limits.

And she, a Naval Academy grad, knew better than to entertain such thoughts as her and him getting way cozier than regulations allowed. Especially given their current circumstances. The tragedy, the trauma, the grief she was supposed to be focusing on.

Absolutely forbidden.

But grief, so foreign to her relatively calm life, did strange things to her. Such as lust after inappropriate men.

It wouldn't have been quite so disturbing if she'd kept the fantasies on a purely sexual level. That would have been normal given that she was a woman with a healthy libido and he was nearly six feet of golden-haired, bronze-skinned, blue-eyed perfection.

But no, when she let her mind wander into forbidden territory, the images were often cozy, domestic vignettes of her and Ensign Drew MacLeod frolicking on a beach or playing around while cooking, acting like a couple in a clichéd romantic comedy. Her fantasies were dangerously close to the kind that meant she was falling into something more than lust with the oblivious younger man. Because he'd never shown a sign of being aware of her as anything more than his boss. He'd always behaved respectfully and properly. As had she…in real life, if not in her mind.

Lieutenant Commander Kylie Thomas tore her gaze from the man she'd been daydreaming about regularly for the past year since he'd been transferred to her office—and dreaming of almost nonstop since their ordeal a week ago—then forced herself to focus on the therapist, Judith, who was leading their group counseling session.

"I'd like all of you to close your eyes and visualize yourselves in a peaceful place," Judith said. "Perhaps in a field of flowers, or on a mountaintop or in a comfortable chair by a fireplace. Find an image that soothes you, and go there…. Breathe deeply, in and out…in and out…"

Kylie had never been in therapy before, and already, five minutes into her first session, she hated it. How the hell would flowers or fireplaces help her accept her failure to perform in a critical moment? It couldn't. Nothing could except working her ass off to regain the confidence of her superiors.

Stifling a sigh, she closed her eyes. The first image that came to mind was that old bumper sticker that read Visualize Whirled Peas.

A giggle erupted from her throat, and she fought to prevent any more from escaping. She had a problem with inappropriate laughter, as well as inappropriate fantasies, apparently. Inexplicable laughter had bubbled out on several inopportune occasions since the shooting.

The other three people in the session glanced at her, perplexed, and she covered her mouth.

"I'm sorry," she whispered when she'd regained control. "I've been doing that a lot lately. The laughing, I mean. I was just thinking of that bumper sticker Visualize Whirled Peas. I guess when you said *visualize* it triggered the memory and, you know, peas are so far from mountains I just found it funny."

Oh dear God, she was rambling now, making no sense.

Judith nodded and saved Kylie from herself as everyone else in the group stared at her as if she'd lost her mind.

"Stress and grief can evoke highly emotional responses that may not seem appropriate to us. It's often our body's way of releasing the stress in a way that feels most natural, safe. Laughter, as a physical response, really isn't so different from crying."

Judith made a point of looking at each person in the circle of chairs, bestowing her gaze on them in soothing little doses—first Ensign MacLeod, then Chief Jones, then Lieutenant Humphrey, then Kylie. This all seemed so contrived to Kylie, so let's-hold-hands-and-sing-"Kumbaya." This touchy-feely stuff was so unlike the rule and regulation-loving Navy that it surprised her the survivors of the shooting had been ordered into this mandatory counseling. Leave it to the military to micromanage the grief process.

Still, mandatory counseling was at least more appropriate than nursing a crush on her subordinate, the one who'd been involved in the most horrific event of her life.

Tomorrow, she'd be here again for an individual therapy session, and she wondered if she'd have the courage to admit her crush. Would she be able to confess she'd been unable to stop imagining them as a couple after those moments alone in that office. There probably was some psychological explanation for the fantasies, but she wasn't sure she wanted to hear it.

In spite of the counselor's soothing words, everyone seemed to be a little ill at ease after Kylie's giggling outburst, so Judith guided them toward talking.

"Has anyone else experienced what seems like an inappropriate response to the trauma you've experienced?" She looked slowly around the room again, waiting for responses.

Silence.

Chief Jones cleared his throat, but said nothing.

Okay, so Kylie was the only nut job in the room.

Or perhaps she was the one with the most incentive to avoid facing her grief, since she'd been responsible for those who'd died. Four of her subordinates. One civilian and three sailors. She'd stood by and watched them die. She'd been powerless to stop it.

Four funerals attended. Six children now grieving the loss of parents. Countless people's lives affected.

When she wasn't engaging in shameful escapist fantasies or laughing at inopportune moments, she was seized by a pain so intense it was beyond her ability to cope.

"Let's start by going around the room and taking turns talking for a few minutes about whatever is on your mind. If you've got a question or issue you'd like to ask the group, you may do that, as well."

Everyone murmured assent.

"We'll start with you, Drew. What's been going on with you since the shooting?"

Kylie watched as he shifted in his hard, green plastic seat. He glanced down at his lap and smoothed his faded jeans along his thighs.

"I've been having trouble sleeping," he said. "I close my eyes and see the shooting happening all over again. I keep thinking how I could have done things differently…and maybe saved someone."

"Those are common symptoms of post-traumatic stress disorder," Judith said. "It sounds as if you felt powerless during the attack."

Drew's expression turned dark. "Yeah, I guess I did."

"Hey, man, if it wasn't for you, we might have all been dead," Lieutenant Humphrey said.

Drew shook his head.

"Hard as it may be to do, it's important to hang on to positive thoughts during this time." Judith spoke directly to Drew before including the other group members. "When you feel your thoughts going in a negative direction, when you begin to berate yourself for what you could have done differently—try to think of something you have control over or something you did that you can feel proud of instead."

Everyone was silent, and Kylie imagined they were

all resisting the encouragement to feel proud about anything in the face of their coworkers' deaths. Clearly Judith had not been there.

Kylie squeezed her eyes shut tight and bit her lip, another wave of giggles threatening to burst out of her at how ridiculous the therapist sounded. Feel proud? Yeah, right. But even mentally mocking Judith didn't ease Kylie's urge to laugh. If she didn't laugh, she'd cry. And if she started crying, she was afraid she wouldn't be able to stop.

And female Navy lieutenant commanders did not ever, ever, ever cry in front of their people.

"Kylie, would you like to take a turn now at talking a bit about what you've been going through?"

Kylie's gaze connected with Judith's, and the sudden pressure to participate without unleashing her inner grief and while showing the leadership and control demanded of her rank effectively eliminated her laughter.

"Okay," Kylie said. "I guess I've been having the opposite problem of Ensign MacLeod. I avoid thinking about what happened, and I find myself daydreaming too much. Thinking about things I shouldn't, just to keep from having to dwell on the shooting."

"What sorts of things do you daydream about?"

Kylie felt herself blush. She hadn't intended to confess to the fantasizing right here and now, but the words had escaped anyway.

"You know, it's sort of like how you were telling us to imagine ourselves in a calm, peaceful place. Like in a field of flowers or something. I keep imagining myself content and living out normal domestic scenes.

Only happier. Like I'm starring in a movie about my life."

"And does this bother you?"

"Well, yeah. I should be thinking about what happened. They were good people and they deserve my attention…my respect…all the time. It was so tragic, it feels wrong to think about anything else. And that's all I do—think about other stuff."

"It's natural to avoid thinking about things our emotional self has trouble processing."

Kylie avoided Judith's gaze. "Yeah, I guess so."

"Isn't it interesting that you're naturally doing what I've advised Drew to do—to think positive thoughts? It's a self-preservation mechanism."

"But isn't it just avoidance?"

"I suggest you allow yourself to think about what happened only as much as you feel you can handle at any given time. Perhaps in individual therapy sessions with me to support you and no audience will be a safer environment for you."

Kylie nodded, though her insides seized at the thought of breaking down and letting out what was building up inside her. Shame, terror, grief—all of it too big and loud to let out in front of anyone.

Four funerals and one memorial service attended, her eyes had remained dry through each one. She was a coward in ways she'd never imagined, because she couldn't face the demons inside herself any more than she could face the challenge of the demons walking around in the world.

Lieutenant Humphrey was talking now, and she owed him her focus. He was talking about things he'd seen, feelings he'd had that day.... He could have been talking for her, their experiences had been so similar.

But her mind refused to cooperate. She pretended to pay attention, while in her mind, the movie began to play again.

A sunny beach. A warm, tropical breeze. Skin bare in the sun. Flesh cooled while sinking into the water, waves lapping at her belly...Drew's hands on her, teasing her, pleasing her, arousing her, pulling her farther toward the surf. His mouth, gentle and demanding at the same time, kissing her, then finding all the places that ached for his attention....

2

"C'MON MAN, KEEP GOING. Don't be a quitter."

The cruel hand pressing down against the middle of Drew's back disappeared, and his muscles screamed for him to stop. Pain gave way to intense burning, and sweat dripped from his brow onto the wood floor beneath him.

Ninety-eight, ninety-nine, one hundred. After the last push-up, he collapsed onto his stomach, his arms jelly after having done all but the last five reps with his buddy Justin pressing extra weight on his back.

Now one hundred sit-ups and he'd be done with his warm-up and ready for his ten mile run. Channeling his energy into training for the S.E.A.L. test was all that kept him sane lately.

"On your back," Justin ordered, and Drew forced himself over and into the sit-up position. Justin planted himself on Drew's feet to hold them still.

"When you make the S.E.A.L. team, I expect you to repay me with many beers, man."

Drew ignored him and began the exercise while Justin counted reps. Justin was a S.E.A.L., and he'd been acting as Drew's coach for the past three months. And since the shooting, he'd been at Drew's side every day, urging him to stay busy. To keep his mind off what it worked over endlessly whenever he was alone or idle. Hell, he'd owe Justin a hell of a lot more than alcohol if he made the team.

Drew had wanted to be a S.E.A.L. for as long as he could remember. His father had been one, but it wasn't carrying on a family tradition so much as spite for the man that drove Drew forward in pursuit of the goal. One of these days he'd show the son of a bitch that he was twice the man his father would ever be.

He'd never walk out on the mother of his children. Or marry a woman half his age. Or forget his kids even existed. And he wouldn't end up with a dishonorable discharge from the Navy, either. If Drew's entire life was defined by being what his father wasn't, then he'd be fine with that.

"Twenty-eight, twenty-nine…" Justin counted.

"I heard a rumor that command might be ordering me on R & R leave," Drew said on an exhale.

Justin didn't respond immediately. "It'll be good for you, you know," he said slowly, as if weighing each word.

"I don't want to have any extra time on my hands. Makes me crazy right now."

"So spend all day training. You're going to need it."

Drew had thought of that already. He nodded, unable to muster any words at the moment.

"Maybe you ought to get away somewhere. Take a trip down to Mexico or Hawaii. Just get the hell out of here so you're not looking at the scene every day."

He'd thought of that, too. He still had a ticket to Hawaii from a canceled vacation that he needed to use.

"Alone?" he grunted.

"Hey, man, I'd go with you if I had any leave left. What about that girl you were dating? Tanya? Tawny?"

"We weren't a couple, and it ain't happening."

"You stopped seeing her?"

"Ages ago. No chemistry."

Justin watched him for a while, counting. Then he said, "I guess everyone's being given R & R, right?"

"So rumor goes."

"You ever notice how Lieutenant Commander Thomas looks at you?"

"No."

"Like she wants to have you for dinner. Maybe you ought to take *her* on vacation."

"She's my freaking boss, asshole."

Justin shrugged. "So what? What happens on R & R is your own business. And no one's gonna blame you for dealing with your grief however you need to."

"Don't be such a prick."

"All right, all right. Sorry. I just think there's something intriguing about that woman."

"I've never noticed."

"Fair enough. But I tell ya, man, if she ever looked at me the way she looks at you, I'd be all over her. Screw rank."

Drew tuned out Justin's comment. Between training and the shooting, seducing his boss was the last thing on his mind right now—or at any other time, for that matter. Besides, regardless of what Justin said, Lieutenant Commander Thomas had never treated him as anything other than a subordinate under her command. She was career Navy and he'd lay odds she wasn't even capable of action outside the code of conduct.

He grimaced as his abs and lats began to burn.

"Hey, you know," Justin said, "I've got a diver buddy who runs a school in Honolulu. I could hook you up with him for a little extreme training if you head out that way."

"Not a bad idea." Drew blinked at the sweat dripping into his eyes, then closed them as he pushed onward.

If the rumor mill was correct and mandatory R & R was forced on his ass, he'd go to Hawaii. It sounded like as good a place to recuperate as he could think of. And the extra dive training along with a ramped-up workout regime might be enough to distract him.

Hell, he might even be exhausted enough to sleep at night.

DREW SAT AT THE BAR next to Justin and did his best not to notice the people crowding the place. He didn't want to talk, didn't want to smile, didn't want to do anything but down a few triple shots of Jameson and get lost in the whiskey's sweet, warm haze. Going out for drinks had been Justin's idea, and it had sounded like a good one to Drew when the alternative was being totally alone.

He was exhausted from his workout. On top of that he hadn't slept for more than an hour last night. Not exactly prime socializing condition, but he couldn't imagine going home alone right now. He didn't want to be in an empty house with nothing but his tortured thoughts to entertain him.

He'd come to think of his constant state of agitation as an adrenaline hangover. Same way he'd felt two years ago during the war in Iraq.

Same as it never was.

Justin caught the bartender's eye and they both placed their orders, then they sat silently, both aware of Drew's morose mood. Drew pretended to be interested in the game on the flat-screen TV across the room. But he saw little more than color and motion. Nothing else registered. He wasn't numb inside. More like numb on the outside while internally, he felt a raging torrent threatening to escape.

He'd seen a friend die in action, but that was war. That was different. He hadn't ever gone into the office in peaceful, easygoing, no-worries San Diego expecting to see his coworkers mowed down by gunfire.

Damn. That train of thought went nowhere good. To distract himself he scanned the room. His gaze landed on a familiar figure near the door.

Justin spotted her only a moment after Drew. He nudged him with his elbow. "Hey, if it isn't the very woman we were talking about before."

Drew ignored him. But he couldn't ignore Justin's earlier comment about how Kylie watched him and how Justin would jump her given the chance. Without even intending to, Drew wondered how good in bed she'd be. Would she issues orders directing his performance? Or would she drop the whole officer demeanor and let loose?

On that tempting thought he took a good look at her out of uniform. Her strawberry-blond hair glinted in the light from the jukebox next to her, and her pale skin and green eyes seemed illuminated. Drew had never really thought of her as attractive, though she clearly was. It wouldn't be a hardship getting busy with her.

What was he doing? He muttered a curse. She was still his boss and no less inaccessible than she'd been this afternoon. Damn Justin for even putting this stupid idea in his head.

He glanced her way one last time.

How *had* she been looking at him?

"She wants you, man. This is your chance. I'll call her over here."

"Don't bother, asshole."

She headed to the opposite side of the U-shaped bar, where no one was sitting. Kylie hung out here often enough. He'd bumped into her now and then, though she'd always been a bit cool and standoffish with him. As a commanding officer, she was good enough, but as a person, he got the impression she was a bit lacking in the heart and soul department.

Tonight she was probably hoping for the same hazy avoidance of what had happened last week as he was. And she probably wanted to find her comfort alone, just as he did. Funny how it didn't occur to either of them to hang together even though they'd been through the same ordeal.

The bartender was busy taking Kylie's drink order, but when he turned to retrieve a glass, her gaze crossed the bar and landed on Drew. He saw some emotion flicker there—fear, perhaps, or dread—then she changed her expression into something that looked more like friendliness.

Justin waved her over.

She rose from her seat and rounded the bar, then took a seat beside Drew with a sigh. "Hi, guys," she said.

"I was just telling Drew how gorgeous you look out of uniform," Justin said, his comment totally inappropriate, especially given her rank compared to theirs.

She smirked, her expression cool. She'd probably had to deal with sexual harassment in the Navy so many times that it didn't even make her blink anymore.

"Sorry I can't say the same for you," she replied.

"Ouch." He made a show of acting wounded. "I apologize, ma'am. Sometimes when I'm in the company of a truly beautiful woman, I lose all my good sense."

Okay. He was laying it on a little thick, and Drew felt an unexpected surge of jealousy. Wasn't he the one Justin thought should be flirting with Kylie?

In fact, now that she was close his thoughts circled back to her in bed. And because he was really looking, he did have to admit she was hot. Beneath her coolness, something about her gave the slightest hint that she smoldered.

He found himself suddenly wanting to find out for himself. And he wanted Justin to get the hell away from her and stop ogling her like she was a slab of beef and he was the hungry shopper.

Thankfully, after a few more minutes of Kylie shooting down his every line, Justin realized he wasn't helping matters with his flirting. He cast a meaningful glance at Drew. "If you two will excuse me," he said, picking up his drink, "I just spotted someone I need to say hello to."

And with that, he was gone.

Drew breathed a sigh of relief.

"How you doing?" he asked. Stupid. He already knew the answer was lousy, but he'd never been schooled in the art of post-mass-shooting small talk.

"I'm…alive."

"Yeah. I couldn't make myself go home to an empty house, you know?"

"I know," she said, wincing.

She waved at the confused bartender when he scanned the bar to see where she'd gone. He placed a glass of clear liquid and a lime in front of her.

"Tequila?" Drew asked.

She nodded. "Don Julio…seems appropriate for a night like this."

The one-week anniversary of the shooting.

Drew downed half his whiskey, then stared at the amber liquid as images of that day crowded his head. He wanted them all gone, so he drank the rest of the Jameson and waited for the haze to come.

The images remained.

"You did your best there, you know," he finally said, figuring she was probably at least as racked with guilt as he was. "There's nothing more you could have done."

"Yeah," she said unconvincingly. "I guess. That's what the therapist keeps telling me."

He looked over at her until she met his gaze. "I know you feel responsible because they were your people."

Her expression went from blank to crumpled with

grief, which wasn't what he'd expected. The Kylie he knew didn't show strong emotions in public. Ever.

Drew put a hand on her back as she fought to regain control, covering her face with her hands. When her hands dropped into her lap, he could see she was on the verge of bursting into tears. His gut wrenched. He supposed even ice queens had to grieve, but he should not have felt so stricken by her emotion. After all, he was grieving, too.

"I can't get any of it out of my head. If I let myself think about it, I see the scene unfold over and over again. Only in slow motion, which makes me think of all the things I could have done. It's driving me crazy."

"Same here," he said, lifting his empty glass at the bartender and nodding for another round. "Hence the whiskey."

Kylie nodded and picked up her own alcohol, swirled it around in the glass, then took one long drink that emptied it. Afterward, she exhaled and closed her eyes. An almost visible peacefulness passed over her features. Drew watched, transfixed.

Why had he never realized Kylie was a beautiful woman? He didn't usually go for girls in uniform, let alone girls in uniform as devoid of femininity as Kylie seemed. So obviously he'd never seen the standard issues.

And yet, looking at her now, he could see something he'd missed. For one thing, she looked vulnerable. Not the invincible admiral-to-be that she behaved like at work, but a real, flesh-and-blood woman. And when her face showed emotion, she seemed pretty in a way he couldn't have guessed. Beautiful like storm clouds, like angry surf.

It didn't hurt that she wasn't in uniform right now. She was wearing a black tank top that hugged her slender curves and a pair of jeans that he couldn't help noticing did the same when he let his gaze drop below her face.

Whoa. Did he just check out his boss? This was Lieutenant Commander Thomas he was having less-than-pure thoughts about, not any old girl in a bar. It was one thing to speculate about her as he had when she showed up at the bar. It was something else entirely to sit beside her and imagine how she'd look after he peeled off that top and got his hands on what was actually an impressive rack now that it wasn't covered by a sexless uniform. He'd bet she had a tight bod—

Damn it. He was doing it again. Entertaining inappropriate thoughts about her. He reminded himself that she assessed his work performance and if he screwed up by offending her, she could deep-six his career in zero seconds flat. But even that sobering thought didn't completely stop the sexual journey his mind was on. Man, what was with him tonight? Must be the grief. Or pain avoidance. Or Justin's innuendo. Or maybe the Jameson was turning him into a mental perv.

"What?" she asked.

He realized he was staring dumbly at his boss like a love-struck schoolboy. Great.

"Oh, nothing. I just—" *What? Was thinking how damn hot you are when you're not being an uptight*

Did you know you could have received this book

before it hit the shops?

Visit www.millsandboon.co.uk

MILLS BOON

For access to all the latest Mills and Boon titles before they hit the shops visit
www.millsandboon.co.uk

For a limited time only, we are offering you **15% OFF** your order when you enter the code 15MAY11 at the checkout. **But hurry**, this offer ends on 31st July 2011.

PLUS, by ordering online you will receive all these extra benefits:

- Be the first to hear about exclusive offers in our eNewsletter
- Try before you buy! You can now browse the first chapter of each of our books online
- Order books from our huge back list at a discounted price
- Join the M&B community and discuss your favourite books with other readers

commander? "I was just wondering if you knew whether we were getting a forced R & R."

"Officially, no. But it wouldn't surprise me. Kind of like the counseling, R & R seems to be the commanders' way of dealing with us." She paused, as if contemplating the situation. "You know, it's the last thing I want right now—to have a bunch of time on my hands to think about things."

"My thoughts exactly."

"So if the orders come down, what are you going to do?"

"I'll probably head to Hawaii. Throw myself into training for the S.E.A.L. test."

"Sounds like the perfect distraction." She caught the bartender's eye and motioned for another drink.

Drew made a mental note to watch out for her and make sure she got a cab home. Someone with her slender build surely couldn't handle too many shots of tequila before things would start to get messy.

"What about you?" he asked. "Any idea what you'd do with the time off?"

"Go crazy."

"You might want to make a more specific plan than that."

Before he could pursue the subject further, Justin rejoined them.

"Hey, something's come up—" he nodded toward a cute brunette hovering near the door "—so I'm outta here. You coming with?"

"Nah. I'm good here." Drew wasn't ready to leave Kylie. Someone had to make sure no one took advantage of her, right?

"All right, then. Lieutenant Commander, a pleasure to see you. Next time I'll keep my senses and show you a much better time than this guy." Kylie rolled her eyes at his boast. "I'll catch up with you at the next workout session," he said to Drew with a slap on the back. Justin walked away, pausing to give Drew a thumb's-up behind Kylie's back. Drew ignored him.

An awkward silence descended.

He marveled at how odd it felt to be sitting here with Lieutenant Commander Thomas, of all people. She'd never talked to him much at work, except to give orders or instructions, and she was always noticeably cold and distant. Now, though, she seemed like a normal woman.

And what had changed? The shooting, of course. If he had to guess, he'd say she'd been humbled by it. The day of the shooting was the first time he'd ever seen her shaken. And that had been the first time he'd realized she was more than just a pencil-pushing officer. In her refusal to escape while she had the chance and her determination to face Caldwell, she'd demonstrated a selfless desire to protect her subordinates. She'd revealed herself to be a true leader who cared about her people and would lay down her life to keep them from harm. It had been a glimpse behind the ladder-climbing officer who played everything by the book and kept everyone at arm's length.

"Why are you looking at me like that?" she said.

He'd had enough to drink that he didn't consider telling anything but the truth. "I was just thinking how brave you were last week, and how if I had to have a leader to go to war with, I'd choose you."

She stared at him for a long time. "Thank you," she

finally said. "I'm not sure I deserve kudos for bravery, but I appreciate you saying it. Really you were the one who saved us from getting shot. I haven't shared how grateful I am for that, but I really do want to say it. Thank you for saving my life."

Drew shook his head. "I didn't do enough. I failed the people who died that day."

Kylie sighed. "That's exactly how I feel. I can think of dozens of actions I should have taken. But your actions were heroic. You have to believe that."

Drew stared at his glass, unwilling to accept her words but not wanting to seem ungracious by arguing any further.

When she placed a hand on his arm, his entire body went on red alert and all his dirty thoughts about her crowded his brain. He'd never have expected her touch to affect him that way.

"Hey," she said, her tone noticeably lighter now. "Will you help me pick some songs from the jukebox? If I have to hear 'Love Shack' one more time, I'm going to start a bar fight."

Drew couldn't help but smile. "Sure, why not."

She stood and he watched her begin walking toward the jukebox. He caught sight of exactly how well her jeans fit her, hugging her ass and accentuating her narrow waist in a way that should have been criminal. An image of the two of them together, their naked limbs tangled together, formed. Kylie's long wavy hair—now freed from the stiff bun she wore at work to cascade down her back—splayed across the pillow. Her delicious ass was cupped in his hands and he buried himself deep inside her.

He fought to banish the lustful image, but it seemed burned on his mind's screen. His boss wasn't just pretty, she was downright smoking hot. So hot, in fact, that if she propositioned him right here, right now, he'd have her bent over the bar before she finished the sentence. Forget the Navy. Forget his career. Burying himself in Kylie seemed worth the cost.

The intensity of his attraction to her blew him away. He knew himself well enough to know that a reaction this strong had something to it. This wasn't grief or Justin's innuendo or the Jameson. Sure, those things might have opened his eyes to the possibility, but his desire was real.

The only question was, what would he do about it?

3

SOMEWHERE BETWEEN her third and fourth shots of Don Julio, Kylie's worries slipped away. She also conveniently forgot why she'd ever been so resistant to indulging her attraction to Drew.

After her fifth shot, she leaned over to kiss him on the cheek, a gesture she'd thought of as comforting, a way to emphasize their newfound camaraderie and perhaps bring him out of his funk. But he turned his head at the last second, and her kiss landed on his lips.

This was a turn of events, so to speak, that she had not anticipated. Things got really interesting when, instead of reacting with shock and pulling away, he kissed her back.

Really kissed her back.

And that was the beginning of the end of their propriety. They both seemed intent on the same goal. There wasn't any question of what was going to happen, on either of their parts.

"Want to catch a cab?" he said when they finally broke apart. It seemed a foregone conclusion they would spend a night in each other's arms.

Ten minutes later, they were all over each other in the back of a taxi. Drew's hands were between her legs, under her shirt, inside her pants…everywhere she wanted them to be. Still she could think of nothing but how badly she wanted more. She'd been dreaming about getting busy with Drew for the past year and it had been twice that long since she'd been with a man. A pure, intense need for sex was driving her. That and the delicious things Drew's mouth was doing.

Somewhere in the back of her mind, the leader in her was making excuses for her potentially career-ending behavior. This was a typical reaction to tragedy. The desire to be a part of life and the living was a healthy way to cope with death, and what better way to feel a part of life than to have sex with someone?

The rest of Kylie wasn't arguing.

She was only vaguely aware of the presence of the cabdriver. So what if he was getting off on watching them make out? She was too caught up in the feel of Drew's body against hers to care about anything else now.

The cab stopped at what she could only assume was Drew's house, and he paid the driver, and then they were alone on a cool, dark lawn, illuminated only by the faint glow of a porch light. Kylie wasn't sure who first fell down on the grass, but once they were both rolling around, kissing, struggling to remove clothing, gasping for breath in their urgency to continue what they'd started, it really didn't matter.

Her head was spinning in a mildly pleasant way that made her feel as though she were in a movie again, the camera circling and circling the frenzy of their activity. Everything was in soft focus for her, except for the intense need that propelled her.

She was naked now, her back against the damp grass, her clothes scattered nearby. She was pretty sure she'd never been naked in public before. Not like this anyway. In the back of her mind, the ever-so-proper Naval officer filed a complaint against this lewd and inappropriate behavior. Thanks to the tequila flowing in her veins, Kylie was able to ignore that uptight prude and concentrate on riding this pleasure trip as far as it would take her.

Drew—bless him for being prepared—had produced a condom and was sliding it onto himself.

And wow, he was naked, too. Gloriously so—his body a wonderland of sculpted muscle and smooth flesh she couldn't stop her hands from exploring.

Then he was on top of her. Then he was inside her. Yes, that was it—inside her, exactly where she needed him to be. She spread her legs and moaned softly into his ear as he stretched her from within, reaching places that had gone sadly neglected for far too long, awakening nerve endings that cried out for stimulation.

She almost came at the sheer relief of being filled up by a man again. There was nothing, absolutely nothing, like the sensation of cradling a man's—this man's—hips within her own.

And then he was moving inside her, his hot, hard body pressed against her, her legs wrapped around his waist as she took him in.

Her head was still spinning, even more pleasantly now.

Time folded in on itself, and she was aware only of the tangle of their limbs, the frantic movements of their lovemaking, the hot dampness of Drew's mouth against hers. Then his mouth caressed her neck, then on to her aching, neglected breasts…and lower still. He withdrew his cock, but before she could protest, his lips nibbled across her belly, down her thigh, and there, *yes*… She gasped as he moved between her legs and began coaxing her toward climax with his tongue.

It didn't take much. She'd already been humming with pent-up desire, and what seemed like only a few strokes of his clever tongue sent her over the edge, crying out at the intensity of her orgasm.

Her inner muscles were still quaking when he covered her with his body again and penetrated her, pumping hard as he brought himself to climax. In a matter of seconds he was there, and the intensity of it gave her a second orgasm on the heels of her first.

She was spiraling upward, breathless, crying out, her body a quivering mass of raw sensation as Drew moaned against her cheek and filled her with a few final, spent thrusts.

She'd never come twice in a row before. This roll on the grass had ranked in her personal top five and all it had taken was a bit of exhibitionism, a man she'd fantasized about endlessly and a few shots of tequila to drop her inhibitions. Even as drunk as she was, she couldn't help but marvel at becoming a multiple-O girl.

Why was she surprised? If any man had the talent to make her come more than twice, it would be Drew. He was everything she'd imagined in her fantasies, and then some. For such a young guy, he was a skilled lover…or at least it seemed so after five shots of tequila.

As much as she wanted to wallow in those two

orgasms, reality started to intrude. The damp grass was cold and itchy. And Drew was heavy. And parts of him dug into her in ways she shifted to avoid.

They roused themselves and made their way out of his front yard and into his house. And once inside, round two proved that the multiple-O version of Kylie was not a one-hit wonder.

KYLIE LAY AWAKE in the dark, her gaze fixed on the ceiling. They had been asleep for a few hours, maybe more—she couldn't be sure how much time had passed since she didn't see a clock from her vantage point and didn't feel quite well enough to sit up and look for one.

She was drunk enough to know she shouldn't attempt to drive home, but sober enough to realize she'd just made a huge, potentially career-ending mistake.

She'd just slept with her subordinate. What the hell had she been thinking? Did all of her effort, all of her sweat and grim determination to climb the ranks mean so little to her that a bit—okay, maybe more than a bit—of alcohol demoed her control and made her so reckless?

Dear God, she'd really done it. She'd acted out the fantasies that had plagued her ever since she'd first laid eyes on Ensign MacLeod. And, yes, rolling around on his lawn—lord, please let the neighbors have been in bed—then tangling in his sheets, was every bit as good as she'd imagined it would be. It was so good that she found herself wanting to linger in the hope that they'd have a repeat performance before daylight came and exposed her indiscretions.

For the first time she could remember in her career, she was seeing a glimpse of the shameful woman she might have become. The one who couldn't control her impulses, the one whose passions outran her discipline, the one who took what she wanted without considering the consequences. That's the kind of girl she'd been. But thanks to some crappy circumstances, at the age of seventeen she'd made the conscious decision to lay that impulsive girl to rest and never let her live again.

She squeezed her eyes shut at the thought, fighting back tears.

She'd become, instead, the woman her strict, God-fearing Iowa farming parents had wanted her to be. Their voices lurked in the back of her head, chiding her whenever she felt the urge to stray from their narrow idea of right and wrong, reminding her of how much she'd almost screwed up her life by following her passions. And for a long time, she'd thought she'd made the right choice in following their rules, and then the Navy's. She'd become the woman everyone else seemed to want her to be, a woman they could be proud of.

But for the past week, her whole life seemed to be in question. She'd begun to suspect it was a total sham. That following everyone else's codes and standards wasn't the secret of her success, but rather the prison that prevented her from following her dreams.

It was strange how the shooting had forced her to confront her own mortality in a way that combat never had. Maybe because it was her job to risk her life fighting for freedom and her country. Maybe because she believed any danger she faced was worth supporting the greater good. The shooting, by comparison, was senseless, serving only to assuage one man's ego and thirst for vengeance.

If life could disappear in the blink of an eye, if any moment could truly be her last, then why was she living the way she was? Why was her career the only thing she had to show for her life? Why was she still, as a woman well into her thirties, looking for the approval of her parents and her superiors at work? Why was she so carefully walking her straight-and-narrow path, not daring to give in to any temptation?

She looked over at Drew sleeping. Somehow he had come to represent everything she'd denied herself. Passion, love, joy…

Why was she living for things that didn't really matter if she died tomorrow?

She couldn't produce any answers to her questions, but she knew she didn't want to live that way anymore.

And yet, reality was creeping in as the sky outside began turning from black to gray. Soon it would be morning. Soon she'd have to face the fact that she'd just slept with her subordinate and she wouldn't be able to wrap up the fallout in I-want-to-be-me rhetoric. She would have to face him every day in the office. She'd have to issue his orders, evaluate his performance and administer any discipline while pretending that she didn't know how good he looked naked and how delicious he tasted. She was pretty sure he could keep things discreet, that he would have just as much incentive as she to act as though nothing had happened between them.

The problem was, she didn't want to act as though

nothing had happened. She wanted to yell from the rooftop that she'd finally done what she'd been long-ing to do, that she loved Drew MacLeod, and she wasn't going to deny it anymore.

Loved?

That was a strong word. But perhaps not a totally inaccurate one. Maybe what she was feeling was lust or infatuation. Whatever label she put on her emotion, it hadn't lessened after having her way with Drew. If anything, it was more intense and looking a lot more like love.

Okay, no. She was really, really drunk. These crazy thoughts were just the tequila combined with a big dose of grief talking. She needed to get a grip and figure out how she was going to handle this disaster she'd created.

She needed to think…think…think…

But damn it, her head was starting to pound. She closed her eyes and willed the sensation to disappear. A little pain reliever was called for. Except, before she could even think where Drew might keep the aspirin, a wave of nausea hit her. It went quickly from being a mere wave to being the certainty that she was going to throw up.

She shot up from the bed and ran to the nearest door praying it hid the bathroom. Luckily it did, because the motion of jumping up and running across the room had done her in. The moment she knelt beside the toilet, she lost her dinner from the night before, along with everything she'd eaten for the past month. Or so it seemed to her aching body.

Afterward, she could only sag in relief. She wiped tears from her eyes that had come with the onslaught.

Drew must have heard her miserable retching. "Are you okay?" he asked from the doorway.

"No," she muttered, her forehead resting on her arms against the toilet seat. "I'm dying."

"I'll get you some water and aspirin."

She could hear him moving around in the small bathroom, but misery mixed with humiliation kept her from raising her head. This was so not a cool way to end a night of amazing sex. The last thing she wanted was for Drew to see her at her absolute worst.

After a few moments, she felt his hand on the back of her head, rubbing gently.

"You drank a lot."

"No kidding."

"It might help to eat something."

Kylie moaned, the thought of food none too pleasing right now.

"I know it doesn't sound good, but I'll make you a little breakfast."

"No, please…" she said, but he was gone.

She listened as his footsteps got farther and farther away. Then she could hear him banging around in the kitchen.

Slowly, the remnants of her nausea disappeared, and she was left with only her pounding head. She couldn't keep sitting here naked on the bathroom floor, so she cautiously stood, rinsed her mouth out, then downed the aspirin and water he'd left for her.

In the bedroom again, she wondered if she was up to getting dressed and leaving. But no, they needed to talk, and it would be cowardly to rush out of there, given the magnitude of what they'd done. Besides, she wasn't sure if her clothes were inside or still scattered about his lawn.

Oh, dear god, his *lawn*. Had they really done that? Had they even waited until the cabbie had driven away to start stripping each other down and getting it on? Thankfully she couldn't remember. That particular time, when the alcohol must have been hitting her hardest, was all a pleasant, hazy blur.

She spotted a robe hanging from a closet door and put it on before lying down on the bed again to wait out her headache.

Whatever else happened, she mused, at least she knew now that if she died tomorrow, she had acted out her greatest fantasy.

That was a comforting thought…sort of.

4

DREW SAT on the edge of the bed next to Kylie, who was dozing quietly. Even hungover, she looked beautiful in the pale morning light. He reached out to brush a strand of honey-colored hair off her cheek, then thought better of it for fear of waking her.

The effects of the whiskey had worn off for him, and he had avoided feeling as awful as Kylie had. The warm buzz of the alcohol had been replaced by a different kind of warm buzz—an unexpected affection for this woman he'd never given a second glance.

This was a different woman than the one he knew as his commander. This Kylie was vulnerable and passionate and real. She was the woman he'd just had the best sex of his life with. She captivated him, intrigued him, made him want more.

Something momentous had happened between them. Okay, maybe it had been fueled by booze. But in his experience, alcohol only lubricated the way for things people really wanted to do. It didn't make anyone do anything they were totally opposed to. And clearly he wasn't opposed to doing Kylie…again and again.

Twenty-four hours ago, if anyone had suggested to him he'd be having a night of crazy monkey sex with his lieutenant commander, he'd have sworn they were nuts. And if they suggested he'd be considering a future with her the next morning, he might have run for the hills. He recalled his conversation with Justin the day before and shook his head. Sometimes friends really did know better than anyone what was best for a person.

Drew and Kylie would have to keep their relationship under wraps for a while since she was his C.O. So they'd have to play it cool in public and sneak around—which could be hot. Once he passed the S.E.A.L. test and moved out from under her command, however, they were good to go. It was a sudden shift for him to go from not noticing her to figuring out how to fit her in his life. But he'd learned to run with his instincts, and they were telling him what he shared with Kylie was real.

She shifted in her sleep, and the blanket slid off her shoulder, revealing her beautiful round breasts in the open neck of his robe. Drew had never noticed that she even had much of a chest, she did such a good job of hiding it under her uniform. Damn, did she ever have one of the nicest sets of tits he'd ever laid eyes on. It took all his willpower not to reach out and caress them right then.

Instead he pulled the blanket back up to cover her. The disturbance woke her and she looked at him through half-closed eyes, a frown on her face.

"How long have I been sleeping?"

"Fifteen or twenty minutes. Feel any better?"

"Yeah, my head's not pounding as much—I guess the aspirin kicked in."

"How about some breakfast in bed?"

"No, I can get up." She started to rise, but he placed a hand on her lap to stop her.

"Stay," he said in a tone that ended the argument. "You shouldn't be exerting yourself right now."

She sank into her pillow and shrugged, a slight smile playing on her lips.

Drew went to the kitchen, grabbed the tray of toast, scrambled eggs, melon, juice and coffee he'd already prepared, and returned with it. Nothing fancy, but it was good, simple hangover fare meant to soothe the stomach more than dazzle the taste buds.

Kylie regarded him with something like awe when he placed the tray on her lap. "Thank you so much," she said. "I'm not sure how much I can eat, but this is… heavenly. I've never been served breakfast in bed before."

"No? How could that be?"

"Well, unless I count eating a bowl of cereal alone in my own bed."

"That just sounds sad. Breakfast in bed, by definition, has to be served to you by someone else."

She adjusted herself against the headboard and sighed. "Thank you. This is really wonderful."

"I'll be right back."

Drew returned with his own cup of coffee and toast and slid into bed beside her.

"This is a lot of food. Want to share?"

"Sure, I'll eat a little," he said, swiping a piece of melon.

She ate silently for a few minutes, taking little bites as if she were testing her body's ability to ingest anything.

She put down her fork and regarded him solemnly. "Listen," she said, "I'm really sorry about what happened last night. Clearly things got out of control, and—"

"Please stop. You don't need to apologize for anything. We were both consenting adults." He wasn't sure he wanted to hear her apologize as if she regretted what had been a life-altering experience for him. He still needed a little time to process what had happened before he dove into talking about his feelings and their future. It all needed to be clearer in his head before they could talk about where they'd go from here.

And, yeah, since the night had been fueled by alcohol, he wanted to give her some time to recover from her hangover.

"True, but we're consenting adults who are a part of the same unit, and we have to consider..." She paused.

"We have to consider what?" he asked, his instincts sensing he was about to hear something he wouldn't like.

She took a deep breath and continued. "Obviously we have to consider how our careers could be impacted by our behavior. I want to make it clear that this won't affect any of our interactions at work."

"Of course it will," he blurted. "I mean, how could it not?"

She blinked, and he could see her cheeks turn red. When she spoke again, it was with much deliberation.

"I'm very aware that I'm your superior. I am in a precarious position because I can't allow sleeping with you to affect how I evaluate your work performance. More than that, if anyone found out about this, about us, I could lose my career."

Drew's stomach turned at her words. He'd been thinking about what a momentous event this had been in his life, and all she could worry about was how it might affect her goddamn career?

"I don't know what to say. If you're worried about me telling people, don't. I won't say a word."

"Thank you," she said, visibly relieved, and he felt then as if she'd kicked him in the gut.

"Sure, don't mention it," he said a bit too churlishly, and she looked at him curiously.

"Are you bothered by what I said?"

"How could I not be? I don't like being considered your drunken mistake or a potential threat to your career."

She blushed a deeper red. "I'm sorry. I mean, I thought you'd understand that obviously, we can't let this go any further than last night."

"I get it," he said.

"No matter how great it was," she added, as if that might smooth things over.

"Yeah, right."

She looked at her food like she couldn't swallow another bite. Drew didn't have much of an appetite now himself. He dropped the toast on his nightstand beside his neglected cup of coffee and lay down, his head spinning now.

Had he fabricated the woman from last night? No, he hadn't. But why had he dared to think the hard-ass Lieutenant Commander Thomas was a different woman from the Kylie who sat with him at the bar?

He was naive, that's why. She had nearly a decade on him when it came to putting her career above all else. Which explained why she was always alone, had never had a boyfriend for as long as he'd known her, as far as he could tell. Then again, maybe her M.O. was getting loaded, picking up guys, then giving them the brush-off after she'd screwed their brains out.

She set aside her tray and rolled onto her side, placing a hand on his shoulder. "I've upset you," she said, stating the obvious.

Great. He was clearly acting like a pouting child, drawing attention to the age difference between them—which, until this moment, hadn't been a big deal to him. Well, he didn't give a damn, because he wasn't about to separate his heart from how he lived his life. If there was anything he'd learned from the past few years, it was that life was fleeting. You had to appreciate the things that mattered and chase after the things you wanted while you had the chance.

"I thought I felt a real connection between us."

She bit her lip, regarding him with a mixture of embarrassment and earnestness. "You did. I mean, of course you did. But I think that's partly because we endured a major life trauma together. Like the shrink says, it makes sense that we'd seize upon something good and life-affirming in the face of tragedy."

"If it's so good and life-affirming, then why do we have to pretend it didn't happen?"

"You know why. The Navy expects us to put what's good for our country ahead of what might be good for us personally. We accepted that when we became officers. And nothing good can come of a commander sleeping with her subordinate, as far as the Navy is concerned."

Drew said nothing, his pride still wounded.

He didn't want her writing off what had happened between them as purely the result of their having endured a tragedy together. It hadn't been that way for him and he didn't want it to have been that way for her. When he'd gotten over the tightness in his throat, he spoke without considering his words. "Last week wasn't the first time I've been through grim circumstances. I've been to war, and two years ago, I lost my sister—my best friend—to cancer."

"I'm sorry," she whispered.

"My point is, I can tell the difference between an emotional response to tragedy, and a real genuine connection with another person."

"We don't get to pursue every emotional connection we feel with another person."

"Neither of us is married, or involved with anyone else, right?"

"Right, but—"

"I don't believe in putting my career above all else. I just can't live my life that way."

It was her turn to be silent. She looked away from him toward the window where the orange glow of sunrise was showing.

Drew wondered how true his words really were. He'd sacrificed a lot for his career so far. And if he made the S.E.A.L. team as he hoped, he'd be sacrificing a lot more. Was he really so different from Kylie?

"Tell me about your sister," she finally said. "I mean, if you don't mind. I'd like to know what she was like."

He'd learned everything he needed to know about life from watching the most important person in his life die: love fiercely, take nothing for granted and never for a second make the mistake of thinking life is fair.

Enough time had passed. He'd finally gotten to a point where thinking about Abby didn't make him unbearably sad. He could remember all that was good about her now, and he held on to those memories for dear life.

"Her name was Abby. We were close growing up because our mother was a wreck, and we didn't have much choice but to take care of each other."

"Was your dad around?"

"Not for long. He bailed when I was six, and my mom never recovered. She went looking for the answer to her troubles at the bottom of a wine bottle, and things kept falling further and further apart."

She listened, not offering any unnecessary condolences.

"Abby was a serious person, but she had a silly side that I brought out of her. She was four years older than me, and she is probably the main reason I've made anything of my life. She looked out for me when no one else did, and she made sure I did well in school, got into college and stayed on track."

"And she died just two years ago?"

Drew nodded. "Exactly a year after she found out she had breast cancer. It seemed like the most unfair thing in the world that could ever happen. It still does."

"It must have been hell to watch her go through that."

"The worst part was, I'd finished college, gotten my commission and went straight to Iraq. I couldn't even be with her most of that final year."

"Oh God, I'm sorry."

"She sent me Web cam photos of herself wasting away. She had a sick sense of humor sometimes, and she was always making jokes about her hair falling out and stuff."

"You must still feel the loss," Kylie said, looking at him earnestly. It touched him that she really seemed to empathize.

He said nothing, but instead cast his gaze toward the window and the sunrise.

He'd never cried on anyone's shoulder, and he really had mourned the loss of his sister past the point of her memory still being painful. But right now he could have curled up beside Kylie and cried himself a pool of tears on the pillow.

Part of him loved that Kylie managed to bring out such strong feelings in him, even while part of him braced for the return of Lieutenant Commander Thomas.

He wasn't sure if he'd been fooling himself about the woman he thought he'd glimpsed in her last night—or if the alcohol had colored his view—but the woman watching him now with so much soulfulness in her eyes was definitely the Kylie he wanted to know better.

5

KYLIE COULD NOT have been a bigger jerk. She had let
the misery of her hangover and her fear of the consequences get in the way of any sensitivity with which
she might have handled the situation, and in her cal-
lousness she'd likely done irreparable damage. She
knew exactly what Drew felt last night, because she
felt it, too. There'd been something incredibly intense
about their coming together, something that, in
another time and place, might have promised so much
more.

She looked at him stretched out next to her, wearing
nothing but a pair of black boxer briefs, and she felt a
rush of warmth between her legs at the sight of him.
They'd had amazing sex—sex that she'd love to repeat.
Not that she could imagine doing anything at the
moment. Her headache might have mostly vanished,
and her nausea had passed, but she still felt weak and
exhausted…on top of feeling like an utter jerk for
blurting out the career talk so quickly and so awkwardly.

And she'd managed to bring the mood in the room
even lower by asking about his dead sister. The tone
in his voice had spoken volumes about how deep his
affection for Abby went. Kylie was touched by that.

Not having a sibling herself, she envied their relationship, even though he'd suffered a profound loss.

That he was mature enough to talk about it as he had also spoke volumes about his character.

"Thank you for telling me about your sister," Kylie said, rolling onto her belly and resting her chin on her hands. "I've never lost anyone like that, so I count myself lucky."

Drew said nothing, just looked thoughtful, and the silence began to weigh heavily between them, making Kylie feel like she needed to fill the space with words.

But what?

She sensed that he didn't want to share any more personal stuff right now, and she didn't see the point of getting more intimate. That direction led to a relationship and the only relationship in their future was a professional one. If she brought up the career impact issue again, she'd only insult him further. If she tried to reassure him she did indeed feel the spark between them, she'd sound as fake as she had earlier.

"I wish the circumstances between us were different," she finally said, bracing herself for the fallout.

He simply looked over at her and sighed. "Me, too," he said without any anger or resentment.

Good. Maybe he had come to terms with reality and wasn't going to make any further noise about pursuing a connection. Maybe they could navigate this situation smoothly, and no one's career would have to suffer.

Kylie, for the first time as an officer, found herself feeling the unpleasant chafing of having to be the responsible, upright one when she would have preferred to flout the rules. She'd gone along with the Navy's idea of right and wrong for so long—since the age of eighteen when she entered the Naval Academy—that she'd ceased to question it. But now…

Now she was thinking and acting like a fool, and she needed to get out of this much younger subordinate's bed before she did anything else profoundly stupid for the sake of a little sex. Albeit fabulous sex.

"Are you finished with this?" Drew said, nodding at the tray of food she'd set aside.

"Yes. Thanks for that. It was good even if I didn't do it justice."

"Don't mention it." He rose, and Kylie watched as he took the food and drinks back to the kitchen.

She needed to get out of here. ASAP.

Tentatively she rolled over and sat up, doing her best not to upset her equilibrium. So far, so good. She went to the bathroom to clean up. When she finished and came back out, she found her clothes lying on the foot of Drew's bed. He was across the room getting dressed.

"I can call a cab so we can get our cars from the bar, if you're feeling up to it."

"Good idea," Kylie said. "I should be getting home. I have to go into the office. With everything that's been going on and the counseling and stuff, I've got tons to catch up on."

"Yeah, me, too, boss." Drew zipped up his pants and sat on the edge of the bed to put on his shoes.

Kylie bit her lip to keep from reacting to the *boss* comment, which was not only inappropriate, but also technically disrespectful, since if he was going to refer to her in a work context, he was supposed to call her

ma'am. Of course, they'd already piled inappropriateness on top of inappropriateness, so now was no time
to be a stickler for the rules. She forced herself not to
watch him, either, as tempting as the sight of him
without a shirt on was.

Instead she found her own shoes that Drew had
placed on the floor near the bed and started to put them
on, then thought better of it when she felt herself
growing queasy again.

"I think I need to lie down for a bit," she mumbled
as Drew picked up the telephone.

"Are you sure you're up for a cab ride right now?"
he asked as he waited on the phone.

"I'll be fine."

He put in the request, then hung up and sat on the
opposite side of the bed. "They'll be here in about
fifteen minutes. Why don't you rest? I'll let you know
when it's time to go."

Kylie was too weak and tired to do anything but go
along with that plan. "Thanks," she said, wishing that
she'd had the good sense not to drink so much.

What on earth had she been thinking?

Oh, right. She'd been trying not to think. That was
the problem.

And then she remembered what she'd been trying not
to think about. At least she'd accomplished that goal.

Her gut wrenched as her mind skirted thoughts of
the shooting. She closed her eyes and forced her mind
in a different direction. As usual visions of Drew filled
her head, only this time reality mixed with fantasy in
a steamy combination. Images of her limbs wrapped
around his, of him over her, under her, pressing his

cock deep inside her, of sheets tangling around them, locking them together, collided in the brain. Hotter than her hottest fantasy, she couldn't resist letting herself taste him again.

Then Drew's voice interrupted her private film clips with news of the cab's arrival. Kylie opened her eyes, realized she'd dozed off and sat up. She wasn't sure how much time had passed, but thank God, the cab was here. She could get as far away from Drew as possible.

They rode in stiff silence to the bar, and once there, Kylie was relieved when Drew didn't make a big deal of saying goodbye. They'd see each other in a few hours at the office anyway.

But as she was driving home, Kylie realized she did not want to return to an empty condo. The closer to her street she got, the stronger her stomach rebelled. She didn't want to hear the echo of her own footsteps on the hardwood floor, or see the dishes from yesterday's breakfast still in the sink waiting for her.

She'd relished living alone ever since she'd escaped the roommate deal first through dorm life at the Naval Academy, then during her years as an ensign, when shared accommodations were practically a necessity on that pay scale. She'd grown to hate navigating the minefields of household chores, bathroom time and overnight guests. Having her own space had been pure decadence after those experiences and she'd basked in having to answer to no one except herself. At the moment, however, answering to herself—not to mention facing herself in the mirror—was the problem. And it wasn't something she could avoid through the distraction of a roommate.

Nope. Her wild indiscretion and her worries over how it would all play out at work loomed. And tag teaming thoughts of work was the echo of gunfire in her head, the screams of her coworkers. A punishing soundtrack for the horrific images of those who'd been shot on the floor of her office. It was unbearable.

She pulled into her assigned parking spot under the carport at her condo. She couldn't go inside. No matter how loud she turned on the stereo or TV, she wouldn't be able to drown out the noise and the pictures in her head. There was no getting away from herself in a place filled with her. She couldn't be home alone right now. But she had nowhere else to go on a Tuesday morning with her hair still disheveled from sleep and wearing last night's clothes. She had to get cleaned up, put on her uniform and pretend everything was okay for another day.

Even if she made it through today, she still had to figure out how to make it through tomorrow, and the day after that, and the day after that, and…

Coping should have gotten easier in the time since the shooting. Instead everything was feeling more and more out of control, as if she couldn't handle one more thing. Hence, her indiscretion.

Maybe having companionship last night had only highlighted for her in big, bold letters how much she didn't want to be alone.

Maybe she should use some of her accrued vacation time to go back to Iowa to visit her parents. Or go up to Washington to visit friends. Or take a friend on a trip somewhere warm and tropical where she could simply lie on the beach for a few weeks and get lost in a paperback novel.

Kylie got out of the car, her options sounding like too much effort for too little reward in her current disconcerted, hungover state. She trudged up the sidewalk toward her door, her chest growing tighter with each step. As she reached the door, it took all her willpower not to turn around and get back in the car to drive away. She wanted to go where there would be people and noise and distraction from the turmoil inside her.

No. She couldn't be this big of a coward. She couldn't run away from herself. She couldn't flee from fear of her empty apartment, for God's sake.

She started to unlock the door, when she felt seized with panic. Her hand shook, and she couldn't turn the key.

She closed her eyes, took a few deep breaths and held on to the door to steady herself against a sudden wave of dizziness. Again the film flashed in her mind in slow motion, each image lingering for maximum torment.

Drew pulls her into that office, telling her to crawl out the window. Caldwell bursts in, his gun aimed right at her. Ensign Brian Buckley appears, in the wrong place at the wrong time. Caldwell turns on him, firing a round. Buckley sprawls against the opposite wall of the hallway and slides to the floor, leaving a streak of blood on his way down.

More movement in the hallway.

"No!" a woman's voice cries out, and Caldwell fires again.

She catches a glimpse of light brown, wavy hair as Marianne O'Brian, Kylie's receptionist, falls.

She's frozen. Unable to act. Unable to protect a single person. When it matters most, she does nothing at all.

Drew springs into action. While Caldwell's attention is turned to the people in the hallway, Drew throws himself on the gunman, risking his life to take the man down. They grapple for control. Drew gets his hands on the gun and jabs Caldwell in the head with the end of it.

Drew is on his feet, gun aimed at Caldwell as sirens outside announce the arrival of the military police.

And still, Kylie does nothing.

Later, an MP pries her hand off the edge of the windowsill and leads her out of the office. To exit the building she must walk past the bodies of the victims. She sees their dying and lifeless faces. She begins to make a low, keening sound that eventually causes the paramedics to wrap her up in a blanket and treat her for shock. Trial by carnage and she fails.

Kylie opened her eyes. She wasn't at the scene of the shooting. She was at her own front door, forehead pressed against the wood, unable to go inside.

Her face was wet…she'd been crying. Her heart still pounded, and her breath was ragged.

She tried to collect her thoughts, figure out what to do next, and her hand went instinctively for her cell phone in her purse. But who could she call, and what would she say?

Hi, I'm at my own front door and I'm afraid to open it for no apparent reason.

No, she couldn't turn this into someone else's

problem. It was her own to deal with. She had to get away. She always kept an extra uniform and an overnight pack of necessities in her trunk. She could just go to work and get herself cleaned up and dressed there. It was early, and whoever was there already wouldn't ask questions if she changed in her own office.

Her own office? Why did that place sound more comforting than her empty condo? Because there were people there.

Her mind made up, she hurried back to her car. Once inside, she realized she was going to have to calm down enough to drive safely. No easy task. Her hands were still shaking, and she was on the verge of hyperventilating. Maybe she needed to call someone after all.

No. She needed to calm down. Take some deep breaths. Exhale. Focus on the task at hand. She wasn't in any danger. She knew how to drive a car.

She could do this.

Kylie put her car in Reverse and backed out, forcing the hysteria from her mind with the mundane task of driving. She drove slowly, deliberately, around the corner, down the road, but then without thinking why, pulled over on a side street.

Now what?

Should she call Drew and tell him she was having a nervous breakdown? He, of all people, would understand. But he, of all people, was also her subordinate with whom she'd already crossed boundaries by sleeping together.

No, she had to leave him out of this. Even if everything about her life was falling apart, and she didn't know what to do next.

She gripped the steering wheel so hard her hands began to hurt. She realized what she was doing and let go. Then she was crying. Loudly. A mournful wail threatened to escape her throat. Worse, from out of nowhere, her nausea returned with a vengeance.

She had just enough time to open her car door, lean out and heave her minuscule breakfast onto the ground. When she was done, she felt some of the tension draining from her body. She fumbled around in the glove box to find a napkin, then dried her eyes and wiped her mouth.

Okay. She needed to get a grip. She leaned back in her seat, reached for the recline lever on the side of it and eased the driver's seat back a few inches. She was feeling tired now. Extremely tired.

So she would rest for a few minutes, and then she'd try again.

6

BY THE TIME Kylie made it to work, the parking lot was almost full, meaning nearly everyone else was there. So she went to the pleasantly noisy military gym a half-block away and dressed in the women's locker room. There, she didn't look out of place cleaning herself up and getting ready for work. And no one was paying close enough attention to notice that she hadn't broken a sweat from working out first.

Being surrounded by normal people going about their normal business was oddly soothing to her frazzled nerves. All that normalcy gave her hope that someday she'd rejoin that team.

When she arrived in her office five minutes late, no one took notice. That is, no one seemed to. No sooner had she settled at her desk to check her e-mail than Drew appeared in her doorway.

"Are you okay?" he said. "I was a little worried when you didn't show up earlier."

"I'm…feeling shaky, I guess."

She tried to turn her attention to her computer monitor, but it did no good. She was hyperaware of his presence now. She could torture herself with accurate images of what he looked like beneath his uniform, or better yet, memories of what he felt like pressed against her and inside her.

He stepped inside her office and closed the door, taking a liberty she was sure he wouldn't have, had they not slept together. Part of her bristled at his forwardness and lack of respect, while another part of her felt a little twinge of pleasure. Before she could stop herself, she imagined him ripping off her clothes and taking her on her own desk.

God, she needed to get a grip. She'd gone from being a woman in control of her own destiny to being one who got turned on by a guy taking charge like a brute.

She was no damsel in distress.

Or at least, she'd never seen herself as one.

Except, last week…she kind of had acted that way. And today, too, for that matter.

Her self-concept was crumbling right before her eyes.

"What can I help you with?" she asked using a no-nonsense tone to remind him—her?—who was commanding officer.

"I came by to make sure you're okay, that's all," he said, shrugging. He made no effort to leave.

She raised her eyebrows. "So now you know I am, and you can go."

"Look," he said, then stopped. And started again, "I just wanted to check in. I mean, after what happened and what we talked about. I don't want you to feel as if your reputation is at stake or anything."

Kylie's throat closed up tight. Her reputation. She never really thought about it, good or bad, especially when it came to those who reported to her. She mostly just did what was required to achieve her current goal. But Drew's words made her think of her parents. Their disapproval. Their disappointment. Her reputation was the kind of thing her father would be concerned about, would say was important.

Without thinking, she blurted, "What exactly is my reputation?"

He stared at her uncomprehendingly. "I'm sorry?"

"What do people say about me?"

"Nothing," he said too fast.

She gave him a skeptical look. "What do you think of me? As a leader?"

Why had she asked him that? It was a ridiculous question that would never get her an honest reply, anyway.

"I think you're a good leader," he said vaguely.

"Don't patronize me."

"If you're worried about last night changing how I view you at work, please don't—"

"That's not what I mean. I want to know if I'm a good officer or not, if I have weaknesses I'm not aware of, if there are things about me that make me difficult to work for."

Drew appeared to be giving the matter serious thought. Was he going to answer her honestly?

And why did she suddenly need to know so badly, anyway?

She had a feeling it was all a part of her crumbling sense of self. Some part of her was itching to smash that foundation all to bits and start over again.

"Well," he said, "if you want brutal honesty—"

"Yes, that's exactly what I want."

"I'd have to say your weakness as a leader is that you're…kind of cold. You're not really approachable when you're in uniform."

"I'm not?" she said dumbly, reeling at how honest he'd been. It was her own fault. She'd asked for it, now she had to sit here and take it. But damn, it hurt.

"It's like you separate everything that doesn't relate to the Navy and don't let it interfere with your duties. And you expect everyone else to do the same. Like you don't think anyone should have human feelings or problems that get in the way of their work."

Oh. Well. That stung.

"Don't hold back," she said sarcastically. "Go ahead with your laundry list of my faults."

He winced. "I'm sorry. Did I go too far?"

"No. I asked for it." She sighed. "But really? I'm cold and unfeeling? Difficult to approach?"

"I could be misinterpreting things," he offered, gesturing with his hands as if it wasn't such a big deal.

Yeah, too bad he hadn't misinterpreted. His words hit home because, she feared, they were spot-on accurate.

Damn it.

"The thing is," he added, "I saw a different side of you last night."

"That would be my drunken side."

"No, it wasn't just the alcohol. You're so much different when you're not the one in charge."

"What's that supposed to mean? When I'm not trying to step out of my place and wear the pants—"

"No. You're just…a hell of a lot more likable and real when you're off duty. That's all."

"Oh."

Kylie's gaze fell to her desk, and she found herself feeling truly sorry she'd initiated this discussion. She didn't need to invite a career crisis into her life at the moment. Regardless, it seemed to be coming on in and making itself at home.

"I'm sorry. I'd be happy to talk to you about it more when we're not feeling so, um, strung out or whatever."

"No, thank you. I do appreciate your honesty."

She stared at him, waiting for him to go, but he just stood there, looking as though he had something on his mind.

"Um, there's another reason I came in here," he finally said.

"Yes?"

"I was hoping you'd agree to have dinner with me. Maybe tonight or later this week. Anytime that works for you, I'll make sure I'm free."

"Oh." After the way things had ended earlier, and after his brutal honesty about how much she sucked as an officer, she definitely hadn't expected to get asked out on a date. What was he thinking? They couldn't go for dinner together. Not the two of them—commander and subordinate with one indiscretion between them already.

"I think it would do us both some good to spend time talking. You know, to someone who truly understands, I mean."

Nice try. But they both knew his invitation had

nothing to do with the shooting and everything to do with their activities on his lawn.

"No," she said. "No, I don't think that would be a good idea." Her tone implied she was done with the subject.

Drew got the message, taking a step toward the door. Then he turned back and said, "See? That's exactly what I mean. When you've got that uniform on, you act like you have no heart."

And with that, he walked out the door, leaving Kylie to mull over whether he was right, or being spiteful, or both.

KYLIE MANAGED to stumble through the next two days of work without completely losing it. But she had a feeling people around her were beginning to notice that she was officially Not Okay.

Like right now, for instance. She was supposed to be conducting the weekly staff meeting to go over the orders for everyone to take leave. Standing in front of what was left of her staff for the first time since the shooting, she was having a really hard time not bursting into tears.

"Are you okay, Lieutenant Commander?" a male voice asked, but she didn't know whose, because her vision was blurry. She sat down hard in the nearest chair.

"Would you like someone else to lead the meeting?" another voice asked.

This one she recognized as Drew's. She looked up at him. They'd barely spoken since he'd asked her out for dinner. She'd been avoiding him at every turn. Maybe…not.

Still the concern in his voice helped her regain a bit of her equilibrium. "No," she said. "I'm fine. I'll be fine."

She looked around the table, and everyone appeared uncomfortable, as if they didn't believe her. Or perhaps, they all thought their boss was a cold, icy bitch who couldn't even admit when she had real human emotions.

"This is difficult," she forced herself to say in an effort to prove she had a human side. "It's the first time we've assembled as a group here at the office since…last week. And I don't want you to feel as if we're to get back to business as usual, without my having any regard for the gravity of what we've been through.

"In fact," she went on, "I've been informed that you will be granted time for R & R, starting immediately. Those of you who have pending work issues that need to be addressed, you're to hand over any necessary files to me, and I'll delegate the work to others while you're away."

She looked around the room at the solemn faces.

Drew's expression was inscrutable, but she had a feeling he wanted to say something to her. She rushed on to fill the silence before he had a chance.

"If you have any further questions, I'll be in my office, and you may speak to me there privately. For now, you're all dismissed."

With that, she stood and left the room, her feet thankfully planting one in front of the other as they were supposed to. No sooner did she reach the safety of her own office than a male figure appeared at her door.

It was Commander Mulvany, her direct supervisor, and a man she admired for his steadfast leadership skills. He'd been a role model to her for the past few years, and it pained her to have to face him now when she was barely holding herself together.

"Lieutenant Commander, I need to speak with you in my office in five minutes," he said.

"Yes, sir," Kylie answered, her stomach flip-flopping at his tone.

Oh God, no more flip-flopping in that region. That sensation usually indicated her tenuous grasp on control was slipping. And she needed all the control she could muster to face her commander.

Why couldn't he speak to her in her own office? The discussion would be less intimidating for her here. But that was the point. Location was a power issue, she knew. The leader was always the one to sit in the comfortable chair behind the desk in his own office, while the subordinate hovered awkwardly on the guest side.

When the requisite minutes had ticked by, Kylie stood and went to the adjacent building where Mulvany's office was located. Once she was standing across from him he got straight to the point.

"You're no good to me like this," Commander Mulvany said, his expression dead serious.

"Excuse me, sir?"

"You can't keep trudging along like nothing is wrong. You look like you're about to fall apart every time I see you. It's not good for morale."

"But sir, I'm seeing the therapist, and I'm feeling better every day. I think showing up for work is helping me sort through things."

"Off the record, you're screwing up, Thomas. You can't lead in your current state."

Kylie felt as if he'd slid a knife between her ribs. She wanted to double over in pain or curl up on the sofa and cry her eyes out. Of course she didn't dare. Instead she swallowed hard and said, "I'm sorry, sir. I admit I've been distracted by recent events, but I promise you I'll be back to my old self right away."

"I don't want your promises. I want you to take leave. You need R & R time to get over the incident, just like everyone else does."

"Sir, I respectfully disagree. I think I'll go crazy if I don't have any work to occupy me."

"I checked, and you're at use-or-lose level on your accumulated leave. That means you haven't been taking enough vacation, which is a problem under ideal conditions. These are hardly ideal conditions. So I'm going to help you with that problem."

Kylie didn't want to be left alone with her maddening thoughts. She didn't want to go on vacation. She didn't want to appear weak and useless in the eyes of her superiors. How would she ever disprove them of that view if she wasn't reporting for duty everyday?

"Maybe if I take a three-day weekend—"

"No. I want you off for a minimum of two weeks. Even a full month if you'd like. I don't want you back here until you're feeling like your old self again. And I mean it. Either you get better, or you don't come back at all."

She frowned, trying to process what he was saying. It sounded like a threat.

In fact, she was pretty sure it *was* a threat that she'd better shape up or her career was done.

"You have to be a leader of the men and women in

our unit, Lieutenant Commander. Since the shooting, you've displayed none of the qualities of a leader. It's an understandable lapse given the circumstances, but the best thing you can do right now is to get out of here until you are ready to lead again."

And what if she was never ready?

That very real unspoken possibility hung in the air between them.

She might never be ready to lead again.

The realization came to her like a thunderbolt in its clarity. It had been lurking around the edges of her consciousness for days. Her lapse with Drew only made her fear all the more valid. She was acting like anything but a leader—cowering in fear, behaving inappropriately, acting on her passionate instincts instead of her rational intellect.

She swallowed the shame that clogged her throat. She'd had nightmares like this in her early days as an officer, bad dreams of getting called into her superior's office and told she wasn't doing her job well enough, that she wasn't hacking it and she'd better step up or step out.

Having her nightmare come true was so surreal she could hardly think what to do or say next.

"You're looking a little pale," Commander Mulvany said, his brow furrowed. "Do you need to sit down?"

Kylie felt cold and clammy all of a sudden. A wave of nausea hit her, and she saw spots. Without any further warning, her head began to spin, and she had the sensation of falling.

When she opened her eyes again, Commander

Mulvany was hovering over her, his face a mask of concern as he talked into his phone. "She's just opened her eyes," he was saying. "Thomas? Can you hear me?"

"Yes," she said.

"Lie still," he commanded when she tried to sit up.

She was on the floor next to his desk, and she had no idea how much time had elapsed. She'd passed out occasionally over the years—a few times while getting blood drawn, and once or twice when she'd been sick with the flu. But fainting in front of her boss after he told her she was doing a lousy job?

Never happened.

She was losing it. She was really losing it.

Commander Mulvany was right to tell her to get out of here.

"She was only out for maybe a minute," he said into the phone. And then to Kylie, he said, "How are you feeling?"

"I'm okay," she said. "I think I can get up now."

"Yes," he said to the phone. "I think she's going to be all right. Yes, mmm-hmm." He paused, listening. "Okay, thank you."

"Really," she said, pushing up onto her elbows. "It's just my blood pressure is kind of low, and I can pass out easily. I can get up now."

"I'm supposed to get you some orange juice and make you rest for a few minutes." He grasped her elbow and steadied her as she stood, then led her over to the sofa. "You lie here, and I'll be right back."

Kylie lay on the stiff tweed guest sofa, feeling like an utter fool. Not only was she an incompetent leader, but she'd just played the helpless female in front of her superior officer. For a Navy officer, she'd committed an unforgivable act of weakness. Was this the kind of behavior she'd display when under pressure? It couldn't get much worse than that.

As soon as the thought formed in her head, she felt like a shit. It could get a lot worse, if she were one of the victims of the shooting, or one of their family members. She needed to keep her ridiculous career problems in perspective. Her own problems paled in comparison to those of other people.

Soon she heard footsteps coming down the hallway, and her commander reentered the room. He knelt next to her and offered a can of orange juice.

"Drink this," he ordered.

A glance at her boss's tight expression told her exactly how uncomfortable he was playing impromptu nursemaid, and she felt flush all over again with the humiliation of the moment. She would never forgive her body for flaking out on her.

"Thank you," she said after she'd taken a long drink. "I'm feeling much better already."

"I hope you see my point now," he said stiffly. "You need a vacation."

She nodded, unable to choke out an affirmative response. Instead she busied her mouth with another sip while she struggled to regain her composure.

"Yes, sir," she finally said.

"I don't want you to come back here until—and unless—you're ready to perform to your previous standards. Are we understood?"

Kylie nodded. "Absolutely, sir."

And she did understand. She had one chance to change the minds of her commanding officers, to convince them she had the fortitude and qualities demanded by the Navy. And, as her body had proven, she was incapable of performing at that level until she had herself back under control. So mental demons or no, she was on vacation.

7

DREW WOKE UP with a scream caught in his throat. His eyes snapped open. He was trying to cry out, but no sound escaped his mouth. Then his brain caught up with his body and he knew he'd had another nightmare.

He glanced at the clock radio on the nightstand: 7:52 a.m.—past time to get up for PT. Except he didn't have to get up at all today if he didn't want to. He was officially on leave.

He was sweating, even though the room was cool. Rubbing his hand over his damp face, he tried to clear his mind of the horrific images. He'd been dreaming of Kylie at the mercy of a faceless gunman. Drew could only stand by and watch the scene unfold, unable to save her. There were variations on the dream, but inevitably, whenever he slept, he had it.

Logically he knew she could save herself. Kylie certainly wasn't helpless in real life. But for some reason, whenever he saw that nightmare version of Caldwell burst through the door, gun pointed at her, Drew froze…and Kylie paid the price. At first he'd thought his fears were doing a number on him. What if Buckley hadn't distracted Caldwell before he pulled the trigger on Kylie? What if Drew had missed when he leaped at Caldwell? What if Caldwell had gotten control of the gun instead of Drew?

But ever since that night after the bar, he'd wondered if the dreams were a sign that he'd had a thing for her long before he realized. And wasn't that just a load of psychological mumbo jumbo. Man, he'd been seeing the shrink too long.

Still, he cursed his inability to sleep without having nightmares. He climbed out of bed, and fumbled around the bedroom getting dressed to work out. Regardless of whatever crap his mind was sorting through, he needed to be in the top physical condition for the S.E.A.L. test next month. He'd decided to take Justin's advice and spend his leave in Hawaii where he'd add swimming and diving to his regimen.

He downed some water before heading out into the cool morning, then tried to take out his frustrations on the pavement outside.

Running was like meditation for Drew. The rhythmic pounding and breathing put him in a zone where he didn't have to think about anything.

An hour later, he was drenched in sweat and his muscles were tight and hot. Exactly where his body needed to be. Too bad his brain hadn't read the memo about running as meditation. He'd failed to get Kylie off his mind for more than a few minutes at a time. He pushed himself hard through alternating sets of push-ups and sit-ups, then showered and dressed for the day.

By the time he was tying his shoes, he'd made up his mind about what he was going to do. He was going to Kylie's house to tell her she'd be a fool not to explore the feelings that had sparked between them.

He believed in following his heart, and if his heart was crazy, then so be it. Thoughts of her had haunted him, proving that it wasn't the alcohol or the grief that instigated the sex. He had to follow this thing between them, see where it took them and worry about the consequences later. He'd learned from losing his sister and now his colleagues, that life was too short not to go for things he wanted most.

Whatever there was between them, it was powerful, and it deserved to be explored. He wasn't going to settle for less than that.

Also, he had to admit, he was worried about her. The ones who exercised as much discipline and control as Kylie never had the coping skills when life tossed shit their way. She was so close to the edge anything could send her over. It was times like these that friends had to look out for one another. Their unit didn't need a suicide on top of the tragedy that had already occurred.

He drove to her condo, where he'd been once before for a holiday mixer, and was relieved to see her car sitting out front. He parked, got out and went to her door to ring the bell.

When she answered the door, she seemed startled to see him, but quickly recovered. She looked a little less haggard than she had yesterday at work when she'd seemed on the verge of passing out in their staff meeting. Her skin was still pale, and there were dark circles under her eyes that showed evidence of tears.

Drew felt bad for waiting until this morning to

come here. He should have come last night. The truth was, he'd wanted to give her space before launching his let's-hit-the-sheets-again campaign.

"What's wrong?" he asked. As soon as the words left his mouth he knew how dense they sounded. The more accurate question was, what *wasn't* wrong?

She crossed her arms over her chest and hugged herself. "What are you doing here?"

"I was worried about you. And rightfully so, given how awful you look." Oops, definitely not the right thing to say.

"Thanks," she deadpanned. Even so, she stepped back and allowed him in. She didn't invite him beyond the foyer, however, so he leaned against the closed door.

"I mean, I suspect you feel like I do—like you need to get as far from San Diego as you can. I want you to come to Hawaii with me."

Damn it, why had he blurted that out so fast? He'd meant to build up to it, to make a case and show her why she needed to listen to him. Instead, he'd set himself up for more rejection. No way in hell would she be receptive to heading off to the middle of the Pacific with him when it was presented so bluntly. He wasn't even sure he would, either.

"Okay," she said, and he almost didn't hear her.

"What?" He blinked.

"Okay, I'll go." She looked so scared and vulnerable for a moment, he almost didn't recognize her.

"You'll go to Hawaii with me?" he repeated dumbly.

She nodded, and relief flooded his chest. She was

going to do it. She'd be with him and he'd have the opportunity, away from San Diego and her Naval responsibilities, to persuade her to give him—give them—a chance. And if they had something as good as he suspected, then they would have time to work out the logistics of how to be together.

"But…" She seemed to be working something out in her head. "You're going there to train before you take the S.E.A.L. test, right?"

"Right."

"I have a favor to ask, then," she said tentatively.

"Sure, whatever you want."

"I want to train with you."

"You want to train with me?"

"Yes. I know I can't become a S.E.A.L., but I'd like to prove to myself that I can at least keep up with the physical rigors. For personal reasons," she added, looking a little embarrassed.

Drew's first instinct was to protest. He'd already been training for so long, there was no way she could just jump in and keep up with him. She'd slow him down, hold him back, at the very time when he needed to be pushing himself the hardest.

Seeming to read his mind, she said, "I won't slow you down. You can think of me as your trainer, if you want. I'll make sure you're being pushed. Anytime I see that I can't keep up, I'll be your coach rather than your partner."

Which was exactly what he needed right now, he thought, without saying it aloud.

And what Kylie needed right now was to feel as though she had power over her life. She wasn't saying so, but he suspected that was at the root of her request to train with him. He could certainly see the appeal of feeling strong and powerful at a time such as this—and of having something all-consuming to throw herself into, so she could forget.

"Okay," he said. "Let's do it."

"One other thing," she added, looking uncomfortable now. "I would prefer to keep the fact that we're traveling together private. I don't think either of us would benefit from our coworkers knowing about this…."

When she trailed off, Drew knew she was hoping he'd jump in and agree right away. And ordinarily, he would have. He was in the military. He knew what was at stake. But his wounded pride held him back. His reticence made no sense. She was only being practical, yet he hated being something she felt she had to hide.

Still, he knew he was.

Finally, he said, "Okay, sure. My lips are sealed."

"I suppose there's always a chance people will find out anyway. If that happens, we'll just have to handle it as best we can—"

"How would anyone find out if we don't tell them?"

She shrugged. "The Navy's a small world. We could bump into someone we know while we're in Hawaii, or on the way to the airport or in the airport…"

"True," he said. "It's not likely, though."

As much as he wanted to assert his position, force her to get over her worries, he recognized that as his superior, she was the one who was taking the much greater risk in vacationing with him. He was being way too hard on her by sulking about it. She hadn't gotten to her position in the Navy by being foolhardy or fraternizing with her subordinates.

"Thank you," she said. She looked away for a moment before meeting his gaze. "I think this trip will really help me."

"Yeah, me, too."

"When do we leave?"

Not soon enough. "Tomorrow morning," he said, deciding to not push his luck by expressing his real thoughts. He'd have her undivided attention soon enough once they were away from here.

"How are you doing?" she asked. "You look more rested than I feel."

"I've been sleeping, but I have nightmares," he said, then realized his error. He didn't want to tell her his feeble attempts to save her tormented him in every single one.

"About the shooting?"

"Yes," he said vaguely.

"Guess that's normal. The therapist told me they should get better, happening less often eventually. Give it enough time. Who knows? Maybe the change of scenery will make them stop."

Drew nodded. He made a move to leave.

"Just one more thing," she said. "I'm going on this trip with the expectation we will move forward as friends and colleagues, not—"

"Not lovers," he said.

"Right."

"I don't see why we can't," he lied.

In truth, Drew could think of more than a few

reasons why they couldn't be just friends. But there was no point in arguing with her now, when he'd finally gotten her to agree to go away with him.

Kylie crossed her arms over her chest, a gesture that emphasized her vulnerable femininity and made his cock stir in his pants. He didn't want to start thinking sexually about her now, so he forced his gaze not to drop to her soft, round breasts encased in the blue cotton shirt. Breasts that were suddenly familiar and obvious to him now that he knew what lay beneath her shirt.

Instead he studied her expression, which had the same hint of vulnerability he'd sensed a moment ago.

Was this Lieutenant Commander Thomas, standing so stiffly before him, really the same woman he'd made love to so passionately? It seemed almost impossible based on the way she'd behaved before. Before the shooting, when he'd spared a thought to Kylie, she'd seemed more a caricature—the career-driven ice queen—than a real woman. He'd been a fool to assume she was so simple.

He admired the delicate lines of her neck leading up to her strawberry-blond hair. The slightest wisp of a curl had escaped her bun, and it took all his will-power not to reach out and touch it.

As if she sensed his thoughts, her posture and expression changed, and suddenly there was nothing even remotely vulnerable about her.

"Good," she said. "If you e-mail me your travel itinerary, I'll be able to make my arrangements to coincide with yours."

Drew nodded, marveling at how quickly she'd changed. This official Kylie, the businesslike, no-

nonsense one, did a fine job of ridding him of his erection. He straightened and reached for the door. "I'll do that right now," he said and headed for his car.

In the driver's seat, he took a deep breath and sighed. With all of her conditions, his campaign looked grim. Some vacation this would be if she had her way. What had he agreed to? A month of blue balls?

Still, mixed with his trepidation he felt excited when he considered what their time in Hawaii could be like. Warm tropical days, hot tropical nights and an even hotter woman…it could be the most erotic experience of his life. Or it could be hell. If she held out on him for an entire month, not only would his libido be out of control, but also his S.E.A.L. training would be shot to hell.

Funny how Drew had never had trouble getting his way with women, but Kylie was a different story. She had an iron will that came with years of being a military leader. And he couldn't presume his charms would work on her the way they did on other women.

No, he couldn't presume. But he could hope.

What really mattered was that she'd be with him. They'd be away from the Navy's influence, away from the rules that governed their lives—especially hers. With that kind of freedom and his persuasion, the island might work its magic on her, loosen her up. At the very least they'd have the chance they needed to explore the potential between them.

He had to be flexible in his approach to Kylie while maintaining the same determination he brought to his training. And like his dream of becoming a S.E.A.L., he wasn't giving up on Kylie without a fight.

8

KYLIE COLLAPSED on her best friend Sonya's couch. After Drew had left with her promise to accompany him, it was as if something had shifted for Kylie. None of her defense mechanisms worked anymore. There was nowhere she could hide from herself. Instead of feeling weak, however, she was liberated. She'd finally been able to admit she was terrified of sleeping alone. She was exhausted, having endured too many nights of little or no sleep.

Being here in the pleasant surroundings of Sonya's Pottery Barn-addicted apartment, with its splashes of intense color and warm atmosphere, seemed like visiting an alien planet after the past two weeks of insanity. Kylie had known Sonya since their years together at the Naval Academy, where they'd become instant best friends. Instead of sticking with the military as Kylie had, Sonya had put in her minimum commitment and gotten the hell out, as she'd put it, to attend law school as a civilian.

She'd always been too headstrong and rebellious for a life of Naval service, and now she put her willfulness to much better use as a civil rights attorney in her hometown, defending San Diego's poor women and minorities.

Now she sat on the arm of a chair across from Kylie, thumbing through her mail, with her sleek black bob half concealing her honey-colored features.

"So where were you the other night when I called?" Sonya asked. "I worried when you didn't answer, you know. I almost drove over to your place to beat on the door."

"I'm sorry," Kylie said. "I didn't mean to worry you."

"You didn't answer my question." Sonya gave her a pointed look. "Where were you?"

"I was, um, sleeping over with someone."

Her friend's eyes widened. "You? Were sleeping over? With a *guy?*"

"Shut up!" Kylie threw a beaded pillow from the couch at her, but it only hit Sonya's knee and bounced off.

"I'm sorry. I know I'm supposed to be saddened by all that's happened to you—and I am—but this is huge. You actually got *laid?*"

Kylie sighed. Was her personal life really so sad that a one-night stand warranted this reaction? "Yes, I did."

"Who's the lucky stud?"

"No one. Just a guy I met at a bar."

"Wait a minute. Why were you out drinking alone, when I told you to come stay with me?"

"I didn't want to impose," Kylie said weakly.

Which was true. She hadn't wanted to feel like a charity case after the shooting. She'd wanted to prove to herself she was still strong and independent.

And look where that had gotten her.

"I don't believe you slept with some random guy. That's totally unlike you, Kylie. Are you sure you're mentally stable?"

No. Definitely not sure.

Sonya knew her too well, and Kylie was a terrible liar anyway. "Okay, so he wasn't totally random."

Her friend raised one eyebrow. Here was the attorney about to go in for the kill. "Who was he?" she asked, then picked up her teacup from the coffee table and took a sip.

"A coworker."

Sonya choked on her tea, then coughed until she'd cleared her throat. "Excuse me? Did you just say a coworker?"

Kylie rolled her eyes and sank back into the over-stuffed sofa. "Stop grilling me. I'm not on the witness stand."

"I'm going to need the details, you know."

Of course she was. Sonya knew about Kylie's every relationship and sexual exploit—or more accurately in recent years, her lack thereof.

"I've been engaging in some rather unsavory conduct, I'm afraid," Kylie said.

No point in hiding anything from her now. It wasn't as if Sonya would disapprove, anyway. She was Kylie's role model for rule-breaking behavior as an adult.

Maybe *role model* didn't quite fit, since it implied Kylie had followed in her footsteps. No, more like, Kylie lived vicariously through Sonya, who made her own rules and thumbed her nose at everyone else's.

"Fraternizing, eh?"

Kylie cleared her throat. "Yes, um…with a much younger subordinate."

Sonya managed to look impressed. "How much younger?"

"Eight years, give or take a few months. Not that I'm counting," Kylie said. Except that last part was a lie. She'd actually checked Drew's military file after their night together for his exact birth date, just to see how much of a cradle robber she really was. She'd also been reminded by looking at his file that he was waiting for a promotion, due to pin on his new rank of lieutenant, junior grade, next month—which meant, too, that he'd be moving to a new job in a different unit under someone else's command. That still didn't make him anywhere close to being her equal in the Navy, nor did it absolve her of the crime of fraternizing with a subordinate.

"Damn, girl. It's about time you get your groove back, and you might as well do it like Stella did."

"Um, yeah. Except I'm not a gorgeous African-American woman with sass and attitude, and I won't be going to Jamaica. But I will be going to Hawaii… with him…tomorrow."

Sonya looked at Kylie as though her head had sprouted palm trees. "You're serious."

"Yes."

Sonya laughed. "Oh. My. God."

"Could you try not to act so entertained by my downfall?"

"Honey, if you're going to go down in flames, you might as well do it with style."

"I'm not going on this trip as his lover," Kylie

added lamely. "Just as friends. I'm going to help him train for the S.E.A.L. test."

"Of course you are, dear. Keep telling yourself that while you screw his brains out."

"Stop it, this is serious. I can't do that anymore. He works for me. *And* he's too young."

"You might have thought of that before you decided to jet off to Hawaii with him. Besides, you know me well enough to know what I think about the Navy's regulations. Might have been necessary to mandate people's sex lives a million years ago, but not now. And who cares if he's younger? Why should that even matter?"

"It feels opportunistic to me, the same way it is when an older guy preys on a much younger woman. The woman might not feel preyed upon, but that's only because she doesn't have the perspective of the older man's age."

"Are you planning to ruin his reputation? Knock him up and then leave him with a baby to care for all alone?"

"Stop being a smart-ass."

"Kylie, he's an adult. He gets to choose whom he goes to bed with, and he's chosen you. What's so wrong with that?"

Kylie felt a wave of nausea hit her again, but this one was minor compared to what she'd experienced yesterday in her commander's office. She closed her eyes and waited for it to pass.

"Oh, sweetie, I'm sorry for being a brat. I'm really happy for you, you know. It's been far too long since you've let yourself have any fun. I think this trip could be the best possible thing for you right now. Screw what the Navy thinks."

"Easy for you to say."

"Sure it is, because I have your best interests at heart. That's one thing you can't say about the Navy."

Kylie knew she was right. And she was too tired to argue about any of it, anyway.

She'd always admired Sonya's rebelliousness, and it occurred to her that Sonya was the kind of woman Kylie might have become under different circumstances. She'd been living vicariously through her friend for far too long, playing by the rules while relishing every time Sonya broke them. Thanks to getting busy with Drew, Kylie had finally measured up to the strong-woman-on-her-own-terms example Sonya set. It did feel kind of good to finally have something juicy to report about her own adult life for once.

Too bad that juicy bit didn't come close to fitting who she'd become—upwardly mobile Navy officer, straight and narrow, always appropriate.

On the surface, she and Sonya seemed an odd pair of friends, opposite as they appeared. But Kylie knew that she'd have died of boredom if she didn't have Sonya around to remind her that there was more to life than adhering to an external set of rules.

"Oh, stop brooding," Sonya said, interrupting her thoughts. "I didn't mean to insult your first love."

"My first love?"

"The U.S. Armed Forces."

Kylie blinked at that idea. Why did it ring so false to her? She'd been living as if it were true for a long time.

Rather than face the accusation, she decided to change the subject. "Speaking of first loves, what's going on with Angelica? She hasn't been around much lately."

Sonya shrugged, uncharacteristically quiet all of a sudden.

A big part of the reason Sonya had left the Navy so quickly was that she'd realized it was no place for a bisexual woman to thrive. She refused to apologize for her sexuality.

"Trouble in paradise?"

"She's got a job offer in New York City and wants to take it."

"Oh God, Sonya. I'm sorry, that really sucks," Kylie said, though she didn't quite believe herself.

Angelica and Sonya had been caught in a stormy, ridiculously passionate on-and-off relationship for years, both of them a bit too strong-willed to ever relinquish control to anyone else. It didn't make for smooth romantic sailing.

"She's talking about moving next month. I guess I haven't mentioned it because I haven't wanted to believe it's really going to happen. I keep thinking she'll change her mind."

"You know, the way you two get along, you might be better off—"

"I know, I know. You think we're awful for each other. But I've loved her almost my whole adult life. What the hell am I supposed to do if she leaves?"

Whoops. There went Sonya's temper, and she was on the verge of tears now, too.

Kylie felt a surge of sympathy that she was sure showed in her troubled expression. She sighed, then said, "Maybe the distance will make things better between you. You could do the bicoastal thing."

Sonya smirked in spite of herself. "You mean like the bisexual thing?"

"You can be bicoastal bisexuals. You'll start a new trend."

"I don't know…."

"Half the time when you're together, you want to kill her. I know you don't like it when I say this, but I really think you two are in sort of an addictive relationship pattern. Who knows? Maybe the time apart will be the best thing that could happen for you."

"I guess if we were really meant to be, she wouldn't be packing up and moving across country, huh?"

"Did she ask you to come with her?" Kylie dared to ask.

Sonya shot her a look. "No. And I don't want to talk about it anymore. You're going to give me nightmares."

"I'm sorry."

Kylie had watched Sonya's various relationship dramas with bemused interest, always half-fascinated and half-glad not to be caught up in such messy affairs. But for the first time, Kylie could honestly admit that she'd been a bit jealous, too. How much bigger would life be with that kind of passion? That inner wild woman she routinely ignored whispered that Drew could provide the answer to her question.

As if reading her train of thought, Sonya said, "Don't think I haven't noticed how you tried to distract me away from your little cradle-robbing escapade. I expect regular phone and e-mail reports from paradise while you're gone."

"I don't know if I'm going to bring a computer."

"You can dial a phone."

"Okay, okay, I'll report to you my every waking move."

"Good," Sonya said, looking satisfied. "I'm going to need something to take my mind off my woes."

Kylie's throat tightened as she thought about what those reports would contain if she were to relax years of rigid control and let her wild side free. "Don't you think it's kind of…I don't know…shameful to be doing what I did?"

"Sleeping with a guy? No, I don't."

"I mean, a much *younger* guy who is also my *subordinate*."

Her friend looked unimpressed. "You're going to have to do a lot more than that to get me to use the shameful word. Maybe stab a puppy dog or push an old lady into traffic."

Kylie sighed at the ceiling.

"Seriously, you need to get rid of that faux Puritan streak of yours, my dear. It belongs to your parents, not you."

"I can't help but hear my parents' voices in the back of my head when I do something they'd disapprove of. Doesn't everyone have that problem— everyone besides you, I mean?"

"I think you're getting a double whammy—the God-fearing parents and the moral authority of the Navy. In my opinion, they both need to mind their own damn business and let you live your life as *you* see fit."

Kylie wasn't sure she could trust herself with such a big task. She'd already proven how royally she could screw up her life operating solely with her own judgment.

"I don't know," she muttered noncommittally.

"You're not a teenager anymore. You're a grown woman, and you can make your own decisions about what's right and wrong for you. I wish you'd start living more like you believed that."

Kylie felt something stir inside her, some little twinge that maybe Sonya was onto something. Maybe she was…right? The Navy *and* Kylie's parents did have an inordinate influence on Kylie's behavior. But undoing that was huge and she was too tired to sort it all out right now. "Well," she said, "thank you for believing in me. I appreciate the vote of confidence."

"I've met your parents, remember. I know there are no two people more in need of a good sweaty roll in the hay than Mr. and Mrs. Farmer Thomas."

"Ew. Spare me the image, please."

Sonya laughed. "Do you think they ever do it?"

"Oh my God, stop it." Kylie fought back a yawn. "Discussing my parents' love life is really fascinating and all, but I hope you don't mind if I crash early."

"Sure, whatever you want. You've had a horrible day—hell, a horrible few weeks. I'm glad you called me. This is where you should have been staying all along, you know."

She stood and left the room, returning with a pillow, some sheets and a blanket.

"Up," Sonya said.

Kylie moved out of the way and watched as her friend turned the couch into a makeshift guest bed.

"By the time you get back from Hawaii, I'm sure

you'll be feeling a lot more healed from your ordeal. So I want you to go and have the time of your life, okay?" she said when she turned back to Kylie. "Forget about all the crap that's gone on here."

Kylie nodded. "I'm going to try."

And as she crawled beneath the covers, she halfway believed she'd made the right choice in accompanying Drew to Hawaii. At the very least she was relieved to be getting far, far away from San Diego.

Perhaps sheer madness had convinced her to go to Hawaii with Drew, but she knew that something else was keeping her from changing her mind and backing out. Some complicated set of feelings she had neither the inclination nor the energy to analyze right now.

9

DREW WAS PACKED AND ready to go. He'd reviewed his itinerary, and he'd gotten the house squared away for a long absence. He had to be at the airport in an hour or so. He was just waiting for Justin to show up to pick up Lola and drop off Drew at the airport.

Last night, he'd had a nightmare that Caldwell had broken into his house and killed the cat while he was gone, which was pretty much impossible with Caldwell behind bars, but it had worried him enough that he'd called Justin to ask that the cat stay with him instead of staying here alone. Ridiculous, yeah, but it made him feel better.

He'd originally intended to have his friend simply come here every other day to feed Lola, because she loathed being moved. With the change in plans, he had to strategically hide her carrier until the very last second so that she wouldn't be clued in that a relocation was about to happen, which would prompt her to seek out the hole she'd made in the bottom of the box springs on his bed. Once inside, no one could get to her.

He knelt on his kitchen floor and waited for the cat to climb into his lap. Lola, a self-satisfied gray Himalayan, had been Abby's cat before she died. He and the finicky little fur ball were a wholly unlikely pairing, and he had no idea what he'd do with her on the long deployments that he'd have if he made the S.E.A.L. team. He'd figure out something because he couldn't give her up. No way. She was his connection to Abby and he occasionally felt as though Lola understood him the way Abby had. The rest of the time Lola treated him like the third-class citizen he undoubtedly was in her world.

She stepped gingerly onto his thigh and glared up at him with an expression that contained both affection and contempt. He imagined she was thinking something along the lines of, "I'm wonderful, and you're not, but I will deign to sit on your lap anyway because you are so pathetic."

"Hey, puss. What's happening?"

This was the most embarrassing habit he'd developed since taking the cat. He talked to her. Constantly. She listened fairly well for a cat, and she was good at keeping things private.

"I've gotta go away for a while," he said, and she blinked at him. She'd already figured out from the suitcase next to the door that he was going somewhere, and she had let out a series of yowls after spotting it, to let him know she was none too pleased to be left.

She'd stayed hidden when Kylie had been over a few nights before, because she mostly loathed strangers.

"I'm going on a trip with a woman—the one who came here the other night. And I need to know what the hell to do with her."

The cat purred loudly as he stroked her chin.

"No, I already know to do this kind of stuff," he said, a wry grin playing on his lips. "The problem is I'm pretty sure she doesn't want me stroking her."

But as soon as he said it out loud, he knew it rang false.

"I think she's torn between her duties and her desires. Not that you'd know anything about that, little hedonist that you are."

"Mrrrow."

"Exactly. And I really think I like this woman. Except, well, she's my boss."

Lola eyed him knowingly. If he hadn't known better, he'd have been sure Abby's spirit inhabited this cat. The two shared plenty of the same facial expressions.

"Yeah, yeah, enough with the guilt trip. So do I respect her wishes and not try to encourage a romantic relationship, or do I go for it?"

A knock at the door interrupted their conversation. Lola's chubby body tensed, and she dashed across the kitchen and skidded around the corner, probably heading for her lookout spot under the living-room sofa.

Drew stood and answered the door. Out of all his friends, male and female, Justin was the one who most liked cats and had the best rapport with Lola. In fact, Drew suspected the cat was a little bit smitten with the tan, good-looking blond surfer.

"Hey, man. Sorry I'm a little late," Justin said as he entered the house. "Where's Lola girl?" He let out a realistic sounding yowl, and the cat trotted gingerly into the room.

Justin knelt and extended a hand to pet her.

Drew decided to take advantage of the distraction to get the carrier. A few moments later, he was sneaking up behind the cat with it, and before she knew it, he'd swept her inside and was zipping up the black dufflelike bag that had been designed with little air holes and mesh windows to carry pets.

She let out an angry growl.

"I'm sorry it has to be like this," Drew said, "but you brought it on yourself with that box springs stunt."

When he'd secured the cat, he showed Justin what to feed her and when, then helped him carry the cat, the food and a litter box out to the car. Last, he went inside and grabbed his suitcase.

Once they were all in the car and on their way, Justin said, "So you've got your final training regimen all laid out?"

"Mostly," Drew said vaguely, not wanting to get into the details, such as who his new coach/training partner was.

"And you got my e-mail about my diver friend's contact information?"

"Yep, thanks for that."

"I envy you, man. Wish I was jetting off to the tropics right about now. Any chance you invited some female company along, like I advised you to?"

Drew kept his gaze straight ahead, trying to appear casual. He made it a rule not to lie to his friends. But he'd also promised Kylie he would remain discreet. His promise to her had to come first. "I'm going solo this time," he lied. "I just want to focus on training."

"Hey, I can understand that. Just make sure you

take a break from it sometimes, too. Otherwise you'll burn yourself out before the test."

"My last week there, I'll probably ease up and relax. I'm scheduled to start the official S.E.A.L. test the week after I get back."

"And that's four weeks of hell you'll need to be fully rested for."

Drew nodded, part of him relishing the idea of having his body and mind put to the ultimate endurance test, and part of him terrified of failing. He'd wanted this for so long, and he'd trained so hard, and it was maddening to think that one little slipup or one off day could cost him this dream.

From the backseat, Lola let out a mournful yowl as they went around a corner, and her carrier slid across the seat.

"Do what you need to do to take care of yourself mentally, too," Justin added. "You're going to need to be in top form in every way possible—"

Drew tuned him out. He knew all this, and he could tell his friend was simply keyed up on his behalf. He'd watched a good buddy prepare to take the S.E.A.L. test—and fail at it—so he knew how hard it was to watch a friend endure such an ordeal.

But even knowing the pitfalls, knowing what he had on the line, nothing really seemed like that big an ordeal after the shooting. Nothing seemed nearly quite so important as it had a couple of weeks ago. Sure, he'd be horribly disappointed if he failed to make it on to the S.E.A.L. team. But he was alive, which was more than some of his colleagues could say. Somehow watching comrades die out of combat for no good reason put life in perspective—sort of the way Abby's death had, only in a more brutal, grimmer way.

And that was why he would continue his campaign for Kylie. He understood a little of why her career meant so much to her that she'd avoid anything that might jeopardize it. But he didn't agree with sacrificing potential happiness for a job. In a way, he had to protect her from the stronghold the Navy had on her.

All of a sudden keeping her from losing herself to the uniform, from becoming only Lieutenant Commander Thomas, seemed like the most important thing he could possibly do right now or ever.

Whether she wanted his protection or not, she was going to get it. He felt an overwhelming sense of affection for her already. And the thought of her never again being the sexy, warm woman who'd shared his bed was almost too much for him to bear. Maybe the strength of his feelings was misplaced—the result of having saved her life and now having a vested interest in ensuring she squeezed the most out of that life. And yet, in a way, his feelings seemed entirely appropriate for the heat they'd generated a few nights ago.

"So," Justin said, his tone announcing that he was about to pry. "Are you ever going to tell me what happened between you and Lieutenant Commander Thomas the other night?"

Drew sighed, tearing his gaze away from the view out the passenger window to regard his nosy friend. "No, I'm not."

"You can't hold out on me forever, you know."

"I'm pretty sure I can."

"Must have been a damn good night if you're

being that tight-lipped," Justin said, and Drew tried not to grin.

"Stop it."

"I'm just saying…"

"It's none of your damn business."

"Wasn't I the one who pointed out how hot she is for you?"

"I'm eternally grateful for your meddling, okay? Are you satisfied?"

He wasn't sure why he resisted telling Justin what had happened. He knew Justin could keep his mouth shut. Drew supposed he wanted to protect Kylie's privacy, but it wasn't only that. It was, he realized with a twinge of shame, that he wasn't sure how he felt about going public with the fact that he'd slept with his boss. He didn't want anyone to think the upcoming promotion he was due was in any way a result of doing his superior officer.

And that quickly, he had an inkling of Kylie's concerns. The insight wasn't enough to convince him to change course on the seduction, but it was enough to help him understand where she was coming from.

"Not at all."

"Then you can just use your imagination and make up whatever it is you hope happened."

Justin smirked. "Dude, I don't want to picture you naked."

"Thank God," Drew muttered, relieved that he wasn't going to be pressed for any more details.

Whatever happened behind closed doors between himself and Kylie was to be the subject for his own fantasies and no one else's.

10

KYLIE STEPPED OUT onto the balcony of her hotel room in Honolulu and breathed in the lush, tropical air. It was harder to fill her lungs here, the air was so thick with moisture, but the ocean breeze made up for the humidity. As did this view. Her room looked out toward Waikiki beach and the Pacific Ocean, where the sun was getting low in the sky now. Soon the sunset would be breathtaking.

Her first assignment out of the Naval Academy had been in Hawaii, and she'd always counted herself incredibly fortunate for those two years spent in paradise. Being stationed here had been exactly how she'd pictured her service. It was the polar opposite of the Iowa farm where she'd grown up, and some part of her had needed that extreme change of settings. The Naval Academy in Maryland had wrenched her out of childhood and turned her into an adult, in every sense of the word. Arriving in Hawaii and realizing that she was truly on her own, a world away from the life she'd always known, had introduced her to the potential that existed beyond her upbringing.

So being here now felt both nostalgic and disconcerting. Nostalgic because she loved this place, and loved that time in her life when assigned here, yet disconcerting because she equated Hawaii with momentous change. She wasn't sure she could come here without being transformed by it.

She sat on the chaise longue and stretched out her legs, letting herself relax into the new setting. Maybe what she needed now was a transformation, after all. Maybe she needed to become someone new, someone different. Or maybe she needed to reexamine her priorities. Maybe she'd outgrown her previous life plan and needed a new one that suited her better.

She closed her eyes. Foolish thinking. She had a good life, a solid career...

And it all felt a little hollow, in the face of the shooting.

Before she could contemplate the matter further, she was interrupted by a knock at the door. Kylie crossed her room to the door and opened it. There stood Drew, smiling and holding two open bottles of beer.

"You work fast," she said, stepping aside for him to come in.

"Flying always makes me thirsty," he said. "And it's room service that works fast, not me." He grinned, and her insides did a little flip-flop.

Damn it. She had to stop responding to him that way. He was eight years younger than her. There was no way anything serious could come of their attraction. And she didn't want a fling.

Okay, that wasn't completely true. She did want something, or she wouldn't have come on this trip. And if a fling was all she could have... She'd be lying if she claimed she'd agreed to this trip expecting they could spend weeks together in paradise without *something* happening.

She just wasn't ready to examine her motives too closely...especially with him in her room and the bed right there.

This was the first time they'd seen each other since he'd issued the invitation, and she felt impossibly awkward. She hadn't been able to get a seat on the same flight as him, so they'd arrived separately, but only a half hour apart. She'd called him when she'd gotten into her hotel room, and he'd promised to bring drinks over.

He stopped at the sliding glass doors to admire her view, so she crossed the distance between them and said, "You've got the exact same view, don't you?"

His room was right next door to hers, after all. That, at least, she'd been able to arrange at the last minute even if the proximity seemed to go against her we-can-only-be-friends position.

So what the hell was she doing? Walking into a field of emotional and physical land mines, most likely.

"Yep, but it's a damn good one."

"Definitely worth the elevator ride up sixteen stories," she agreed, then turned and said, "Cheers."

He clinked his beer bottle against hers. "To vacationing in paradise," he said.

Kylie took a long drink of her beer, an ice-cold Dos Equis that went down deliciously smooth. As she swallowed, she realized Drew was staring at her.

"What?" she asked self-consciously.

"It's amazing how different you can be. I mean, your demeanor at work doesn't fit with how you act away from it."

Kylie felt her cheeks warm at his observation, particularly because his expression made it clear which aspect of her he preferred. Then she cursed herself. She was no blushing schoolgirl, and she shouldn't have let a guy's attention affect her that way. It was absurd.

"I don't know what you mean," she said to cover up her embarrassment. "I'm the same person as always."

He shook his head, not buying it. "No, you're different."

"How so?"

"You just seem so much more…womanly, away from work."

Kylie glared at him. "That's sexist bullshit."

"No, it's not. You can't convince me you don't suppress some part of yourself at work."

"Everyone does. It's not a phenomenon relegated to women."

"I didn't mean to suggest it was. But you especially seem to turn off some essential female part of yourself."

Kylie couldn't deny that. She supposed a lot of women did it to survive in male-dominated subcultures.

"In case you haven't noticed, the Navy isn't exactly a bastion of femininity."

"No, and you're probably smart to keep yourself…restrained or whatever."

"I don't ever want to be accused of using my gender to get a promotion."

Drew nodded, appearing thoughtful. "What made you decide to become a Naval officer, anyway?"

"Long story," Kylie said, walking out onto the balcony.

She sat on the chaise again, and Drew followed her, taking a seat on the other chair.

"Great thing about vacation is, we've got nothing but time on our hands."

She sighed. "My dad always talked about his time in the Navy with such pride and wistfulness—completely atypical for him. My parents are God-fearing Iowa farmers. Anyway, he made his service years sound so romantic that I grew up fantasizing about joining the Navy myself. I just pictured it being this idyllic life at sea, traveling to exotic places and all that."

"You must have been a good student, to make it into the academy."

Kylie nodded. "Straight A's. I was a good girl…at least on the surface."

"Do you ever regret it?"

She took another sip of her beer, wanting to avoid such a probing question. A month ago, she'd had few regrets, certainly few she'd acknowledged. But lately they seemed to be crawling out of the woodwork. "Yes, sometimes I do. I think maybe I wasn't cut out to be a leader, since it's partly my fault what happened—"

"No," Drew said sharply. "Don't put that on yourself."

Kylie shook her head, refusing to listen to him. "I could have done things differently. When I think about how I handled Caldwell…"

"You did the best you could at the time, and there's no way his behavior is your fault."

"I think I did treat him unfairly," she blurted. It was her first time admitting it to herself, let alone saying it to anyone else.

"How so?"

She took a long drink to rid herself of the sudden dryness in her throat. "I overreacted. He was accused of rape by a female seaman, and I was in charge of the investigation. In the end, there wasn't enough evidence to be sure what really happened. And...I took her word over his."

"But there was some evidence that he'd raped her," Drew argued.

"It wasn't definitive."

"What made you decide against him?"

"My gut," she said quietly.

"Even if he feels he was treated unfairly, that doesn't justify shooting up an office building full of innocent people."

"I know," Kylie said. "It doesn't. But I'm haunted by the thought that I could have prevented the whole thing."

"So am I. I mean, for different reasons. It's a natural reaction to this kind of thing," he said in an attempt to make her feel better.

It wasn't going to work. Kylie knew her role in the tragedy. And it was maddening that she couldn't turn back the clock, make a different decision in the rape case....

"Stop doing that to yourself," Drew said. "I can see the wheels turning in your head."

She sighed heavily, then drained her bottle.

"I'll try to stop," she said. "Maybe if I drink enough, I'll forget."

"That's a slippery slope we've both already gone down," Drew warned.

"Yeah, and it's only a temporary fix."

"But it sure feels good while it lasts," he said with a wry smile.

Kylie couldn't help but laugh. It had the pleasant effect of easing some of the awkwardness she felt.

"What about you?" she asked to change the subject. "Why'd you join the Navy?"

"Pretty much the same reason you did."

"Didn't I hear somewhere that your dad was a S.E.A.L.?"

"He was, yeah."

"Is that why you want to become one?"

"Hell, no," he said, a sudden harshness in his voice that shocked Kylie.

"*Okay* then. Never mind that question."

He glanced up at her, looking chagrined. "Sorry. I don't have any good feelings about the man."

"Then your reasons for joining the Navy aren't anything like mine. How about giving me the real story?"

The beer, on an empty stomach, had given her a light buzz, and she felt herself loosening up, relaxing as her thoughts and words became less clouded by inhibition.

"What I meant was, I grew up with those same notions in my head of a life in the Navy, traveling across the ocean and all that. Visiting exotic ports, sleeping with exotic women." He grinned.

"Yeah, yeah. That wasn't part of *my* fantasy," she said, and he laughed.

"By the time I was a teenager, I hated my dad for leaving us the way he did. I guess I wanted to prove to myself and to him that I was twice the man he was, that I could walk the same path as him, but do it a hell of a lot more honorably."

"Was he an officer?"

Drew nodded. "Yeah, but he got a dishonorable discharge for conduct unbecoming. Bastard deserved it, I'm sure."

"What did he do?" Kylie dared to ask.

"Had an affair with another officer's wife, but that was long after he left my mother. He was married to his second wife then, and my sister and I hardly ever saw him."

"Well, I'm sure you've already proven yourself. You've got the makings to be a great officer, you know."

Drew looked a little uncomfortable at the compliment. "I guess the real question is whether I can make it past the S.E.A.L. test."

"I'm sure you can," Kylie said, though she knew there was no way to be sure. The test was incredibly strenuous, and one slipup could spell doom for an otherwise perfect candidate.

"Want another beer?" Drew asked, indicating her empty bottle.

"Actually, yeah, I do."

He nodded, then stood and left the balcony, then she heard him opening the door to her room. A few minutes later, he returned carrying a bucket of ice filled with beer. He smiled when he noticed her eyebrows raise. "I ordered a six-pack, but didn't want to seem too presumptuous by showing up with all this beer at once."

He opened a bottle for her and she downed another

long drink. The cold beer tasted heavenly in the warm, tropical air. She should probably eat something before drinking any more, but she never felt hungry these days. Her stomach was tied up in knots half the time.

She looked at Drew, at the way the late afternoon light shone golden on him from the side. It was the kind of light photographers loved, and seeing him now, she wished she had her camera. He was too gorgeous for words, and she could hardly believe she was here with him now. Why did he have to be her subordinate? And why did he have to be so damn tempting? And eight years younger? And not even remotely appropriate for her?

He caught her staring, and curiosity sparked in his eyes. "Can I ask you something?"

"Sure," she said cautiously, "but I can't guarantee I'll answer you."

"Why do you work so hard to ignore the attraction between us?"

"Because it's inappropriate," she said, her cheeks burning again. Yes, she knew a fling was a distinct possibility between them. She was even anticipating it. But that surety and anticipation did not change any of the reasons he was wrong for her.

"Is it really?"

"How could it not be?"

"Pretty soon you won't be my rater anymore. And then what?"

"Then I'll still be eight years older than you."

"So?"

"I've been twenty-six before, Drew. I remember what it's like."

"Everyone is different. You can't claim to know me based on my age."

"No, but I know more about life than you do. I can pretty much guarantee that."

"That's arrogant of you."

"Perhaps," she admitted. "Just as it's arrogant of you to assume you know as much as I do."

"I never said I did."

Kylie wasn't sure what point he was trying to argue. "We both have our careers to consider. I think we'd be setting ourselves up for a painful ending if we entered a romantic relationship."

"I don't think there's any reason to assume that," he said, staring at her defiantly.

Kylie took another drink and felt her resistance slipping. Maybe if they both kept the right perspective about things… If they both understood that this could only be a fling, with no hope of a future together…

She recalled that rush of emotion she'd had after her first night with him, when, for a moment, she'd been sure she was falling in love. That clearly had been her libido, so overjoyed to finally have had sex again, doing the thinking.

If she didn't confuse her libido with her emotions, maybe she could play Mrs. Robinson for a few weeks. Maybe tearing up the sheets would help them heal. Help them forget.

"If anything happens again between us on this trip," she heard herself say. "We have to understand it can't go anywhere."

Drew's expression was unreadable. "What kind of

things might happen?" he finally said, daring her to spell it out.

"You know what I mean."

"Sexual things?"

She stared at him silently, refusing to take his bait.

"What happened to all that talk about inappropriateness?"

"You're being a shit right now."

He took a swig of beer. "You're right. I'm sorry."

"I guess I'm not in any shape to be acting like my most virtuous self at the moment."

"And you think we both might benefit from a little sexual healing, don't you?"

Kylie looked out at the ocean to avoid his gaze. She shrugged, unwilling to admit it out loud.

"It's okay to admit you're human, you know."

"I think I have more than admitted that."

"I don't want to sleep with you if you consider it shameful and wrong," he said, a note of challenge in his voice.

He was backing her into a corner, trying to get exactly what he wanted, rather than accept only what she was willing to offer.

Is that what she felt in her heart? That sleeping with Drew was shameful and wrong?

No.

No, it wasn't. It was the kind of thing her parents might think, or some of her superiors, but it wasn't really what she thought, she had to admit. Otherwise she wouldn't have been able to do it and enjoy it so much.

The real Kylie didn't like living by anyone else's

rules but her own. The person she'd kept buried deep inside for so long made mistakes—sometimes huge ones—but she also lived passionately, fully engaged.

She'd thought she'd banished that part of herself for good. An accidental pregnancy at the age of seventeen had taught that impetuous part of her hard lessons— lessons she never forgot.

But something about the shooting had brought to life long-dead parts of herself. She wanted to be free of her self-imposed constraints and any other con- straints that no longer worked for her. She didn't want to feel passive or not in control ever again.

"That's not what I think," she finally said. "What we shared wasn't shameful, nor could it be."

"Then what do you think?"

"I think we're two adults who should be able to do whatever we want in the privacy of our own beds."

And as soon as she said it aloud, she knew it was true. And she knew it was exactly what she intended to do.

11

MIDWAY THROUGH her next beer, Kylie realized she needed to eat something substantial or she was going to have another horrible hangover in the morning. Nursing a sore head and queasy stomach was not how she planned to spend her first day in Hawaii.

She and Drew had continued to hang out on her balcony, talking right through sunset. Because she'd lacked the energy to go out to eat, they'd ordered room service. Drew was at the door of her room paying for it as she lounged, lazily staring up at the night sky.

"Dinner's served," he said a moment later, appearing next to her.

He wheeled the cart to the door of the balcony and began setting their plates on the small drink table between their chairs.

Kylie sat up and felt her belly rumble. She'd ordered a cheeseburger and fries—the perfect accompaniment to beer—and it looked even better than it had sounded on the menu.

But when she looked over at Drew, all thoughts of dinner disappeared and were replaced by more carnal ones of him in her bed. As tempting as it was to tackle him on the spot, another part of her was equally resistant to the idea. Was he worth ruining her career and her self-respect over?

Certainly not. But hadn't her therapist said to watch out for signs of serious depression, like self-destructive behavior? Was that what this was?

Was she using Drew to self-destruct?

She pushed the thought aside, mostly because she was just buzzed enough not to care too much about consequences right now.

"You're looking awfully serious over a quarter-pound of beef. Is something wrong?"

"Oh." She smiled. "No, nothing."

"I don't believe you," he said, watching her closely.

He had the ability to read people's emotions—or maybe only hers. He wasn't a typical guy that way. He seemed to know exactly what he was feeling at any given time, and appeared unafraid of those feelings. His emotional astuteness was as keen when it came to others. She'd never been with a man who could look at her face and have any inkling what was going on in her mind, and it was a little bit disconcerting.

"Well, to be honest, I was wondering if my attraction to you might be self-destructive behavior. Perhaps a sign of depression."

"Wow, you sure know how to overthink an issue."

"Well, the therapist warned me about uncharacteristic behavior. And I have to say the way I've acted for the past two weeks has been a tad uncharacteristic," she said defensively.

"Beware of listening to therapists too closely. Their job security depends on perpetuating our neuroses."

"That's a pretty cynical way to look at it." Although she did agree with him.

"I don't think most of them set out to intentionally do it. I just think too much navel-gazing and too little living one's life leads to neurotic thoughts and behaviors."

"Am I behaving neurotically?"

"Maybe a little," he said, a teasing smile playing on his lips.

"Okay then, I'm going to shut up now."

She picked up her burger and took a bite, then moaned at the greasy, oozy, delicious mess of it, fairly sure that there was some sort of condiment dripping down her chin.

Drew had ordered a steak, which he was cutting a bite of when she looked at him.

"Don't worry," he said. "I'm not staring at the ketchup on your chin."

"Good." She picked up a fry and used it to catch the extra stuff dripping from her burger. "So, I'm wondering, if you don't recommend thinking too much, then how do you ever grow as a person?"

"By always trying to be a good person," he said, shrugging.

"Don't you have to do a bit of self-reflection sometimes?"

"Sure, but not to the point of torturing myself with it."

"Good thing you're perfect, huh? That must make life so much easier."

"It really does." He grinned and stole one of her fries. "Anything you need to know about life, just ask me. I've got the right answer."

She knew he was joking, but his emotional confidence was undeniably sexy. She supposed it was a big part of what attracted her to him so powerfully.

"I think I have a weakness for people who seem to have all the answers," she said, thinking out loud.

He cocked his head to the side, appearing to give the idea some thought. "Interesting. Do you think maybe that's part of the appeal of the Navy for you? The military's always ready with a set of strict rules to live by."

"Perhaps," Kylie said slowly. "I've always been a little afraid of the results of totally living by my own rules."

"You strike me as a person with good judgment."

She shrugged. "Yeah, but…"

She didn't want to get into any more navel-gazing, especially not after his recent comments on the subject. She had a feeling he was absolutely right.

"But what?"

"But this cheeseburger is far more interesting than my little problems. Want a bite?"

"Sure." He leaned forward as she brought the sandwich to his lips.

He was making a show of being sexy about it, and she couldn't help but laugh.

"What?" he said around a mouthful of burger. "Wasn't that hot enough for you?"

"Smoldering." She pretended to be interested in a French fry, because she was afraid of her feelings showing too much on her face.

She couldn't help but be utterly mesmerized by him. They chatted as they ate the rest of their dinner, and

Kylie felt herself growing exhausted from the day of travel, the alcohol and the heavy dinner. She yawned noisily, and Drew took that as his cue to leave.

"We should probably get some rest, eh?" he said, stacking their dishes on the room service cart.

"I'm so tired all of a sudden," Kylie said. Despite the exhaustion she had the urge to drag him straight to bed and strip off his clothes.

But…not tonight. If she was going to risk all to have a fling with Drew, she had to do so with a clear head. No more diving into bed with him again thanks to the effects of alcohol. That might be a too-in-control Kylie kind of notion, but it felt right.

Drew's gaze lingered on her as she stood and stretched.

He paused, his hand on the cart that he was about to wheel away. "It was really good talking to you, getting to know you better. I'm glad you came on this trip with me."

"The feelings are mutual. It's been a huge relief already, thinking about something other than…" She didn't want to mention the shooting and ruin the night.

"Yeah. Definitely," he said, rescuing her.

She followed him to the door. "Well. Um…good night."

He looked into her eyes, and she got a little shiver of excitement. It was as if he could undress her with that one little look.

Amazing.

Then he leaned in, and Kylie's breath caught in her throat. Her insides turned warm and oozy at the idea of his kiss, and she closed her eyes. But instead of landing on her mouth, his lips touched her cheek gently, then disappeared.

Kylie opened her eyes and sighed inaudibly. Damn it.

"Good night," he said, then gave her one last sexy appraisal and left the room.

Kylie bit her lip in frustration as she stood alone, staring at the closed door and its instructions for escape routes to take in case of fire or emergency.

He'd given her exactly what her rational mind wanted—a time-out to sort through her thoughts with a sober brain. She should be thanking him, grateful that he hadn't put her in an awkward position by hitting on her and forcing her to turn him down. Or, worse, regret it in the morning. Yes, she should be pleased.

But she wasn't.

Not even close.

WATCHING KYLIE stroll on the beach wearing her swimsuit was enough temptation to drive any man crazy. But particularly the man bent on a slow seduction. The extreme contrast between the bikini of today and the stiff Navy uniform of most days was startling, like an electric shock to Drew's groin. All his reminders to himself not to stare fell on deaf ears.

Surely she felt his hungry gaze on her, could read his dirty thoughts. But she pretended not to notice. In fact, she seemed totally oblivious to his tortured state.

He had to distract himself before he grew an erection big enough to make him the talk of the beach. He'd been thinking of going for a swim, but the moment he saw the surfboard rentals, he got a new idea. "Didn't I hear you like to surf?" he asked Kylie.

She nodded, her gaze following his to the rental booth. "I used to," she said, "but I haven't in a while. I've never quite gotten used to the frigid water off the California coast."

"Then you're in the perfect place to start again."

They were close to the water's edge, and when the next wave came in, she let her feet get wet. "Oh, yeah," she said. "That's more like it."

"Want to go for a surf?"

"God, I'm so out of practice…I haven't gotten wet in a couple of years at least."

"C'mon, it'll be fun."

She looked a little wistful. "This is the beach where I learned to surf, actually," she said. "I was stationed here right out of the academy."

"Really?" Drew hadn't known she'd lived in Hawaii.

He wondered what she'd been like back then. As career-minded and focused as she was now? Probably. Most Naval Academy grads were.

"Yeah, you know, back at the dawn of time," she said wryly.

He chose to ignore her remark. She was only trying to emphasize their age difference, and he wasn't going to bite. If it didn't matter to him, maybe she'd eventually be comfortable with it, too.

"Let's go," he said, taking her by the elbow and guiding her toward the surfboard rental. "It'll be fun, and we'll get a morning workout."

She didn't resist. Thank God, because he couldn't look down at her again right now. His body shouldn't have reacted so strongly to her in that little red bikini, especially since he'd gotten up close and personal with her totally naked body a week ago. But there was something about a healthy, beautiful woman in a swimsuit… Make that woman Kylie, and apparently he had a recipe for his own undoing.

Once they'd gotten their boards, they made their way down the beach to the spot where the waves broke. They were easy, clean, beginner-worthy waves, but Drew didn't mind. It would give Kylie a chance to get her confidence built up, and he could use the practice himself. He wasn't a frequent surfer like Justin was, since the Navy and his training kept him too busy for many time-consuming sports.

They started paddling out. It was still early, but a few surfers were already in the water, and the June air was warm enough to make the cool water refreshing. Drew found himself falling a bit behind so he could watch Kylie's long graceful strokes, the muscles in her shoulders and back flexing. Predictably, his gaze stuck on the unbelievably sweet curve of her ass barely concealed by the bikini and accented by that narrow waist and fabulous legs.

He forced himself to pay attention to the water before he drowned himself or something.

Once they'd gone out past the surf break, they found spots far enough away from the other surfers to keep from getting in each other's path, and they waited.

Kylie looked over at him, squinting her eyes. Her hair was soaked now, slicked back from her face. "You take the first good wave, okay?" she called out.

Drew nodded, and they waited as other surfers took

their turns. Then a new set came in, and Drew saw a perfect wave come along. He started paddling fast, then he was up, his arms out, the force of the wave propelling him forward. It was exhilarating in a way few other things were. He managed to stay up for a respectable amount of time, until the wave broke and he fell into the surf.

By the time he had gotten back on his board and was paddling out again, Kylie had caught another wave from the same set, and she was looking anything but tentative. Her stance on the board suggested she was plenty comfortable, and she appeared like a surf goddess gliding across the ocean.

He watched until the wave dissipated and she took a smooth dive into the water. Perfect execution from the Naval officer. Yet another way she'd managed to surprise him. He could not wait to find out what else she had to hide under that seemingly cold facade.

And if he had any say in the matter, he wouldn't be waiting long. Tonight, he didn't have any intention of spending his time in an empty bed.

12

KYLIE COULD NOT remember the last time she'd had a day packed with so much fun—or a night, for that matter. She wasn't sure when exactly she'd decided to throw caution to the wind, but she had. In a big way.

After the surfing, they'd rested on the beach, gone for lunch, then strolled around town to get themselves oriented. A late afternoon workout had wrapped up their day. Although none of it was particularly eventful, Kylie had been pleasantly surprised to discover that she enjoyed Drew's company.

He was funny, and playful, and smart and quirky. He clearly enjoyed making her laugh as much as she enjoyed laughing at him, which was worth quite a lot when Kylie considered how seldom she laughed in her everyday life.

Even now, as she recalled the joke he'd made about the swordfish, she giggled.

Okay, so there was something to be said for hanging out with a younger guy. He had youthfulness in spades, and not in the annoying way most twentysomethings she knew did. He wasn't overly cocky and sure of himself while being devoid of wisdom.

Not at all. In fact, he did seem pretty wise for a guy

so young. She'd already sensed that about him from working with him, but she had a much more solid impression of him now. She was taken aback at how much she liked everything she was coming to know about Drew.

Of course, there were the negatives, too. Like…

Um.

There had to be something.

Kylie had just gotten out of the shower and finished drying her hair when she heard a knock at her door. Still wrapped in her towel, she went to the door and peered through the peephole. It was Drew, looking all polished and clean and ready for a night on the town.

Dear God, she was in trouble.

She opened the door and stood aside for him to come in, forgetting for a moment that she wasn't decent. But his appreciative glance down at her towel reminded her.

"Hey, I like what you're wearing tonight," he said.

"Is it too much for dinner, do you think?"

His gaze lingered on her barely concealed body. "Uh-uh," he said slowly.

She could feel the heat in his eyes, warming her wherever he looked.

Yep, she was in big, big trouble.

"There's just one thing," he added, reaching out as if she had a piece of lint on her outfit. "It looks like this would fall off easily."

"Oh?" She watched as his fingertips brushed the edge of the towel, below where she had tucked in the corner.

It felt as if he was moving in slow motion, but she didn't try to stop him as he gave the towel a gentle tug. It fell to the floor, and she stood there naked.

"See what I mean?" he said casually.

"Um, yeah," she said, looking down at herself, not sure what to do.

She could only marvel at the intensity of the raging heat that started low in her belly and caught fire where her legs met. Her nipples tightened at the sudden burst of cool air on her skin.

Drew traced his finger along one breast and around the erect nipple. "Oh, no, you're cold. I'd better help you warm up."

How they got from the doorway to the bed was a blur. Kylie registered only his mouth on her, his hands everywhere she needed them to be. She didn't remember much about how he got his clothes off, but soon he was naked against her, and she was straddling him, kissing him frantically, touching him as if he were the last man on earth.

He'd produced a condom, and slipped it on right before she hovered over his erection and shifted her hips so that he eased inside her, where she was already hot and wet.

She moaned in relief at the sensation, rocking fast and hard to keep him pumping into her, to keep that wild need inside her at bay. This was so good—*he* was so good. How had she gone all day without touching him?

She understood now that she'd been practicing supreme self-control that dissolved in the instant it took a towel to fall.

DREW TRACED his fingertips along the smooth skin of Kylie's belly. He loved the way the glow of the lamplight shone on her skin, the way it highlighted the tiny blond hairs and cast every part of her body in gold. He swept upward, gently tickling the lower half of her breast, then down again, over her belly button, to her hip bone, and along her bikini line to the mound of hair where her thighs met.

His cock stiffened, but he had no intention of rushing things again. Dinner all but forgotten, he figured they could order room service when they got too hungry to go any further. For now, though, he wanted to take things as slowly as possible, to draw out the foreplay until the delicious torture was too much for either of them to bear a second longer. He wanted to know every nuance of her body, and all the ways he could pleasure her best.

She squirmed her hips, urging his fingers lower, but he didn't give in.

"Will you show me how you like to touch yourself?" he said, studying her reaction.

She smirked at him, her cheeks flushing a bit. "No, I will not. Not with you here to do it for me," she said, teasing.

"I'm serious. I want to learn what you like best. Plus it's really hot to watch you get off."

She sighed. "I don't think I can do that."

"For a woman who's so good in bed, you sure do act like a prude sometimes," he said, knowing the taunt would get to her.

She narrowed her eyes at him. "I do not!"

His gaze dared her to protest. Then, unexpectedly,

she slid her hand down to his. Guiding his hand, she put it between her legs, moving his fingers to explore wherever she wanted them. She purred in the back of her throat and shifted her hips to give him easier access.

Drew couldn't complain about her loose interpretation of his request, not when he was so damn aroused.

"It feels really good when you move your fingers like this," she said, guiding his hand in a gentle circular motion.

"Yeah? What else?" He had a good sense of how to please a woman, but he'd had enough experience to know that every woman was unique, and what might have felt like heaven to one wouldn't feel so great to another.

"You've been doing a fine job on your own. I don't know why you think you need my help," she said, but she was clearly getting into the game, her eyes halflidded and her voice a little breathless as she continued to rub his fingers against her slick, hot flesh.

"Tell me what else you like," he persisted, savoring how beautiful her body looked as she writhed against his touch.

"I like this," she said, moving his fingers again, this time so that they barely brushed against her.

"Yeah?"

"Mmm-hmm."

"How about this?" he said, sliding one finger inside her to find her G-spot, while continuing to rub her clit with his other fingers.

She gasped and closed her eyes. "Yes, that feels… amazing."

Drew leaned in and kissed her neck as he continued to explore with his fingers. Then he whispered into her ear, "Show me something else you like."

For a moment she did nothing. Then she slid one hand up and began rubbing her breast, at first tentatively, but soon without inhibition. She gently pinched her nipple, then tugged at it. "This feels great, especially when I'm about to come."

"Mmm. That's good to know. What else?"

"If you kiss my neck…"

He did so again. "Here?" he whispered.

"Back a little…yeah, right there. It feels almost like an orgasm."

Her body responded with head-to-toe gooseflesh.

Drew trailed his tongue across her neck and up to her earlobe, then nipped at the soft flesh with his teeth. He moved lower, to her collarbone, then her breast, the one she wasn't massaging herself.

"How about this?" he said right before he took her breast into his mouth and gently tugged at the nipple with his teeth.

"Oh!" she gasped again, but arched her back toward him. "Yeah, that's good."

He bit down a little harder, to see where the line was for her between pleasure and pain. She responded with another moan of pleasure. He tried a slightly firmer bite, and she gave a squeal of pain. He made a mental note of this, too. He wanted to know her body as if it were his own.

His own…

He wanted her to be his, pure and simple.

He moved to her other breast, nipping at her fingers, then, when she slid her hand around to the back of his head, he turned his attention to her nipple, sucking and tugging gently with his teeth while he continued to explore between her legs with his hand. By her breathing he could tell she was getting closer to orgasm, so he soon backed off. He knew he could give her an orgasm—or two or three—but this time he wanted to make her wait for it. He wanted to know just how long he could tease her—and himself—before it became too much to bear.

Positioning himself on top of her, he stopped stimulating her and said, "Tell me one of your favorite sexual fantasies."

She blinked in surprise. "Um…"

"It's okay. I don't care if it's weird or innocent or anything in between. I only want to know what really turns you on."

"You clearly turn me on," she said, squirming a bit.

"Besides me."

"I don't know…"

"Yes, you do."

She smiled sheepishly. "Why don't you go first."

"Nope. It was my question. You have to answer it first."

"I don't remember agreeing to those rules."

"I thought I had you at my mercy and could get you to heed my every command."

She made a weak attempt to wriggle out from under him, but her heart clearly wasn't in it. "I suppose you do, but I'm curious to know what sort of leverage you intend to use other than brute force."

"Oh, you know, the sexual kind, since you don't

seem too keen on touching yourself in front of me. If you want to be touched, you'll have to follow my rules."

She narrowed her eyes at him and gave him a swat on his bare ass. "That's pretty cruel, you know."

"Not really. I have your best interests at heart." He rested his head on his hand, emphasizing that he was waiting for her to talk.

After a few silent moments, she cast her gaze up at the ceiling and sighed. "Fine, I'll tell you a fantasy."

13

KYLIE HOPED her cheeks weren't flaming red. She'd never talked about sex out loud with a lover before. That probably made her the prude Drew had accused her of being. But she'd never really thought of herself that way. She was pretty uninhibited, and she loved sex, but talking about it…was something entirely new.

No guy had ever asked her exactly how she liked to be pleasured before, and the whole idea of articulating her preferences was revolutionary to her. Was this an uninhibited twentysomething deal where talking was another tool in the foreplay arsenal? Or was this Drew wanting to know everything he could about satisfying a woman, satisfying *her?* The idea of having her own personally trained lover was tantalizing. Almost enough to entice her to spill a sensual image or two that got her off.

"I've always found something really arousing about water, so my favorite sexual fantasies involve being in water."

"Yeah? Interesting. Go on."

She stared at the shadows on the ceiling cast by the lamplight and continued. "Sometimes, I imagine a romantic night on a boat, just me and a lover, someplace tropical. The water is warm, and we come upon a sea of bioluminescence. We decide to go for a skinny dip, swim around in the glowing light, stroke each other, tease and play in the water. Then we end up on the steps to the boat, our bodies still submerged."

She paused. This was the part where she'd actually have to describe stuff. Sex stuff. Out loud.

"And?" Drew asked.

"And I sit on the steps, and you hold on to the rails and make love to me right there. It's just the water, the boat and the dark, with the glow of the bioluminescence…and the sex, of course."

"So, is the sex slow and sensual, or fast and frenzied, or both?"

"Hmm, I guess both. Depends on my mood when I'm having the fantasy. Sometimes I imagine it raining, too."

"That's a nice start, but I'm going to need more detail."

"Can't we leave anything to the imagination?"

"Nope."

"Of course not," she said wryly. Still there was something wildly liberating about exposing the long-hidden parts of herself, saying things aloud that she'd never spoken before. It made her feel as though she was getting intimate with Drew in a way she never had with any man—in a way that created a deeper bond than she thought it was possible to have.

No. Scratch that. She was getting way too carried away with the romantic thinking. They were simply titillating each other with pillow talk. That was all.

"I'm waiting," Drew said, his gaze half-lidded. He was thoroughly enjoying this, obviously.

If he was going to insist she do detailed and explicit, then she could make him suffer. Get him all hot and bothered then not let him have what he wanted for a while…

When she thought of it like that, the task didn't seem so daunting.

She slid her hand down his side, between their bodies until her fingers brushed his erection. He shifted his weight to the side to give her easier access to him. She gripped him gently, and began exploring him with her fingertips.

"You swim to me underwater and surprise me, slide between my legs, tease me for a while until you know I can't take it anymore."

"How do I tease you?" he said, his voice noticeably tight now.

Kylie resisted a smile of satisfaction.

"At first you use your tongue until you run out of breath and come to the surface. Then you press your erection against me and rub it back and forth, arousing me without entering me. You get me so hot and wet, I beg you to take me right then."

"And do I?"

"No, you keep torturing me. Finally I get fed up and go for the boat, thinking you'll follow, but you stop me and turn me around. You grab on to the boat's stair rails while we're still in the water, and while I brace my arms against the lowest step, you slide inside me and we have passionate, frenzied sex. And it's so good suspended in the water. We can move in ways that are impossible on land."

"Mmm, nice… That wasn't very much detail, though."

"What more do you want to know?"

"How does it feel to have me inside you?"

"It feels like…hmm…like having a full stomach after hunger pains, but better. Like…having an itch scratched in a place you can't reach yourself…" She giggled nervously, hating the way she sounded. "Those are pretty lame descriptions."

"No, not lame. I think these kinds of things are hard to describe because there's nothing else quite like it."

He could be awfully insightful for a twenty-six-year-old. "I suppose you're right."

"Want to know how it feels to be inside of you?"

"Sure."

The corner of his mouth twitched. "Like…um… having an itch scratched in a place I can't reach myself?"

"Except, you can reach it."

"Oh, right."

They both laughed.

"Aren't you going to show me how you like to touch yourself?" she asked. Like everything else about him, she suspected the reality would be so much more intense than her already sizzling mental images of his hands on himself.

"Hell, no. Are you crazy? That's way too embarrassing."

She slapped his arm playfully. "Stop it! I want to see you do it."

"Or what?"

"Or…" She tried to think of some appropriate revenge, but she wasn't likely to withhold anything from him in her current mood. "Or I'll be really annoyed."

"Ooh, big talk."

Kylie tried to keep her expression serious, but she failed. As he rolled onto her and came in close for a kiss, she was nearly overcome with desire and longing and an emotion that wouldn't bear scrutiny if she wanted to keep this fling in I-can-walk-away territory. It was becoming clear that she was in deep, deep trouble, in ways she was only beginning to fathom.

DREW HAD SLIPPED into a meditative state, his mind focused solely on his breathing—in and out, in and out. He and Kylie had been running for a solid hour, first through the jungle and now along the beach. His body had moved beyond the point of pain and was now operating as a machine doing exactly what it was made to do.

Keeping pace beside him, Kylie uttered not a single complaint. When they'd set out, she'd talked, but as the exertion began to tire her, too, they'd slipped into the silent meditation of breathing and running.

Finally they neared the end of the beach where they'd agreed to stop, and they both slowed to a walk. It was only then that the pain of the workout registered. His leg muscles burned, and his lungs ached.

They'd been in Hawaii for five days now—five of the best days of his life. A combination of the company, the setting and the sheer relief from the angst-filled situation they'd left in San Diego had created a wildly heady feeling between them. He knew Kylie was feeling it, too, because he'd never seen her smile and laugh so much.

There was something growing between them that he was happy to nurture, but he could tell Kylie was not.

He banished that thought from his head. No point in ruining a perfectly good time with gloom and doom predictions.

He was happy with the way his training was going. They'd been doing two long workouts daily, and yesterday had been a full day of strenuous hiking. Kylie surprised him with her ability to keep up regardless of the activity. And she was a hell of a coach, pushing him when he lagged and encouraging him when he most needed it.

An afternoon storm was moving in over the ocean, its dark clouds promising rain any minute now. Kylie was looking up at the sky as they walked. She loved the storms—said they reminded her of the epic weather in Iowa that she never really got to experience in California.

They reached a rocky area and stopped, having cooled down sufficiently to do their stretching. He watched Kylie from the corner of his eye, admiring the graceful lines of her body as she stretched her hamstrings, then her calves, then her shoulders.

"What?" she asked when she caught him full-on staring at her.

"I was just thinking that you're beautiful, that's all."

She smiled, but he could tell she was a little uncomfortable with the compliment.

"Yeah, right. Good answer."

"I was also thinking I'd like to strip you naked right

here and take you on the sand like an animal." Not only was his comment true, but also it put her at ease. She seemed more comfortable with the sex than any words or action that suggested emotional attachment.

As it to prove his theory, she burst out laughing.

"I'm serious."

"I know you are. That's why it's funny."

Drew looked around at the rare stretch of deserted beach, and the shelter of the rocks where they stood. "We probably wouldn't even get caught."

"I'm not sure I want to test that theory."

"There goes that conservative streak of yours again," he said, half disappointed at her reluctance to be daring, and half wanting to get to the heart of why she was afraid. This wasn't the first time he'd butted up against her fear, but it was the first time he wanted to really push the issue.

A hurt expression crossed her face before she recovered and presented her usual cool mask of detachment to him. Thanks to this time together at least now he knew it *was* only a mask, and not an accurate representation of her real feelings.

She sank onto the sand, her legs out in front of herself, and reached for her toes without commenting.

A wave of frustration hit Drew. He wasn't going to let her avoid the topic.

"Seriously, Kylie. Why does it seem like there are two sides of you that are so different?"

She sighed. "I don't know what you're talking about. Lots of people wouldn't want to have sex in a public place. I don't think that makes me emotionally flawed."

"It's not just that. It's the way you present yourself

to the world. At work, you're an ice queen, but since we've been together this past week, you've been so warm and passionate and real. But when I least expect it, the ice queen comes back."

"Like now?" she said sarcastically.

"Yes, exactly."

"Your male ego won't let you accept even a minor rejection, so you have to blame it on me being frigid, right?"

Drew winced at the accusation. "That's not fair, and it's not true. This has nothing to do with my ego. And I wouldn't classify this as you rejecting me at all."

"Then what's the problem?"

He knelt in front of her and took her hands in his, forcing her to look at him. "I just want to understand. *Really* understand."

"Understand what?"

"You."

She blinked at that, clearly unsure what to say.

"Why?" she finally asked.

"Because I'm interested. You're someone I care about. How could I not want to understand you?"

She took a deep breath and drew her legs up into a crisscross position, then rested her elbows on her knees. She looked out at the approaching storm.

Fat drops of rain began to fall on them. After a few seconds, the drops morphed into buckets, and they were forced to seek shelter. A rocky outcropping near-by formed a sort of half cave, and they dashed for it. By the time they were beneath the cover, they were drenched. But the rain went a long way toward cooling him after that hard run.

Kylie sat on the sand to watch the rain fall over the ocean, and Drew sat beside her, patiently waiting for her to speak.

When it seemed like she would remain silent forever, Kylie said, "I guess I should explain. This happened to me a long time ago. I never talk about it, but my whole life changed then. And I changed."

"What was it?"

"I was seventeen, and I was known as the town wild child. I'd always been a good student, and on the surface I followed the rules well enough to keep my parents happy and get into a good college when it was time. But I had this part of myself that desperately needed to rebel."

"And that's the part of you I've been getting glimpses of, right?"

She shrugged. "I guess so. It's been a long time since I've let myself even bend a rule, so maybe you're right."

"What did you do to rebel then?"

"I snuck out and partied. I drank, I experimented with drugs…and I had lots of casual sex. My parents would have been horrified if they'd known the half of it."

"They never found out?"

She shook her head. "I was an expert at sneaking. And because I kept up my grades and went to church and did what they asked, it never occurred to them that I wasn't what I seemed. They trusted me so never checked on me after I went to bed. I'd climb out my window and meet up with my friends. They were older and didn't go to my high school, so the chances of my rebel life intruding on my daily life were pretty remote. You know what's funny? I was doing all this crazy stuff and no one bothered to look past the good-girl persona to see that I was heading for a whole lot of nothing good. People only see what they want to see."

"So what changed? Did you get caught?"

"No. I got pregnant. The game was up."

"Oh, wow. That must have been rough."

"It was absolutely terrifying. One broken condom showed me exactly what a shallow, reckless brat I was. I'd gotten accepted into the Naval Academy and suddenly I wasn't so clever for juggling this double life and pulling a fast one on everyone. Instead my stupidity threatened my future—I couldn't go to the academy with a kid in tow. Worse, when I told my parents, they were devastated. I don't think I'll ever forget the look on their faces—like I was a deceitful stranger who'd stolen their precious daughter."

"So what happened to the baby?"

"I knew I wasn't ready to raise a child, especially not alone. I didn't even really know the father. He was just some guy…"

Her voice trailed off, and Drew felt a pang of sympathy for the scared girl she'd been. It could have just as easily been him or any of his friends who'd made such a mistake.

She continued. "My parents wanted me to have an abortion, even though they'd always been opposed to it. They were so afraid of me messing up my life. They were so desperate to have their plans for me work out, as if by maintaining my grade point average then going to the academy, we'd be able to put this unfortunate incident behind us and I'd be the daughter they'd thought I was. There were times when I was convinced their plans for me meant more to them than I did." She sighed. "Despite their pressure and expectations I decided to go ahead and have the baby, then give it up for adoption."

"And did you?"

She swallowed hard and looked away. "I had a miscarriage when I was almost three months pregnant. I guess everyone considered it a blessing of sorts. But I didn't. I just felt so sad."

Drew wanted to comfort her, but words escaped him. He really couldn't begin to imagine how she'd felt.

"It was impossible to explain to anyone why. I got really depressed after that—stopped talking to my friends, stopped going out. I just went through the motions of my final semester of high school in a daze."

"You'd gone through a major trauma. It makes sense that you were depressed."

"Everyone around me was so relieved. My parents kept saying it was God's will, that I was given a second chance—stuff like that. Yet it all felt so wrong and so sad. No one seemed to care that a baby—my baby—had died."

"Yeah, they were probably too caught up in worrying about your future to look at it that way, huh?"

"I guess." She paused, biting her lip as she watched the rain. "It's so strange to talk about it now, after all these years. I really haven't talked about it to anyone."

"Ever?"

"Ever."

"I'm honored that you're sharing it with me," he said, feeling lame even before the words exited his mouth. They weren't adequate to express how he really felt. "How did you get past it so you could go on to the academy?"

"I don't know. If anything, the academy did it. That first year was so grueling, and such a different world. I was so physically and mentally exhausted that I could only think about surviving each day. It kind of helped me forget."

"I guess that's the intent. That first year breaks down who you were and turns you into someone new." He'd never attended a service academy, but he'd heard the stories of how brutal they were.

"Right. In a way that's what I needed."

"I've heard one way to cure depression is to get your mind totally engrossed in something new."

Kylie nodded. "I never thought of it that way, but yeah, I suppose that's what cured me."

"Except, everyone needs someone to talk to about this kind of thing. Holding it in for all these years is a pretty big burden."

She looked at him, and he was surprised to see what appeared to be an expression of gratitude in her eyes. "Especially around my parents. I think it's always bothered me that the pregnancy and miscarriage have become a taboo subject no one ever mentions. We pretend that part of my life didn't happen."

"You don't have to pretend, though. You can't control what your parents do or say. If they're ashamed or embarrassed, that's on them, not you. You have to make your own peace with your choices. Past and present."

Outside, the rain fell heavier, and the waves crashed closer and closer to the rocks where they sat. Drew was pretty sure the tide wouldn't reach them, but he kept an eye on its movement just to be safe.

"You're right," she said. "It's odd how we can get trapped into the roles our families set out for us. We never think of questioning them."

"I don't have that same pressure since it was mostly me and my sister trying to survive. There wasn't much in the way of parental expectations."

"I don't know why I let mine become so influential. It's like all that rebellion as a teenager never took place. I've spent my whole life since then trying to be the perfect daughter, trying to regain their trust and redeem myself."

"Guilt can do that."

She nodded.

"Maybe you need to forgive yourself."

"I think what I really want," she said, her voice sounding uncharacteristically shaky, "is for my parents to forgive me."

He reached out and put a hand on her thigh. He wanted to pull her close and hold her, but he knew she'd resist. He sensed she had more to say. "They've never given you that?"

"Not overtly, no. Like I said, they act as though those months didn't happen. But they're cautious around me, as if they're braced for the next big revelation about my true character, the next disappointment."

"Maybe you should tell them how you feel."

She laughed out loud then, a bitter, harsh laugh. "God, that would blow their minds. We don't talk about how we really feel in my family. We stay tight-lipped and pretend everything's okay, all the time."

"Do you think some part of you has always been rebelling against that?"

"I don't know if it's that complicated. I was a kid, and I wanted to have fun. I felt a lot of pressure, being the only child, to be the perfect daughter. So I blew off steam—albeit in a self-destructive way."

"It makes sense. They were probably way too strict, right?"

"Yeah. I don't know why, but I've always felt like their way was right and anything else was wrong. Maybe because their way was so close to what I heard in church every Sunday."

Drew thought of how she had always seemed so controlled, so exacting, and it made a hell of a lot more sense now. "You don't have to follow all the rules all the time to be a good person."

She shook her head. "I'm halfway through my thirties and haven't figured that out yet?"

"You've been doing a pretty good job of doing your own thing lately."

"Yeah," she said quietly. "I suppose I have."

"Maybe you just need to relax and go with it."

Thunder boomed overhead, and a warm breeze whipped at them. Kylie pushed her hair out of her eyes as they watched the storm bending the palm trees outside. Drew understood her a lot better now. Her duality, the way control and uninhibitedness seemed to battle inside her. She was even more attractive to him now that he knew how she'd come to be the woman she was.

A coy smile played on her lips then. "You think?"

She slid across the sand closer to him, taking his hand and moving it up her thigh. Then she straddled his lap and dipped her head to kiss him.

Right before her lips met his, she cupped his half-erect cock and whispered, "Still up for action?"

14

KYLIE WASN'T SURE what had gotten into her. She normally didn't consider talking about her parents or her checkered past a prelude to sex, but at the moment, she couldn't think of anything she'd rather do than get Drew naked right here on the beach. The rain had chased away the last of the beachcombers and swimmers, so whatever bit of modesty had been holding her back was gone.

Thunder rumbled overhead as she tugged off her top. Drew stared at her, looking a little stunned.

"I'm glad you took my advice so quickly," he said when his gaze dropped to her now-bare chest.

He slid his hands up her belly and cupped her damp breasts in his palms. Between her legs, she could feel his erection growing harder.

"I'm all sweaty," he said. "Want to swim first?"

"I want you inside me," she said, her voice husky with desire. She nipped at his earlobe, then his neck, kicking off a wave of sensation in him.

He let out a ragged breath and grasped her hips, pressing himself harder against her. "You'll have me inside you soon enough."

Then he set her aside and stood, grabbing her hand and pulling her up.

"You're going to make me wait now?"

He smiled a half smile and shrugged. "C'mon, let's take a dip in the rain."

Kylie loved the feel of the rain against her skin, so didn't argue further. She peered out around the rocks to make sure the coast was clear, then stripped off her shoes, socks and bottoms. "This is the part where I admit I've never been skinny-dipping."

"Not even as a teenager?"

"Nope."

"You've been missing out."

He was naked now, and he took her hand to sprint across the sand into the crashing surf. The wind and rain on her skin was one of the most luxurious feelings she'd ever experienced, and she squealed with the delight of it.

When they reached the surf, Kylie waded in without hesitation, Drew just ahead of her. Once he was waist deep, he turned and pulled her to him, lifting her in the water so that she was a little deeper than him, her bare chest concealed by his. The waves lapping at them concealed that they were both naked.

"There, you're safe now," he murmured. "No one can see you."

But safety was the last thing on her mind. She felt carefree, intoxicated by the sudden freedom she felt— a freedom that was both literal and figurative.

She wrapped her arms around Drew's shoulders and her legs around his thighs before kissing him for all she was worth. There was no worrying about anything at the moment. She wanted nothing more than the sensations of his body against hers, of the rain and wind and ocean on her skin. She wanted to absorb it all so that she'd never forget the luxury of it.

His tongue lapped hungrily at hers. From the hardness of his erection nudging her, she knew that he wanted her as badly as she wanted him. Only then did she remember that he wasn't wearing a condom.

"I don't have any protection," she said.

"Neither do I."

She felt a moment of panic. She took birth control pills—just in case—but she'd always considered condoms a necessary precaution.

"I've been tested recently, and I'm clean," he said.

"Me, too," she said, but still that deep-seated phobia held her back.

"Are you worried about getting pregnant even on the pill?" Once again he astounded her with his perceptiveness.

"I know it's safe. I'm just…" She shrugged, at a loss to articulate such an irrational fear.

"Hey, I get it. We don't have to do anything, okay?"

His willingness to concede to her neuroses put it in sharp focus. She was safe with him. "No," she said firmly.

This was her chance to prove she could accept the risks inherent in living a full, rich life. She was going to take it. She needed to prove to herself that she could.

He looked at her with those enigmatic blue eyes, and she couldn't help but melt under the power of his gaze.

"I want to do this," she said, to make sure he understood, and she shifted her hips then to allow him easier entry.

He positioned himself at her opening and slid inside, just as a wave broke nearby and the foaming surf washed past them. She moaned at the pleasure of it, and rocked her hips in time with his, accepting him as deeply inside as he could go.

Her clit rubbed against his abdomen, causing her enough stimulation that she felt on the edge of orgasm after only minutes. He pumped into her slowly at first, but his thrusts came faster until Kylie could only hold on for the ride.

He was panting against her neck, moaning softly under his breath, as she felt herself start to go over the edge. She cried out at the suddenness of it. The startling intensity overtook her as another crack of thunder sounded overhead.

Kylie cried out, gasping as the waves inside her body became so much more intense than those surrounding them. She realized, as the orgasm passed its peak and the waves of pleasure slowed, that she was reacting as much to the sensation of his bare, unsheathed skin inside her as she was to any of the other stimuli.

Having him bare inside her was physically intimate in a way nothing else they had done together was. And she understood, in her extreme caution, yet another pleasure she'd been denying herself all these years.

Drew's thrusting quickened, then faltered as he reached his own climax. He held her so tightly she almost yelped.

He gave a final thrust and groaned against her ear, then reclaimed her mouth in another hungry kiss as his breathing calmed.

They ended the kiss, yet remained quiet, as if unwilling to break their connection. The moment stretched, until she started to feel too vulnerable and exposed. With his usual insight Drew changed the mood by licking a raindrop from Kylie's nose, then he smiled at her and sighed heavily.

"Wow," he said. "You don't mess around."

"Me? Far as I could tell, it took two of us to do that."

"I was just along for the ride, babe."

"You were leading the cavalry." She backed up and splashed him, which was ridiculous as an assault since they were already soaked.

He laughed and pulled her closer. "What do you say we get out of here before we get struck by lightning or washed away in the downpour?"

"We've been safe so far," she said, then threw herself into the surf to float.

"We've been pressing our luck," he said, but his gaze was fixed on her chest rising above the surface of the water.

He was probably right. Yet Kylie was still in the process of proving to herself that she could live on her own terms. It was all such a new, thrilling, exhilarating idea to her. She felt like she needed to stick with it to make it real.

She began a lazy back crawl that took her farther from shore, her body gliding easily over the surface of the water as waves bobbed her up and down.

Drew dove in and swam beside her. "How far you going out?"

"I dunno."

"Is it safe to swim after sex?" he asked with a wry grin.

"Hmm, good point. We might get leg cramps or something, huh?"

"Personally, I might collapse from exhaustion."

"So go back to the beach. I'll be there soon."

"I'm not leaving you," he said.

"I'm a strong swimmer."

"I know you are, but I'm still not leaving you."

A loud clap of thunder sounded again overhead—this one stronger than any of the previous ones. Okay, there was a fine line between being a risk-taker and being stupid. She rolled onto her belly and started swimming toward shore. Drew followed.

As they reached the sand, she ran toward the rocks and started getting dressed, but she was so wet, getting back into her clothes was no small feat.

"How about we run for the car?" Drew asked. "There are some towels in the trunk."

"You mean, naked?"

"Sure, why not?"

She glanced around, reminding herself about the whole living in the moment thing she'd been determined to do just minutes ago. She could handle this. No big deal...

She gathered her things then bolted across the beach to where they'd parked the rental car on the side of the road earlier. Drew quickly caught up to her.

This was ridiculous. They were two grown adults, totally naked in broad daylight running through a thunderstorm. They could get arrested, or electrocuted, or photographed by weirdoes or all of the above.

She started laughing and couldn't stop. Soon she was laughing so hard she had to slow to a walk.

"What?" Drew asked, smiling at her laughter.

"Us. We look ridiculous," she said between laughs as she held her aching stomach.

"No, we just look naked. From my angle you're looking pretty damn hot. *Ridiculous* isn't a word that comes to mind at all."

Kylie tried to catch her breath, ducking as a car drove by. No, she really didn't care. This would probably be a moment she'd look back on in her old age and see as one of the highlights of her life. If she couldn't enjoy it fully now, then she was a sorry excuse for a human being.

And with that thought, she relaxed. Another car went by, and she didn't care this time. She grabbed Drew's hand and pulled him to her, then kissed him long and hard. When she broke the kiss, he looked both pleased and stunned.

"Where'd that come from?"

"From me, to say thank you."

"For what?"

"For this." She kept walking, leaving him to catch up as he contemplated what she meant.

"Sex on the beach? Anytime, babe. I'm your man."

They reached the road, and dashed for the car while the coast was clear. A few minutes later, they were sitting in the shelter of the front seats, toweling off and struggling to get into their clothes.

Kylie succeeded at putting on her top and shorts, but she didn't bother with her shoes.

"Have you ever had a moment in your life when everything is suddenly clear to you, when you feel like you're right where you're supposed to be, doing exactly what you're supposed to be doing?"

Drew gave the matter some thought. "I think I felt that way the first time I went diving."

Drunk with her own happiness, she felt as though she could say anything. "That's how I feel right now."

It was true. She couldn't remember the last time she'd felt more like herself than she did right here and now—and she never wanted to lose this feeling.

15

AFTER ALMOST TWO weeks in Hawaii, it amazed Kylie how easily she forgot about her life in San Diego. Those fantasies about Drew she'd entertained had seemed so far beyond her reality a few weeks ago. Now she'd not only acted them out, but also she'd discovered how much better reality could be than fantasy—how much more detailed and satisfying. If she weren't so blissed out, she'd be concerned about her lack of imagination and creativity.

She tried her best to avoid thinking about how soon her visit out of time with Drew would come to an end. But every once in a while, she'd get a pang of fear when she thought about how tenuous her grip on this existence was.

Such as right now. She and Drew were strolling along the marina, a flaming pink and orange sunset on the horizon. It was romantic and dreamlike and she hated the thought that these moments were soon going to end.

"What are we doing here?" she asked to distract herself from the nagging worry.

"It's a surprise."

"Well, let me guess…it has something to do with a boat, since we're surrounded by them right now."

"I'm not telling."

He was acting like a little boy on his way to the candy store, and Kylie couldn't help but be charmed by his excitement. He'd been mysteriously planning something all day that he wouldn't share. She suspected it had something to do with the boat fantasy she'd described to him when they first arrived in Hawaii.

She blushed at the thought of acting out the fantasy—especially such an elaborate one—even while she was tantalized by the possibility. If her imagination proved to be as lacking in creating a fantasy as it had with the others, she was in for a scorching experience.

They reached a small yacht, and Kylie saw a candlelit dinner set up on the deck. She laughed. "Are you serious?"

Drew smiled, took her hand and led her across the gangplank to the deck.

"I'm serious about being hungry," he said. "Hope you like oysters."

"I love them. Who set all this up?"

"It's magic. I snapped my fingers, and—"

"Oh, stop it."

"I can't ruin my mystique by telling you the inner workings of my plan."

"Of course not. Sorry I asked."

He pulled out a chair for her, and she sat.

"I thought we'd better eat before leaving the dock, if that sounds good to you."

"Absolutely." Kylie surveyed the food on the table and could hardly believe how good it looked—a delicate red beet salad with goat cheese, orange slices and walnuts, baby asparagus, fresh French bread and a selection of oysters on the half shell. A bottle of chilled white wine had already been opened and poured, probably only minutes ago.

She looked at Drew and shook her head. "I'm amazed."

"Good." He picked up his glass of wine and toasted. "To fantasies," he said.

She smiled shyly and touched her glass against his, then looked out at the water and shook her head at how ridiculously perfect it all was—better than her fantasies.

Growing up in landlocked Iowa hadn't afforded Kylie opportunities to experience life aboard a boat. The Navy had changed all that for her; however, no matter how challenging serving on a military vessel got, she'd never quite gotten over her romantic ideas about the seafaring life. Blending her once-in-a-lifetime fling and her love affair with all things nautical was almost too perfect to be believed.

The boat rocked gently on the water, and Kylie looked out at the open ocean as she imagined what was on the other side. Japan, China, all of Asia.

"What are you thinking?" Drew asked.

"I was just imagining faraway ports of call."

"Have you ever been to Asia?"

"On deployments. And I got to travel around Thailand for a while after one tour."

They chatted about traveling as they ate. Drew hadn't been to many ports of call yet, but he would soon enough. Kylie had a feeling he was going to make the S.E.A.L. team. The more time she spent with him, the more she recognized that he had the drive and the focus to do it.

By the time they finished dinner, she had a slight buzz from the wine. A waiter appeared from the cabin bearing dessert. He lit a plate of bananas on fire, then made quick work of serving them over ice cream.

"Wow," Kylie said. "Bananas Foster?"

Drew smiled. "It's a little showy, I know. Too much?"

"Not at all. I'm just amazed—it's my favorite dessert."

"Really?" He looked pleased with himself.

"Really." It was one more absurdly perfect detail to emphasize that this was a whole state of fantasy they existed in.

Kylie tried to ignore the uneasy feeling in her belly that this was too good to be true. She could live this way forever, she knew, pretending sunset dinners aboard yachts were real. But they weren't. She was still Drew's commander, and this affair was still forbidden. There were still two disparate lives they'd left behind in San Diego.

After the waiter had served them, then disappeared, Drew leaned across the table and took her hand.

"What's wrong?"

"I'm sorry, it's nothing. This is all really perfect. Thank you."

She felt like a total shit for feeling anything but thrilled at all the effort he'd put into the evening.

"No, don't lie to me. I saw that expression that just crossed your face."

What could she say? That she was too caught up in

her Mrs. Robinson role and had forgotten that it was just that—an act?

No.

Not now, anyway. She owed him the enjoyment of this night he'd planned for her.

"You're too damn intuitive for your own good," she said, hoping to distract him.

"Were you thinking about San Diego? What happened?"

Kylie nodded and cast her gaze down at her dessert. That was close enough to the truth. "Yeah. I guess I had a moment of feeling guilty that we're here having so much fun, and other people…aren't. You know?"

"Yeah, I know. It hits me sometimes, too, at the oddest times."

An awkwardness descended. Kylie didn't want to ruin this night, especially after Drew had gone to so much effort for her. She picked up her spoon and forced herself to take a bite. The flavor was exquisite enough that there was no way not to enjoy it.

"This is amazing," she said.

Drew was still watching her. "This trip really is helping us heal, you know," he finally said.

"I know. I can feel it. Sometimes I don't believe I'm entitled to be happy so fast."

"We have to hold on to happiness whenever we can. There's no rule that says we have to suffer constantly to mourn the loss of people we care about."

"I guess you'd know about that better than I."

"One hard lesson I learned was that it's impossible to go on with your life and stay sad. We're not really honoring the dead when we do that."

"No, I suppose we're not," Kylie said quietly, stirring the bananas and ice cream.

"The only way to honor the dead is by living life to its fullest. As cliché as it sounds, life is a gift. It's gone too fast not to cherish every second of it."

Kylie shifted uncomfortably in her seat at the raw, unvarnished sentiment behind his words. Cliché, yes. But the thing about clichés was they often revealed the most basic truths about life—the things everyone experienced.

"You're right," she said. "Thank you. I need to learn not to feel guilty about being happy."

"Yes, you do." He went quiet for a moment, then leaned in close and added, "Because I've got more fun planned."

She couldn't help but smile at his leering expression. "I don't know. We might have trouble finding bioluminescence tonight."

"That's okay because I brought the next best thing," he said, leaning over and retrieving a box from beneath the table.

"What is it?"

"Glow sticks."

Kylie bit her lip when he pulled out a little plastic tube of green liquid. "Perfect," she said.

He set the box aside and dug into his dessert.

His thoughtfulness humbled her. When was the last time a man had taken such care to ensure she was happy, her wishes fulfilled? When was the last time she'd *allowed* a man to do so? That Drew had listened to her then recreated her wishes down to the last detail of her favorite dessert and glow sticks overwhelmed her. What a barren wasteland her emotions had been.

How many wonderful experiences had she cut herself off from while trying to keep herself under control? Drew had given her a bigger gift than he'd ever know.

She reached across the table to clasp his hand. "Thank you," she whispered around the tightness in her throat. "Thank you for this trip, for this night…for the romance. It's been far too long since I've experienced something like this."

"Yeah?" He turned over his hand so their palms touched and their fingers entwined. "Why is that?"

She shrugged. "The usual. Too caught up in my career."

"That sounds like an excuse."

"Maybe it is. I don't know."

"When's the last time you had a serious relationship?"

"Define serious."

"You know. In love with someone."

"In love?" she said, stalling. There had been only one time when she'd thought she was in love—the first time she slept with Drew.

"Yeah, head over heels, crazy in love."

"I…um…haven't been."

"Ever?" He looked stunned.

"Ever."

"How could that be?"

"Maybe my definition of love is too strict. Maybe I've played it safe and never let anyone get close."

"Haven't you ever dated anyone long-term?"

"Oh, sure. I've had a couple of relationships that lasted a year or two. But even at the time I knew I wasn't fully engaged. It was real easy to let the next deployment or the next promotion be an excuse to walk away."

"I don't get that. Why'd you stick around if you weren't into it?"

"Companionship?"

"Did they fall in love with you?"

Kylie winced. "They claimed to."

Drew wore a disbelieving expression as he withdrew his hand. "So you strung along these saps until, what? You got bored? Or until you got promoted and could cuddle up to your new rank. Man, that is cold."

The warmth and affection she'd been nurturing from Drew abruptly ceased as he continued to stare at her. "That's harsh. Those relationships have nothing to do with you."

"Don't you get it? They have everything to do with me—with us. You hold yourself apart, never letting yourself commit. Meanwhile the guy, the poor sap, is turning himself inside out trying to get your attention. But there's no point, is there? Because no man can compete with the mighty Navy for you esteem, can he?"

He stood and began to pace. "God, I've been such an idiot. Here I've been busting my ass to show you that we could have something amazing together and you're just looking for exit."

Panicked, Kylie couldn't speak. Not only was his attack out of left field, but also the real possibility she could lose him—had already lost him—froze her in place.

"Well, aren't you going to say something?" He paused, then turned his back on her. "Of course you're not."

Seeing those broad shoulders averted spurred her into action. She rose and approached him, hesitating only a moment before wrapping her arms around him and resting her cheek on his rigid back. "Drew, I swear it's different with you. I have no proof of that. I can only tell you I feel things for you I've never felt for anyone. You mean more to me than the Navy, than my job, and that scares the crap out of me."

Something about her clumsy apology seemed to have an impact on him because his muscles relaxed as he turned to embrace her. The relief flooding her system made her knees weaken.

"I'm sorry, Kylie. I shouldn't have said that shit to you. Guess I freaked a little at the thought I might not be important to you."

"You are, Drew. I just don't know how—"

"Let's not worry about the hows tonight, okay? We'll figure it out. In the meantime, we've got a moonlight cruise and some glow sticks that need our attention." He said the last with a leer that made her laugh.

As the yacht's captain navigated the vessel into the open water, Kylie worked to restore the flirtatious mood between them. Despite her best efforts, however, she couldn't replace the sad, bleak look in Drew's eyes.

AFTER THEY'D ANCHORED and the crew remained discreetly hidden, Kylie and Drew stripped down and dove into the dark Pacific. The air was warm and humid, the water felt refreshing. Despite his earlier blow-up—or maybe because of it—Drew had every intention of making this experience better than her wildest fantasy.

He handed her a glow stick. "So you don't get lost," he said, grinning.

He pulled her against him and kissed her. She tasted like saltwater and wine, a perfectly intoxicating combination. Her naked legs wrapped around his hips, and for a few moments the pumping movement of his legs suspended them both in the water. But his energy could be put to much better use. He guided them to the boat's ladder where he could hold on as they floated.

As she held on to him, he lowered his own glow stick between her legs and rubbed the side of it gently against her clit.

She squirmed and laughed. "Is that what I think it is?"

"I hope you're not opposed to creative uses for safety lights."

Her eyes fluttered shut as he continued to stroke her. "Mmm. I…think…I'm fine with whatever you just said."

She slid one hand down his back and around his waist to his hard cock. When her fingers wrapped around him and began stroking, he gave a little gasp of pleasure. "I'm going to forget how the fantasy goes if you keep doing that," he said in a tight voice.

He slid the glow stick inside her, teasing her with it gently, then moved it back over her clit in a rhythmic motion. "Oh," she gasped. "That's…okay. I…can't remember it, either."

He watched pleasure play across her features in

the moonlight. Having her this relaxed, this into the moment and him, almost erased the hollowness and fear that her relationship history had left him with. This was the Kylie he was fighting for.

"Mmm."

"You are the most beautiful woman I've ever seen," he murmured.

She opened her eyes and looked at him with a mixture of disbelief and gratitude.

"You are," he insisted. "Inside and out."

"You're too much."

"I meant inside as in, your personality, not your… but that's beautiful, too," he said, and she burst out laughing.

"Oh, this is so romantic," she said when she recovered. "I never imagined being seduced with a glow stick."

"Hey, it was working for a few minutes, wasn't it?" He hadn't intended laughter to be part of his get-busy-in-the-water scheme, but it seemed to be working if the intimate look in her eye was to judge.

"Yes," she said. "This is wonderful." But she couldn't contain her laughter.

It only got worse when he put the glow stick between his teeth and wiggled his eyebrows at her. "Sexy, no?" he said around the tube of glowing green plastic.

"Wildly."

"Am I ruining your whole fantasy?"

She stopped laughing and pulled him close, her fingers clasped around his shoulders. "Not at all. It's like you said, the reality blows the fantasy all to hell. I never could have dreamed this up."

She took the glow stick from his mouth and kissed him long and deep, while Drew cupped her ass with one hand and guided her to his erection. With little effort, he slid into her hot pussy, and the delicious sensation of it caused him to gasp against her mouth.

She moaned softly as he thrust deeper into her. He held the railing to the ladder as he found a rhythm, and she clung tightly to him, rubbing her clit against his body as they moved together.

He could feel her growing hotter and wetter around him, could feel her inner muscles tensing as she built toward a fast climax. It would be one of many for her tonight, if he had his way. He'd chartered the boat for the whole night, and he intended to make it around to the other side of the island in time for sunrise.

But right now, he lost all thought of past and future as his own body edged near climax. He heard himself gasping as his cock strained inside of her, then she came. Her body quaked against his, her insides growing even tighter and wetter, sending him over the edge on the heels of her orgasm. He spilled into her in great spasms, his body stimulated further by the ocean.

After a few moments, their climaxes passed, and he kissed her again, this time more gently. Now he was feeling the strain in his arms. She noticed his muscles quaking.

"Let's get back in the boat before we get eaten by a shark," she said.

And he watched her glorious backside as she pulled herself up onto the ladder. If he hadn't been so spent, the sight would have made him instantly hard. He followed, and they went to a blanket he'd spread out on the deck and lay down on it, then gazed up at the stars.

"Thank you," he said into the silence after a few minutes.

"*What?* No, thank *you*. It was incredibly sweet of you to put together this whole night for us, based on my silly little fantasy."

"My pleasure. But I do thank you for giving us this time together. It's been one of the best times of my life."

He hadn't meant to go all sentimental on her after his earlier outburst, but the stars, the night, the setting…there was no way around a bit of heartfelt sentiment.

But her relationship history and her continued reticence about any commitment to him held him back from what he most wanted to say—that he could have spent his whole life happily making Kylie's fantasies come true.

16

"I TOTALLY beat your time!" Kylie insisted the next day as the cool air of the hotel lobby enveloped her. The spacious area was crowded with people checking in and guests chatting or reading in numerous chairs and sofas scattered about. In her sweat-soaked workout gear she felt a bit underdressed and disheveled.

Drew, walking beside her, shook his head. "You did not. I was an eighth of a second ahead of you, at least."

"Liar!" she said and swatted him on the shoulder.

They'd just completed a sprint from the beach, and Kylie had been thoroughly impressed with herself for staying neck and neck with Drew the entire way. She wasn't about to admit defeat. So what if he'd been a little tired from diving all morning—she had to have something to give her an edge against his stamina.

He caught her against his chest and held her with her arms pinned at her sides. "If you don't admit I won, I'm going to tickle you until you pee on yourself, right here in front of all these genteel hotel guests."

"It'll probably embarrass you more than it'll embarrass me. People will just wonder why you're harassing that poor incontinent girl."

"That's it, you asked for it," Drew said and dug his fingers into her rib cage.

Kylie squealed. She'd never been able to tough out being tickled. And she'd made the mistake of confessing to Drew recently how easily it made her wet her pants.

A few people in the lounge area cast disapproving glances at them.

"Okay, okay," she said, gasping. "I give up!"

"You admit I won?"

"Yes…"

He stopped the tickling and loosened his grip on her enough that she could turn to face him. "Yes?"

She was going to tease him some more, but the happiness in his eyes struck her. The bleakness from last night had vanished and the result left her almost breathless. She wrapped her arms around his neck and kissed him.

He pulled her against him, and the kiss got a little more passionate than perhaps was appropriate for a public place. Kylie moaned softly at his tongue coaxing hers. Reluctantly she pulled away before anyone could tell them to get a room.

They already had a room, after all. They might as well go use it.

Before turning away, she placed one more light kiss on his lips as a promise of more to come as soon as they could get a little privacy. "Let's go get naked," she whispered.

As they headed toward the elevator, hand in hand, Kylie caught sight of a familiar face waiting in the check-in line. She stopped in her tracks.

She was screwed.

And not in any way she wanted to be screwed.

The entire passionate exchange with Drew had been witnessed by one of their superiors.

And not just any superior. Admiral Dunmead, the commander of the entire Naval unit she and Drew were assigned to was staring at them, a frown on his face. He looked different in his civilian clothes, but there was no doubting his identity.

Drew followed her line of vision. "Damn, isn't that—"

"The admiral."

"Oh, shit," he said under his breath.

"We'd better go say hello," Kylie said weakly, her heart sinking to her knees.

She should have known better. She *had* known better, but had chosen to ignore her own good sense. Hawaii was a frequent destination for military stationed in San Diego, for work and leisure. And many personnel stayed at this hotel that catered to the military. It was only a matter of time until they ran into a coworker. And they had—the worst possible coworker.

Releasing Drew's hand, she marched across the lobby with him at her side. She supposed there was a small chance the admiral wouldn't recognize Drew, given his lower rank and infrequent associations with the admiral. But Dunmead knew her.

She forced a calm expression on her face. If ever there was a time to invoke the ice queen, this was it. "Admiral Dunmead. It's so good to see you, sir." She extended her hand, and he shook it in his typical vise grip.

"Lieutenant Commander Thomas," he said evenly. "What a surprise." His gaze swept her head to toe and never had Kylie wished for the protection of her uniform more.

"And Ensign MacLeod, as well," he said to Drew, shaking his hand in turn.

"Hello, sir. What brings you to Hawaii? Business or pleasure?"

"Business. But apparently you two are here for pleasure." The admiral's tone made it absolutely clear that he did not approve.

"We're, um—" Kylie cleared her throat "—on mandatory leave. After the shooting."

"Right. I remember discussing it with Commander Mulvany."

"You were right. Getting off base was necessary. We—" What was she doing bringing Dunmead's attention to the fact she was here with Drew? "That is, I have appreciated the leave," she said, feeling like an idiot as she babbled on. "It's been a healing time."

"Lieutenant Commander, I'd like to speak with you privately when I'm done here."

Kylie nodded, her mouth going dry and her stomach twisting into a knot. "Yes, sir. Should I wait here in the lobby for you?"

"That's fine."

With a nod, he dismissed them both. Kylie cast a worried look at Drew as they walked away. He sighed and shrugged.

"I guess I'll wait for you in the room," he said as they neared the lounge area.

She could only nod, her mind reeling with dread.

After he left, she sat alone, waiting to hear her death sentence. This was her worst career nightmare come true—behaving inappropriately in front of her superior officer. She never should have agreed to this vacation. She should have stayed in San Diego, stayed on the job and dealt with her crap. She could have proven her worthiness as a Naval officer by persevering under pressure. She could have shown Commander Mulvaney that the little fainting episode was an anomaly and that she had control of herself.

Instead she'd let a moment of weakness dictate her actions. She'd jumped Drew at the first chance and continued to make one bad decision after another.

And she'd gotten so caught up in her lust for Drew that she'd let it happen, when it could have been prevented.

Damn it. Damn it. Damn it.

She wanted to kick herself.

What would she say to the admiral? Would she try to excuse herself? Plead temporary insanity? She hated the idea of making excuses.

No. She would face the music. She'd been wrong, she'd acted inappropriately and she deserved whatever punishment she got.

Agonizing minutes later, Admiral Dunmead finished checking in and approached. Kylie straightened.

"Lieutenant Commander, I assume you are aware that fraternizing with direct subordinates is conduct unbecoming an officer."

Hearing the words spoken aloud was a shock to her system. "Yes, sir," she said quietly.

"I confess, I'm surprised by your behavior. You

have an exemplary service record and this is the last thing I would have expected from you."

Under his sharp regard, Kylie's insides shriveled. Once again she'd disappointed, she'd failed someone in authority whom she'd sought to impress. The weight of it threatened to buckle her.

"However, I'm aware you've been operating under mental duress lately. Because of that and your record, I'm prepared to offer leniency. I will report your behavior to your commander and let him decide what your punishment will be. Understood?"

She more than understood. She'd been granted a temporary reprieve that she did not entirely deserve. She could still face severe consequences, but not right now. "Yes, sir. Thank you, sir."

"And I don't want to see you fraternizing with that ensign—or any other—again, do you hear?"

"Yes, sir," Kylie said, barely able to meet his gaze.

The admiral, finished with her, turned on his heels and marched away, leaving Kylie to seethe in her own shame.

Her parents had been right all those years ago. She had awful judgment, and she should never be left to her own devices. She was an incompetent fool. Worse, her superiors knew it, too.

Kicking herself every way she knew how, she went upstairs to end her fling with Drew.

KYLIE WATCHED the people on the dance floor, her own body still soaked in sweat. She and Drew had danced until her feet, clad in strappy high-heeled sandals, couldn't take any more, and now they were sitting at the bar having a drink.

She'd spent the afternoon since talking to Admiral Dunmead feeling miserable, knowing she'd have to leave Hawaii and all the comfort she'd found there with Drew. He'd been so concerned for her that she hadn't had the heart to tell him they were over. Cowardly, she knew, but her low spirits had needed the care that only Drew gave her. Tomorrow, she promised herself. She'd tell him tomorrow. For tonight she'd absorb every last drop of enjoyment she could. It wasn't likely the admiral would be here at this club, so she could have some fun.

Except, she didn't seem able to escape her thoughts. They cycled through her demolished career to breaking the news they were over to Drew. She wasn't sure she'd even be able to say those words aloud.

She was so very grateful to him for helping her heal. The thought of hurting him now tortured her.

And he would be hurt. She'd sensed he had a lot invested in this fling, although she'd managed to skirt most attempts to discuss what was between them. Still, he'd done nothing to deserve it.

Forcing the gloomy thoughts away, she sipped her beer and elbowed Drew. "I had no idea you had such rhythm," she teased.

"I don't like to reveal all my tricks in one shot."

"You certainly don't need a strategy for how to impress the girls."

He pulled her close. "There's only one girl I'm interested in impressing, and I've got my hand on her thigh right now."

Kylie looked down at his hand creeping up under the

hem of her dress. "Be careful what you start," she warned.

He smiled mischievously. "Be careful what you promise."

She felt a slight warmness in her cheeks. With little provocation she knew he'd drag her into the nearest bathroom to have his way with her.

Next to them, a drunken man raised his voice at someone else, then stumbled sideways into Kylie.

When he didn't apologize, Drew put his hand on the man's arm and held him firmly. "Watch it, man."

"Oh, sorry," the guy slurred, then turned his attention back to the guy he'd been talking to.

"Pretty rowdy crowd in here tonight," Kylie said, glancing around the busy bar.

On the stage across the room, a cover band played dance music, and the enthusiastic group on the dance floor had spilled into the rest of the bar, creating a wild energy in the place.

"You want to get a little fresh air?" Drew asked, and Kylie gratefully nodded.

She followed him through the crowd to the lobby, where they got their hands stamped and ducked outside into the sultry evening air. It wasn't that much cooler, but the relative quiet and lack of people were a relief to her senses.

No sooner had they escaped the noise, though, than a buzzing sound came from Drew's pocket. He pulled out his cell phone and looked at the display.

"It's the friend who's watching my cat. I'd better answer," he said, then flipped open the phone and said, "Hey, man, what's up?"

Kylie started to turn her attention elsewhere to give him some privacy, but she couldn't help listening in a little bit.

"It's awesome. I'm having the time of my life."

He was?

"Yeah, hey, it's good to hear from you, but I'm kind of in the middle of something… No, I'm here alone… How's Lola?"

Lola? Was that his cat?

"Is she eating her prescription food okay?"

Definitely the cat. Kylie tried not to smile at his choice of names as she walked ahead of him. The breeze did a wonderful job of cooling her skin. She was wearing a little green sundress with spaghetti straps that crisscrossed her back multiple times, and a pair of gold heels that were going to be the death of her feet if she didn't get out of them soon.

Drew joined her. "That was my friend Justin. You remember him from the bar, right?"

"Yeah, sure. I've seen him around the base, too."

"I have a feeling he suspects something's up. Ever since that night he's been pumping me for information about you. He's convinced something happened between us and doesn't believe I came on this trip alone."

"Technically, you did, since we were on different flights. Guess it's impossible to avoid speculation."

"You know, he mentioned a story about Seaman Caldwell's arraignment being on the news today. I haven't watched any news since the shooting happened."

"I only did once, and I immediately regretted it." Seeing the horrific events she'd experienced firsthand reduced to a sensational headline and a few talking points had emphasized the tragedy. She'd been so angry at the way the media treated their lives—hers and the victims' and the families'—that she'd wanted to throw her TV at the announcer. Perhaps the day would come when she could again view news coverage without the urge to do bodily harm.

"So," she said, eager to change the subject. "I was eavesdropping on you. Are you really having a great time?"

Drew closed the distance between them. "I really am," he said and took her into his arms to kiss her. "Can't you tell?"

"Um, yeah," she said. "I can tell."

Kylie closed her eyes and felt a wave of happiness mixed with regret wash through her. When Drew pulled away, she took a deep breath and looked up at the starry sky.

"Beautiful night," she said, trying not to sound sad.

"Beautiful girl," Drew murmured, watching her. "It's nice to see you looking carefree."

Thank God he'd misinterpreted her expression. He hadn't been as worried by Admiral Dunmead's admonishment as Kylie was. Drew thought that the admiral deferring her reprimand to her commander was a sign of how lenient the Navy would be with her so there wasn't any real reason to let the episode ruin their vacation.

If only Kylie could be so genuinely carefree.

He took her hand in his and led her along the walkway toward the beach. They passed other couples taking advantage of the romantic setting, and soon they came to the edge of the beach and an empty bench.

"Let's sit," he said. "Rest your feet."

She sat and he tugged her feet into his lap. When he took off her shoes and began massaging her left foot, she moaned gratefully.

"Oh God, that feels good. Thank you."

"My pleasure."

She smiled. "Is this the part where I discover you're really a robot lover and not an actual human guy?"

"If I were a robot lover, I'd be a terrible swimmer, I'm pretty sure."

"Good point. Nonetheless, sometimes you seem too good to be true."

He looked at her seriously then. "You seem so much more happy and relaxed than you did in San Diego."

"Yeah, I guess this trip accomplished what it was supposed to, huh?"

"For both of us."

"I'm in the best shape of my life," Kylie said. "Both mentally and physically."

"Mentally, too? Really?"

She nodded. "I think so."

"That's great. I was afraid you'd let the admiral get to you too much."

She shrugged. She was about to clarify that her improved mental state had taken a serious hit from the admiral, but she didn't want to ruin Drew's vacation, too. "No, it's okay. I agree with you—there's no use worrying about the consequences now."

"Good. The rest of the world can wait for us."

"Yeah. I'm not letting it dominate my every thought," she said, then realized she'd gone too far and had started sounding as though she was trying to convince herself of her own words.

Drew cast an odd look at her, but said nothing.

"I've loved being here with you…" Her voice trailed off again. God, now she was sounding as though she was saying goodbye.

Why couldn't this go on forever? She'd been avoiding thinking about how it would feel to leave Drew. It was going to hurt like hell, no way around it.

She didn't want to go back to San Diego.

Since that night on the yacht and Drew's outburst she'd felt a shift in her feelings for Drew. His comments about her past and behavior toward him had opened her eyes to how much more she wanted from… from herself. That shift terrified her. She was getting too attached.

"Hey," Drew said, catching her mood change. "It's going to be okay, you know. We'll have each other to get through the repercussions, just like we do now. Whatever happens, I'll stand by you in whatever way you need me to."

She couldn't look at him so faced the ocean. Moonlight reflected on the waves, and she tried to keep all emotion from her face. They wouldn't have each other. And she was too lacking in courage to admit to him that she couldn't continue their relationship. She needed to steer this conversation in safer directions.

"I still feel like I can never trust the universe the way I used to. Like any minute now, it could all fall apart." The shooting was much safer.

"That's one of the hardest things about life, that there aren't any guarantees. But that doesn't mean we can't relax and enjoy ourselves as best we can."

"I guess," she said.

"I haven't had any nightmares in two weeks," Drew said.

"You know, whenever I went to bed I'd feel the weight of those deaths on my chest. I couldn't sleep. The weight was unbearable. Soon as I got to Hawaii, the weight went away."

"Maybe none of it will come back."

"Whatever happens, this trip has been good for me. More than I can even say. Thanks for inviting me."

She didn't want to veer into smarmy territory, but he deserved to know that she hadn't completely sacrificed this time for her career.

"I'm glad it's helped you." He smiled then. "And I'm hoping this foot massage has helped enough to keep you dancing with me a little longer tonight."

"My feet feel about a million times better. Thank you."

She slipped on her shoes and let him lead her back toward the nightclub. As they neared, the music and din of people got louder. Once inside, they had to squeeze close together to maneuver through the crowd.

They found their way to the edge of the dance floor, and they were about to start dancing when several people started yelling nearby. Angry voices rose above the music. Drew looked over to see what was going on, and people began to scramble out of the way.

A fight had broken out near the bar. Two men, one

of them the drunken one who'd bumped into Kylie earlier, were pushing each other and hurling insults, while onlookers seemed more interested in watching than intervening.

Kylie looked around for a bouncer, but there wasn't one in sight. Then she saw that several men were distracting the bouncer at the front entrance. They must be friends with the brawling men. She muttered a curse.

Someone screamed, and when she glanced around, she saw that one guy had drawn a gun and was pointing it at the drunken man. She felt a cold bolt of terror shoot through her.

Not this.

Not again.

She grabbed Drew's arm.

"Get out of here!" he yelled, pushing her toward the door. "Go for cover."

But she couldn't leave him behind. She couldn't live with herself if anything happened to him. In her mind she saw Campbell shooting at her coworker, turning the gun on Drew, on herself…

No.

Courage would not abandon her again. She knew what to do.

Chaos had erupted, and the man fired a warning shot. It hit the floor. The drunk hurled himself toward the shooter, trying to grab the gun. They fell to the ground, grappling and throwing punches.

Kylie saw the gun slide free and, without thinking, she dove for it. Drew, seeing what she was doing, threw himself at the men and pinned them while she got her hands on the weapon.

A moment later, she had it firmly in her grasp, and Drew was holding one of the men while the bouncer, who'd finally gotten into the room, restrained the other.

She felt tears welling. It was over. In a matter of seconds, her life had flashed before her eyes, along with Drew's, along with everyone else's that she'd seen die in her office that day.

But this time it was different. She watched as the two men were dragged out of the bar, and four police officers entered and took over. One of them relieved her of the gun, another started asking her questions. She answered as best as she could, concentrating to keep the two incidents separate in her mind.

She kept looking around for Drew, wanting reassurance over and over that he was safe. And he was.

He was safe.

Later, after the scene had calmed down and the police had finished taking reports, after she and Drew had walked home in stunned silence, there weren't any words.

Kylie only knew that she felt a relief like no other she'd experienced. A relief like rain after a long draught. She felt as if something about their fates had changed, that they'd gone from being the ones who had no control to being the ones who could turn the tide.

She'd trained to defend, and this time she hadn't let her training down. She might never again have complete confidence in her ability to perform in a crisis, but she'd proven that she could, when called upon, react appropriately in an emergency.

She could save someone after all.

She never questioned or considered resisting what started happening once they were back in her hotel room. Drew stripped off her clothes, then his own. He turned on a lamp beside the bed, and he covered his body with hers as they lay down together.

He kissed her with overwhelming emotion. Maybe it was her imagination, but she didn't think so.

He ran his hands up and down her torso, over her breasts and her neck and her face and her hair, down her hips and over her thighs and calves. He cupped her bottom in his hands and pulled her to his mouth, plunging his tongue into her, teasing her most sensitive spots. He did it all hungrily, as if he'd never been with her before, as if he was proving to himself that he could really have her.

Kylie grasped at the sheets and gasped at the delicious sensations between her legs as he licked her. As she neared climax, her every coherent thought vanished. She rocked her hips in time with his tongue. When he finally plunged his fingers into her, she climaxed, crying out at the blinding pleasure.

Her inner muscles contracting, she writhed against him until the orgasm passed. She pulled him up to her, kissing him as he entered her, then burying her face in his shoulder so he wouldn't see the tears in her eyes.

She didn't want this to end, but there was no place for them to go. And if she stuck around any longer, she'd never be able to leave.

17

KYLIE AWOKE to the familiar feel of a warm body next to hers. Before she could snuggle into Drew again she got the horrible sinking feeling that she had to leave. Now. In the middle of the night. Like a coward.

But if she lingered until morning, she wasn't sure she'd have the courage to go. She couldn't face him right now and explain that she didn't have the balls or whatever it took to pursue a relationship, given their circumstances. Let him think the worst about her—that she'd again chosen her career over a man, that she'd never been fully engaged with him. Whatever it took for him to forget her.

Not that she'd be forgetting him anytime soon.

She muttered a silent curse that she was again buckling to external pressure. The carefree woman she'd been in Drew's company couldn't withstand the scrutiny of Admiral Dunmead and the Navy. One harsh glance from a senior officer and she was once again a new recruit desperate for approval.

However wonderful she felt in Drew's arms, she still felt ashamed. Around him, she was, quite simply, a reckless fool. She was supposed to be the more mature one of the two of them, the one with more wisdom, experience and self-control. She had none of those qualities. She wasn't brave enough to defy the Navy and embrace a possible future with Drew. So, by default, the Navy won—they got to keep her.

When she looked at his sleeping face, so perfectly handsome and kind, the air of strength and courage that surrounded him all the time apparent even now, she knew he deserved better. He deserved to live his life with someone who would put him first. She had too much baggage to be capable of that sacrifice so she needed to leave him before she did something really stupid, like fall in love.

Like fall in love.

Oh dear God. The moment she let the words cross her mind, she knew it had already happened. That feeling that had struck her their first night together... she'd hung around long enough for it to take root and grow.

She'd provided it with sunshine and nutrients and water, and it had blossomed into something that couldn't live.

Her heart thudded double time. There was no doubt. She was in love with Drew, and she had no one but herself to blame for the pain their breakup would cause.

Outside the window, the sun was cresting the horizon, casting a slight glow on the morning sky. With no idea where she would go or what she would do, Kylie eased herself out of the bed, quietly dressed and gathered her belongings into her bag. She cast frequent nervous glances at Drew, but he slept on in oblivion.

When she was ready to go, she paused at the door,

and her stomach bucked at the idea of walking out this way. Drew would never abandon her without saying goodbye. But she couldn't face the anger or disappointment in his eyes, or hear his arguments for why she should stay.

There wasn't anything for her to say in her defense. She had to salvage her career because she knew who she was serving—her country. Anything else was too big for her to handle. He might not be happy with her decision, but he would understand.

But she couldn't go without even leaving a note. She glanced at the desk across the room, with its hotel stationery and pen. Then she crept silently over to it and began writing.

I'm sorry I can't stay anymore. I hope you can understand. Good luck. You'll make a great S.E.A.L.

Ugh. It was lame, and awful, but better than nothing. She folded it in half, tiptoed to her pillow and placed the note on it.

Then she went back to the door and eased it open silently. Blinking away the dampness in her eyes she stepped into the empty hallway alone.

"DAMN IT! Answer your phone, Kylie. I'm going to keep calling until you do!"

Drew hung up his cell phone, threw it on the bed and muttered another curse, this one to himself. He'd dialed Kylie six times today, but each time he'd only gotten her voice mail. Ever since he'd woken to find her missing from the hotel room with nothing but a vague, pointless note left behind, he'd been angry, shocked and bewildered.

But the longer he went without talking to her on the phone, the more he was forced to face the fact that she'd simply done what she'd been itching to do from the start—run away from him. History repeated itself. That didn't make the reality sting any less.

He paced across the room outside to the balcony. Suddenly Hawaii seemed like a dreary place, in spite of the beautiful scenery and sunshine. Having her disappear out of the blue, just when he'd been sure they'd really connected, made him itch to blow out of paradise.

Damn it, Kylie. Damn it, damn it, damn it.

He should have known. She'd never wanted a relationship with him. She'd made that clear from the start.

Well, sort of clear. She'd wanted him for sex, but she hadn't wanted the accompanying emotions.

He should have known a thirty-four-year-old woman who'd never been in love before was a woman to be avoided with a twenty-foot pole.

Spotting the note she'd left that morning, he crumpled it in his hand, then threw it into the garbage. He had so much pent-up rage, he hardly knew what to do with himself. He'd channeled as much of it as he could into working out earlier, but still he seethed. He wasn't going to feel any relief until he talked to Kylie.

He grabbed the phone from the bed. This time, he dialed her home phone rather than her cell. She had to be back home by now, and if he was lucky, she wouldn't have caller ID.

After four rings, she answered.

"How dare you leave me here with nothing but a note," he said by way of greeting.

Silence on the other end of the line.

He hadn't considered how best to keep her on the phone.

"If you hang up on me, I won't stop calling. You have to talk to me sooner or later. You owe me that."

She sighed. "You're right. I'm sorry."

"How do you think it felt to wake up and find you gone?" he said, his voice thick with emotion.

"I—I couldn't face you. I knew you'd talk me out of leaving. And I had to leave."

"No, you didn't. You just did what was most convenient for you and your goddamn career."

"That's not fair."

"Isn't it? You used me to distract yourself, and when you were done, you wanted out as easily as possible."

She didn't respond.

Maybe he'd touched a nerve. Rather than backing off, he said, "So much for your flawless character. Turns out you're just as big a coward as you feared you were, huh?"

He knew he was hitting her where it hurt most now, and he had no intention of letting up—until he heard her crying.

Almost immediately, his anger drained, and he fell silent as he listened to her sob and sniffle. Cruel as it was, it felt good to know she was in pain, too. He didn't want to believe she could simply walk away from him and feel nothing.

But finally, she spoke, her voice remarkably free of emotion. "I am very sorry I've hurt you. I understand your need to lash out right now, but please know I want the best for you, and that is why I left."

She sounded like Lieutenant Commander Thomas again, not the woman he'd known as his lover. Calm, cold and stiff, he pictured her in her freshly starched uniform, her hair restrained in a bun.

"Oh, really? Your actions were totally selfless?" Sarcasm oozed from his tone.

"Of course not. No one's are. But I did consider you in making my decision. I'm not the right woman for you, Drew. You and I both know that."

"Don't tell me what I know. You don't get to order me around in my personal life the way you do at work."

"You're right, but much as you may not want to admit it," she said coolly, "the Navy dictates a lot about our personal lives. You know it's part of the reason we can't be together."

Drew bit his lip. He wanted to yell at her, to rail and rage and throw the phone out the window, but he felt as if he wasn't even talking to the same woman he'd fallen for. This other Kylie he barely recognized. She was the straitlaced boss he hadn't even given a second thought.

He imagined her more passionate side being held hostage inside her stiff facade, and his anger dissipated. If this is how she had to be to survive, if she was too afraid or fragile to be the vibrant, passionate woman he cared about, then truly, all he could do was feel sorry for her. Because this other version of her…it was no way to live.

Was she going to spend her whole life trying to be perfect—or this warped version of it—in order to get other people's approval?

If so, then yeah, she'd done him a favor by walking away.

"I feel sorry for you," he said, then hung up the phone.

18

DREW'S WORDS ECHOED in Kylie's head all night. She'd tried her best to forget their final conversation, but she'd never had anyone slap her in the face with a statement of pity before.

She deserved his anger, but not his pity. Anything but that.

She tried to tell herself he was lashing out in the cruelest way he could, but something about the tone of his voice suggested he hadn't spoken in anger at all. He'd been sincere, she feared.

Kylie parked her car in her assigned spot at the office. It was 8:00 a.m. and her stomach twisted tighter and tighter as she turned her thoughts from Drew to her task at hand. She had to face Commander Mulvany and admit her wrongdoing. She wasn't sure if he'd spoken to the admiral yet, but it didn't matter one way or the other.

The honorable thing to do was to confess the whole story herself and face the consequences. She walked slowly toward Mulvany's office, the morning air still heavy with coastal fog. For a moment, she wished she was still in Hawaii.

But no.

She was here, in her own life where she belonged, not there, living out a fantasy. All was as it was supposed to be. And she deserved to feel as awful as she did.

Inside the building, Commander Mulvany's secretary wasn't at work yet. Her desk sat empty, and the door behind it stood open with the light on. Kylie stepped into the doorway and knocked gently to get the commander's attention.

"Lieutenant Commander, come in," he said, distracted.

She stepped into the room and took a seat across from him.

"Welcome back from vacation," he said as he put down the document he'd been reading and gave her his full attention.

"Thank you, sir."

"Did you get plenty of rest?"

"Yes, sir."

"That's great. You're looking a lot better than the last time I saw you."

"I'm feeling better, too. You were right, I needed the break."

"You've still got more time off, don't you? Are you ready to return to work?"

Kylie hesitated. Was she? She didn't know what to say to that, so she decided to cut to the chase. "Actually, sir, I came here to speak to you about a different matter."

"Yes?"

He must not have known, or else he'd have brought it up by now, wouldn't he? Maybe he was waiting for her to do the right thing and confess.

"I accompanied one of my subordinates to Hawaii, sir—Ensign MacLeod."

"Right, he was one of the survivors of the shooting, I recall. Quite the hero that day," Mulvany said solemnly.

"Yes, well, MacLeod and I developed an inappropriate romantic relationship after the shooting. I've ended the relationship, but I am ashamed of my behavior nonetheless."

Her commander cocked an eyebrow at her. "Why are you confessing this to me now?"

"I—I'd like to say it's purely out of my own sense of honor and duty, but I'm sorry to say Admiral Dunmead saw MacLeod and I together in Hawaii. I wanted to let you know, in case he hasn't talked to you yet, so that you wouldn't be taken by surprise."

"I talked to the admiral yesterday, but he didn't mention seeing you."

Kylie wasn't sure whether to feel relieved or bewildered by that. "I suppose he's got much more important matters to think about than my personal life."

"As we all do. I suggest you keep this matter private and move forward, behaving with the utmost professionalism from this point on."

"Yes, sir, but…" She paused, confused by his lack of a reaction. "I'm not sure if I can continue to work with Ensign MacLeod in the same way I have in the past."

"Are you saying a reassignment is necessary?"

"No," she said, surprised at how sure she sounded even though she'd never considered this option. "Actually, I'm not. MacLeod is due for a promotion, and he's about to take the S.E.A.L. test, so he won't be working under my command for much longer."

"Then what's the issue?"

"What I should have said is, I'm not sure I'm cut out to serve anymore at all."

His expression lit up with surprise. "What leads you to this conclusion?"

Good question. She was as surprised as he was to hear herself saying it aloud.

"My time in Hawaii gave me a chance to reflect. And of course, my relationship with Ensign MacLeod has brought into question my moral fitness as an officer—"

"You used poor judgment, but given the set of circumstances—the trauma you two have been through—there's not a jury that would judge you as harshly as you seem to be judging yourself."

"But—" Kylie felt the absurd urge to defend her belief that she'd behaved reprehensibly.

"There's no question your actions were inappropriate, but unless the admiral cares to make an issue of it—"

"No, sir. He said he intended to leave the matter to you to handle."

"Good. I'm inclined to move forward as if none of this happened. If, however, I hear the slightest word of your consorting with your subordinates again, there will be serious repercussions."

"I'm afraid, sir, my heart isn't in service to the Navy anymore." She was making it up as she went along, but it was true.

"Are you saying you want to leave the Navy?"

Leave the Navy. The phrase washed over her like a

breath of fresh air. She exhaled all the tension in her body and nodded.

"Is this because of the shooting? Because of your relationship with MacLeod?"

"No, sir. Well…yes and no. It's because of everything. I think recent events have only forced me to face a realization I've been coming to for a while. I'm ready to move on to the next phase of my life, and the Navy isn't a part of it."

He nodded solemnly. "I'm sorry to hear that. I don't suppose I should try to talk you out of it?"

"No, please don't. My mind is made up."

"Okay, well, let me know what I can do to help you in the transition to civilian life."

"I will, sir. And thank you for being so understanding of my recent actions."

She stood to leave, and they said their goodbyes. When she was alone again, she felt tears sting her eyes. Tears of relief, she realized. She'd owned up to her bad behavior, and this time, she'd been forgiven.

She'd been forgiven. It had seemed too easy, but Commander Mulvany had hardly blinked at her confession.

Kylie swiped at her damp cheeks and laughed at herself. She was amazed that she hadn't seen before what she needed to do. She was leaving the Navy, and the decision made the weight of her entire adult life lift from her shoulders.

The world was wide-open for her to explore anew. And one thing was for sure—she was done being her parents' daughter, living by their rules and consequences. She was ready to be fully her own woman.

Maybe she'd never get their forgiveness, but that was okay.

It was time to forgive herself.

19

Six weeks later…

KYLIE'S ENTIRE BODY ached from the cold water and the long workout, but she couldn't stop smiling. She'd just caught one of the best waves of her life, and Sonya had been on the beach videotaping the whole thing.

Until today, she hadn't been surfing since Hawaii. She'd nearly sold her surfboard a few years ago, it had collected so much dust, but now she was glad she hadn't. The time in Hawaii had reminded her how much she loved the sport. And when she had officially retired from the Navy, she was going to surf as much as she wanted.

She hauled her board to where Sonya sat on a blanket, then dropped onto the sand next to her friend.

"That was awesome," Sonya said. "I got the whole thing."

"Excellent."

Kylie stretched her back and shoulder muscles as they watched the crashing surf.

"So you're really going to do it, huh?" Sonya asked.

"Retire, you mean?"

"Yeah, it's just, I can hardly imagine you not being a Navy officer."

"You won't have to imagine, because you'll be face-to-face with the reality in another week."

"So, seriously. You spend a couple of weeks on a tropical island and you're ready to toss your whole career and start over?"

Sonya knew Kylie too well. She fixed Kylie with a stare as if her patience for allowing Kylie to share the sordid details in her own time had just expired.

Kylie usually told her friend everything, but this time, she felt afraid to divulge the whole truth. Partly because she wasn't sure she wanted to admit it to herself, and partly because she wasn't sure she understood everything that was happening to her.

"C'mon. What's really going on?" Sonya prodded.

"I wish I could explain it clearly…" When she trailed off, Sonya sighed.

"Does this have something to do with that twenty-something guy you've been suspiciously vague about?"

Kylie felt her cheeks redden. She knew in a flash that she was afraid of how her friends and family would react to the idea of her investing deep feelings in Drew.

"It does, doesn't it?"

Kylie glanced at her friend, then looked back down at the sand and nodded. "Yeah, I haven't told you everything that happened with him."

"Gee, let me guess. You go off to Hawaii with a hot young guy and you…um, let's see, *fall* for him, perhaps?"

"Is it that obvious?"

"Kylie, don't be stupid. You haven't gotten any action since the Dark Ages. Of course it's that obvious.

Besides, you came back glowing like you'd gotten thoroughly laid."

"I did?"

"Yep." Sonya leaned back on her elbows, sunning her belly. "So spill. I want all the dirty details."

There wasn't any point in hiding the truth now. So Kylie launched into the complete story of how she fell for Drew and how she'd crept out of the hotel room like a coward. Her friend nodded and murmured encouraging sounds as she listened, and by the time Kylie reached the point where she'd decided she couldn't live her life for the Navy anymore, Sonya was looking at her as if seeing her for the first time.

"Wow," she said when Kylie went silent. "You've really seen the light."

"I guess so. I mean, when I went to my boss to confess what had happened with Drew, I opened my mouth and out came my decision to leave the Navy."

"Good for you."

"And yeah, there's nothing like losing your big chance at love to make a girl wake up and smell the retirement papers."

"But how do you know he wouldn't give you another chance?"

Kylie felt a bit of tension drain from her shoulders. "So you don't think my relationship with him was horribly inappropriate?"

"Why would I?"

"Because he's eight years younger than me? And he's my subordinate?"

Sonya shrugged. "I've always thought those military rules you follow are crazy, and age ain't nothing but a number, babe. If you meet a guy and you dig him and he digs you, why get caught up in worrying that he grew up listening to the Backstreet Boys while you listened to George Michael?"

Kylie rolled her eyes at her friend's simplification of the issue. "You know it's more than just that. It's about maturity, and life experience and—"

"And you being afraid to go for it?"

"No!"

"Let's look at the situation. You're a smart, attractive, thirty-four-year-old woman who hasn't gotten laid in at least a couple of years. You haven't even had the prospect of a relationship—not even a *date,* for God's sake."

"I've been busy!"

"Even the leader of the free world manages to have a personal life, while you—"

"The leader of the free world doesn't have to deal with sexism, far as I know. I felt like I needed to focus totally on my career at the time, but now I've seen the error of my ways, okay?"

"I'm only trying to keep it real. You can't tell me you haven't been afraid of getting involved with a guy."

Kylie felt like arguing further, but really, what was the point? To protect her silly pride? "Okay, fine. I've been a total chicken shit. Are you happy now?"

"Absolutely." Sonya's expression was vaguely triumphant, but her eyes twinkled with mischief. "I just wanted to hear you say it."

She was joking, but Kylie realized by the sudden lightness in her chest that saying it really did count for something. Better yet, accepting it was true…it mattered. She really had been afraid.

She thought of the safe feeling that came with making all the safest choices, with walking the narrowest path possible, following a course someone else's good intentions had laid out for her. It all amounted to an imminently safe—and utterly boring—life.

"You know," Sonya said, her tone softer now, "you're not a teenager anymore. You can bend or break the rules without your whole world coming to an end."

Kylie could hardly think of her teenage years without seeing expressions of pain and disapproval on her parents' faces. It was ridiculous. She was too old to be letting a mistake she'd made at the age of seventeen affect her life so much.

"I know," she said. "You're right."

"So what are you going to do about it? Let true love pass you by?"

Kylie sighed. She hadn't heard a word from Drew since that last horrible phone conversation, when he'd told her he felt sorry for her. He hadn't called, and she mostly felt relieved by that.

Mostly.

She knew he'd passed the S.E.A.L. test, but he wasn't due to arrive in San Diego until tomorrow. And of course she was keenly aware of his impending arrival, in spite of her repeated insistence to herself that she had moved on.

She had received an invitation to his promotion ceremony. He'd been waiting to pin on his new rank for months, thanks to the limits of government money dedicated to promotion raises, and finally the ceremony was scheduled for next week. He'd probably only invited her out of formal obligation since she was his boss for now, but…it would still be appropriate for her to attend the ceremony.

"No, I'm going to give it a try," she said quietly, not quite sure what that meant.

Sonya leaned over and gave her a squeeze around the shoulders. "That's my girl," she said.

And suddenly, Kylie knew what she had to do.

20

DREW STOOD STRAIGHT and tall as the new rank of lieutenant, junior grade, was pinned to his collar. His expression carefully blank, he looked out at the crowd of his friends and coworkers. This should have been one of the happiest moments of his adult life—his first promotion as a Naval officer—second only to learning last week that he'd made the S.E.A.L. team. But something was missing.

He'd scanned the crowd at the start of the ceremony, and the one person he'd hoped against hope to see among the faces had not been there. He should have known she wouldn't come. And he'd told himself she wouldn't. But now, he realized by the heavy weight of disappointment in his chest, his promotion meant very little to him without her there to celebrate it.

Then, a strawberry-blond head in the last row caught his eye, and he saw her. She must have slipped in partway through without his noticing. His chest swelled with relief and other emotions he didn't want to consider now, and he blinked away a sudden dampness in his eyes.

Kylie was here, after all.

It was his turn to talk now, to address those who'd gathered to celebrate this moment with him. He'd had a speech planned out in his head, and he took the written version of it from his pocket as he stood at the lectern, but his entire being was focused on her. There was no way he could stand here and read the dry speech he'd prepared last night.

Instead he spoke freely into the microphone and the words flowed out of him.

"Ladies and gentlemen," he began. "Thank you for joining me to celebrate this momentous day of my career." As he spoke, his gaze never left Kylie. "As I stand here, I see among you people whom I owe gratitude for all of my growth and achievement as an officer. I see colleagues and mentors who've selflessly passed along their wisdom, and I am deeply indebted. I could not have grown as a person or as an officer without your guidance. You are the very embodiment of heroism. In your quiet, everyday acts of courage, you exemplify what it means to be an officer of honor and integrity."

As he wrapped up the speech with a few closing words, he caught the welling of emotion in Kylie's eyes. She understood he was talking about her. She may not have believed those words about herself, but it meant the world to him that she knew he believed them.

No matter what happened between them personally, she was a hero in her own right, and she deserved to know it.

When the ceremony ended, he had no choice but linger and talk to those who wished him well. He only wanted to talk to one person. His gaze sought her out repeatedly as he accepted congratulations and listened to small talk. She was frequently watching him, too.

It was the first time he'd seen her since returning from Hawaii. She looked more relaxed now. Her tan hadn't faded, but the tension around her eyes had.

When he finally made his way over to her, she smiled warmly and hugged him.

"Congratulations," she said. "You've got a great career ahead of you."

He didn't want to hear more small talk—not from her. "It's good to see you," he said, the huskiness in his voice revealing more depth of emotion than he'd intended.

"Good to see you, too," she said seriously. "I was hoping we could talk privately after this."

"How about right now?"

"But your guests—"

Around them, caterers had set up tables of food in the outdoor pavilion. Appetizers and drinks were being served, along with a cake that Drew would be expected to cut soon. He didn't give a damn, though. Not now.

"They won't even notice I'm gone."

She looked doubtful, but she said, "Maybe we could walk out to the beach?"

He nodded, and they headed away from the hotel garden where the ceremony had been held, toward the sounds of seagulls and crashing surf.

What could she want to talk about? He didn't dare to hope. She'd already made her feelings clear. She probably wanted to give him some sage career advice, pass on whatever wisdom she'd gained as an officer.

Which would be nice, he supposed, but the very thought of it was a punch in his gut. Wisdom wasn't what he wanted from her.

They reached the sand, and Kylie slipped off her heels to carry them. Drew tried not to notice how she looked, but she was too gorgeous to ignore. She wore a white sundress that revealed a hint of cleavage, her hair upswept so that her neck and shoulders were exposed. The light dusting of freckles on her shoulders made him want to reach out and touch her. He knew how soft and warm her skin would be, just as well as he knew how she'd smell like sweet citrus...

No, he had to stop that kind of thinking right now. No more, he told himself. Not another thought.

They reached the waterline where the sand was cool and damp from the waves. Kylie stopped walking and turned to face him, her expression serious but otherwise inscrutable.

"I wasn't fair to you," she said.

"Wasn't fair to me how?" His chest tightened, afraid of what she might or might not say.

She looked up at him, her big green eyes brimming with emotion. Her soft pink lips turned up at the corners, forming the slightest of smiles. "I shouldn't have held your age against you. You're clearly old enough to know what you feel and what you want, and I denied that. I'm sorry."

"Thank you," he said stiffly, wishing that wasn't all she had to say.

But then she spoke again. "I realized something else."

"What?" he asked, his voice barely audible above the sounds of the waves.

"I've fallen in love with you."

He blinked, the news striking him momentarily dumb. Even he hadn't dared to hope she'd say *that*.

"You have?"

"Yes." She was watching him carefully, probably anxious for his reaction. "I've done a lot of soul-searching since I came back from Hawaii, but that was one thing I didn't have to do much searching to figure out."

She smiled tentatively then, and he could see that she needed desperately to hear his response. But he was afraid to believe the answer to his happiness could be this simple. There had to be a catch, a problem—something. Questions swirled in his head.

"But what about your career? And what about caring what everyone else thinks?"

"None of it matters," she said, sounding both vehement and frustrated. "I *love* you!"

"I love you, too," he said, unable to pretend it wasn't true.

Then he took her in his arms and bent his head to kiss her. She felt better than he remembered, her lips eager but pliant. She kissed him with enough enthusiasm that he couldn't doubt she was happy to be in his arms again.

When they broke the kiss, she said, "I don't want to be apart from you again."

"If you'll marry me, you won't have to be."

Her eyes widened in shock at his words. Then she smiled again. "Are you serious?"

He hadn't planned on saying it, but he'd been speaking from his heart, he knew. He'd known from their first night together that there was something incredibly special about them together, and it hadn't taken him much longer to know she was the woman he wanted to spend his life with.

"Dead serious," he said. "Will you marry me?"

She wiped a tear from her cheek and nodded. "Yes," she said. "I will."

Drew felt like doing a cartwheel right there on the beach, or letting out a victory yell, or… The idea of them never being apart again might sound nice, but given his new assignment as a S.E.A.L., and Kylie's steady rise in the ranks of the traditional Navy, they were going to spend months—even years—of their lives apart.

His heart sank.

As if she sensed his sudden change of mood, she said, "I decided to take early retirement."

Drew stared at her, stunned and uncomprehending. "But… You're a great officer. I thought you loved your career."

She shook her head. "I used to love the challenge of it. But it was always what my parents wanted for me. It wasn't until we were in Hawaii together that I started realizing what I want for myself."

"What is that?"

"I want a life, not just a job. I want a family someday, and a partner, and time to spend with my partner. If I stayed in the Navy on the track I'm on, I'd never have any of that."

"But some people manage it," he argued weakly, not really wanting to change her mind, but feeling obligated not to take her away from something she loved.

"True, but I know in my heart that I couldn't, and I don't want to do the important stuff halfway."

"What do you want to do, then?"

"Training with you in Hawaii reminded me of how much I love diving. For now, I'm taking a job as a diving instructor here in San Diego. And I'm going to get back into taking pictures, maybe specialize in underwater photography. See if I can get a freelance gig going with it. When you move to your next duty station, then I'll figure out what to do there."

"Wow," Drew said, stunned.

This really could work. They'd still have the inevitable separations of the military, but they wouldn't be compounded by dual careers with dual deployments.

"You'll really get early retirement?"

She nodded. "The Navy has more officers of my rank than it needs right now, so they're happy to get rid of me."

He took her hand, and they walked toward the hotel garden and the promotion party.

"What made you change your mind?" he asked, his wounded pride finally having a chance to smart now that he felt secure that he was getting what he wanted so badly.

"I didn't really have to change my mind. I always knew I wanted you, from the first time I ever laid eyes on you. But I did have to allow myself to face the truth. In some ways you're more mature than I am, and I had no business thinking age had much to do with it."

He grinned. "Age does have something to do with it."

"Oh?"

"I'm old enough to recognize a hot old chick when I see one."

She slapped his shoulder in mock outrage. "Don't push your luck, buddy. I may be old, but I'm stronger than I look."

He caught her hands in his and pulled her against him. "Don't ever doubt for a second that I think you're the hottest woman I've ever laid eyes on."

Her eyebrows shot up suspiciously. "Hottest for an old chick?"

"Just plain hottest."

"I don't think I believe you."

"Wait until after this party and I'll show you exactly how I feel." He pressed his pelvis against her abdomen so that she could feel his stiff cock.

Her gaze turned mischievous. "What if I can't wait?"

"Then we'll have to bow out early."

"Like right now?"

"Sounds pretty reasonable to me," Drew said, suddenly changing direction to head for the parking lot.

With Kylie at his side, nothing was out of the question.

* * * * *

THE RANGER & HOT-BLOODED
(2-IN-1 ANTHOLOGY)

BY RHONDA NELSON & KAREN FOLEY

The Ranger

Will Forrester—former Army Ranger—has his work cut out for him. Rhiannon Palmer's the most stubborn, flat-out sexy woman he's ever encountered. And he can't keep his hands off her.

Hot-Blooded

First Sergeant Chase McCormick isn't a chauvinist. But he does believe that women have no place in combat zones. Why? Because his men forget their training! He wouldn't do that!

3 SEDUCTIONS AND A WEDDING
BY JULIE LETO

Jessie might not forgive Leo for his long-ago betrayal, but after one scorching kiss, she can't fight the chemistry any more. But a girl can't base her future on great sex. Or can she?

MY FAKE FIANCÉE
BY NANCY WARREN

Chelsea Hammond will live with David Wolfe temporarily in order for him to clinch a massive promotion. Newly returned from Paris, she'll use his kitchen for her new catering business. *Strictly business...*

**On sale from 20th May 2011
Don't miss out!**

*Available at WHSmith, Tesco, ASDA, Eason
and all good bookshops*

www.millsandboon.co.uk

0511/14

MILLS & BOON®

are proud to present our...

Book of the Month

Come to Me
by Linda Winstead Jones

from Mills & Boon® Intrigue

Lizzie needs PI Sam's help in looking for her lost
half-sister. Sam's always had a crush on Lizzie.
But moving in on his former partner's daughter
would be *oh-so-wrong*...

Available 15th April

Something to say about our Book of the Month?
Tell us what you think!

millsandboon.co.uk/community
facebook.com/romancehq
twitter.com/millsandboonuk

BAD BLOOD

A POWERFUL
DYNASTY,
WHERE SECRETS
AND SCANDAL
NEVER SLEEP!

VOLUME 1 – 15th April 2011
TORTURED RAKE
by Sarah Morgan

VOLUME 2 – 6th May 2011
SHAMELESS PLAYBOY
by Caitlin Crews

VOLUME 3 – 20th May 2011
RESTLESS BILLIONAIRE
by Abby Green

VOLUME 4 – 3rd June 2011
FEARLESS MAVERICK
by Robyn Grady

8 VOLUMES IN ALL TO COLLECT!

www.millsandboon.co.uk

BAD BLOOD

A POWERFUL
DYNASTY,
WHERE SECRETS
AND SCANDAL
NEVER SLEEP!

VOLUME 5 – 17th June 2011
HEARTLESS REBEL
by Lynn Raye Harris

VOLUME 6 – 1st July 2011
ILLEGITIMATE TYCOON
by Janette Kenny

VOLUME 7 – 15th July 2011
FORGOTTEN DAUGHTER
by Jennie Lucas

VOLUME 8 – 5th August 2011
LONE WOLFE
by Kate Hewitt

8 VOLUMES IN ALL TO COLLECT!

www.millsandboon.co.uk

GIVE IN TO TEMPTATION...

As the champagne flows beneath the glittering sun,
three scandalous affairs ignite...

It's going be one wickedly hot summer of sin!

Available 3rd June 2011

www.millsandboon.co.uk

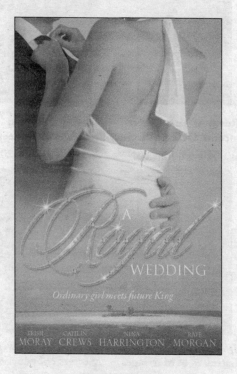

*Royal Affairs – luxurious and
bound by duty yet still captive to desire!*

Royal Affairs: Desert
Princes & Defiant Virgins

Available 3rd June 2011

Royal Affairs:
Princesses & Protectors

Available 1st July 2011

Royal Affairs:
Mistresses & Marriages

Available 5th August 2011

Royal Affairs: Revenge
Secrets & Seduction

Available
2nd September 2011

Collect all four!
www.millsandboon.co.uk

Intense passion and glamour from our bestselling stars of international romance

Available 20th May 2011

Available 17th June 2011

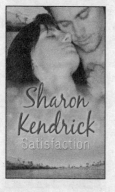

Available 15th July 2011

Available 19th August 2011

One night with a hot-blooded male!

One night in MILAN

MICHELLE REID · INDIA GREY · KATE HEWITT

18th February 2011

One night in RIO

ANNE MATHER · JENNIE LUCAS · OLIVIA GATES

18th March 2011

One night in BUENOS AIRES

MAGGIE COX · CHANTELLE SHAW · SARAH MORGAN

15th April 2011

One night in MADRID

KATE WALKER · JENNIE LUCAS · ABBY GREEN

20th May 2011

MILLS & BOON

www.millsandboon.co.uk

2 FREE BOOKS
AND A SURPRISE GIFT

We would like to take this opportunity to thank you for reading this Mills & Boon® book by offering you the chance to take TWO more specially selected titles from the Blaze® series absolutely FREE! We're also making this offer to introduce you to the benefits of the Mills & Boon® Book Club™—

- **FREE home delivery**
- **FREE gifts and competitions**
- **FREE monthly Newsletter**
- **Exclusive Mills & Boon Book Club offers**
- **Books available before they're in the shops**

Accepting these FREE books and gift places you under no obligation to buy, you may cancel at any time, even after receiving your free books. Simply complete your details below and return the entire page to the address below. You don't even need a stamp!

YES Please send me 2 free Blaze books and a surprise gift. I understand that unless you hear from me, I will receive 3 superb new books every month, including a 2-in-1 book priced at £5.30 and two single books priced at £3.30 each, postage and packing free. I am under no obligation to purchase any books and may cancel my subscription at any time. The free books and gift will be mine to keep in any case.

Ms/Mrs/Miss/Mr_____ Initials _____

Surname _____

Address _____

_____

_____ Postcode _____

E-mail _____

Send this whole page to: Mills & Boon Book Club, Free Book Offer, FREEPOST NAT 10298, Richmond, TW9 1BR